Sisters *of* Heart
and Snow

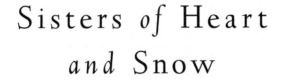

Sisters *of* Heart *and* Snow

MARGARET DILLOWAY

G. P. PUTNAM'S SONS
NEW YORK

PUTNAM

G. P. PUTNAM'S SONS
Publishers Since 1838
Published by the Penguin Group
Penguin Group (USA) LLC
375 Hudson Street
New York, New York 10014

USA · Canada · UK · Ireland · Australia
New Zealand · India · South Africa · China

penguin.com
A Penguin Random House Company

Library of Congress Cataloging-in-Publication Data

Dilloway, Margaret.
Sisters of heart and snow / Margaret Dilloway.
p.   cm.
ISBN 978-0-399-17080-5
1. Sisters—Fiction.   2. Domestic fiction.   I. Title.
PS3604.I4627S57   2015   2014040675
813'.6—dc23

Printed in the United States of America
1   3   5   7   9   10   8   6   4   2

BOOK DESIGN BY AMANDA DEWEY

Penguin
Random
House

For Cadillac

In a realm of his own.

Why did you vanish
into empty sky?
Even the fragile snow
when it falls,
falls in this world.

—Izumi Shikibu (CA. 974—CA. 1034)

Some Warriors look fierce, but are mild. Some seem timid,
but are vicious. Look beyond appearances; position yourself
for the advantage.

—Deng Ming-Dao

Obedience: Yoshinaka's Mistress Tomoe, from the series
The Eight Virtues *by Utagawa Yoshikazu*

Photograph © 2015 Museum of Fine Arts, Boston

T omoe held the round bronze mirror with steady hands, fighting her nervous pulse. A warrior stared back at her, in full battle dress. The close-fitting wrapped jacket and ankle-length pants worn under her armor, her *hitatare*, were fuchsia silk, embroidered in a repeating light pink depiction of the Minamoto crest, bamboo leaves fanning above a gentian flower. Over this she wore her armor, a crimson damask cover hiding the sturdy bamboo plates.

A bronze crown of intricate scrollwork served as her helmet, with long red tassels dangling near each high cheekbone. Her full lower lip and pronounced Cupid's-bow mouth stood out crimson in her pale face.

Behind her, Yamabuki's dark eyes shone like wet pearls. If Tomoe's skin could be called pale, then Yamabuki's was white, luminescent as sea life in the deepest waters. Yamabuki's hair was black, too, but shot through with silver and white strands.

Yamabuki worked through Tomoe's thick long hair with a tortoiseshell comb and fragrant camellia oil, her small hands working quickly to undo the knots. "There. You are ready, my captain. Your hair is so well oiled, a typhoon cannot disturb it."

Tomoe's throat went dry. Yamabuki had begun as her rival, but soon she found that she needed Yamabuki as much as Yamabuki needed her. Tomoe the warrior, Yamabuki the poet. The strong and the gentle. Two sides of one coin. Now she could no more imagine her world without Yamabuki than she could imagine cutting off her own arm.

Yamabuki blinked rapidly and Tomoe grasped the other woman's hand. "And you? Are you prepared?"

"As ready as I need to be. What can I do? Offer the enemy some tea? Play him some music?" Yamabuki stood and retrieved Tomoe's short sword from the corner. The tiny woman staggered under its weight. Tomoe watched her, knowing Yamabuki would refuse any offers of help. "I do not understand how you can carry this, much less fight with it."

Tomoe took the sword. Their fingers touched. Tomoe's insides seized, and she took a deep breath to steady herself. "I should stay here and protect you."

"No." Yamabuki retrieved the quiver of arrows and bow next. "You must go." For a moment, she looked again like the girl she had been on her arrival. A wobbly newborn chick finding its way among piebald eagles. "I will be all right."

There was a saying for a dear female friend you held as close as a relative. Sister of heart.

Unlike Yamabuki, Tomoe had never been good at putting what she felt into words. Instead, she retrieved her *naginata*, a small sword attached to a long pole, from its place in a corner of the room. With a bow, she presented it to Yamabuki. The woman didn't move. "Take it." How Tomoe wished Yamabuki would heft up the *naginata* and arc it through the air with a shout. Stab at something. But the woman could barely wrap her tiny fingers around the pole.

"*Arigato.*" Yamabuki inclined her head toward Tomoe, and laid the *naginata* carefully on the floor. "And I have something for you," Yamabuki added, reaching into her pocket. It was a piece of braided red cord, hung on bright blue fabric. A good-luck amulet. "An *omamori*. To protect you."

Outside, the army chanted for her. "Tomoe, Tomoe!" The drums and horns sounded and the men stomped their feet on the ground, banging swords against metal. Tomoe felt the vibrations in her eardrums, in her heart.

Yamabuki took a step back and bowed deeply. Tomoe bowed in return. Both filled with unspoken words that would always remain so.

One

P eople in my family are pathologically incapable of asking anyone for help. It's probably the only tradition we have. Call it pride or stubbornness or fear of rejection, even—each of us is our own island. No matter what anybody's going through, we pretend *everything's fine, just fine, thanks for asking*, and we soldier on.

Take my mother. My mother never asked me or my sister for anything. Not for help with the dishes or cooking. Not for a Christmas or birthday present. Not even for a simple hug.

But I always believed that my mother had deeper needs. Wants she would not express out loud, even when she could still communicate. Maybe even desires I was afraid to ask her about, in case I couldn't help her.

Except for today. Today she broke through her cocoon and, finally, now of all times, asked.

I'll do anything I can to help her. I wish she'd always known that.

I put one hand on top of the other, palms down, and rock the soles of my feet back and forth into the smooth concrete pool deck. Goggles and ear-plugs and nose plugs and swim cap and plain black Speedo racerback swim-suit all in place.

You wouldn't know it, but there was once a day when I could have handily beat every single person standing on the pool deck next to me. That sleek woman to my right. The barrel-chested old man in the unfortunate Speedo to my left. Even the twenty-year-old man already kicking through the water. In fact, there's still a plaque in the La Jolla High gym that bears my name. Rachel Snow, 100-Meter Freestyle record. Still unbroken, says a handwritten note below it. That was who I used to be. Unbroken.

The noon sun covers me in a prickly blanket. It's October, and still oven-warm here in San Diego. Only a few people are in the public pool in the middle of the weekday, parents splashing in the shallow end with their toddlers. Later, it'll be filled with water polo teams and after-school swim clubs.

Usually swimming clears my head, but not today. My brain turns over and over what happened this morning, when I visited my mother in the nursing home. I shake my shoulders loose, take a deep breath in. One, two, three. I release it, take another, stare at the shimmering blue-white water. Yes, there it is. That particular ache I get whenever I think about Mom.

We had a good visit today. Not because my mother knew who I was, but because we had a nice time together. Being quiet. Looking at foam on the waves and cloud formations in the sky. This was a beautiful facility, situated as it is right by the Pacific, and its expense matches its views—and my father can afford it without a single sacrifice.

My mother and I ate ginger and lemon crème cookies, dipping them into our decaf black tea. She ate a whole sleeve. Probably not on her approved diet list, but really, if I were in my mom's situation, I'd be eating a daily pound of See's. You might as well enjoy the time you have left. The truth is, she's never going to get better.

After we finished our snack, Mom continued staring out the window. I sat in another slipcovered armchair next to hers.

Mom's coarse black hair, white at the roots, was standing up, and I reached over to smooth it down. "Hikari Sato." My voice was so loud I hurt my own ears. Most of the time, people ask me to repeat myself. Mom didn't turn at the sound of her name. I wondered what she was thinking about. If she remembered her husband, my father.

I haven't seen or talked to him since I was sixteen. I'd become a problem child, breaking the rules, acting the wrong way, and my father had abruptly told me to get out, forbade my mother to see me. I've heard, since then, of other parents doing the same for various reasons—often because they disapprove of their child's partner or lifestyle or sexual orientation. Some people have an unshakable internal morality. As far as he's concerned, he has only one daughter now, Drew. I'm not sure I'll ever talk to him again. If you can say anything about Killian Snow, it's that he will never give up.

"Hey." Mom took my hand in her paper-dry one. "Look out there." She pointed to the parking lot below, where a man shimmied out of his wetsuit, his surfboard leaning against the open trunk of his sedan, having finished some morning surfing. His broad shoulders glistened with salt water. "Check out that surfer. He's changing. I can see everything. Back and front." She giggled, a throaty, mischievous sound, then leaned over and rapped on the window. "Woo!" she shouted like a teenager, and he looked up, searching for the source. "That cold water didn't hurt him any."

"Mom!" I giggled, too, my laugh echoing hers perfectly. A flush rose up my neck. The man waved, believing it was me yelling, not the tiny innocent-looking Japanese woman sitting next to me. Oh well. I leaned back out of sight and checked the time. "I have to go, okay?" I stand, kiss the top of her head. "I'll see you next week."

"Wait." Mom grabbed my upper arm, hyperalert. Wrinkles suddenly cracked across her face like riverbeds on a relief map, cutting across the high mountains of her cheekbones. "Wait, wait." She yanked with sudden Hulk-like strength on my arm, and I sat right back down.

Mom wanted something.

I gently pried her hand off my arm, no small feat. "What is it, Mom? What do you need?" I thought perhaps she'd ask me for a box of her favorite cookies, Mallomars, or maybe even tell me to bring my twenty-year-old daughter, Quincy, and my fourteen-year-old son, Chase, around next time.

Her mouth opened, forming words I couldn't catch, her voice raspy and low. Like she couldn't quite expel the syllables hard enough.

"Say it again." I leaned closer, trying to make out her meaning.

Mom cupped my chin with her hand. "Rachel." Her eyes met mine, purposefully now, not with the usual randomness, as if my eyes were another piece of furniture in the room. "Rachel, Rachel."

Mom was back. If only for a moment.

"Mom?" I leaned forward, my mouth going dry. "What is it you need? Tell me. I'll help you." Tell me. Make up for all the other times you didn't ask. Or when I couldn't help.

Mom took a gigantic gulp of air, as if she'd been diving hundreds of feet under water. *"Hon, hon,"* she whispered in Japanese.

I didn't speak the language. *"Hon?"* I whispered back, though I wasn't sure why we were whispering. We were all alone in the calm, white room. The plastic vertical blinds rattled in the breeze. Mom blinked and screwed up her face like she'd tasted something sour. "Sewing room," she said finally, with tremendous effort, in English. "Drew knows. Drew will help."

My little sister. Not that she's been little for a long time. Younger, I corrected myself. *I will always be younger than you,* Drew liked to say. "What does *hon* mean, Mom?"

Mom took her hand out of mine and stared back out the window, at the ocean waves pounding. Another car pulled into the surfer's vacated spot. I bent into her face, searched her gaze for a sign she knew me. But it was like looking at the blank dark screen of a laptop. Only my own reflection.

Now I hesitate on the pool deck, straighten, crack my shoulder and stretch it out, considering my mother's request. Small pins of pain shoot up across my back, to my spine. *Hon.* I had looked up the word. *Hon* means "book."

My mother wants me to get a book.

From her sewing room? Or what used to be her sewing room? And

4

Drew, of all people, knows? As far as I know, my sister's never set foot in that room. That was Mom's sacred space. I'm going to have to call my little sister. Which means bumping up our phone calls from birthday-and-holiday-only to an out-of-the-ordinary one.

I imagine Drew's voice, smooth as melted sugar, coating over her real emotions. It used to be so easy, second nature, to tell what my sister was thinking. Now there's a thick invisible wall between us, and it's like we're little girls again, our beds on each side of the wall, tapping and hoping the other will hear, after the other one's already deep asleep.

Drew coming home from the hospital is one of my very first memories. I was four when Drew was born. I wasn't too excited about having a baby in the house. I didn't even like baby dolls.

Mom told me to sit quietly on the couch. She put Drew in my lap. "Hold her while I get her bottle ready," she instructed me. "Do not move." Drew lay perfectly still, wrapped up like a sausage in her blanket. I thought Mom had tricked me, brought me a heavy doll. I stared at her. She slept, immobile. Boring. She smelled like sour milk. Her head was pointy, her face wrinkled and homely.

I poked her in the cheek with my finger, dimpling the soft skin like dough. I poked her again, a little harder. "Wake up."

Drew opened her eyes and stared right at me. Her eyes were the deepest gray-brown then, like polished obsidian mixed with dark chocolate. Her stubborn little arm busted free and her tiny hand clutched my finger.

My heart stuttered. "Hello," I whispered, and I swore to God she smiled, though everyone said newborns couldn't. I kissed the spots where I'd poked her. That night, I slept in her room, on the floor next to her crib, until Mom caught me and made me go back to my own bed.

It was my sister who taught me how to love.

"Feel like a race, Rachel?" the sleek woman to my right says. Shelley, another mother who swims laps here regularly. She pulls her dark goggles down over her tanned face and white swim cap and stretches her wide, muscular shoulders. "It'll be good for both of us."

My own shoulder gives a twinge of anticipatory pain. "That's okay. You go on with your bad self."

She sticks out her lips. "You're no fun."

"I know, I know." I wave her off and she dives in. Wet blanket. Hey, somebody's got to be the sensible one, even if it's not much fun sometimes. I bend over again, grabbing for the water, diving in without a splash. Perfect, even when nobody cares.

Water has its own time. Inside, under the water, you can't hear anything but muffled sounds from the people onshore. Bubbles and sloshing from whoever or whatever's in there with you. Nothing to look at but the white lines painted on the bottom of the pool.

Usually I don't think of anything at all while I swim, which is why I love it so much. Even with my bum shoulder, which still flares up like a barometer on thunderous days.

But today. Today I do my usual crawl, two strokes and then a breath, two strokes and then a breath, my big feet like turtle fins propelling me along. I look down at the white lines and instead I see the familiar faces of my mother, my sister, and my daughter. The three women closest to me.

It strikes me that even though I could sketch all these faces in my sleep—even though one gave birth to me, one inhabited the same womb I did, and I literally grew the other one inside me—all of them are really strangers now. Unknown to me, really. And I'm unknown to them. Because isn't that what happens when we grow up? We leave each other.

I close my eyes and swim faster.

Drew decides to drown this afternoon's humiliation in a diet Pepsi. What she really needs is a kick-in-the-sternum Jack and Coke. Jack, like the musician she met today. She almost giggles at the reference. "I'm losing it," she whispers to the photo of the English sheepdog drooling over a Milk-Bone.

She opens the mini fridge under the desk, hoping that she missed a little whiskey or vodka bottle amid the old bagged salads and half-eaten Dannons. It's turned up too high, ice filming over everything. She pushes a spot clean on the desk, amid papers and tufts of dog hair in blacks and tans and whites. She cracks the can open slowly, and pours it into a child's plastic take-out cup, pleased to see that the soda comes out the consistency of a Slurpee. Perfect. This, at least, is the bright spot in her day. She sits back in the ergonomic chair her employer, Liza, bought. An awfully expensive chair, considering this office is essentially a storage closet.

This is Dogwarts Dog Grooming, located in a little strip mall off of Beverly Boulevard. Not the Beverly Hills part of Beverly Boulevard, but farther east, next to an all-night burrito joint and a legalized marijuana shop, the parking lot always crowded with red-eyed, sleepy people. The interior looks like a preschooler's approximation of an English castle, with fake stone walls and a built-in turret on which a fake sleeping dog sleeps, his nylon-furred, black-and-white sides moving up and down eternally. Dogwarts is closed today, because Drew had another job and Liza is off on what she called a "cleansing cruise" for the next three weeks, where she'll get her aura purified and lots of hot stone massages, or something of that nature.

Drew's not a hundred percent sure. She only knows that Liza, a never-married woman in her late fifties, has called Drew three times during her vacation and requested wire transfers of thousands of dollars. It's making Drew nervous, this hemorrhaging when there's so little coming in; but tomorrow she's got two groomings, an overgrown Labradoodle and a Newfoundland, so that will eat up at least half the day. The viola gig came at just the right time.

The viola gig. Drew takes a big pull of the soda, getting a chunk of ice. Today was the final recording session of Drew's backup strings for an alternative rock band, Time in Purgatory, working along with ten other classically trained instrumentalists.

Everyone else had already left the studio, except for Drew and the lead singer. Drew fiddled with the locks on her viola case, feeling, she thought, a warmth between them.

This band's about to take off, U2 style. Radio stations are already playing tracks off the second album, and everybody's talking about the release of this one. She's still humming the song they recorded today. It'll be one of those songs they play ten times a day until you're properly sick of it, like it's some radio conspiracy to make people hate songs they once loved. But right now, it's still new.

A musicians' agency books Drew for these gigs. She's played viola for chocolate and lotion commercials, for Italian restaurant radio ads (she's always playing that cheesily romantic "Bella Notte" song from *Lady and the Tramp*), for educational baby DVDs. (Drew still can't believe anybody lets babies watch television—her sister, Rachel, would have rather poked her own eyes out than let her precious babies be stunted by television. Okay, exaggeration. But not by much.)

These gigs aren't bad work by any means. Not that steady, but Drew's got it better than most musicians. The occasional gig supplements her dog-grooming job. And who knows—one could turn into something one day.

Maybe even a relationship.

Drew sinks down into her comfortable chair and takes a pull so strong on her soda that she gets brain freeze. Relationship. Yeah, right. She'd rather forget.

How Drew had smiled at the lead singer, Jack, as he packed up reams of sheet music into an accordion folder, carefully sorting by instrumental part. It reminded her, with a twinge in her stomach (regret? annoyance? she couldn't identify which feeling; they felt interchangeable sometimes, in her untrustworthy gut), of the old days, when Drew used to arrange music for the rock band she was in, Out Stealing Horses.

Drew quit grad school at twenty-five to be in that band, quit for her boyfriend, Jonah, because she didn't want him traveling, having fun, without her. They didn't want a viola player, so she banged the tambourine, standing in the background, stage left of the drummer, hundreds of cables swirled around her ankles like chains. Her most important role was that of the music arranger, as Drew was the only one with a music degree and the only one who could do notation.

For seven years, off and on, with Drew always working some job that could easily be left if need be, they'd traveled from one club to another, to every dive on the West Coast until they were signed by a minor label; then to every county fair and second-rate musical festival in the country. The crowds grew at each venue. Drew wrote some music, hoped she'd prove her worth and get a larger role. Once she wrote an entire song, "Out of Bounds," with a beautiful viola part that backed up and supported the other instruments, like the frame of a house. *That's not the kind of music we play, Yoko,* the bassist said. *The guitar's the frame, not you.* Jonah told her it wasn't quite right for them. She told herself it didn't matter, that she was only sticking around because of Jonah, The One. She wouldn't have put up with that for anyone else.

That's what you get for putting all your eggs in one basket. Her literal ovarian eggs—nearly all of them wasted on Jonah. They'd broken up almost two years ago now.

Drew was lucky to be doing anything even semi-professional with music. Most of the other music majors in her year went into other fields after graduation, their student loans and then mortgages and weddings and babies absorbing their freshly hatched ambitions. Drew would see her old friends and they'd tell her, *You're so lucky to be doing what you love. I just became a corporate cubicle slave.* And Drew would feel a glimmer of gratitude and pride.

Finally, Jonah's band signed with a big label and embarked on a European tour, and Drew was unceremoniously released from both the band and the relationship. "It wouldn't have worked out long term anyway," Drew told Jonah, wanting to be the one to say it first. Jonah, staring at Drew with his large Siamese cat eyes, had at least been kind enough to give her that courtesy. "If we had kids, both of us can't be traveling the world, and I hate being left behind." This was absolutely true. At least this all had ended before Drew hit her mid-thirties, and really lost all of the best years of her life.

And so Drew returned to Los Angeles, to her viola and her side jobs. Then, at some point, her side job became the viola instead, and the side job became the main job, the transition taking place so fluidly that Drew didn't notice it had happened until Rachel had asked her about it last Christmas. "Are you spending most of your time at the grooming salon these days?" Rachel asked, encased in the bubble of her perfect family. "Not too many music jobs in this economy, I suppose." Rachel couldn't see how much this question hurt Drew. Or possibly she did. Drew could no longer tell.

Drew put her viola case on the floor with a bang. *Snap out of it,* she told herself. Here she sat in this studio, wasting her chance with Jack as she questioned every life choice she'd made since high school graduation.

Jack turned to her. "How do you think the final version sounds?"

Drew's eyes snapped up to meet his green ones. She was unable to think of anything to say except, *Quit talking and kiss me.* "Um, good," she said instead, and wished she hadn't. She hated it when someone told her she was "really good," after a performance. Good could mean anything—*Okay, Great, I was asleep.* Good meant you didn't care. "Fantastic. It's going to be a hit."

He nodded and looked back down at the papers with a pleased smile. She wasn't attracted to Jack because he was about to hit it big. Drew liked him because of his clear, wavering tenor; because he closed his eyes when he sang; because he had tousled blond hair like a Lab puppy's; because the muscles of his tanned skin were visible under his white T-shirt. And when he smiled at her (often and more than he smiled at anyone else—Drew counted), pleasant shivers, as if she'd just tasted an ice cream cone, traveled all over her body. "More robust," he said to Drew after the first rehearsal this morning.

"Robust like Arabica beans?" She nodded toward his coffee.

"Robust as those coffee beans they have to dig out of squirrel poop." Everyone laughed.

All day they'd been flirting, bantering, and now Drew thought this was her big chance. She stared at him from under her thick ebony lashes. In certain lights, her eyes were as amber as pieces of petrified tree resin, the effect magnified (she hoped) by the thick black eyeliner that had been Drew's signature look since the age of fourteen. Without the eyeliner, Drew thought her half-Asian eyes disappeared into her face.

She glanced at her phone. It was nearly three, and the traffic on the 405 was only going to get worse. If she wanted to get home, she'd have to leave immediately or be gridlocked for two hours. That was what her love life came down to: traffic-based decisions. *Come on,* she willed. *We haven't got all day.* She smoothed down her denim mini and crossed her long legs in a casual attempt to get him to look at her.

"Hey," she said huskily to Jack, who finally finished organizing his papers. "Feel like getting a drink?"

Jack blinked, blatant surprise and mild dismay on his suddenly awfully young-looking face, though he was her exact age. A mottled flush settled over Drew's fair skin. Well, shit. She'd read that wrong? Really?

She'd been doing a lot of that lately. Reading things wrong.

To cover herself, she rolled her shoulders. "Alcohol. Relaxes the muscles. You know." She pointed vaguely at her chin, which she knew bore the mark of her chin rest. "My neck. It's super sore."

"Ah, yeah." Jack snapped the folder closed. "We're meeting at the Black Crow around the corner. If you want to join us." He flashed her a quick, friendly smile. But that was all it was. Friendly.

The studio door opened and a young woman walked in. At least ten years younger than Drew, who was thirty-four and therefore decrepit by Los Angeles standards. She smiled at Drew, her big teeth so juvenile they still had those serrated edges. "Hey, Jack. Ready to load the van?" She had long brown hair, like Drew, and high cheekbones and full lips. All not unlike Drew. Even her frame, a tallish five-seven and bones thin enough to wrap a hand around and overlap a finger, was about the same size as Drew. But this girl had that youthful sleekness Drew was starting to lose, as if

Drew's skin had already begun pulling away from her bones. It didn't seem fair, to deteriorate physically so fast in her mid-thirties, before she even had the chance to have a baby. Drew swallowed, aware suddenly of the gap between her and this woman, the unspoken biological need that made men desire younger and younger women, no matter how close to her age the men were.

When she first moved to L.A. for college, Drew had been horrified by all the plasticky-looking people. Women with enlarged lips looking for all the world like wax candy, with their bolted-on breasts and shiny waxen skin. The weirdest thing, she thought, was that nobody acted like this was anything out of the ordinary, these aliens walking among them. Now she seriously considered joining them.

Back then, Drew felt so superior about her own skin situation. "Half-Asian skin, baby," she told people, and held her hand up for a high-five. "Doesn't get wrinkly until you're at least sixty." The indestructible twenties, when you're superior to everyone and everything. Back then, she would have been this girl, smiling with perfect confidence at this elderly inter-loper. Nobody could take a man from Drew. How bitchily powerful that had felt. She hadn't felt like a bitch at the time, of course, but now she sees that she probably was.

Jack lifted his beautiful face for a kiss from the other beautiful face. "Priscilla, Drew."

"Hello," Priscilla chirped, picking up the accordion folder. "Nice to meet you."

"Nice to meet you," Drew echoed numbly.

"See you at the bar, maybe." Jack nodded at her and exited the glass-walled studio, Priscilla close behind.

Drew dropped her head, staring at the pocked black plastic of her viola case. There was no sound in here except for the air faintly whistling through her nose, a by-product of seasonal allergies. Suddenly she saw herself how Jack must see her. A semi-employed cougar, practically *Basic Instinct*–ing herself at him. Pitiable. She caught sight of herself in the glass between the sound booth and the studio. Her eyeliner was streaked into the fine lines beneath her eyes. Well, great. The cherry on it all.

In the pet grooming office, Drew shudders at the memory and pretends that this soda is making everything all better, forcing herself to drink it all fast so she gets a throbbing headache. "That hit the spot," she says to a picture of a hairy mutt, a grooming guide stuck up on the wall, arrows pointing at all the places that needed trimming with various shear sizes.

She fires up the laptop so she can wire Liza another two grand, her stomach tensing at the dwindling balance. Honestly, she isn't sure how Liza stays in business. Liza comes from a rich family, the offspring of someone who'd invested early in Wendy's, so this business is mostly a way for Liza to stay busy. A vanity operation. But lately money hasn't been being deposited, and Drew doesn't know where it's gone, or if it's gone for good.

Drew waits for the laptop to hum to life and regards the empty plastic cup sitting in front of her, where Mickey and Minnie Mouse hold hands and proclaim, in Gothic script, *The Happiest Place on Earth*. She doesn't know precisely when her life turned into this big sticky oatmeal cookie of a mess. One, two wrong turns—detours, really—and she'd veered completely off the path to wherever she was headed. But Drew kept thinking that if she only turned around, turned right, she could find her way back.

If she had a destination. Something's got to change.

She takes a small black spiral-bound notebook out of her bag. She's carried one around since she was a kid, to write down ideas for song lyrics and music notes. Drew used to set it on the toilet tank outside the shower because that's where she thought of her best ideas, and the notebook would get wet and curled, the ink running. When she was in the band, she'd fill up one every two weeks.

This one still looked factory-new. She opens it to the second page, the first page having been filled with a grocery list, and stares at the dogs on the wall and tries to will a new song to come to her.

All she hears is the refrigerator whirring.

Her phone buzzes again and she lifts it to her ear. "I've almost got it done, Liza, but you need to deposit more money by the fifteenth for the rent." It's October 2, she notes.

"Hey." A younger voice, not Liza's raspy twang. As familiar to Drew as her own. Her big sister. Rachel clears her throat.

"Rachel," Drew says. She wasn't expecting her sister to call. Fear laces up her insides. "What happened? Mom? One of the kids?"

"Everybody's fine."

Drew exhales. She talks to her sister on the phone a grand total of maybe five times a year, if they're lucky, and lately they hadn't been. Their conversations had grown shorter and shorter over the years, until it was simply an exchange like, "Happy birthday! The kids want to talk to Aunt Drew." On major holidays, Drew stops by to see the children, but she's never felt quite comfortable staying for too long. Like she's intruding on her sister's impenetrable family unit. That's just how it was between them. Rachel getting kicked out had turned them into virtual strangers.

When Rachel and Drew were young, they were inseparable. Or at least Drew had felt that way, tagging along after her older sister wherever she went, until Rachel hit her mid-teens and became the problem child, leaving Drew behind as the everlasting gobstopper in her family. Drew, the musical talent. How her parents had pinned their hopes on her.

Then their roles had reversed. All of Drew's potential had evaporated when she picked up the tambourine for the band. It is Rachel now who has it all. Rachel who turned her sinking ship of a life around and made it into something beautiful, with her great kids and truly great husband. Pillar of the community, that Rachel.

Drew has the feeling Rachel gave up on her years ago. Wrote her off as Eccentric Sister, she who will never get her life together. Drew can actually feel Rachel rolling her eyes through the phone every time they speak. It's that visceral. The Rachel Glare. Her sister's never been good at hiding feelings. Drew's teeth grind automatically, thinking of Rachel's judgment. She's got bigger problems. Her phone beeps again. A Liza call awaits. "Can I call you back in like two minutes?"

"No." Rachel sounds determined. "This is really important. It is about Mom, though."

The office phone rings now, and an e-mail pops up in front of Drew. WHERE ARE YOU CALL ME, Liza has written. Drew groans inwardly, and, fed up with Liza and her constant demands, silences the office phone and swivels away from the computer. "What can I help you with?" She sounds formal yet cheerful, how she imagines a midwestern front-desk clerk to be. Maybe that's where she'll move. Where people aren't so concerned with appearances, and she can be a real person.

"I went to visit Mom today," Rachel says.

Drew sits up straight, her spine popping. "How is she?"

Rachel takes a big breath, and Drew knows she's trying not to cry. "She was Mom again for a minute, and she told me to get something from her house."

She pictures her mother's face, *Mom again,* as Rachel says, Mom with recognition in her eyes, instead of the blank Mom they know now, and bites her lip hard. These moments are getting rarer. "Did she tell you about a secret treasure chest buried in the backyard?" Drew says, both to keep the tone light and to tamp down the stinging in her own eyes.

Rachel either doesn't get or ignores this bit of humor. "No. It's some kind of book. In the sewing room," Rachel continues. She hesitates. "I don't know what kind of book it is. She said you would know. Do you remember her showing you a book in there?"

Drew shuts her eyes, pictures her parents' house, which she'd left as soon as humanly possible, at the age of seventeen and a half, escaping to USC. The sewing room is downstairs. Drew rarely ventured in there. Sometimes, when nobody else was home, Drew would go in and look around, just because she was bored and lonely and nosy. But all she can remember are fabrics and a big sewing machine. A material-cutting table. "I can't think of her showing me any book. I'm sorry. Did she say why she wants it?"

"No. But I just know it's important, Drew. You should have seen the way she grabbed me. Her expression. It was like she was starving and asking for food." Rachel's voice is flat, which means she's afraid. There's no reason to be afraid about a book, Drew thinks. They'll go find it. No big deal. Rachel's always overreacted. Always has. Once, a huge gray moth flew into the family room while they were watching TV. Rachel grabbed Drew and threw her off the couch, out of the moth's path. "I thought it was a monster," Rachel had said later. "I was protecting you." Drew had a bruised thigh for two weeks from that protection.

Drew pictures all the books she's ever seen Mom handle. An Italian cookbook. *Curious George. Amish Country Quilting.* Her mind goes blank. Their mother was never known as a big reader. Besides, Drew was never close to her, the way Rachel had been. "Why don't you just go over to Dad's and look?"

"Yeah." Rachel gives a little bark of a laugh. "I should. I will. I was just wondering if you remembered, so I'd know what I was looking for."

Oh. Yeah. Getting a book out of their father's house should not be a two-person operation, but Drew had forgotten, for a second, that their father had disowned her sister. Does she want Drew to come down and help? Then she should ask, Drew thinks stubbornly. Is she supposed to be a mind reader?

Yet something in Rachel's voice gives her pause. Rachel hates, more than anything, to admit weakness. She's the type of person who'd bleed all over the place instead of just accepting a damn Band-Aid from you. Does she want help, but is afraid to ask? Afraid Drew will blow her off?

Drew's phone buzzes again. Won't Liza leave her alone for just a minute? Drew hits Send on the bank transfer. The page refreshes itself, and her pulse skitters. The balance is down. A lot down.

DREW CALL ME IMMEDIATELY, Liza's text reads.

She clicks the screen dark on her phone, turning her full attention to her big sister. Rachel's never asked for help with Mom. Not once. *You're too far away. I can take care of her. Tom and the kids will help,* Rachel always said, rebuffing Drew's offers. No doubt Rachel thinks this makes it easier for Drew, but instead it makes her feel unwanted.

Drew goes down to visit sometimes, on the weekends, where she sits with her mother, trying and failing to think of anything to say. She usually reads a book aloud, out of the library cart, to fill the time. Then she heads back to L.A. before traffic gets too bad, thinking, sometimes, of calling her sister—but then thinking there's really no point, because Rachel will just say, *Oh, we're really busy today, not going to be home until bedtime.* Which was probably, in fact, a hundred percent true. Anyway, Drew had stopped trying.

Drew clears her throat, imagining going down to help for a couple of days. Suddenly, walking away from this store, from this nonlife, seems like a pretty damn good option. She needs to recalibrate.

She hears her sister breathing on the other end of the phone. How Drew always tried to crawl into bed with Rachel, to be lulled to sleep by that sound. Drew has an urge to put her arms around her sister, to tell her both of them will be okay. She thinks of her niece and nephew—Chase a teenager, Quincy in college—and it feels like someone pitched a ball into her stomach. They're so old now, and Drew has mostly missed it all. If she doesn't know them well, who will come visit Drew when she's in Mom's situation? She wants to see them, too.

Does Rachel want her help? Will she be offended if Drew offers? Drew pauses. "I could come down there and help you find the book tomorrow. If you want, that is. It's not a problem." *Please want,* she prays.

There is a silence for a moment. "Yes, I would appreciate that, thank you," Rachel says softly, and that's all that Drew needs to hear. She closes the laptop with a snap.

The Story of Tomoe Gozen

MIYANOKOSHI

SHINANO PROVINCE

HONSHU, JAPAN

Spring 1160

I f left alone, objects remain in the same unchanging state for all of eternity. An object at rest will remain at rest unless acted on by an unbalanced force. Boulders sit on mountaintops, worn down over thousands of years by rain. Trees untouched by lightning or fires keep on growing.

But then that unbalanced force appears, and suddenly stationary objects are set in motion.

So it began for Tomoe Gozen, the greatest woman warrior who ever lived.

The daughter of a samurai retainer, Kaneto, and a mild-mannered wet nurse, Chizuru, Tomoe started life as an unremarkable little girl living in the mountains of central Japan in the late twelfth century. Her younger brother Kanehira and their foster brother, Yoshinaka Minamoto, lived a quiet life on a farm. Yoshinaka and Kanehira were the ones meant to be samurai, to fight for the title of shōgun. Tomoe's father rescued Yoshinaka from the murderous Taira clan, who killed Yoshinaka's father, or so they had been told.

Tomoe might have been content to stay a normal little girl. To grow up and marry a boy from a neighboring farm. But then Yoshinaka and the stick set her in motion.

Had it been a thin, reedy branch off the dead plum tree, the kind of twig that crumbled into dust with a touch, Tomoe would have forgiven the quick pain. Instead, Yoshinaka chose a thick length of sticky pine, a proper switch, the kind used on prisoners.

That cool spring morning, seven-year-old Tomoe squatted in the square kitchen garden on the north side of the house, picking moth larvae off her spinach plants. All of her concentration was on looking for the bugs, placing each wriggling green worm into a basket to feed to the chickens. The earth was soft and damp from watering, black and fertile. She hummed to herself, a melody of her own making.

"I'm very sorry," she said to the third worm. "But you're making far too many holes in my plants."

The worm twisted in her pinched fingers, its white jaws grasping at the air. She threw it into the basket and examined the tender sprigs of spinach. Soon she would pick these, and she would help her mother prepare them for supper with some soy sance and a bit of sesame oil. She imagined her father closing his eyes at the rich, salty taste. "What a good gardener our Tomoe is!" he would say. Her foster brother, Yoshinaka, would have sauce dripping down his chin. *"Oishikata!"* he would roar. Delicious. The dish was his favorite. One of his favorites, anyway—the boy ate everything.

Then something solid hit Tomoe's left rib. A stinging slap. She fell over, knees and hands in the dirt, pebbles embedding in her hands, so rough for a girl of only seven. Her blue-black hair escaped its head wrap and fell over her face. All she saw was a blur of legs going past. She didn't need to see to know who was to blame.

Tears stung her eyes, mixed with hurt and anger. What had she done? That was a real hit. An ambush.

"Ha ha!" a boy called from the other side of the garden. Yoshinaka. He wore a gray kimono and loose pants, doing a dance in his bare feet. He waved the branch in his hand. "Taira scum, come get me."

Kanehira joined him. "You can't catch us."

Those ungrateful troublemakers. She was always saving them. Tomoe had pulled Yoshinaka out of a frozen pond the previous winter. Always impetuous, he had run ahead onto the ice, not bothering to stop to check its thickness. Tomoe had seen the dark, semi-frozen color and shouted, "It's not safe!" Then she heard the cracking. Yoshinaka turned to her with an expression of surprise before the icy water swallowed him up. Kanehira ran to help and fell through, too. Tomoe lay on her belly, reached out her hand and hoisted them out, first Yoshinaka, then Kanehira.

She put her hand on her throbbing side. The flesh swelled around the bones. How dare they? What if they'd missed and hit her eye? Or caught her in the abdomen? She could be half blind, or dead.

A strangled cry erupted from somewhere in the distance, sending white egrets flapping skyward in a giant cloud. Tomoe stood. What had made that noise?

The sound had come from her. Rage, pure and hot, floated in her center. She let the sensation guide her, move her limbs.

Those boys had better run.

From across the field, she saw the whites of their eyes. The boys took off like rocks out of a slingshot, across the meadow. She chased.

Yoshinaka dropped the branch into the tall grass. Tomoe bent and picked it up without stopping. The boys had made it across the field to the northern pinewoods, disappearing up the hill. She searched for footprints. All their lives, Father had taught them how to look for animal and human tracks. How to cover their own. If the boys were smart, they would have been careful.

She brushed her hair out of her eyes and sniffed the air. That distinctive unwashed boy scent of mud and dogs and mashed grass presented itself, and she pushed her way farther into the forest. It went abruptly dark, the evergreen trees interlocking above her head. Here and there were still patches of snow, untouched by sun. She shivered. Her feet were bare. Tomoe kept moving. Those boys would be cold, dressed as they were in light kimonos. She fought back an urge to call them, tell them it was all right. She had spent her whole life wiping their faces clean. She could not mother them anymore.

At last, through a copse of thick short pine trees ahead, she heard voices.

"Did you hear that?" Yoshinaka said suddenly. He was chewing.

"It was a bird. She'll never find us here," her brother said.

"Right. She's only a dumb girl." Yoshinaka chewed some more, smacking his lips.

Tomoe's hand combed the dirt through the pine needles until her fingers closed around a rock. She threw it, her arm parallel to the ground, so it skipped across the boys' toes as it would skip across a pond.

"*Ai!*" Yoshinaka was first up. Kanehira followed. Their toes pointed away from her. "What was that?"

Tomoe rolled out from under the trees, jumping upright. The boys had their backs to her. Without pause, Tomoe swung the branch low, knocking their legs out from under them. They collapsed, breath gone, turtles on their backs.

Immediately she put her foot on Yoshinaka's chest. He grimaced. His eyes were the rich brown-red color of azuki beans, ringed with thick lashes, and she felt a momentary surge of pity. She wanted to let him up, but something stopped her.

"Oh, hello. Did you think you were hiding?" She turned her attention to Yoshinaka's hand, still gripping the food. Dried persimmon. She pried open his fingers and took the fruit. "Mmm. At least you didn't drop your treat to fight me off. Food shouldn't be more important than your life."

"Let him up!" Kanehira, her scrawny younger brother, tugged at her free arm, knocking her off balance. He tugged on her arm again; she tugged back hard, then shoved him with her other arm. He tumbled backward.

"You are both idiots." They blanched—Tomoe had never dared call them an idiot before. A girl could get beaten for that. Tomoe didn't care anymore. *Let my father come for me*, she thought defiantly. *I am right.*

She casually ate another bite of persimmon, the stickiness all over her hand now. *After all I do for you*, she added in her head. Getting their meals, scrubbing their clothes, making sure they didn't perish. She was only a year older than they. She did not want them to see how much it hurt her. She would not be weak. "Never call me Taira." She ground her foot down.

"Tomoe." Rough fingers closed around her ankle.

"Especially you, Yoshinaka," she added reproachfully. His chest rose and fell under her foot, but she kept her gaze on Kanehira, who sat farther off, pouting.

Now, as Tomoe pinned Yoshinaka down, Kanehira kicked at the ground, sending a cloud of needles upward. He stomped his feet. "Stop it, Tomoe!"

"Tantrums are for babies, Kanehira." She transferred the fruit to her other hand, wiping her palm on her trousers. "But I suppose that's to be expected from you."

"You just wait, Tomoe." Kanehira took off through the copse. Tomoe considered going after him, but decided against it.

"Ah, going to get Father, I suppose." Tomoe spoke as if she didn't care, but her stomach seized. There would be a consequence to her retaliation. Father would not be happy. They were supposed to be guarding Yoshinaka, not beating him up. Though he'd legally lost his title, he was still Lord Yoshinaka in the eyes of the Minamoto clan. Tomoe's family were but his servants.

"Tomoe, I can't breathe." Yoshinaka's fingers played a tune on her ankle-bone. It tickled. He squeezed her calf, rubbed the muscle. "Let go."

She took her foot off his chest and sank into the damp new grass. Yoshinaka sat up so they were side by side, facing each other. His face was streaked with dirt. His hair, normally pulled back, was loose around his face. His eyes, normally impish, were sad.

Beaten. Thoroughly beaten. She couldn't stand to see him like this. She leaned over, the last bit of fruit in her palm. For a moment he ignored it.

"Come on," Tomoe said, moving the fruit under his nose. Always, the boy could be swayed by food. She put it to his lips and he glared at her— she thought he'd smack her hand away. He opened his mouth instead and allowed her to feed him.

Two

T he next morning, I pull my minivan into the absurdly long middle school drop-off line, behind the fleet of identical minivans. These minivan car dealers must lurk outside hospital delivery rooms, capturing new parents. "What's going on today? Any tests?" I brake as two kids leap out in front of the car and scurry into the school. I turn up the music. The group's name, The Naked and Famous, pops up in digital letters on the display. "Young Blood," my favorite.

I flip down the visor mirror and put on a little lipstick, singing along. I look good, I think. No makeup, but my skin's kind of glowing, no doubt thanks to the hijinks my husband initiated this morning. I flip my ponytail sassily and grin, showing most of my teeth. I even remembered to brush before we left. A pretty big accomplishment.

Chase shoots me a withering look and turns down the volume. "It should be illegal for a mother to listen to a band with a name like that."

"Oh really? What about moms dancing to it?" I shake around in my seat, flailing my arms around, and he slides down as far as he can, pulling his hoodie over his eyes.

You can't tell my children are one-quarter Japanese. Chase has light hazel eyes and curly light brown hair perpetually bleached blond by the sun. Quincy has hair that was full-on blond when she was little and turned to medium brown when she get older. Quincy and Chase are taller than I am—Quincy about five-ten, Chase already nearly six feet—and both are athletically built.

Perhaps they don't look Asian because I don't, either—I've got reddish brown hair and a smattering of freckles. My face turns red when I drink. I look more like my father's side, of indeterminate Western European heritage.

I dance some more, not caring who sees.

In the past, I was *that* parent. The one who had no life outside of school. The too-into-it room mother who sends out thirty-page e-mails detailing class potlucks and craft projects. The one who takes carpool duty as seriously as military service.

And that's who I wanted to be. I wanted my kids to have a CHILDHOOD: *Now Without Traumatic Family Dynamics.* To glance up from their timed math tests and know that somewhere, on campus, their mother hunched over a miniature table, cutting out eighty construction paper hearts for the first grade. To know in the very marrow of their bones that they'd come home to a hot dinner with a vegetable and a whole grain and a lean meat, and a father who'd play catch and never, ever tell a single lie to them.

My phone buzzes and I glance down. My daughter Quincy's photo lights up the screen. Her engagement photo, to be precise. *Got our proofs.* A lovely picture, the afternoon light making her long light brown hair and skin glow as if candlelit. Her fiancé Ryan's hair is shaved to the skin on the sides and back, the top left an inch long in a high-and-tight military haircut, wearing his dress blues.

Yes. There's also this. As if there isn't enough already happening. My twenty-year-old *college student* is getting married in June. Twenty. Yes, I said twenty. "Look." I show the photo to Chase.

He nods absently, sighing at the carpool line. "Yup, that's Quincy."

I put the phone down.

Only two and a half years earlier, Quincy had yet to meet Ryan. She was looking at college brochures with me at the kitchen counter, her face alive with fresh dreams. She trailed her fingertips along the photos. "I've got it all planned out, Mom. I'm definitely going to do grad school. Maybe a double MBA/engineering. That'll get me on the executive track."

Her wide hazel eyes, today leaning more toward brown, as they did when she was in emotional disarray, waited for my approval. I felt the same way I had when she stood up to a playground bully twice her size in second grade. Plain old awe. I kissed her forehead. "I have no doubt you'll achieve whatever you want."

I can, of course, think of dozens of objections to her marriage. Any reasonable parent can. Her fiancé is only four years into his Navy career, still deciding whether or not to stay in for the full twenty years. "The world's too uncertain to wait, Mother," Quincy told me. "Have some optimism," I told her. If you're a cynical parent, you might as well give up and move to a bunker buried in a hillside. Then again, Ryan's already been deployed, seen action. I could understand why Quincy feels he might not be around forever.

I have to keep my mouth shut. After all, what can I possibly say about her getting married? She's doing what I did. Only better, because she's already got two years of college behind her and she's not even pregnant.

I have to trust her. But another part of me worries we've messed up somehow. Overlooked some crucial parenting key, and Quincy now wants to escape our family the same way I'd wanted to escape mine.

Parenting. It's not for the weak.

I peer at the sky above the middle school. Two more cars and we're there. This takes up the biggest chunk of my morning by far. "Don't forget your umbrella. It's supposed to rain." October is the month of strange weather. One day it will reach the nineties, with the desert blowing in hot Santa Ana winds. The next, a storm from up north might cause the temperature to drop twenty-five degrees and rain to fall. Clouds sit low over us today, thicker than the coastal fog that usually burns off by noon. We call this part of town inland, though it's only fifteen minutes to the beach, in the middle of San Diego.

Chase puts his hand on the door, ready to jump out. "Mom. I play water polo in the rain all the time. I don't need an umbrella."

He's got a point, but I don't want to concede. I inch the car forward. "If you catch a cold, I'm going to be mad."

"That's not actually how you catch a cold," Chase says. "You catch cold from a virus, not from actual cold air. Science, Mom."

"Some things science doesn't know. *Mothers* know." I smile sweetly at my son.

"Um, okay, Mom. You are all knowing. Greater than science." He rolls his eyes dramatically. I used to think only my girl would do that.

He leaps out with a shouted good-bye.

I pull forward. Now the kids are older, and I need something new to occupy me. Quincy sure won't need me after next summer.

I can see the blank years unspooling themselves like a roll of new register tape. Once Chase graduates, I've got years before my husband can retire. Years I've got to fill. It's terrifying and exhilarating. Like starting out fresh, as if I'm eighteen.

Except, yeah, I'm not eighteen. I'm thirty-eight.

Okay. Like starting out fresh, but WISER. That sounds much better. I'm wise, not old.

Besides, I've got everything I ever wanted. A fantastic, loving husband. Two healthy kids who make me laugh. A house to tinker with. What else do I need? I'll figure out something. I always do.

I wave at a clutch of women standing on the lawn ahead of the drop-off zone, where the curb's red. One of them, Susannah, stands out with her long flowing hair dyed flame-red, like a comic book heroine. She motions at me to roll down my window. "You going to help with the science club bake sale?" she calls.

I'm usually the one in Susannah's place, shanghaiing the unsuspecting into service. But this time, with me preoccupied with my mother, the honor's gone to her instead. I feel instantly guilty. "Sure thing. I can make, um, cupcakes with those gummy earthworms and Oreo cookie crumbs that look like dirt."

"Fan-tastic." Susannah hops over to the driver's side and leans in through the window, so close I can smell traces of the cinnamon oatmeal she had for breakfast. I've known Susannah for fifteen years, since our older two were in kindergarten. Quincy and Sam. We always said their names sounded like a detective show. Now Sam, her son, is away at Berkeley. The last time I saw him with her, I didn't know who he was. Susannah looks the same as she did fifteen years ago, but her son's a man. In my memory he's still about three feet tall. It's like there was a blip in the space-time continuum.

We clasp hands briefly, my left in her left. "Your mom okay?"

I hesitate. I can't get into details right here and now, in the carpool line. And even if I had the time, I'm reluctant to share all the gritty details of my family's feud.

This morning, our family attorney, Laura, forwarded a cryptic note from my father, the latest in a year-plus battle to gain power of attorney from me. The battle that could actually go on forever, because my father's sure not going to run out of money. *If Rachel truly has her mother's best interests at heart, she will do as I say. There are things Rachel doesn't know about her mother. Ask Rachel if she'd rather keep Hikari safe, or if she'd rather keep the power of attorney.*

"Do you have any idea what this means?" Laura had asked. "If you did, we could be prepared. But if he drops a bombshell during the hearing . . ." she trailed off. "I told his attorney we need more info, and he said he'd ask Killian at their meeting this afternoon."

I knew what Laura meant. We'd lose. "I have no idea," I'd said, my stomach dropping. Of course there's a secret. Everything our parents do revolves around secrets. Keeping things hidden. Unspoken. It could just as well be an empty threat.

When my mother first got diagnosed, when her doctor said she was still able to understand the consequences, Mom gave me instead of Killian power of attorney, enabling me to make decisions about her care and well-being.

In truth, I wanted to say no. Just the thought of how my father would react, his cold eyes boring into me, made my stomach turn. "What do you think Dad will do when he finds out?" I asked Mom. "Why not Drew? He gets along with her."

"I know you won't go along with what he wants." Mom gripped my arm and told me the name of the home Dad had chosen for her. "I saw the paperwork," she whispered. "It's a cheap home. He's done with me. He'll throw me away."

I checked out the assisted living home my father wanted. It smelled of dirty diapers and moldy apples. The disheveled residents stared at blank walls; the staff were brusque and distracted. I wished that I could rescue every single one of those people. I stood in that lobby imagining my mother living there, unable to speak up for herself. Of my father sitting on his pile of wealth like Scrooge McDuck. Mom deserves better.

I know it's the loss of control, not the money, that bothers my father. The fact that his disowned daughter has popped back up to prove him wrong. That's what he doesn't like. He's been fighting me, saying I coerced Mom into signing.

I glance down at my steering wheel, then back into Susannah's sympathetic, deep blue eyes. I shrug. "Mom's spending the day checking out hot surfers and eating cookies. There are worse ways to live out the end of a life, I guess."

She squeezes my hand. "I'm sorry, hon. Let me know if you need anything."

I nod mutely, appreciative. Knowing I'll never ask.

Somebody honks, and I salute Susannah and drive away from the school, thinking about when I'll have time to make those complicated treats. I don't even know when the bake sale is. The truth is, I'm going to forget about it all by this afternoon.

Drew pulls up just as the heavy black Mercedes backs out of the driveway and accelerates down the quiet residential street. Her father's gray head is visible above the driver's seat. Eighty-nine, still driving, with shot reflexes and eyes scarred from imperfect cataract surgery. The last time he failed a behind-the-wheel test, he just went up to the DMV in Palm Springs and took it there, where they were much more sympathetic to the AARP crowd. Drew hadn't been surprised. Her father always finds the right angle to get what he wants, even if just to prove that he can.

Darn it. Drew slumps down so he doesn't see her. It would have been simpler if her father was home and Drew could have walked in alone and looked for the book. She doubts he'd care a bit if she took it.

Drew's not exactly close with her father, but she's not at war with him, either. Drew once heard a radio therapist advise people on how to get along with difficult family members: Just *pretend* that you get along. Don't engage them. Let everything slide right off. That's what Drew's done her entire life, and she didn't need a radio personality to tell her that.

After Drew left for college, she rarely spoke to her parents, calling occasionally out of a sense of duty. They never contacted her, leaving Drew to wonder if they'd even notice if she stopped calling. It didn't occur to Drew how strange this was until she mentioned it to her roommate, Brenda. "My mother calls me every week if I don't call," Brenda said. Brenda received care packages full of fresh apples from Washington state, her home. "Your family's kind of messed up."

Drew hadn't said anything to this. To her, it was just how her family was.

So, during sophomore year, Drew had conducted an experiment. She hadn't called them for the entire fall semester, just to see if they'd notice. She figured her mother was glad to be rid of her, secretly relieved that

Drew wasn't calling. After Rachel left, they hadn't gotten along. It was passive-aggressive of Drew, perhaps, but Drew was only nineteen.

Finally, in December, just when Drew figured she'd spend her holiday break in a near-empty dorm like Ebenezer Scrooge in his memory of Christmas Past, her mother phoned her and asked if Drew was coming home. But her mother, rather than sounding like she wanted Drew home, sounded irritated. "You cannot just ignore us. You owe us some respect. We're your parents. You need to call us."

"Tell her we don't have to pay her tuition. It's not required," Drew heard Killian say in a petulant voice. "She should be thanking us, not the other way around. Tell her that good daughters call their parents and only good daughters get their education paid for."

Drew's heart constricted. Her mind flew to what she'd do if he didn't pay tuition. "I'm sorry. I was busy," she said lamely. "I have to practice a lot."

Hikari sighed. "Just come. Two hours on Christmas. Your father will be happy."

What about you? Drew had wanted to ask, but was afraid to. She might not like the answer.

So Drew had gone over there, figuring a couple of hours making small talk with Killian and Hikari was better than forgoing a degree. After college, she continued to come home at Christmas, without fail. It wouldn't kill her, she thought every year.

"You don't have to go every time," her ex-boyfriend Jonah said to her once a few years ago. "They're your parents, but look at how they treat you. You don't owe them anything."

Drew thought about it, how Jonah blew off his family because he'd gotten a more fun vacation offer, or thought his uber-conservative mother talked politics too much (though, Drew pointed out to him, his mother tolerated his liberal views without kicking him out). After she was out of college, she had no compelling tangible reason to go. "They're my family," was all she could think of to say. "I'm here and alive. Don't I owe them something?"

Drew taps her hands on the steering wheel. She tried all night to think of what book Rachel could be talking about, but she had no memory of it. Now the curiosity's eating away at her.

This home of Drew and Rachel's childhood is on a hill in La Jolla, a wealthy community north of San Diego, the houses on this hillside large and worth millions. This was not a separate city from San Diego, though the residents have tried to secede several times. Across the street, the trees that once blocked the house's ocean view have been cut down. The trees were Torrey pines, a rare and protected type of tree that grows only in certain coastal areas. The trees must have become diseased—it's the only way to have them legally cut down. That was another thing her father tried to do for years: have those "infernal trees removed." Drew wouldn't be surprised if her father had planted some kind of destructive beetle on them, just so he could claim the trees were compromised.

Killian has been known to skirt the law to get what he wants. During one Christmas visit, Killian told Drew to go in his office and get his checkbook, so he could write her the gift check. On top of a stack of letters, she'd seen a notice from Killian's lawyer regarding the FCC investigating a company called Himalaya Telecommunications, which was owned by a company that was owned by a trust, which was owned by Killian. Drew stopped breathing—she'd seen Himalaya on the news—they'd roped phone subscribers into illegal contracts, charging them exorbitant fees. The upshot was that Killian had protected himself with layers of trusts and shell companies, enabling him to keep his money while preventing people from collecting.

If it wasn't cloudy, even at four o'clock, Drew would be able to see the ocean. October is actually a great time of year to go to the beach in San Diego—few tourists, warm water.

Liza's big message to Drew was that her cruise was taking longer than she thought. Drew asked her if she was okay, if she needed any help, and finally, bluntly, "You know there's not enough to cover rent."

Liza shrugged, or Drew imagined she shrugged. Drew couldn't see her through the phone, obviously. "You know what, the business hasn't been profitable for a while. Give the keys back to the owner. I'll mail you your last check."

And then Drew should have shouted at Liza, told her off for being so flippant with someone else's life. It shouldn't have surprised Drew. An employer who made Drew look like a sensible far-thinking thrifty person was definitely not someone Drew should have trusted. Berating Liza wasn't worth it—she'd just hang up. Drew's got enough in the bank, thanks to a few music jobs, to cover herself for a couple of weeks. And she could always ask her father for money. She hates doing that—has eaten ramen for days and sold her television to avoid it in the past—but the reality is that her father doesn't miss it any more than she'd miss pocket lint.

Drew still has a key to his house. She could just walk in without Rachel and look for the book. Her mother, still legally married to Killian Snow, has the right to get her stuff out of the house, does she not? Especially because Rachel has power of attorney.

Drew shifts on the leather seat, her backside sticking uncomfortably to the upholstery. Power of attorney is number fifty or so on a long laundry list of the reasons why Rachel and Killian are still bitter toward each other.

To outsiders, Killian Snow seemed like a genial, gentle man. With his cheerful baritone and big teddy-bear build, Killian charmed everyone who met him. He'd played high school football and skipped college, starting a business providing window glass to high rises, as well as many other investments they didn't really know the details about, like that telecommunications company. He was one of those guys who could sit down with a stranger in a bar and come away invited to the family reunion. Someone people didn't believe could do any wrong. "Your dad's so charming," Drew's friends would tell her. "That's because he's a white-collar grifter," she always wanted to reply, but of course did not. To his family, he was someone else. It was like he erected a new and happy public face every day that slowly crumbled into dust by the time he got home, revealing his true nature.

The earliest memory Drew has of her father is from when she was maybe three years old. Rachel was seven. Drew asked her father if Santa would bring her Spanish Barbie, a doll with a swirling red flamenco skirt and long brown curls.

"Nah. Santa's going to bring you a lump of coal," Killian said, his eyes twinkling.

Drew began to cry. Back then, she'd believed everything her father told her. "I don't want coal."

Killian turned the page of his newspaper. "Well, that's all you're going to get. A big lump of coal."

Drew tried to remember what she'd done that was so bad. She couldn't think of anything. "But I've been good."

Now Killian was unable to back away from the narrative he'd started. Never, not at anyone's expense, could her father cut his own pride. Never could he admit he was wrong. "That's how Santa works, Drew. What can I tell you?"

Her big sister, Rachel, reading a book across the room, put her book down. "That's mean," Rachel said quietly. "You shouldn't make her cry."

Killian looked at Rachel, his forehead wrinkling in surprise. "I'm just teasing her. I always say: hope for the best but expect the worst."

Rachel curled her upper lip and Drew put a couch cushion in front of her, bracing herself. "That's not telling her to hope," Rachel said. "That's just being mean."

Drew looked around for their mother, but she was in the kitchen, out of sight. Drew heard her banging a pan in there. Besides, even if they told their mother, she couldn't do anything.

Annoyance settled over Killian's face. He ground his teeth lightly. "Well. Maybe you'll get a lump of coal, too, my smart little Rachel." Back then Rachel was Killian's favorite. And Drew did find Spanish Barbie, wrapped up under the tree in white tissue paper that looked like it'd been pulled out of an old gift bag. She doesn't remember what Rachel got.

Drew's lesson from that was to keep low, out of her father's mind as much as possible. Be compliant. Let harsh words roll into one ear and out the other, the way you do if you're an Army private and a sergeant's yelling at you at boot camp. She never cried again at anything her father did.

Instead, she retreated into her music, staying in her room or at school to practice for hours on end. She ought to thank her father for giving her that discipline. That's how she got so good.

Rachel was another story. Rachel hadn't ever learned to keep to herself well. She'd always step in, tell Killian he was wrong, or do the things he told her not to do—and that was just like dangling a goat in front of a tiger. She pushed him too far.

Still, Drew thinks that Rachel should have gotten over their childhood by now. Sure, their father's kind of a sociopath. Sure, he was intelligent enough to know better, but it was just his personality. He couldn't harm Drew or Rachel.

Rachel's almost forty, a full-grown woman with a loving, devoted husband and two smart, capable children. Her sister has so much more than most.

She turns up her stereo, tuned to her iPod, to her current favorite song. "Time Won't Let Me Go," by The Bravery. They could make a musical out of her life and this song would be playing right now, she thinks, then laughs at her own melodrama. But still.

Drew shuts off the music.

Her father, Kaneto, ate the last of the rice. Tomoe waited, willing herself not to speak. Would she be punished for her actions against her brothers? Outside, her mother and her brothers laughed. At last Kaneto pushed away his empty rice bowl and spoke. "Tomoe, I have left off your education for too long. When the men are away, it is you who must defend our home."

Tomoe blinked, surprised.

Kaneto rose and went to the large oak trunk in the corner of the room. This trunk held his possessions from his time as a retainer. None of the children were allowed to touch it. The boys did, of course, when their parents weren't around, so Tomoe knew what the trunk contained: swords and armor.

But it wasn't the trunk Kaneto opened. He shoved it aside and bent to the floorboards, prying one up with his fingertips and reaching into the depths of the house. Kaneto fished around for a minute, then straightened. He held something Tomoe hadn't seen before. It was a curved blade about two feet long, glinting in the dim light, set atop a wooden pole much taller than Tomoe herself.

"A *naginata*." He gestured for Tomoe to come closer. She took the pole in her hands, holding it up. It was heavy, but she could manage. She hefted it and took an experimental swing. With this, one could reach far. It was like having an eight-foot-long arm.

Kaneto grunted approvingly. "You may think this is a sword for women and therefore less useful, but this is what the fierce warrior monks use." He looked at her appraisingly. "Your being female has advantages, Tomoe. You are nimble and light. And you have more natural fortitude. You will make the boys work harder. They will fear being shamed by a girl."

Tomoe swung the sword up, stopping short of the ceiling. She had no wish to shame anyone.

Kaneto knelt and looked her in the eye. "You understand, Tomoe? I give you permission. Be yourself. Be the best. Nothing done by half."

Permission to be herself.

A weight lifted from her shoulders, a weight she hadn't even known existed. Her breath came easily. She smiled up at Kaneto, and he touched her cheek gently as he stood.

Her father glanced toward the door; Chizuru had gone. The boys chased a squawking chicken. Tomoe couldn't tell which was making more noise, fowl or boy. Kanehira slipped and fell on his face in the mud, laughing and pulling Yoshinaka down with him. Kaneto sighed. "Tomoe, go clean them up."

Tomoe handed the sword back to her father and bowed.

Three

R achel's minivan pulls up behind Drew's car, and Drew watches as her sister kicks open the door with her sneakered foot. Though she's wearing just yoga pants and a tank top with her hair pulled back, she's still as beautiful as ever, with her lean, curvy build. Drew supposes this is the eternal way of younger sisters, to admire the elder. Rachel had always seemed so poised, holding her head erect and regal like the ancient Nefertiti bust. Drew was certain she could never be as great as Rachel. When Rachel grew breasts, eight-year-old Drew had been awed, stuffed her own shirt with oranges, wondering when it'd be her turn. "You don't want your period," Rachel said flatly. "Do you think it's fun to bleed out of your vagina for a week?"

"I don't know. Is it?" Drew asked, not knowing. Bleeding without dying seemed kind of miraculous. Maybe it was fun, too, in a way she couldn't understand. After all, she was only eight.

"Dope." Rachel shook her head, laughing. "You'll believe anything."

Drew has always looked at her sister and hoped it would be her turn next. Drew's turn to leave. To fall in love and get married and have kids. Some things didn't happen.

Drew opens her car door, waiting for Rachel to leave hers. Would

Rachel still be her champion? From the stiff smile on her sister's face, Drew suspects not.

My sister sports dark hollows under her eyes that I don't think have anything to do with her makeup. She looks like she could use a big bowl of soup and a long nap. I wonder if she's taking care of herself, working too much or partying too hard. With Drew it could be both. If I had nobody to take care of, I think, I'd sleep for about twelve hours a night. I put my arms out. "Hey. Thanks for coming down so quick."

"No problem. I'm sort of dying to know what book Mom's talking about now." Drew steps forward and we hug awkwardly, leaning into each other like old fence boards crushed by wind. Neither of us were huggers. I splay my fingers along her back, the way I do with Quincy. Secretly checking the meat on their bones. Yes. She needs soup and probably a big juicy steak. Drew's always been a grazing, forgetful eater. A handful of baby carrots here, a few peanuts there. Ever since she was a toddler, Drew was more interested in action than in sitting down for a proper meal. I want to ask if Drew's taking a calcium supplement, if she's getting enough vitamin D, if she's sleeping well. Drew releases me abruptly.

Once I left home, I rarely talked to Drew. I rarely talked to her in the last years I was still home. But she had her music and Killian's good graces. It could be worse. Sometimes she'd call me when nobody was around, or I'd pick her up someplace so my father wouldn't find out. After I had a baby, we could barely relate. I knew we'd never be as close as we were when we were little. No matter how much either of us wanted to be.

Mom brought her to see me for my twentieth birthday. Drew was sixteen, and all she could talk about was high school, the music competition coming up.

"Dad said he was going to buy me a car. He wants me driving in something safe and new," Drew said, and though I knew she wasn't specifically saying it to brag or hurt me, it was just a fact, I still felt a raw pang. Killian didn't care if I had something safe and new.

"Not an expensive car," Hikari said.

"He said Mercedes." Drew ate a piece of pizza. "He said that's the best. Built like a tank."

The pizza cheese turned to glue in my gut. Drew and I were in such different places in our lives. I shared an ancient Maxima with Tom, which he drove to work. If I wanted to take Quincy anywhere, I walked or took the bus, which in San Diego is like waiting for a covered wagon. "Good," I said quietly. "Good for you." I put my fork down. At that moment, I realized how much of the carefree high school experience I'd missed. How I was jealous of Drew for still being able to go have fun at the drop of a hat, have no responsibilities. I looked over at Quincy, shoving pizza in her mouth with her chubby hands, and told myself you can't have everything.

Mom reached over and touched my hand.

Drew frowned. But my mother was just letting me know she understood me—I was never her favorite, like Drew thought I was. Parents can't have favorites, I thought. Shouldn't, anyway. Mom was just trying to make up for my father.

My sister shoved a fat slice of pepperoni into her mouth. "Yeah. Yeah. Yeah. Did I tell you? I got into the Juilliard summer program."

"That's wonderful." I meant it. I'd always loved hearing her play. I'd often wondered where the musical talent came from—perhaps some people way back in our lineage.

I waited for Drew to ask me how things were going, how things were for me, but she just talked about herself without taking a breath. Now, as an adult, I know that I was hoping for too much from a teenager. But our relationship had begun its downhill slide.

So my sister and I stand on the street in front of my father's house. Eighteen years later and nothing's changed. "Fog's not burning off here," I remark. Drew nods. A silence settles between us. "How's work?" I ask, to fill it. "Any new gigs?" Drew works with some big-name bands sometimes, whenever somebody wants to add a bit of classic zip to rock, which seems popular now. She posts pictures of herself on Facebook posing with the band members, with captions like *So much fun!* "How's the dog-washing business?" Even this job is interesting—Drew's washed the dogs of some actors. Not A-list, but regular working actors you'd still recognize.

"Fine. Got a few days off." Drew blasts me with one of her smiles, looking like the old Drew, shaking off any hint of exhaustion. "And how are the kiddos?"

I inhale, thinking of Quincy and her fiancé. Chase and the bake sale. Drew doesn't want to hear all the boring nitty-gritty. "Great. They're great."

"Your kids are perfect." Drew walks briskly in front of me. "I saw Dad jetting out of here. It's safe to go in."

I suspect that my father is heading downtown to yell at his attorney. Hence his e-mail to me. I wonder all over again what he could be talking about. Is there a secret will? Maybe it's enough to overturn the decision.

But I will carry out Mom's wishes as best as I can, no matter what. Right here and now. I swallow down the rising acid in my throat. Everything is fine. I'll do this and I'll go back home to my own house, my own family, whom I love and who loves me.

Drew watches me expectantly, a key in her hand. My younger sister doesn't understand all that is between me and Killian. The way I still feel so helpless where he's concerned. She thinks it's all in my head, because she's his favorite, and she can still call him and ask for help whenever she gets in too deep.

The house where we grew looks so American, so *Leave It to Beaver*. From the outside, you'd never know our mother was from Japan. Or the inside, for that matter.

Drew jiggles the key in the lock and swings the door open into the living room. Everything's quiet, dust floating in the air. I look over the dark, heavy leather furniture, the brown paneling that's unchanged since the 1970s. My father's tastes. He's wealthy, but frugal. The only sign of modernity is the eighty-inch television screen that hums lightly against one long wall.

I switch on the light in Mom's sewing room, then sneeze four times in succession, big sneezes that threaten to empty my bladder. I stand perfectly still, clenching unseen muscles, until the fit passes. More than a decade after my last child, you'd think I'd be totally recovered from pregnancies, but sometimes it feels like my body's This Old House: creaky and leaky.

"Are you all right?" Drew pushes past me.

"Fine." I sniffle, too embarrassed to tell Drew the truth. No kids—she won't understand.

This room is packed to the brim with boxes. White cardboard file crates, big plastic bins. A bulletin board holds fabric squares. The sewing machine is set up on a long table below, navy blue thread ready to go. I pick up a quilting project, hanging off the sewing machine. She made wedding ring quilts for Quincy and Chase, big enough to fit on king beds, given to us five Christmases ago. "For the future," Mom had said. It was almost like she knew she wouldn't be around long enough to see them get married.

Drew has a wedding quilt in here someplace, too. Mom made it for her right after I got married. Drew didn't want it. She said she wasn't ready for it, but she clearly hated it. I was there when Mom gave it to her on her twenty-first birthday. The stiff smile on Drew's face. "Gee, Mom, it's so beautiful, but I'm a long way from getting married," Drew said, putting the pink and yellow and purple quilt back into its enormous box. "Maybe you could keep it for me until then."

"Sure," Mom had said, an identical polite smile on her face. Why was I the only one who knew what they felt and didn't hide behind this mask? All I could do was watch and pretend, too.

I exhale a long, slow breath and let the quilt fall. "I'm surprised Dad hasn't packed up her stuff yet."

"He says by Christmas." Drew slides the closet door open. "If you want any of it, I could probably ask him for you."

I make a noncommittal noise. Drew lives in a different city, but she knows more about our father's day-to-day existence than I do. He may as well be a stranger. "Are you going to help him?"

"Dad and I aren't close, no matter what you think, Rachel." Drew sounds irritated. I stop talking. If I pretend that Drew and I get along, then we will. It's my coping method.

The closet's just stacked with boxes, too, no clothes hanging from the bar. I can see the clear boxes are full of material, so I take out a cardboard one and look inside. Papers, ancient water bills and warranties. "Great. Looking through all these is going to take about six months."

"Are you sure Mom didn't give you more of a description?" Drew glances at me from where she's dug out boxes.

"I would have told you if she had," I retort, taking out another box. I'm not going to bicker with my sister, as if I'm twelve and she's eight again. *Be calm! I can't tell whether you're fighting or playing,* Mom used to say. *It all sounds the same—like somebody's going to get hurt.* My kids have a bigger age gap, six years, and Quincy's almost like a second mother to Chase. From the time he was born she was able to carry him and change his diapers. Drew and I were either best friends or bad rivals. Nothing in between.

An aroma like a museum storeroom, musty and woodsy, wafts up. I take out a different box. This one has recipe clippings and citizenship awards from elementary school, fading Mother's Day construction-paper flowers and other random bits. Swimming medals for me, fancy embossed certificates for Drew's viola competitions. I hadn't known Mom was so sentimental. I run my hand over it. "Drew. Did you know Mom saved all this?"

Drew glances in. "Junk. Not important."

I put my hand around a heavy bronze medal. First place, CIF state champion, freestyle. The trophy for the team is still displayed in a glass case in the high school office. "Mine are."

"Well. I don't need mine." Drew turns away with a shrug.

She'll want them one day. Drew often talks first, thinks later. I dig into the bottom layer of the box. A sturdy but slightly crushed brown cardboard shipping box, about eleven by fourteen, held together by disintegrating brown packaging tape, emerges. It's covered in stamps and postmarks with Japanese writing as the return address, and my mother's name and address printed in careful English. I wish I could read the Japanese, but as I said, I'm Asian in heritage only.

Who sent this to her? My mother kept in contact with nobody in Japan; as far as I knew, her whole family was gone. Her parents died when she was a young adult, in a train accident, I think. No siblings. Not even any cousins.

The shipping box is postmarked June 20, 1972, the year my parents married. I open the side and slide out the contents. A book. Or a big antique photo album, brown leather softened by the touch of hundreds of hands, bound with delicate red silken thread. A book, I realize, turning it over. The back of the book to us is the beginning in Japan. I'd learned that from looking at Chase's manga, Japanese comic books.

"What is it?" Drew peers over my shoulder, her breath on my ear, loud and moist. I twitch in annoyance, the way I did when she used to read over my shoulder. *Whatcha reading, Rachel? You're not really reading, because your mouth isn't moving. You're pretending. Stop ignoring me. Why won't you read to me?*

"Recognize it?" I say.

Drew opens the cover with an awful crackling sound. We freeze. "Let's be careful."

We sit on the floor and hold the book between us, resting each side on one of our knees. The cover features an embossed horse with a samurai astride it, accented in gold leaf, no color. The samurai has long, flowing hair and waves a sword. A story about a warrior? A history book?

"It looks vaguely familiar," Drew says. She twists her mouth into a pout and taps her chin with her left index finger, the Drew thinking pose she's had ever since she was about two. She used to do it for the drama, and it stuck. Sometimes I do it, to imitate her.

I open the album to the first page. It's made of yellowed parchment, the edges rough, and smells of ink and old paper. The characters are handwritten, each symbol a work of art in and of itself. I, of course, have no idea what it says. I turn the page.

On this one, all by itself, is a painting like an image out of an illuminated manuscript. A young Japanese girl holding a sword stands in front of a full-grown samurai, as if she's fighting him. Two little boys are in the background, grinning. Farmland stretches behind them to a nearby mountain range.

I turn the page. A beautiful Japanese woman in a red kimono rides a white horse wearing fancy crimson dress regalia. The woman holds a bow and arrow. Another arrow speeds toward a frightened monk in an orange robe. A whole crowd of monks stand before him, seemingly ready to turn on their heels and run. Behind the woman is a male samurai on a big black horse, his face contorted into a scowling mask, an army behind him. The woman is in the lead.

I've never seen anything like this. A woman warrior, in Japan?

Another picture, the same woman. Now her horse leaps, her dark hair flows in a banner behind her, as if the hair itself is the battle standard. A Mona Lisa–like half smile tugs her lips. A man cowers below her, a severed head, drawn in gruesome detail, rolls off a body and under the horse. I gasp.

And another, this one depicting the samurai woman kneeling at what seems to be some kind of ceremony. A long low table, laden with food, is behind her. A smaller woman, in a rich-looking kimono, kneels beside the samurai. She holds her hand out to the warrior, and the warrior reaches toward her.

"Oh yeah," Drew says, her voice loud. "I remember this now."

"Now? Just now?" A twinge of annoyance. Why didn't Mom show this to me?

Drew shrugs. "I didn't really think of it as a book. It's bound like a photo album. I don't know. I didn't remember." She traces the samurai woman with the tips of her fingers.

"Did Mom tell you the story? What's it say? Who are these women?" My pulse pounds hard. Below the women, in faint pencil, so light against the color of the paper that I can barely see it, my mother has written our names.

Rachel.

Drew.

I hear her small, high-pitched voice as clearly as if she's in the room. My diaphragm contracts sharply, without my cooperation, hurting my ribs.

Our mother is not a warrior. She is—was—the opposite. If there was anyone who fit the stereotype of a passive Asian woman, it's Hikari Snow. She sat in the backseat if we had a male guest. Never questioned our father, no matter what outrageous thing he'd done. She had our father's dinner ready and his laundry done without his asking. Once she'd even left Drew's school concert early so she could switch the wash into the dryer. I couldn't count the times she blindly accepted things my father wanted, even if they adversely affected her. Or me.

Growing up, when people asked about my parents, the way people do with their half-masked nosiness after they observe that my mom's Asian, I've always given them the plainest vanilla answers. These days people probably wouldn't care, but back then they still did. "Yes, she speaks English. Yes, she's a citizen." The most unusual thing I've let out is that Mom came over in the 1970s to marry my father. "Was he in the military?" they always ask next.

"They met through business," I answer, leaving out a word. They met through *a* business.

I never tell the interesting part of the story, the thing that would make their jaws drop. Only Tom knows. None of Tom's family or my best friends or even my children know this part.

My mother, Hikari Snow, was a thirty-three-year-old secretary working a dead-end job in Tokyo in the early 1970s when she submitted her photo and biography to a mail-order-bride catalog called *Satsuma Blossoms.* Just like the picture brides of the turn of the century, ordered by Japanese men working in Hawaii and California, Hikari wanted to get out of Japan but had no means to do so besides offering herself up for marriage to a stranger.

My father, Killian, a divorced businessman older by sixteen years, was charmed by Hikari's mastery of English and her orphan status. No pesky family matters tying her to home. He promised her a life without want, where she wouldn't have to live in a filthy third-floor walk-up with four other women. Where she wouldn't have to decide between paying rent or buying food. In return, he imagined he'd get a supplicant wife who'd bear children and keep house. Which he mostly got.

"Just tell people I met your mother in Japan when I was there on business," my father told me when I was small. I remember him saying so over ice cream on the patio, my earliest memory of him. One of my friends' mothers had been asking about Mom, and I must have been almost four when I asked my father how they'd met, because Killian's hair still had some blond in it and Drew wasn't born yet. I had to squint at him, the sun halo-bright around his head, and all I can remember is his hair color as he spoke. "Your mother's what people call a gold digger, Rachel. People will think we're no good."

I glanced up at my mother, who cleared our empty bowls without expression, her I'm-staying-out-of-it face. "Isn't a gold digger a miner? That's not bad."

Dad laughed. "No, it means a woman who married for money. Not love."

"You love Mom, don't you?" This worried me. I knew certain things to be true. Santa Claus came on Christmas Eve, the Easter bunny never hid eggs where you couldn't find them, and married people loved each other, like Cinderella and Prince Charming. Childhood lore.

Mom carried the bowls inside, sliding the screen shut behind her. Dad leaned forward, coming into full focus, and ruffled my hair. Unlike Mom, Dad had bags under his eyes, wrinkles by his mouth. He'd been fifty when I was born, and was often mistaken for my grandfather. "People get married for all kinds of reasons, Rachel. That's how the world works. Now, don't tell your friends, or they might not be allowed to play with you." He chucked my chin. "And we had you. A sweet, perfect little girl. Hopefully we'll get a little brother one of these days."

Of course, we did not. And it wasn't long before I grew out of being his sweet, perfect little girl for good.

Because I was never perfect to begin with.

Once, only once, and not until I was ten, did I ask Mom directly how she and my father met. "Do you still have the letter?" I asked. I imagined it to be grand and romantic, full of hearts and expressions of love. Maybe she'd written back and squirted perfume all over her reply. Maybe she kept his letters tied up with a silk crimson ribbon, high up on a closet shelf.

"No," she said. "It wasn't a letter like you think. It was a form."

"A form?" I didn't understand.

She nodded. "It had boxes for what he preferred. Hair: Long. Height: Short. Wants children: Yes. Speaks English. That kind of thing. Then the catalog people wrote to me and asked if I was interested."

"He ordered you? Like you were a television set?" I had never heard of such a thing. All my classmates' parents met during high school or college or at some young adult job. "Could you have said no?"

"He was the only one who wanted me," Mom responded matter-of-factly. "Now, what do you want for dinner?"

It seemed like a blatant, crass transaction. The woman who wanted to be kept. The man who wanted a subservient Asian female. In our community, where girls weren't told to keep their mouths shut, I kept mine shut. I was embarrassed to have such a nonfeminist stereotype for a mother.

When Quincy was in middle school, one of her classmates' parents was a Russian woman known to be a mail-order bride. She was in her late twenties, married to a taciturn biotech executive twenty-five years her senior; she dressed flashily, in short skirts and low tops and high heels, even on field trips, with lots of diamonds. She was a centerfold come to life, and completely intimidating. No one spoke to her. She spoke to no one and never smiled.

"Typical," Susannah had said. "She doesn't love him. She just wanted his money."

Was that how others perceived my mother? I remembered my father telling me my classmates might not be allowed to play with me if their parents knew. Did I harbor a similar prejudice against the Russian woman?

I focused on Susannah. "Hey, if it works for them, who are we to judge? It might be acceptable in her culture. It works for the man, it works for the woman."

Susannah stared at me. "There are some things that aren't right no matter what the culture. What about all the brides who don't get a good man? They're stuck here, without anything. Maybe even abused. It's basically slavery."

Images of my mother and father flashed across my mind, and my body went cold, my hands numb. No, I wasn't going to think about that. I turned away from Susannah without another word.

I take a breath and scan the sewing room closet. Maybe I'll find some swords stashed away next. Mom might have been a ninja, for all I know.

I hear another car pass outside. I push the box aside without looking at the rest of the items, and throw the quilts back to where they were. This is what Mom meant for me to find. For when she forgot. Is there a code in here, too?

For all I know, the book isn't a story at all, but a long letter to her daughters. I gingerly turn the pages again.

Drew shifts away from under the book, pushing it into my lap. She gets up and dusts off her backside. "I don't know what it's about, Rachel. Mom never said. One day, she told me to come in here and get something for her and I happened to see it. She said, *Oh that's just an old book from Japan. I might use the woman in a quilt.*" Drew shrugs. "I didn't think any more about it."

"But look." I point to our names. "She wants us to read this."

Drew stares at our mother's handwriting, her eyes turning liquid. "How?"

I close the book, put it in the box of treasures. I'm taking the whole box. It belongs to me and Drew. I would have gotten it before if I'd known. "We'll get it translated. There's got to be a starving student who needs cash."

At the word "starving," Drew's stomach growls and Drew coughs, covering it up. "Yeah. I'm sure there is. Ready to get out of here?"

I narrow my eyes theatrically at my sister, my patented Rachel evil eye. *Stop staring at me like a vampire, Rachel! You stared at me first, Drew!* She rewards me with a flash of a grin and I know she's remembering the same thing. "Want to come over and have something to eat?" I ask.

T omoe peered down from the top of the swaying pine tree. She
stretched her fingers toward the violet and pink sunset. Almost
close enough to touch. This was higher up than she'd ever been.
Small branches ripped off and fell away to where she couldn't see them.

She'd won again. Pride and guilt mixed in her. Now her brother was
relegated to picking weeds in the garden for losing, and Yoshinaka would
join him. And now both of them would hate her even more.

Below her, Yoshinaka shouted. "It's not fair! She's lighter. She can go
faster." He shook the trunk.

Tomoe yelped, hanging on. "Stop, Yoshi."

They made their way back down the tree to where Kaneto waited. "Yoshinaka, if you know Tomoe is quicker, then you'd better think of what else
you can do to win."

"What do you want me to do?" Yoshinaka brushed pine needles off his
robes, his face red. "Pull her off and throw her to the ground?"

"That's what I'd do." Kanehira stood in the kitchen garden, his arms full of thorny weeds, and a snarl on his face. "Father, it is a dishonor to our family. Having a girl fight with us. Why don't you just have me and Yoshi put on geisha clothes and become entertainers?"

"You're just mad because you always lose." Tomoe couldn't help smirking at her brother, as he had done so many times to her. He threw down the weeds and clenched his fists. "Loser." She turned away, focusing instead on walking to the outhouse.

"Take it back!" Kanehira shouted, coming toward her.

Tomoe didn't stop or respond. He would do nothing in front of their father. Suddenly something knocked her over. Fists beat onto her back and head. "You stupid girl!" Kanehira pounded her. She heard her father shouting at him to stop.

Tomoe rolled over. A punch caught her in the face. She kicked at Kanehira's ankles, causing him to be off balance, then scrambled away. Kaneto grabbed his son in a bear hug as Kanehira erupted into angry tears. Tomoe bent over, trying to catch her breath.

"Go inside," Kaneto whispered to his son. Kanehira ran off, no doubt to be comforted by his mother. Yoshinaka followed, shoulders slumped.

Tomoe stood in front of her father. "Do you think I dishonor you, too, sir?" Her own lip trembled but she willed it to be still. Her back and ribs ached. She wouldn't complain.

"You know better than that, Tomoe." Kaneto's face was serious. He was being a trainer now, not her father, Tomoe thought. "This is a lesson for you, Tomoe. Did you see Kanehira before you turned away?"

Tomoe sniffled, thinking. "Yes."

"And what was he doing?"

"He looked angry." Tomoe stared at the needle-covered ground. "He had his hands in fists. He was walking toward me."

"So." Kaneto stooped to her level, putting his hand on her shoulder. "You turned your back on someone who was threatening you."

She nodded. "I thought because you were here, he wouldn't do anything."

"Well, Yoshinaka would not have done that, nor I. But you know your brother well." He patted her shoulder. "Some who look weak do so on purpose, to make you let down your guard. You must always be ready."

"He's my brother." Tomoe wiped at the errant tear that escaped her eye. Dirt scratched her skin.

Kaneto stood. "I know, Tomoe. But he counted on you to turn, so he could attack from behind. Never turn your back to an attack. *Ichi-go, ichi-e.* All you get is one chance."

"But . . ." Tomoe wanted to defend herself. Was she to always be on guard against her flesh and blood?

Kaneto held up a finger. "Only one chance. Sometimes, you must be the first to attack. Do not wait until it's too late." He left her there and went into the house.

Tomoe stayed where she was for a moment, thinking. She smelled rice and fish. Dinner cooking. But she did not go in. Instead, she went into the garden and finished pulling the weeds, ignoring the thorns that scratched her hands.

Four

There's a Japanese saying, *Ichi-go, ichi-e*. Literally, it means "one encounter in a lifetime." Figuratively, it means you don't get doovers in life. Sometimes you make decisions that irrevocably send you down one path instead of another. When you're young, everything seems reversible.

But making a few wrong choices can trip you up forever.

My father was the one who taught me that phrase.

I spent my childhood on swim teams, winning meets all over town. It was the one thing that made my father really notice me. I saw his proud expression when the other parents congratulated him, how he took photos when I went up to claim my medals. If I lost, he critiqued my performance on the car ride home, telling me how the other swimmers had bested me, how I could improve my time and my form. The thing was, though he'd been a football player, he was often correct. He was not one of those parents who said that doing my best was enough. Winning was enough. I agreed, then.

And it was also what I was known for in school. I was Rachel the Swimmer. The girl who got up before dawn to swim and would surely be in the Olympics one day.

I worked harder than anybody else on the swim team. We practiced in the mornings, and I went back to the pool in the evenings to perfect my strokes, ignoring little stabs of pain shooting up to my neck. Ignoring how I'd stopped my periods and how tired I was every day in class. When my blood sugar dropped too much, I drank coffee and ate a banana and a candy bar and pushed myself to go further. I wanted to be number one.

When I was sixteen, during January of my sophomore year, I dislocated my shoulder during a swim meet. I felt a deep pop, a wrenching sensation, and then the purest pain I'd ever feel, besides childbirth. I sank, my mouth opening in a soundless scream, lifting one arm aloft to get help.

I'd never again be able to swim at the same level. At that age, it felt like the end of the world. Suddenly I wasn't Rachel Snow, Winner of Gold Medals. I was just Rachel Snow, average student. A nobody to anybody, especially to my family.

And so I found comfort in other ways.

My friends had all been on the swim team. We'd traveled to meets together, spending entire days huddled together on cold pool decks or applying sunblock to each other's backs on the hot days. Suddenly I had nobody. I could have been manager, somebody who kept score and gathered up goggles and brought out water, but I couldn't stomach the thought of watching them all do something I could not.

Killian treated me differently, too. Apparently, swimming was the only thing interesting about me. He had no reason to take me anywhere or even talk to me anymore. But what could I do about it? It's not like we had the kind of relationship where our family went to the movies together.

No longer working out every day, I put on weight and needed new clothes. I had to ask Killian for some money. He stopped drinking his Old-Fashioned to look me up and down, how my thighs strained against my Guess denim mini, my stomach pooching over the waistband. A look of plain disgust crossed his face. I shrank inside. "Better stop eating so much," he grunted. "No boy will like you, the way you're going."

"Thanks," I said, in response to the cash he handed me. I'd trained myself not to respond to his barbs now, not the way I had when I was little. When somebody is like him, you expect all kinds of mean things to come out of his mouth. It barely affects you anymore. Or so you think. It's like swallowing something sharp without realizing it, the object sitting undisturbed until years later, when your insides suddenly begin to bleed.

I had no idea why Killian Snow was the way he was. He didn't tell stories about his childhood. I knew he grew up on a cattle ranch in central California that his father had lost in a drunken card game when Killian was sixteen. He had no siblings. Probably his childhood was unhappy. Who knew what had happened to him? All I knew of my father was how he was with us. And of course, in high school, I didn't spend a second of time wondering why.

At lunch one day, tired of being alone and deciding I didn't need any more calories that day, I'd wandered out to the school parking lot. Back then you were still allowed to leave school for lunch, and in the chaos some kids would hang out in their cars in the far corners of the expansive lot and smoke.

I walked slowly past a truck bed full of these students. "You're Rachel, right?" a boy with a floppy mop of dark hair said. A clove cigarette stuck out of his mouth. "The swimmer?"

I inhaled the sweet scent of the smoke and smiled at him. He had blue eyes and dimples and made my heart race like it did right before a meet. I didn't recognize him from my classes. "Not anymore."

He offered me his hand to help me into the truck.

My mother tried to warn me. I was on my way out one evening, my pockets clinking full of mini booze bottles I'd stolen from my father's collection, when she materialized before me in her white bathrobe, like a ghost. "Rachel, you have to stop. Your father won't forgive you." Her face was lined, worried. "Some . . . boy's mother called. She said you got him drunk."

I stopped, wondering which boy she was talking about. Because there had been more than one. At parties in strange houses, buzzed on watery beer, I'd hook up with almost any boy who'd wanted me. Which, since they were teenagers, was pretty much all of them. "Do you think I'm pretty?" I would say, standing naked before each one. I felt powerful, wanted. "Yeah," each boy had said.

I stood in front of my mother and recalled all of this and felt nothing. Numb. Little pieces of my soul were getting chipped out and thrown away, and I didn't care anymore. Being numb was better. "He wanted to," I said. "It's not a big deal."

My mother rubbed her temples and looked at the floor. We hadn't known, but she was probably already experiencing the first stages of dementia. Sometimes she struggled to find words, used the wrong ones—I just thought it was because English was her second language. Looking back, I think that's why she had so many unfinished quilting projects. But I was young then, and not searching my parents for signs of illness.

I waited for my mother to speak. I wanted her to forbid me to leave, to order me back to my room. To tell me I still had some worth, even if I couldn't swim. I could not articulate any of this. Couldn't even think it consciously. Instead, I pushed past her and she clutched onto the railing. My mother had no power. She knew nothing about my life. She was a figurehead, not a parent. "Just leave me alone." I knew she'd do as I asked, because it was easier, and she did.

The following week, another kid reported he'd seen a bag of weed in my locker. My father stood in the principal's office stone-faced as the principal asked if I had anything to say for myself before I was expelled.

I said nothing.

"It's not hers," my father said. "She told me her friend gave her a paper bag, said it was a sandwich. Asked Rachel to hold on to it until lunch. How was she supposed to know? Her friend probably saw the dog coming."

The principal furrowed his gray-white brow. "And who is this friend?"

My father shrugged his big shoulders. "You want her to be a pariah on top of everything else? Tell you what." He stood up. "You should decide what'll be more expedient. You can expel Rachel and get a lawsuit that you'll end up settling for a lot of money, maybe with your job—or you can give her a one-week suspension."

I hadn't told him any such thing. For a second I had the urge to tell the truth. Yes, it was my weed. Yes, I deserved anything thrown at me. But that would make it worse. My father would flip out. I held my tongue. My stomach churned and I began to cry.

The principal didn't answer. I wondered what power my father had that my principal knew about.

Killian gestured to me. "Come on, Rachel."

The principal looked right at me. I remembered him shaking my hand after I won a CIF championship. Saying hello to me in the hallways. All the wrinkles of his face seemed to drop to the center of the earth. "Is this true, Rachel?"

No, I whispered in my head. I nodded.

"Tell him, Rachel," my father prompted.

They were waiting. I swallowed. "I guess somebody stuck it into my locker while I was getting my books out. I didn't even see it."

The principal sighed. "Well, you're a good kid. I'm inclined to believe you." He shook hands with my father. "Too bad about the swimming."

"It is too bad." My father smiled his easy Cheshire Cat grin, the one nobody seemed to see through but me. "She'll find something else. She's a great kid. The best."

I followed him out to the car, tears streaming down my face. I was shaking and I wasn't sure if it was because I'd narrowly escaped punishment, or because I hadn't gotten it.

When we got in the car and shut the doors, he turned to me, his eyes burning with fury. "What do you have to cry about?" he said. "I just fixed it for you. You're a damned idiot, Rachel. First the swimming. Now this."

Through my tears, I was stunned. "I couldn't help the swimming." Then I realized. Oh my God. He was right. I'd worked out too hard.

It was all my fault.

He turned on the car. "If you'd listened to me about form, you wouldn't have gotten injured. Very simple. You've never listened to me." He started backing up. "Just do me a favor. Keep out of trouble until you're out of school. I have business in this town, and I don't need you fucking it up with your antics. Got it? No more, or you're out on your ass." He slammed his palm on the steering wheel, beeping the horn. "No more!" he screamed.

I nodded mutely and bit my tongue, concentrating on that pain so I'd stop crying. I swallowed down the hard lump in my throat. I didn't worry about getting kicked out because I was going to be good from now on. "I won't mess up again. I promise."

We didn't speak of it again. I stopped going out to the parking lot at lunchtime, knowing that the principal would be specifically watching for me, waiting for me to mess up. I ate lunch alone, in a far shady corner of the campus, behind the P.E. building, where couples went to make out. At nights I lay awake, imagining creatures out of the dark shapes in my bedroom, wondering what I was going to do with my life. Wondering what the point of it all was. My grades had dropped so much this semester I doubted any college, even the local state school, would take me. I wasn't able to bring myself to care anymore. I'd have to live at home and go to the community college. And what would I do after that, marry somebody, end up like my mother?

I longed to talk to her, to cry into her shoulders, and several times I almost did. I went to her quilt room where she sat sewing, sewing, sewing, like she was in some kind of factory with an imaginary deadline. As I stood in the doorway, watching her head bent under the orange yellow desk lamp, I knew two things to be true. She had her own demons. And because of those, she'd be unable to be a mother in the way I needed a mother.

Mom looked up at me and if she'd invited me in, maybe things would have been different. She didn't say anything, just waited, blinking blearily. The sewing machine hummed. She frowned as she searched my face. As if I was a door-to-door salesman bugging her.

I reached out and grabbed the doorknob and shut the door. I felt like I was standing on the edge of a bottomless canyon, looking down, and very much wishing I could jump.

I retreated into my room and locked the door. All I could hear was the sound of my own breathing. I longed to cry, but nothing would come. I felt like I was inhabiting some permanent dream world, where I'd never be the slightest bit happy again, or even sad.

I went to the window, imagining what would happen if I leaped out onto the concrete driveway. It was only two stories. With my luck, I'd probably just break my neck and need to live with my parents forever. I went to my closet, looked at the clothes bar, wondering if it'd support my weight. I pushed down on it experimentally. Maybe. I picked up a belt, made it into a loop. Would suffocation be quick?

Somebody pounded on my door. "Rach?" The sound of Drew's still bell-sweet little girl voice jolted me back into reality. My heart restarted. I gasped, tears springing into my eyes. I threw the belt down. "Do you want to watch *Jeopardy!* with me?" We used to watch that together as we did our homework, each of us shouting out answers, usually a few seconds too late.

This was not what I wanted. It would most likely be my sister who'd find me. I couldn't do that to her. I sank to the floor, shaking uncontrollably. I took several breaths. I made my hands into fists until the nails cut my palms, the pain giving me something else to concentrate on.

"Rach?" Drew knocked again, rattled the doorknob.

"I'm busy," I said, my voice sounding more brusque than I'd intended. "I have homework." I couldn't talk to Drew about any of this. She was still an innocent little kid. I needed to protect her.

I heard her shut the door to her room. The strains of Stravinsky's "Elegy" floated through the walls. Drew bought the sheet music for it almost two years earlier, when she was just ten. It'd been too difficult for her

SISTERS OF HEART AND SNOW

at the time, but now here she was, performing it perfectly. *Holy shit. When did my sister get so good?* I wondered, listening to the low, sad melody.

Then Killian pounded on Drew's door. "No playing after nine," he shouted. I touched my shirt. It was soaking wet from the tears I hadn't realized I was shedding.

I wouldn't admit what I was thinking about that night to anyone, ever, I promised myself. Drew had saved me, jarred me out of my lowest point, and she would never know. It was too shameful and too burdensome to confide. So I just kept managing my pain as badly as I knew how. At least I knew for certain I'd never leave my sister. Not like that.

A couple of months after the drug incident, on a summer night, my father caught me parked in a car, late, with another boy. The boy was dropping me off and I hadn't wanted to be dropped off yet, so I'd whispered, *Why don't you park down the street?* and there we were, steaming up the windows a few houses down, where the streetlight was out. I don't remember the guy's name or what he looked like, particularly. He was just another boy who paid attention to me, and that's what I needed. Suddenly there was a violent rapping at the window. "Unlock this car right now." My father pounded the glass with his palm. He was, though then sixty-six years old, still a big, burly man.

I screamed and fixed my clothes. "Don't unlock it."

But the boy, scared, unlocked the car, and my father opened the passenger door and yanked me out by my sleeve. A glass bong fell out of my pocket, shattering on the asphalt. He put his arm around me tight and ushered me back up the street, my arms pinned to my sides, and into the house, slamming the front door as hard as he could. He turned to me. "So it's boys *and* drugs. What are you, a prostitute?"

I looked around for Mom. Nowhere. "No," I whispered, edging toward the stairs. My heart thumped and I suddenly became drenched in sweat. I needed to get to my room, where I could lock my door and cry.

"I will not have you bringing shame into our family," Dad said, his voice low. He leaned into my face, his breath smelling of old garlic and sulfurous red wine. Broken capillaries lined his red cheeks, a map with roads leading nowhere.

I gripped the banister and took one step up. "I'm sorry." I wanted to hide my face, to crawl under my bed like a little kid, holding on to my stuffed Easter bunny for dear life. "I won't do it again. I promise. I'll be good."

"You already promised that!" Dad shouted. "How many chances do you think you get, Rachel? I'm not taking care of any baby. I'm not bailing you out of jail. I'm done."

Drew appeared at the top of the stairs, her face white. "Rachel? Dad? What's going on?"

"Go back to bed!" I shouted. I didn't want her to see this.

"Now you're a slut and a dope addict? Fantastic." He straightened and took in a deep breath. I had the impression he was getting himself under control. He closed his eyes. "You need to get out of my house."

"What?" I thought I must be dreaming; Dad was talking like a bit player in an after-school special. I flushed, heat spreading from my torso up to my face. Mom appeared behind him. "Mom?" I said, hoping she would stand up for me.

She didn't. "I wish you'd listened to me."

Dad folded his arms, his face turning a normal color. "There's a Japanese saying." He stared at me emotionlessly. "I'm surprised your mother hasn't taught it to you. *Ichi-go, ichi-e.* One chance, no mistakes. You make a mistake, you have to live with it. Now. Get your stuff and get out." Dad stepped aside. "Tonight."

"I'm only sixteen." A wail worked its way into my voice. Oh my God. Was he really kicking me out? Where would I go? Nobody in our neighborhood kicked their kids out unless they were serious drug addicts. Was I one?

My mother came out of her sewing room and moved to the middle of the living room, her gaze fixed on my father as though he was a wild tiger.

He glared at me. "I left home at sixteen. You need to get your head on straight."

At last my mother spoke up. "Give her until morning." Her voice was assertive.

My father's eyes opened wide, genuinely surprised, as if he'd forgotten the existence of my mother altogether. Some of the bluster deflated out of him. "Be out by eleven a.m. I'll be back from golfing then."

All night, I ran through a mental list of people I could call and ask for help. I couldn't stand the thought of their sympathetic, polite voices. My swim team knew what I was up to. I saw them whispering at school as I walked out to the parking lot at lunchtime. *Sorry, my parents said no,* I imagined them saying, while secretly thinking, *You brought this on yourself. Deal with it.*

I had to pick someone, though, or else I'd be sleeping on a park bench. Who would be most likely to help? Who had the kindest mom? I chose Jenn. We didn't talk much anymore, only cursory hellos in classes, but she'd been on swim team with me since grade school. Her family lived in University City, another suburb on the other side of the mountain from La Jolla, a few miles more inland. I used to go over to her house to play, after swim practice sometimes. She was an only child—her mother wanted more, but couldn't have them—and her house was the kind of Kool-Aid-and-cookie place a kid longs for. More often than not, I'd whisper-ask Jenn if I could eat dinner with her, and she'd ask her mom.

Jenn came to my house only a handful of times, where we'd play Barbies for a couple of hours after swim practice, until her mother came to pick her up. "Can I eat dinner here?" Jenn asked once in third grade.

It seemed only fair, though I was afraid of how my father would act. "I don't think you'll like what we're having," I said.

"It doesn't matter. My mother says you say yes to the company, not the food." She grinned her cheerful gap-toothed grin. "I can pretend to like almost anything. Except anchovies. You're not having those, are you?"

I admitted we were not, and went to ask. My mother, after hesitating a moment, agreed. We needn't have worried, for my father smiled cheerfully at my friend and complimented her swimming skills. "One of the best, for sure! Keep it up, you're going places," he'd said, and passed her a buttered roll. But we'd gone to different junior high schools, and in high school we'd been friendly, but never hung out at each other's houses again.

I called Jenn at the mostly decent hour of eight-thirty in the morning. Her mother answered. "Rachel! Oh my goodness. I've been wondering how you are." Barbara was one of those comforting moms who wore sweat-shirts with pictures of kittens on them and had a pleasant, huggable layer of natural padding.

Though I hadn't meant to, at the sound of her kind voice, I burst into tears again and blubbered out the whole story.

I thought she'd be surprised at how I'd acted, how my father had acted, but she passed no judgment. "You'll stay here," she said firmly.

"It's just for a few days." I thought my father would cool off, change his mind, that at the very least my mother would contact me.

Instead, I was erased.

I saw my mother a week later when Jenn and her mother drove me to pick up my things from the house. "I can go in there, if you like," Barbara said. "You can wait in the car."

Mom stood in the garage, glancing nervously down the driveway as if she was afraid Dad had enlisted the neighbors to spy on her. I knew my father had told her not to contact me. As far as he was concerned, they had no daughter. "No," I said.

All three of us got out of the car, Jenn at my side, her blond hair in a ponytail, arms crossed and feet planted into the ground like she was my bodyguard. Barbara squeezed my arm. I felt braver with them. I addressed Mom. "Where's Drew?" I hadn't even had a chance to say good-bye to her. "I want to see her."

"At music lessons. I'll tell her you're at Jenn's." Mom's voice sounded normal. Not cheerful, not sad.

I hesitated, then nodded, taking this to mean I'd still get to talk to my sister occasionally. This, at least, lifted some of the burden from my chest. "Tell her to call me. When Dad's not around."

"I will." Mom kept her hands behind her back, as if that absolved her of any complicity. It made me angry to see her standing there so emotionlessly. As if she didn't care. I won't care, either, I told myself. Not a bit.

We started loading boxes from the garage to the car. After a few minutes, she turned abruptly and went inside.

"Not even a good-bye." Jenn shifted, shook her head. "Shit. That's cold."

"Jenn, language!" Barbara took in a deep breath. "Rachel. Your mother loves you. This has to be hard for her. She doesn't have many choices, so she *has* to do what your father says."

"Nobody has to do what a man says. It's America!" Jenn flung out her arms.

Barbara folded a box top closed. "This is why I'm raising you to be independent, Jenn. Why it's important to have a college degree. Even if you end up getting married to a great man, he could get injured or die. You always need a backup plan." Barbara hefted up a box that was too heavy for her and heaved it into the trunk. If Barbara had any faults, it was her tendency to lecture. Maybe Jenn had heard it all before, but I soaked it up.

Jenn rolled her eyes. "You're such an optimist, Mom."

Despite my hurt, I understood. Mom was completely dependent on my father. "You can't work," my father would tell her when she wistfully mentioned finding a job. "It's impossible. Besides, who'd want you? You haven't worked for almost two decades."

We finished loading the boxes into the trunk. I stood there mute, my insides churning. I wished my sister was there to say good-bye. I wished I could take her with me. Well, she was barely home anyway, and my parents still liked her—she'd be all right.

Barbara shut the hatchback of her station wagon and regarded me with a furrowed brow. She didn't fully understand our family dynamics, couldn't comprehend my father's nature.

"Come here, sweetie." Barbara opened her arms. She hugged me in a way I did not recall my mother doing since I was tiny, patting my back. I leaned into her peach-colored sweatshirt with a scene of lambs playing in a field, smelling her drugstore Coty musk. I sobbed, letting myself release all the tension, dribbling snot all over the lambs. I was nothing. My parents could let me go so easily. Like I was a cast-off in one of those boxes. Jenn thumped my back.

Barbara rocked me back and forth. "You're not a bad kid, Rachel," she whispered into my hair, her breath warm on my scalp. "You have a good soul. You're just in pain, that's all."

I looked at the lambs through blurred eyes. Nobody had ever told me anything like that. "How do you know?"

"I just do." She pushed the hair off my sweaty forehead. I tightened my arms around her.

The garage door began grinding closed. I looked back to see Mom, her hand over the button, watching us with a pale face. The door hit the concrete with a final thud.

"Yeah, really. What do they know? Fuck 'em all." Jenn flipped a middle finger toward my house.

"Jenn!" Barbara slapped her daughter's hand down in horror. "What's with the potty mouth?"

"Sorry. I've been hanging around with the swim team boys too much." Jenn flashed me a grin. "Hey, Rach. Our summer league needs a manager. You might as well do it. It'll be fun. I promise." She leaned over to my ear. "It's co-ed."

I had to laugh. Boys were the last thing I needed, except maybe as friends. But with Jenn there, it'd be all right. "Maybe."

"Maybe. Not maybe. For sure." Jenn got in the station wagon, patting the backseat beside her. "Come on, Rachel. Let's go."

"Nobody wants shotgun?" Barbara asked. "What am I, a chauffeur?"

So this was what a regular family was like. I relaxed a little bit, feeling less nauseated. Barbara would take care of me, I was certain. I shut the door and buckled in.

. . .

I lived with Jenn's family until I finished high school. "We could probably legally force your parents to take you back," Barbara said, "but it's up to you." I didn't want to go back. The only regret I had was at leaving my sister, but whenever I saw her, Drew seemed fine. We seemed to have lived different realities within a single family.

Barbara and her husband refused to take any rent, allowing me to keep the money I earned from a job I had cleaning up for an elderly neighbor. Later, Barbara and her husband, Harvey, got an affidavit to be my caregivers, so they could sign me up for school activities and medical care.

They moved back east shortly after I married Tom, and Barbara passed away from cancer ten years ago. Jenn's working for the State Department in Europe now, but we keep in touch to this day, exchanging Christmas cards and occasional e-mails. I honestly don't know what would have happened to me if it weren't for Jenn's family. Through them, I got to know what a normal family was like, in stark contrast to mine.

That was the last time I saw Mom until I was pregnant with Quincy.

When I remember this, it's like it all happened last week instead of twenty years ago. A pit opens in my stomach and that feeling of abandonment, of being yesterday's stinky fish, hits me all over again. I wish I could time travel back and find teenage Rachel and give her a big hug like Barbara had. Lots of big hugs.

My father should've tried a heck of a lot harder. He hadn't even made an attempt to help me, the way I would if Quincy or Chase started acting out like that. I wasn't entirely horrible—I never stole, I wasn't robbing anyone. I was just lost.

In short, he should have been a parent. So should have my mother. Parents help guide their children. They're not just these guardians who provide money and shelter, who pay attention only when their kids shine.

For two years after the big to-do that got me kicked out of the house, my mother had obeyed my father's orders. I'd seen my sister a handful of times—it was easier for Drew to claim she was doing something else so she could meet me—but never my mother. I'd given up on my mother, knowing she either couldn't or wouldn't risk my father's ire.

During the last month of my pregnancy with Quincy, my mother appeared at our house with two armfuls of gifts, calling first to make sure we were home. It felt like we were making a mutually inconvenient but necessary appointment, as though she was coming for a root canal. I'd opened the door to her reluctantly. After I felt Quincy flipping in my womb, awakening with loud music or kicking at the sensation of Tom rubbing my belly, I couldn't understand how my own mother could have let me go. What, exactly, was my father holding over her head? Maybe it was my crazy primeval pregnancy hormones talking, but if someone had tried to come between me and Quincy, I'd have cut off his leg and beaten him to death with it. Needless to say, at eighteen, I was still angry at my mother. At her impotence and passivity.

But Mom said she had something very important to give me. Entering my house, she stood nervously behind the couch, brightly striped gift bags held awkwardly in her hands. I hadn't seen her for two years, but she looked as if she'd aged ten, with deep new creases between her brows and at the corners of her mouth. Doing a lot of frowning, but not much laughing. My poor mother. Still, I didn't want to take the gifts. She was supposed to have fought for me. Determined to make this as uncomfortable as possible, I sat down and waited.

Tom swooped in, though, scooped up Mom's bags and enveloped her in one of the big warm Italian-family hugs he gives without reservation. "I'm so glad to meet you!" Tom squeezed my tiny mother. Only his parents had attended our wedding. I waited for her stiffness, for her to step back.

To my surprise, her arms flew up and she squeezed him back. When he stepped away, her eyes were bright. She let out a large sigh and smiled. "I'm happy to meet you, too."

Was that all she was feeling? No sadness? No apologies? I gulped down the lump in my throat. She could not just waltz back into my life, I thought fiercely. I wanted something—for her to say she regretted what her husband had done. That she had missed me. Anything.

Tom touched my shoulder. "I'll be in the bedroom if you need me," he whispered, and left.

Mom sat down, playing with the black pocketbook on her lap. She was dressed not in one of her customary Chanel suits, as I'd expected, but in sweatpants and a sweat jacket, the kind of thing she would have worn only while out walking. She stared at the rickety old trunk that served as our coffee table while she spoke. "Your father does not know I'm here," she said slowly, enunciating each word.

My mouth went dry. "What will you do if he finds out?" Who knew when my father would embark on another crazy whim and force her away? She would comply. She'd shown me that.

Mom smiled wryly and spread her hands out. "It is not your worry. He cannot keep me from seeing you." She reached into the bag, drawing out a large floppy gift wrapped in pink tissue paper. "I have something for you and Tom, and some things for the baby." She bowed, as if I were a stranger. Which I was. I made no move to take the package.

"Mom. I don't need anything. We're set." In fact, we were not, but if I took her gift, I'd be accepting her back into my life. I couldn't handle the disappointment if she left again, not while I was pregnant and vulnerable.

"Please." In that low light, her irises blended into her pupils. I was looking at a dark reflecting pool.

I took the package and unwrapped it. I knew what it would be as soon as I felt the softness through the paper. It was the wedding ring quilt, repeating interlocked circles of blue and yellow and green. My favorite colors. I ran my hand over the stitching, admiring the tiny stitches that hadn't been touched by a machine.

"I did it by hand," Mom said. "For you. It will bring good luck."

"I don't need luck," I said, still prickly. I felt Quincy move inside my stomach, pressing her tiny hands against my belly button as she flipped upside down. "Tom isn't Dad."

Her face went still. She took out another package. "And for the baby."

I unwrapped the other gifts. Knitted green booties, a cap, a soft pink receiving blanket. The booties looked vaguely familiar.

"They were yours." Mom settled back in the couch and gazed at some spot behind me. "I made them for you."

My chest felt like it was on fire. This was my mother's apology. Her love letter. She didn't need to use words. All at once I felt how much effort it must have taken for her to come see me, afraid I'd turn her away or be mean to her. I wiped at my eyes. "Thank you."

We stopped talking then. Only a mantel clock ticked away.

"And some new clothes." She pointed at the other bag. "Only yellow and green. Good for a boy or girl."

"It's a girl," I said.

Something akin to disappointment flickered over her face. "Oh."

"I'm glad it's a girl," I said. "I can't wait to raise a girl. She's going to do everything. Whatever she wants."

"How about Tom?" She nodded toward the door where he'd gone.

"Tom's happy. He says he can do anything with a girl that he could have done with a boy. Take her camping. Play sports." That had in fact been what Tom had said, but now I desperately wanted him to come out and confirm the story. "Tom!" I shouted.

He came running out as if he'd been waiting on the other side the door, his eyes wide. Those days, every time I called his name, he was afraid I was going into labor. "Are you okay?"

"Tell my mother you want a girl." I grabbed his hand.

"Of course I want a girl," he said, his voice laced with puzzlement. He glanced at my mother, her expression as unreadable as a doll's. "What's the question?"

After that, Mom came by sporadically. Always in the daytime and never staying for more than a couple of hours. She couldn't come on Christmas or other holidays; that would make Killian too suspicious.

But she appeared often enough for my children to call her 'Bāchan, which means "Grandma" in Japanese. She always had candies in her purse, saltwater taffy and caramels, gooey stuff the kids loved. They were always glad to see her, though mostly Mom just sat on the couch and watched as they played. We never spoke of my father.

K aneto took them to the town of Kiso-Fukushima to buy supplies. They brought along Yoshimori Wada, the nine-year-old son of another local farmer Kaneto had recruited to the cause. "His grandfather was a Minamoto noble," Kaneto said. "Descended from Emperor Kawa. He is like us. Samurai blood."

Yoshimori Wada seemed unremarkable to Tomoe. He was barely her height, with a medium build and a placid face on a ball-like head, his straight hair falling into his eyes. He looked like a dull wooden doll. Tomoe greeted him with a small bow when they were introduced, then faded back behind Kaneto so she wouldn't have to talk. She focused instead on walking the horse they had brought to carry the goods back.

Tomoe loved going into town, which she rarely got to do. This town was tiny, only two streets long, but compared with the farm it was a bustling metropolis.

Kaneto paused at a stall where a man sold clothing, asking about woven bamboo body armor. "You may each buy a sweet," he said, giving them each a Chinese copper. Tomoe grinned. Such a treat was usually reserved for special occasions, like New Year's. This was a noteworthy occasion indeed.

Tomoe and Yoshimori Wada walked slowly to the sweets stall. The two younger boys danced in front of them, kicking up plumes of yellowish-brown dirt in their wake. Tomoe sneezed. "Watch out!" Yoshinaka yelled to the townspeople, doing a high-kick for their benefit. "Minamoto coming through." Several old people nodded approvingly at him with toothless grins. Tomoe doubted these people would state their support aloud, however.

Tomoe glanced back at her father, expecting a reprimand for the showy display. Kaneto did not turn. It was young Yoshimori Wada who stepped in and clapped Yoshinaka on the back roughly.

"Stop it," he said sharply. "You are getting dirt in Tomoe's face."

Yoshinaka glanced back at her, surprised. "She doesn't care if she gets dirty."

"I care." Yoshimori Wada put his face next to Yoshinaka's. "You're her brothers. You're supposed to protect her."

Tomoe stepped forward. "It's all right, Wada-san."

"Call me Yoshimori." But he straightened from Yoshinaka.

"I like Wada. Wada-san." She bowed with a smile. It wasn't polite of her to call him by his family name. Surnames were given as an honor by the emperor, and should not be bandied about so casually. He might have punched anyone else who tried it. But instead Wada's face brightened and blushed. Perhaps he wasn't dull after all, Tomoe thought. Of course, Kaneto would never consent to training a dull boy. Tomoe would watch the boys to make sure they didn't die by their own clumsy hands, and Wada-san would watch after her.

A group of little girls stood in front of the candy vendor. They were merchants' daughters, clad in cotton kimonos of light pinks and yellows, their hands soft and untarnished by heavy work, tall in their wooden *geta* sandals, platforms built on sideways blocks. They looked at Tomoe and giggled.

"Is that a boy or a girl?" one of them asked disdainfully.

"She's as dirty as a boy, and she's with boys," another girl said.

Tomoe's face burned. But what did she care what these little girls thought? In Japan, merchants were below farmers in society. One day, they would pray for protection from people like her and her family. The real warriors.

Head held high, Tomoe walked up to the sweet vendor. Her mouth watered at the display of multicolored candied fruits and the mochi candies. The air here was sweet. She inhaled and looked over the prices. She had money for the fruit, but not for the mochi, her favorite.

The vendor, an elderly man whose wrinkles nearly pushed his eyes closed, leaned over.

"What would you like, pretty one?"

"One candied loquat, please." To her left, Tomoe heard the girls continue to chatter about her. Loneliness welled up. She wished she had a girl for a friend. Just one girl, to play dolls or some other nonviolent activity. She had to put Kanehira in a headlock at least once a day to make him behave. She admired the girls' clean *tabi,* the socks worn with their *geta.* They had no dirt beneath their fingernails. She imagined what it would be like to stroll, instead of run, to giggle with friends.

The vendor handed her change. A thought made her heart pound faster; Tomoe bought several candied loquats, golden and juicy, and turned to the girls. "Would you like one?" she asked, holding them out on the palm of her hand.

The girls eyed her with distaste. They said nothing. They turned away.

Then Yoshinaka was there, muscling up alongside her. "Answer Tomoe."

A girl with catlike eyes wrinkled her nose. "I smell dung and despair. It must be a Minamoto." The others laughed openly, several little boys joining in as they sensed excitement afoot.

Tomoe stiffened, sure that her young foster brother would retaliate. But Yoshinaka only laughed and stuck one hand into his kimono. "One day you'll wish to be a Minamoto, too, and don't think I won't remember who you are and what you said." He stared at the girls with an expression that reminded Tomoe of their dog when he was hunting a rabbit. The girl blanched, unwilling to escalate a conflict with the unpredictable Yoshinaka, and wobbled off, her friends following. "You don't bother Tomoe, you hear?"

Wada, as she now thought of him, pulled her backward. "They're not worthy of you, Tomoe," he said. "Come on, Yoshinaka. Kanehira. Let's find your father." Linking her arm with his, they left the stall.

"Here." Kanehira was at her side. He handed her a mochi cake, heavy, filled with candied fruit. This was the most expensive thing at the stall, because of the cost of the rice. Rice was so valuable in Japan that it was even used to pay taxes. Kanehira must have used his whole coin, maybe even two. She glanced at Yoshinaka and saw that he had no treat. Neither did Wada. All three of them had bought this for her. They did not acknowledge her, but kept walking, eyes forward.

These boys were her truest friends. Both by blood and by chance. They were the only ones she could depend upon, who truly understood her. When the world turned against her, they would form a shield.

They came from the same place, after all.

Tomoe knew they did not want thanks; it would embarrass them. Instead she held out the loquats. Each of the boys popped one into his mouth as they went back to locate Kaneto.

Five

D rew does wonder, sometimes, what became of the quilt her mother made for her. When she thought she was going to get married, she imagined putting it on their bed. Then her mother tried to give it to her when Drew knew her boyfriend would never marry her. Every time she saw the quilt, she thought of her almost-fiancé. She feels guilty now, thinking of all the work her mother put into it; but getting the quilt then was like receiving a baby outfit after you know you can't get pregnant.

Besides, Drew had never been as close to Hikari as Rachel had been. Drew figured she'd been the boy her father never had—they gave her this unisex name, after her father's father, Andrew—and Killian generally gave Drew whatever she wanted. Maybe her mother had allied more with Rachel as a result.

Drew kept busy in school, with music lessons, gone from before dawn until late at night, and that had seemed to be fine with Hikari. After Rachel got kicked out, Hikari became more withdrawn from the family. Further away from Drew. Instead, her mother spent most of her days sewing in that room downstairs.

"How many quilts can a person make?" Drew asked her mother once, when she was twelve. No one else was home. She felt a vague irritation, seeing her mother so involved in the task. Not involved with her. She stood in the doorway, watching Hikari piece together a crazy quilt. "I mean, we're in California."

Her mother hadn't even looked up from the sewing machine. "It is for the process, Drew." She heaved a sigh. "Go someplace else. If you can't find something to do, then practice your music."

Drew didn't understand what her mother meant by the "process." She knew only that her mother preferred the company of her buzzing sewing machine to Drew's chatter. Drew didn't want to be alone, playing her viola. She watched her mother sew for another minute.

Hikari stood up, obviously struggling to be patient. "Do you need something?"

Drew shook her head.

"Then go." Hikari shut the door in her daughter's face.

Drew paused, listening to the machine start up again. She banged on the door. "I hope those quilts keep you warm, when you're old and alone," she yelled. Her mother hadn't even slowed down the machine. Quite possibly, she hadn't heard.

Still, it wasn't the nicest thing a girl has ever said to her mother. She was acting like Killian, petulant, selfishly angry at the loss of attention.

Drew shakes off the memory.

She pulls up in front of Rachel's house. Rachel lives in a split-level on a hill, with a partial view of Lake Murray. Like all the lakes in San Diego, this is a water reservoir—you can take out slow speedboats or fish from the shores, but not swim. They call it a lake, Drew thinks, looking at the low water level, but it's more like a really big pond. People who live by, say, a really big body of water, like Lake Michigan, would be disappointed.

Rachel and Tom bought this house right after they were married. It's a

nice area. Homes built in the 1970s, remodeled and restuccoed and sometimes knocked down and rebuilt. Middle class. Far beyond what Drew can
afford in her foreseeable lifetime.

What happened was this: Rachel got knocked up when she was just
eighteen, and both of them quit school, so his parents used Tom's college
money for the down payment. Tom's a contractor, employed at the company his father started; and it's a case of the shoemaker's kids having no
shoes—the house still needs a fair amount of fixing up. The stucco's peel-
ing off and the deck surrounding the house needs to be sanded and
stained. Every time Drew visits, Rachel complains about the house, about
its various leaks and cracks and termites. It's annoying, Drew thinks. Like
somebody complaining about their secure job to someone who's been un-
employed for years.

Drew locks the car, following her sister in through the garage, passing
through the laundry area. "Sorry the kitchen's a mess," Rachel calls over
her shoulder. FRESH LINENS, a Pottery Barn–type sign proclaims in antique cream. The washer and dryer are cherry red, pristinely clean, with a
deep spotless white sink on one side and a white Formica counter on which
to fold laundry on the other. Drew, having spent most of her adult life
doing laundry in laundromats, is impressed with her sister's attention to
tiny details. If Drew ever owns a house, she decides, not a word of com-
plaint about anything, ever, will cross her lips.

Seeing Rachel makes Drew look back on her missed opportunities.
Most of the people Drew counted as financially successful now had part-
nered up early, gotten responsible jobs, and bought a house before the
prices shot up out of reach. Or they'd struggled in their twenties, or had a
lucky break that let them climb up out of their debt hole. When she was
younger, Drew hadn't understood how difficult it could be to attain
middle-class-dom. How fast opportunities slipped away.

But Drew also remembers Rachel encouraging her after she finished
college and she was thinking about joining Out Stealing Horses. "I just

don't know if I can do it," Drew had said. "What if they make me play the tambourine forever and ever?" It was Thanksgiving, and Drew had stopped by to give the kids matching stuffed turkeys that squawked. (*Thanks*, Rachel said in her cool, polite voice, and Drew knew she'd made a mistake with the noisy toys.) Her parents were taking her out to dinner. "Besides, I see people more talented than I am every day."

Rachel sighed impatiently. She stood at her kitchen counter—then a broken yellow Formica—mashing potatoes for dinner in a big ceramic bowl with what looked like an entire package of butter. Both toddler Chase and little girl Quincy clung to her legs. "Don't be such a . . ." she glanced at her kids, "frickin' Eeyore."

"I'm telling the truth." Drew felt a wash of self-pity. Even though she knew Rachel would tell her to suck it up. Her parents would just look at her uncomprehendingly. *So marry somebody rich and quit chasing that Jonah guy,* Killian would say.

Chase wiped his nose on Rachel's jeans. Rachel grimaced. "Go see Grandma Jean, you guys." Quincy stood up and grabbed her brother, hauling him off with her. Rachel stopped mashing. "Are you saying you don't know any working musicians who play worse than you?"

"Yeah. Of course." Drew can name a dozen offhand, and that doesn't include the pop stars who sing off key when they're not autotuned.

"Somebody is always going to be better than you, Drew. That's true for everybody." Rachel smiled with the kind of benediction Drew craved. "But all I know is when you play, I get goose bumps. And I don't get goose bumps for pretenders. If they won't let you play the viola, you can always quit. Talent doesn't mean anything if you don't use it."

"What's your talent?" Drew asked curiously, and immediately regretted it. Rachel took it wrong. A shadow fell over her sister's face.

Rachel attacked the potatoes with renewed vigor, fluffing them into mounds that almost looked like whipped cream. "See what I mean?" her sister said. "Talent means nothing if you don't use it. Or lose it."

. · .

Now Drew follows her sister into the kitchen. The old yellow counter-tops and decrepit cupboards are gone. The kitchen's been remodeled, ex-panses of tawny spotted granite with soft spotlights on the big gas stove and farmhouse sink. The large island is covered in letters from school, fly-ers about bake sales, and library books. The kitchen smells like marinara sauce, tomatoes and basil and garlic, coming from a bubbling Crock-Pot plugged in next to the coffeemaker.

Tom sits at the island, eating a bowl of Honey Nut Cheerios. "Drew!" He stands up, enfolds her in his arms. "Good to see you."

"Tom, why are you eating cereal? It's almost six o'clock." Rachel hangs her purse on a hook by the door. She holds out her hand and Drew gives her her purse, too. She puts the samurai book, in its bag, on the counter.

"If it's good enough for breakfast, it's good enough for dinner." He takes another bite.

"But I'm making dinner." Rachel points at the Crock-Pot. "If that was a snake, it would've bit you."

"Oh. Didn't see it." Tom shrugs. "Don't worry. This can be a snack. I'll digest this in six seconds, and then I'll eat your spaghetti."

This makes Rachel smile. "Okay, then."

Drew sits next to Tom, the stool squeaking. "Six seconds? What's that mean?"

Rachel waves her hand in the air. "It's something Chase used to say when he was a little boy. He'd get full at dinner, and we'd say, *Oh, you better wait a while for dessert.* He'd say, *Don't worry. I digest food in six seconds.*"

Inside joke. "Oh." Drew wonders what other family-specific sayings they have. She can't remember any that she and Rachel had, from growing up. Maybe it takes a certain kind of family to have those.

She watches her sister bend to kiss Tom, how his hand still grabs the back of Rachel's head to pull her in close. Tom the Steady. She still doesn't know her brother-in-law very well, even after all these years. She knows he's friendly, and that you should never mention foreign cars around him—the man was obsessed with Corvettes and Mustangs and American-made engines. He keeps an old project Corvette in the garage that he'd been working on for the last decade.

"He's so boring," Drew had said to Rachel after she and Tom first started dating. Drew was fourteen, Rachel eighteen. "A football-watching, American beer–drinking, early-to-bed early-to-rise typical . . . dude." She trailed off for lack of a more descriptive word. She pointed at Tom's old New Orleans Saints T-shirt that Rachel was wearing as a maternity shirt. "You're going to turn into one of them."

"One of who?" Rachel asked.

"One of those super-boring suburban PTA moms." Drew shuddered. "You'll be old before you even have a chance to do anything with your life." Drew wanted adventure. She wanted to be free of her family. Of all obligations.

"I *am* doing something with my life." Rachel patted her belly. "Just in a different order than I thought I would. I'll finish college when this one's in school. I'll only be twenty-three."

Twenty-three seemed ancient. Drew persisted. "Has he ever been in an art museum, or to the symphony? Or does he just watch football and drink beer?"

"Of course." Rachel's neck got blotchy. She was getting angry. "He's not morally opposed to culture."

Drew should have backed off, but she kept going. She was kind of prone to doing that. "I think he's just pretending to like the stuff you like," she said. "Men do that. Then you marry them and you find out that you've been tricked."

"Where on earth did you get that?" Rachel asked.

Drew stared hard at her. "Um, to begin with, Mom and Dad." She didn't know this for certain, but she imagined it couldn't have happened any other way. Killian must have pretended to be far nicer than he actually was, for Hikari to agree to marry him.

"Well, Tom's not like that," Rachel said. "He's the worst liar you'll ever meet. Even white lies. He turns red."

Remembering this, her naive snobbery, makes a flush creep up to Drew's hairline. She'd followed her own advice for a while. Kept up with Jonah because she thought he was going places, clinging on to him like Yoda clinging on to Luke's back as he did his thing, trying to shoehorn her way into his life and music. Tried out some accountants and engineers, but never clicked with them. Rejected other guys because they were too low on their job totem pole—she wanted someone who was already successful, not somebody who *might be* successful. Because you couldn't count on "might be."

Now all her friends have children or partners, or both, had moved to the Valley or other distant suburbs. Drew could use a dose of something true and solid in her life. It's worked for Rachel.

Drew leans over to her sister's husband. "Hey, Tom."

"Hey, Drew." He leans toward her, too. At forty, he's still got all his hair, and his active job's mostly kept away any middle-aged spread. He's wearing a white T-shirt and faded flannel pajama pants decorated with snowmen. "What's up?"

"Do you know anybody I could, you know, go out with?" Drew leans her elbows on the counter. "Who doesn't drink too much?"

"So the only criteria are sobriety and a pulse. That shouldn't be too hard." Tom laughs, puts his bowl in the dishwasher.

Rachel shakes her head and pulls off the Crock-Pot lid, stirs the contents. "Drew, you live in L.A. How can you date someone here?"

"I've tapped out the L.A. dating market. I'm too old." Drew takes a paper napkin out of the chrome holder and folds it diagonally. Her heart pounds. She looks at Tom's kind face and decides what the hell. Just tell the truth. "Besides, my employer kind of quit on me. The shop's closing." She keeps her gaze on the napkin, folding and refolding it until it forms a crane, or a semblance of one.

Tom clucks sympathetically. "Oh man. That's tough. I'm sorry."

Rachel drops the Crock-Pot lid with a clang. "Drew! You just told me work was going fine."

"My work *was* going fine. The business wasn't." Wetness springs into her eyes and she wipes at them, embarrassed. Rachel purses her lips and puts her hands on her hips. Drew knows what she's thinking. Rachel figured out decades ago that Drew often cried just to get attention, even when she didn't do it on purpose. When she was tiny, Drew would make huge fusses over tiny scrapes, just so Hikari would comfort her. She made up nightmares and monsters when she couldn't sleep, so Rachel would let her sleep with her. And truthfully, Drew's feeling a teensy bit sorry for herself. It'd be nice if someone could put a metaphorical Band-Aid on her. Tom obliges, patting her hand, which only makes Drew even more teary.

Rachel takes out a large pot and fills it with water, shaking her head all the while. "I knew that woman was a weirdo flake. I never trusted her. Do you have something else lined up? Did you know she would do this?"

Drew shakes her head back. Of course Rachel saw this coming. When Drew first took the job, Rachel had asked dozens of questions. How long had the woman been grooming dogs? *Never.* What was different about this business? *It's cute. It's called Dogwarts.* Does she provide benefits? *No.* And on and on until Rachel drove her point like a stake into Drew—that Drew was an ignorant fool who would never succeed at anything. Not that she said that in those words, exactly. Or that Drew had done anything except give her one-word answers and nod. She tried hard not to fight with Rachel.

Drew should have seen the signs. She should have gotten a job that went somewhere ages ago. But there were always the music gigs. And the fact that their father gave her a generous Christmas check every year that filled in the income gaps. Drew had grown comfortable in her stasis.

Tom smiles at her, his eyes crinkling. "Well. You can stay here as long as you want. We have that guest room. We'd love to have you. I feel like we never see you."

Drew's head lifts. She hadn't considered staying more than a night. Rachel swivels her head to stare at Tom. The Rachel Glare. Tom doesn't backtrack, just lifts his eyebrows back at her sister. Drew stifles a smile. How lucky is her sister that she found a man who will actually stand up to her? Because even though Drew loves Rachel, she has to admit that Rachel can be a teensy bit stubborn. Rachel looks down. "Tom, I've been having trouble with the TV remote in our bedroom. Can you show me?"

Tom shrugs, stands. "Sure." Rachel's already moving toward the living room.

T omoe weighed each green bean in the palm of her hand for heaviness before attempting to twist it free. If it did not give way immediately, she knew it was not ready. Such fruits were good only when the mother plant released them.

She knelt in the crumbling black earth, feeling in the leaves for the beans she couldn't see. The morning was still cool, the heat not yet oppressive. This was sixteen-year-old Tomoe's favorite time of day, and often she would arise in the first wan light to begin her chores. "Tomoe is more reliable than our rooster," Kaneto would say. He was the second one awake, going out to oversee the rice paddies. Tomoe always began her work with feeding the chickens and helping her mother start breakfast. Then it was time to wake up the boys. She saved the garden she'd attended as a child for last, weeding and watering, deadheading blossoms and picking ripe vegetables.

This morning, Kanehira and her parents had gone to town, taking eggs and some rice to barter for silk—Chizuru wanted to make them both kimonos. Yoshinaka was already out in their rice fields, supervising the dozen or so workers Kaneto employed.

The *clop-clop* of hooves caused her to look up. Yoshinaka dismounted and came at her, full-force. "Tomoe! You'll never guess."

Tomoe stood, upsetting her basket of beans all over the ground. She knelt again and picked them up. "What's wrong?" she said, annoyed.

Yoshinaka grinned, his eyes big with excitement. "Come on! I have to show you something."

She looked at the rows of beans she had not yet touched. "I cannot. I am not done."

"Tomoe. This is important." His voice took on an authoritative, deepening tone. Tomoe had overheard Yoshinaka bragging to her brother that he already had hair in places where only men had hair. The thought made her blush. Now Yoshinaka took her hand, his tone softening. "Come with me. Please. I promise you'll like it. And bring that basket."

She allowed him to lead her to the horse, a sturdy brown mare the boy was riding bareback. An excited, nervous giggle escaped her. Where were they going? Was he trying to get her in some deserted bushes? She trusted him, though. "All right. But can't you give me at least a hint?"

He laced his fingers together to give her a foot boost. "No." He scrambled up behind her. His growing strength surprised her. She could feel the strong muscles in his thighs, alongside her buttocks, squeezing her into place. Yoshinaka wrapped his arms around her and kicked the mare. She put the basket between her legs and held on to the horse's mane.

The breeze whipped through Tomoe's hair and she enjoyed the sensation on her face. It blew back onto Yoshinaka's face, fanning over his head like a bolt of silk. "It's like I blindfolded you," she said teasingly.

"I can ride blind," Yoshinaka said, "but I want you to close your eyes."

She shut them, her heart fluttering. What was he going to show her? She hoped it wouldn't be a terrible schoolboy prank. That he wasn't taking her to see an animal corpse or something equally disgusting. Sometimes she didn't know if Yoshinaka could tell the difference between her and her brother, his assistant in mayhem.

They rode for a while. Tomoe could tell by the sounds they moved beyond their fields and into a forest. The sunlight on her face and shoulders disappeared into shadow. She held the coarse horse mane a bit tighter. She could feel Yoshinaka's pulse beating through her light summer robe, into her spine. "Are we almost there?"

The horse stopped abruptly, but Yoshinaka held her still. "We are." He jumped down, then reached for both of her hands. She landed upright. "Keep your eyes closed." She heard him moving a branch, the crack of the wood breaking, and felt a sudden shaft of warmth on her torso. They were not in the woods. She heard birds singing, many of them, their song loud as though they were inside an aviary.

"Open your eyes," he commanded.

She blinked. They were standing before a cherry orchard of about half a dozen trees. Ripe fruit in shades varying from yellowish pink to dark red hung from every branch. This was what the birds sang about; they darted in and out of the trees, gorging themselves on cherries. Tomoe didn't blame them. If she were a bird, she would be here, too. Cherries were her favorite, and they didn't have any trees.

Yoshinaka bowed to her and swept his arm toward the booty. "Welcome to the Minamoto private orchard," he said. He reached up and plucked off a cherry. It was a brilliant primary red, so crimson it seemed as unreal as if it had fallen out of a painting. "For you."

She opened her palm for it, but Yoshinaka broke off the stem and placed the fruit on her lower lip. "Open," he said.

She obeyed, and he let it fall into her mouth. The sweet juices exploded against her tongue, and she couldn't prevent the smile from overtaking her face. She savored the fruit meat, crunching it off the pit and spitting out the seed. Yoshinaka stood watching her with a satisfied smile. He rubbed his hands together.

"See? Worth it," he said.

She looked around. Beyond the orchard was another field, and behind that a wood. Surely some neighbor had planted these trees. Whose land were they on? Would they get into trouble? "Yoshi," she said, "whose orchard is this?"

He popped four cherries into his mouth, then grabbed more handfuls, tossing them into her basket. "What does it matter? They are too lazy to pick them. They'll go bad if we don't."

She pictured arriving back home with a basket full of stolen cherries. Kaneto would have a fit. "You know Father won't like it. It's thievery. And why are you out wandering around instead of supervising?"

"Our workers don't need me to watch every second. Kaneto said so. It makes them feel downtrodden." Yoshinaka lay down on his side on the flattened green grass, patting a spot beside him. He spat out a pit. "Let's eat them here, and then we won't have to deal with your parents."

She sank to the ground and accepted the cherries, eating slowly, savoring the sweet, tangy flavor. "We could trade for them," she suggested.

Yoshinaka exploded, throwing over the basket. "Stop, Tomoe. We don't need to trade. This orchard belongs to the Wada family. And Wada-chan won't care. They'll be happy they didn't go to waste. They have too many other worries." He turned from her, stepping on the cherries in his haste.

Tomoe watched the cherries rolling away into mud. She looked at Yoshinaka accusingly. "You just wasted these," she said. She hadn't known, in all their years of being neighbors, that the Wada family had this treasure trove. She would have thought Wada would bring some cherries to her family. How often had she and Chizuru picked eggplant, beans, spinach from their gardens and given them to Wada-san to take home? Nearly daily, in the summer.

Yoshinaka stood, grabbing the basket. "I'll pick more."

"I've no appetite." She got to her feet, shaking out the bits of dirt and grass from her *yukata* and pants. "Don't eat yourself sick."

"Tomoe!" Yoshinaka grabbed her arm. He put his face very close to hers, pressing himself into her side, length to length. "Do you think me a child?"

She stared hard into his eyes, that warm brown-black-red color. A miniature Tomoe reflected back darkly at her. Their breath, through their lips, matched. His pupils dilated and his lips parted, close enough for her to feel the moisture from his mouth. His hand slid off her arm, around her waist, back up to her breast, caressing her. She put her arms around him. A hardness between his legs pressed on her stomach. She gulped. Her heart began beating wildly, sending unfamiliar shoots of warmth all over her body. He was going to kiss her. Perhaps more. Perhaps she hoped he would.

Frightened of her own strong response, she took a step away. He was no child. And he was not her brother. "I have to go finish my chores."

"Take the horse," he said, turning away.

She did not see him until that evening's meal, when he returned on foot, dirty and sweaty and without the basket. Yoshinaka sat quietly, eating, as Kanehira tried to jostle him out of his dark mood. Always his accusing eyes fixed on Tomoe. She ignored him.

Later, while her parents talked softly by the lamplight and Tomoe unrolled her sleeping mat, there was a knock at the door. Kaneto slid open the door. "Yoshimori! What brings you here at this hour?" Kaneto whispered. Wada said something indecipherable, and her father bowed before closing the door.

"What is it?" Kanehira said, sitting up. Tomoe looked, too. Kaneto held up a gift, wrapped in a bright red square of silk with a small note.

"A note from Wada-chan's mother. *We have been too busy and ill to pick these, but Yoshinaka helped us out today,*" Kaneto read aloud. *"Please accept our gift with our gratitude, as always."*

Chizuru unwrapped the silken knots. "Cherries," she said, holding aloft a handful. She smiled. "Ah. I had forgotten they had an orchard. Yoshinaka, what a nice thing that was to help."

Yoshinaka nodded modestly, but stole a glance at Tomoe.

Impulsively, she got up from her futon and ran across the room to give him a quick peck on the cheek. "Very nice," she whispered.

Yoshinaka's grin broadened. "I know they are Tomoe's favorite fruit," he said.

Six

T om wants to talk sense into me. I already know it. He's the commonsense yang to my emotional yin. His hand feels warm and steady. Tom still has the sandy brown hair he had when we first met; all the men in his family keep their hair. Many are also remarkably long-lived, active into their nineties. Good genes. He'll outlive me. It's why I picked him.

Also, I fell in love with him when he walked into my community college Introductory Biology class. He had the best posture of anyone I'd ever seen, his neck and shoulders strong. Confident. An easy smile, which he was directing at the person behind him. I admired him, feeling my whole body freeze up, my vocal cords included. I'd never talk to him. I'd want to, I already knew. I'd content myself with a semester of staring at the back of his well-trimmed head, with the soft hairs meeting his neck.

Then he tripped on my backpack, which I'd carelessly left too far out in the aisle, the straps a booby trap for passersby. He face-planted with a worrisome crack. The chatter in the room stopped. I froze. I thought he'd yell at me, and rightfully so. I forced my muscles into action and rushed to him though I was shaking in fear. "Oh my God. I'm so sorry. Are you all right?"

From the floor, he lifted an arm. "Don't worry. I'm okay." He got up and brushed himself off. There was an alarming red mark on his chin.

"I'm so sorry," I managed again, in a tiny voice. I could feel my eyes tearing up, everyone looking at me.

"No worries. Nothing broken. Probably." His lively green-brown eyes, the ones our children would inherit, met mine. I was so close I could see tiny dots of blue, deep within the green, the browns underneath that, as if his eyes were soil and grass and sky. Every nerve in my body sang. I took a gasping breath, speechless again, then looked away in embarrassment at my own reaction. He smiled, the kind of smile you'd use to tame a skittish dog. He sat next to me.

There would be jokes about that lethal backpack for years.

I think about that day sometimes. How if I hadn't been so thoughtlessly careless, I would never have met my husband. How so many tiny accidents lead us to who we are. Who we create.

We make it to the living room, to the bottom of the stairs, before I stop and turn to my husband. "With everything that's happening with Mom, I can't handle another thing," I say. I run my hands over my hair. I need a shower. My sister's an adult, but she needs as much tending as a guest. "And I'm not ready for a guest. There's a bunch of laundry in the guest room. It needs new sheets. The bathroom's dirty."

"All of which is no big deal." We get to the base of the stairs. "She's your sister," Tom whispers. "She's not just any random person." This room has a vaulted ceiling and voices echo too much off the hardwood. Over the years, with thin walls and hollow doors, we've perfected both the near-silent fight and the clandestine sex with each other's hands clamped over our mouths. "She can help you with your parents. You just don't like not having total control."

"Not true," I protest in a whisper, even as I think, *Yeah, maybe it is a little true.*

Tom knows this. But I'm a planner. He's not. And he's also got a much more generous nature than I do. It's something I work on. This opening up to the world and letting whatever wants to happen, happen.

During our first Thanksgiving together as a proper little family, with six-week-old Quincy, Tom had been gone for a weeklong project and got home on Wednesday. Tom's parents were off visiting one of his brothers, so it was a perfect opportunity for me to practice, screw up, and get it right for other years.

Cooking your first Thanksgiving turkey is a huge milestone. Making sure it's not disgustingly dry. Defrosting it for the right number of hours. And this was before the Internet was in full swing—you couldn't easily Google recipes. You had to have a book, or know how to do it.

Growing up, Thanksgiving was barely a blip on my family's radar. If we had no guests that year, we'd eat take-out—Killian installed in front of the television, watching football, Drew and me in the kitchen, my mother someplace else in the house. If Killian wanted guests, if he had some out-of-towners to impress, we'd hire someone to come in with a full dinner and present the turkey on a rented silver platter.

I wanted to make my new family's traditions special. Perfect. One day, Drew would be out of that house and I could invite her to mine, I thought.

So, the whole week Tom was gone, with my two-month-old in tow, I prepared. First I got one of those complete Thanksgiving recipe magazines they sell by the checkout stand. I bought every food I could think of—yams and marshmallows, potatoes and cream, Italian bread and seasonings, pastry crust and canned pumpkin.

By the time Wednesday night rolled around, when Tom was due to be home, I'd called it quits. Quincy had a cold. In three days I'd probably slept for three hours, sucking yellow-green snot out of her nostrils and sitting up with her in a steamy bathroom. Our apartment was scattered with burp cloths and laundry, and the turkey floated in a pool of ice water in the sink. Dirty dishes were stacked on the counter—I had no dishwasher.

I sat on the couch, topless, my stuffy-nosed baby on a semicircular

Boppy pillow, and tried to get her to latch on. Quincy kept bawling because she couldn't breathe through her nose and therefore couldn't nurse well. It was this domestic scene that met Tom when he sauntered through the door, followed closely by a lanky man who smelled strongly of cigarette smoke. "Rachel, this is Larry. His family's in North Dakota. I invited him here for the holiday. He can sleep on the couch." Tom spoke before he really looked. I reached for a blanket, but it was too late. Tom turned beet red.

Larry averted his eyes. "Hello," I said through gritted teeth, resisting the urge to throw the pacifier at a hundred miles an hour at my husband's face. What was I going to say? *Fuck off, Tom, you're too fucking nice, bringing people without families to our home?* I couldn't.

"Sorry to intrude," Larry said, keeping his gaze away. "I thought Tom cleared it with you."

This made me feel worse. It wasn't Larry's fault that Tom didn't think this through. Or call. A call would've been nice. Now Larry would think I was a horrible wife, a lame cook, an incompetent mother. He and Tom would sit and watch football and I'd have to clean up everything, take care of the baby, and cook a meal that was looking further out of my grasp every second. "I'm just . . . surprised, is all."

Tom picked up Quincy, cooed at her, kissed her face. "Little girl. I missed you."

"She's sick." I reattached the hooks on my nursing bra and slid on my T-shirt and offered a real smile to Larry, who had produced a six-pack of Corona that neither Tom nor I was old enough to buy.

Larry excused himself to wash up, and I beckoned Tom close to me. "Next time you bring someone home like this, I'd like a warning. I don't like surprises," I whispered. "How am I going to entertain him? This house is a mess."

"Everything in life is a surprise," he whispered back, pointing to Quincy. He kissed my head. "Don't worry. I'll take care of everything."

I moved my head away. "Whatever." I hadn't met a man who could cook a meal or was willing to clean up. I stood up, aware of the fact that I couldn't remember the last time I showered. I decided not to worry about judgment. That's all women do, worry about who's going to think what about them. As though Larry was going to report back to the Mothering Authorities, and a contingent of Good Wives would show up at my door and give me demerits. I was too tired to care anymore. Let Tom deal with it. "I'm going to bed."

I stayed asleep until the next morning. My first full eight hours since Quincy was born. Larry, it turned out, knew how to cook a turkey. Tom mashed the potatoes and steamed some vegetables and bought a frozen pie. All I had to do was put on some cleanish clothes and show up at the table. To our first holiday meal, which kind of turned out perfect. I didn't really need or want to cook up a huge Norman Rockwell feast. What I really needed was exactly what I got—time to sleep. Somebody else to cook and do dishes.

That was when I figured out that although my husband didn't do things exactly the way I did them, his intentions were generally good. Which forgives a lot. And that sometimes he knows what I need before I do. Difficult as that is for me to admit.

Now I wonder if by inviting Drew to stay with us, he's seeing something I don't. It really would be nice to have Drew here when I woke up in the morning. We haven't been in the same house like that in eighteen years. We've never gone on vacation together. When she comes on the holidays, she stays somewhere else and visits me and our parents separately.

"Hey you." Tom clamps his arms around my waist, his hand interlocking his wrist. This is what he does, when we fight. He pulls me in so close that I can't get away, puts his mouth right next to my ear so my skin's a quilt of tingles. "You have to give her a chance," he murmurs. "She's a good person."

"I know she's a good person. I practically raised her." I think about the easy camaraderie Tom has with his two brothers. They tease each other mercilessly and nobody ever has hard feelings over it, the way Drew and I always do. Tom says they've done this since childhood. Maybe boys are different.

"Rachel." Tom leans into me. "The past is past. You have to let go and move forward. Time is a gift. That's why it's called the present."

For a second I'm about to compliment him on his depth. Then I have to laugh. I recognize the line. "You got that from *Kung Fu Panda*." One of Chase's favorites. We've probably watched it fifty times. "You need to come up with your own stuff."

"It doesn't matter. It's true." He circles his arms behind my back, pulls me into him forcefully. As if we're doing a tango. "Do you know you look hot when you're angry?"

"So that's why you want me all the time." I put my arms around his neck and lean against him. "Okay. I'll see if she wants to stay."

"You're sisters. She's family. You need to be close." He tweaks my nose. "I know things, Rachel."

I roll my eyes. "You try."

"Such a bad attitude." Tom smacks my bottom.

I yelp and laugh and glance guiltily into the kitchen. Drew's bent over her phone, her hair hiding her face. Her long legs are all angles on the stool. As if she feels my gaze, she lifts her head and meets my eyes, and I feel that electric jolt of surprise and warmth. Like I did when she was a newborn. "Hey," she says. "I found a translator. Goes to UCSD. Hopefully he's not a serial killer."

"Great," I say.

Tom holds my hand. "You okay?"

"Yeah. Help me get dinner on the table." I let go of my husband and go into the kitchen.

Drew knows that Rachel's telling Tom that he shouldn't have invited her. Drew's inadvertently started a battle. "I don't actually think I can stay," Drew says when Rachel returns. This is why it's better for Drew to keep her mouth shut. "I've got stuff to take care of at home, too. Like finding a new job."

"No. I don't mind if you stay," says Rachel, just as quickly, and one of those fake smiles Drew hates stretches her sister's face. "Stay as long as you like. I can use the help. Really."

Drew gets up and opens the Crock-Pot lid, considering. Chunks of onion float around juicy meatballs. Drew inhales. This is Tom's mother's recipe, Drew knows—she's had it before, and it's the best red sauce she's ever had. Fresh herbs float in the pot. The meatballs are not uniformly shaped. Homemade. When did her sister have time?

She takes a spoon out of the drawer (of course the utensil drawer is next to the dishwasher—unlike Drew's kitchen, Rachel's kitchen makes sense) and scoops out a meatball. It's juicy and tender and—surprise—has a morsel of creamy mozzarella hiding in the middle. She closes her eyes, suddenly famished, and has to stop herself from scooping out another one—she could eat this whole pot, no problem. The last time Drew had Italian, it was a can of Chef Boyardee she got on sale for a dollar. Yeah, she's definitely staying for dinner. She can go home after that.

"Can you make the salad?" Rachel nods at the refrigerator.

Drew opens the doors. The veggie drawer's stuffed. Two kinds of lettuce, something called "Power Mix" (prewashed three times, it proclaims), carrots, fresh herbs, broccoli, cucumbers. Drew usually gets the premade salads where you just have to open the bag, add the dressing. "With everything?"

"Whatever you like." Rachel puts a wooden cutting board on the island.

Drew hopes she can meet Rachel's unspoken standards. Or, worse, for Rachel to pretend that she liked the salad when in fact she hated it. When they were little, Rachel detested raw tomato. She'll leave those out, just in case. It's salad, Drew thinks. Not some huge symbol of their relationship. When their mother made salad, she put all the ingredients in different little bowls, so people could add what they wanted. "So, mixed in? Not like Mom?"

"We eat everything." Rachel hands her a chef's knife. "Go crazy."

Drew washes a cucumber and finds the peeler. It's all so cozy here. So different from anyplace Drew's ever lived. Until Rachel left, Drew hadn't noticed the tension of her family. There was always Rachel, the buffer, capturing her parents' attention.

Rachel had been a swimmer for as long as Drew could remember. If music was Drew's special talent, her passion, swimming was Rachel's. She started at the community pool swim team, then joined competitive leagues. Rachel scooped up all the awards from early on.

Drew loved watching Rachel swim, sitting on the bleachers, shielding the sun from her eyes. Seeing her sister's long arms cut up out of the water, faster and faster. A machine. A hero.

"This one's going to the Olympics," Killian would say proudly.

Then, at the CIF state championship meet, something happened. Drew remembers watching Rachel's lane, the feet, the arms churning, she and her father and mother cheering on Rachel until their voices were hoarse. But the arm stopped and Rachel sank.

She burst back up, treading water with her legs, holding her useless arm, her eyes and mouth opening in a silent scream. The shoulder had dislocated, tearing the ligaments around it. She'd never swim competitively again.

After that, Rachel hadn't been the same. Their father stopped saying Rachel was going to the Olympics; he barely spoke to Rachel at all. Disappointment hung in the air. Her swim team friends fell away. Her grades slipped, and she'd stay out late, sneaking in late and reeking of Coors Light and marijuana. Rachel would call herself in sick to school, spend the day sleeping and listening to music, the nights sneaking out.

Drew watched all this happen with increasing worry. She was only twelve at the time, still a good girl. She practiced the viola even more to make up for Rachel. Wanting to give her parents something to be proud about. Worrying about Rachel gave her stomachaches and made her into an insomniac. She'd knocked on Rachel's door one night. Her sister cracked it open, showing only reddened eyes. "Why are you doing this?" Drew said. "Do you want to end up a loser?"

Rachel said nothing. No hurt, no anger. Nothing. Like Rachel was so numb and beyond any emotion that she might as well have been a corpse. A sharp sliver of fear hit Drew. She kicked the door. Rachel pushed her into the hallway, flipped her off, then slammed the door.

Finally Drew approached Hikari, who was in her sewing room, of course, cutting out little squares of yellow and green calico, laying them into tall piles, her lean hands working as if they had a mind of their own, her dark hair bound back into a ponytail. If somebody painted a portrait of Hikari, it would be of her at the sewing machine. Drew came into the room and closed the door behind her. "Mom, Rachel needs help."

Hikari continued cutting. "She must go through this alone, Drew. She will be all right. She's just sad about her shoulder."

"No, she won't be all right." Drew's voice rose. Why did her mother always ignore her? "She's using drugs. Go in there and find out for yourself. Can't you smell it?"

Hikari put down her scissors and stared at her sewing machine. "It's incense," she said finally, and looked up at Drew, meeting her eyes.

Drew wanted to tear apart every quilt in the room. Why was her mother being so dumb, on purpose? Drew wasn't thirteen yet, and even she could see the problem. Parents were supposed to help their kids, not pay attention to them only when it was convenient. Everyone else she knew had parents who cared. Who would ground them or tear apart their rooms or send them to rehab. "She's going to end up pregnant or in jail." Drew's voice choked with a sob.

A deep line furrowed between her mother's brows, and Hikari stood up, brushing her slacks. "You're a child. You don't know the best way. Now, please get out. Calm yourself."

"You're nothing more than a maid. No, we have a maid. You're not a mother. You're not a maid. You're not even a babysitter. What good are you? Why are you even here?" Drew was yelling. Deep, primal. The neighbors heard her. The fish in the ocean heard her.

Hikari stiffened to her full height. She opened the door. "Get out."

Drew picked up the quilt squares and threw them into the air, sending them into a hail of material all over the floor. "I hate you!" She stomped her feet. "I hate you, I hate you, I hate you!"

Hikari stared at the material flying through the air. She turned to Drew with a terrifying expression. Years of repressed anger and sorrow and who knew what else mixed together. Before Drew could react, Hikari slapped Drew soundly across the face, her nails indenting Drew's flesh.

Drew stopped her yelling, shocked. She held her stinging cheek, not knowing what to do.

"I hate you, too. What do you think about that?" Her mother's bottom lip trembled, as if she, too, was about to cry. Her cold gaze met Drew's.

Drew ran out of the room.

This is what Drew can't forgive her mother for. Her inaction. Her passivity when her children needed her help. Why didn't she step up for Rachel? Sure, Killian would have flipped out, but Drew thinks his reaction was worse because things had been going on for months. If he'd known earlier, it might not have been so bad.

And also, there's this—Drew's pretty sure that if she ever has kids, even if they tell her they hate her, she won't respond in kind. No matter how down and shitty her life was. Never. She'll always respond with love.

KISO-FUKUSHIMA TOWN
SHINANO PROVINCE
HONSHU, JAPAN
Summer 1170

O
n the grounds of the Kozen-ji temple, one of the grandest in the area, with ten buildings on its premises, all the families gathered to celebrate the wedding of Wada's sister. To Tomoe, the main temple looked like a palace with a long sweeping curved roofline, perched on a high hill. The grounds were surrounded by forest and gardens, ponds and cherry trees.

Thick wisteria vines, purple blossoms cascading down, shedding sweet scent, crisscrossed the patio roof where the feast was set up. The guests had brought dishes to share at low rectangular makeshift tables set up in rows beneath the flowers. Petals and dropped leaves crunched under Tomoe's feet. Lit lanterns swung over the revelers. A man banged a small *taiko* drum in a rhythm like a heartbeat while another played the *hichiriki*, a high-pitched recorder, in a dissonant yet cheerful melody. Drunk people danced, arms linked, laughing. It was a perfect warm summer night.

Tomoe sat on a cushion and picked at her mother's lotus root dish while she looked around for Wada.

Last year Yoshimori Wada—through the combined efforts of Kaneto, his new brother-in-law, and several Minamoto cousins—won an assistant clerk job in the capital. "I will be your eyes and ears on the inside," he promised Kaneto. But Tomoe doubted Yoshimori would risk his new job to help them. Wada was probably already carrying on with the higher-class women there. He had written to Tomoe once. *Look, Tomoe, fine paper at last. Working on my poetry. I won't send one until it's perfect.*

Instead of Wada, she spotted Yoshinaka. He was talking to a girl older than Tomoe, his head bent low. The girl was small, her face pale and round, pleasantly chubby. Yoshinaka gestured occasionally; Tomoe imagined he was lecturing the girl about something, like battle strategy. She will get bored soon and leave, Tomoe thought.

But then the girl laughed, the sound cutting through the din as clear as a gong, and put her hand on Yoshinaka's neck.

Tomoe swung away, the lotus roots turning to lead in her mouth. She swallowed. Why should she care? Yoshinaka was sixteen, a man by most people's measure. He could do what he wanted. Tomoe put her hand to her stomach to staunch the sudden pain there.

"Tomoe."

She recognized the voice immediately. She looked up, but there was a lantern behind him and his face was in shadow.

"Hello, Wada-san." Her voice sounded calm, thankfully.

He cringed, and then smiled. "You are the only person existing who may call me that."

He took her hands and helped her up. His face had lost some of its roundness, and he had grown older in the year since she had seen him, but he looked like the same old Wada. He grinned impishly, and Tomoe noticed a dimple at the left corner of his mouth. How had she missed that before? His sons would inherit that dimple, she thought, and did not know why Wada's future sons should come to her mind.

They walked out of the courtyard. The moon hung low and impossibly huge on the horizon, shaded in hues of orange. "It looks close enough to touch," she said.

"The moonlight suits you." Wada still held her hand.

Tomoe felt her heart beating harder in anticipation. Would he kiss her? She tried to decide how she would react, and could not. "How long will you be home?"

"Long enough." Wada smiled. "I start back in two days."

A soft wind blew up, rustling the trees around them and cooling Tomoe's skin. A thrush sang out. Tomoe stopped. "Listen."

Wada stopped, too, putting his hand on Tomoe's cheek. "A thrush's song is not half as sweet as your voice, Tomoe. I've missed you."

She gulped and took a step away. "Oh, Wada-san. You've been studying poetry in the capital." She whistled the thrush's song, and the bird sang back in reply.

"Tomoe. Can't you be serious?" Wada dropped his hand to his side.

"I am serious, Wada-san. It's you who are not. I know you will not marry me, because I cannot increase your rank." She studied his face to confirm her blunt statement. He had the grace to blush. "So you will excuse me if your poetry leaves something to be desired." She knew what he wanted—a quick tryst. Something to occupy him while he was home. It would only be trouble for her.

"You are in love with Yoshinaka, aren't you?" he asked quietly.

She stopped moving. Was Wada right? The breeze shot up her sleeves, rustling the leaves in the distance. The crickets played their lonesome song, louder than the distant wedding music. Louder still was the sound of her inner heart. *Yes,* it said in quiet.

"He will never marry you. You cannot increase his rank, either," Wada said. "You will be a concubine. A novelty in his army, a dancing monkey who can fight with a sword."

Tomoe turned away so he could not see her face, gazing up at the moon. He was correct, of course. Her choices were limited. But she knew her place, for now, was with her family. In Yoshinaka's army as an *onnamusha*, whether or not he took her as his wife. This was the life she had, and she could choose no other. "Yet I would rather be a warrior in his army than a kept woman in the capital," she said.

The thrushes and crickets went quiet all at once. The *hichiriki* wailed a high note and faded, the drums stopped. Tomoe went still. Neither she nor Wada breathed. Something was wrong.

In the next instant, screams rose and people began running like ants from boiling water. Smoke filled the air. Tomoe exchanged a glance with Wada and as one they broke into a full run. Tomoe felt for her short sword, feeling its reassuring heaviness in her palm.

The main temple's roof was on fire. They ran into the wedding pavilion and saw shadowy figures fighting with swords, the banquet table kicked aside, the carefully arranged dishes strewn across the muddied grass.

Tomoe rushed into the fray. Wada fended off two men with swords. Tomoe guessed these were employees of the Taira, probably wandering samurai hired for a fee. The Search and Punish crew.

"Surrender!" she yelled. "Surrender and you can join the Minamoto clan."

The men made no answer. The one closest to Tomoe reached down to the table and grabbed a rice ball, shoving it into his mouth, the bits of rice sticking to what was left of his beard. It was only a second of distraction, but it was enough for Tomoe. Her sword connected with flesh where the man's arm met his shoulder, sliding cleanly into his torso. He screamed through the mouthful of rice, staggering to the ground.

Tomoe looked about for Yoshinaka and Kanehira, but couldn't see them. Wada turned to her, his elegant robes spattered with blood. Somehow he still seemed unruffled. "This way."

They ran to the back of the pavilion.

"Tomoe," she heard from the ground. It was so quiet she thought she'd imagined it. Tomoe stopped.

"Here." Her father lifted a hand into the air.

"*Otōsan!*" She rushed over to him. Blood seeped from his midsection.

"*Ichi-go, ichi-e.* My one chance is gone." Kaneto put his head back. "Where's your mother?"

"I don't know." She put her hands over his wound, her front becoming soaked.

"No use, Tomoe." Kaneto coughed up blood.

Wada and Yoshinaka returned. "Is he hurt?" Yoshinaka said.

"Find my mother," Tomoe shouted. Wada ran off.

"Tomoe," Kaneto said, his voice so low she could barely hear it. "Take care of Yoshinaka, of all of them. They are lost without you."

"Of course." Tomoe pressed down harder. "But you will be fine." Perhaps Chizuru knew how to stitch up a wound this vicious. Tomoe fought off her rising panic. "Help!" she screamed. "Okāsan, where are you?"

"Tomoe!" Chizuru called, hurrying to her daughter's side, her face covered in soot. She stumbled to the ground and covered Kaneto's wounds with a folded cloth. "Move, Tomoe. Let me try."

She could not imagine this world without her father. Not yet. Kaneto would die an old man, she told herself, breathing in and out until she stopped shaking. She stood. The pavilion roof flamed. People tossed buckets of water.

"Nine Taira," Yoshinaka said with disgust. "Idiots. Why would they send such an unlucky number?" Nine, or *ku*, also meant pain and suffering. "If they think this will stop me, they are fools."

A woman wailed long and loud, a storm blowing through a grove of pine trees. Tomoe jumped, at first not knowing from where the sound originated. "*Ie, ie, ie.*" Chizuru howled out the two syllables. "No." Her breath gone, Chizuru put her head down and cried quietly.

Tomoe took a step toward them. The face, already turning blue, had open glassy eyes, like a caught fish. Dark blood pooled around him. *"Otō-san?"* she whispered.

The fire snapped behind her.

This isn't real, she thought. It cannot be. But of course it was.

Their lives had changed in an instant.

Yoshinaka put his hand on her shoulder. He squeezed. She spun and embraced him, and he held her up. She would always hold on to her family. No matter what else happened.

"We will make him proud, Tomoe," Yoshinaka whispered. He released her, then picked up her father and carried him away.

Seven

I n the late morning of the following day, Drew and I go up to UCSD and walk over to the Geisel Library. The translator Drew found last night is a grad student in Medieval East Asian history, and he agreed to meet us here.

Quincy wants me to take her shopping this afternoon, so Drew's of-fered to chauffeur my son on his after-school activities. Win-win for me. It's like having a Rachel clone, which I've always needed. "What kind of job are you going to look for?" I ask her as we walk across campus. All the students seem to be in shorts and flip-flops. Another hot October day.

Drew shrugs. "I need to let that simmer on the back burner for a while."

"How about a music job?" I try to think of different ways she could make a living. "Could you play for a TV show or at Disneyland or in another band?"

Drew's shoulders visibly stiffen. "It's not that easy, okay?" She doesn't look at me. Which means she doesn't want to talk. "Let's just concentrate on this."

We open the door to the library. Named after Dr. Seuss, one of La Jolla's most famous residents, the library looks like a blocky, mirrored dia-mond encased in concrete prongs. The samurai story hangs heavy on my shoulder.

I'm glad to step into the humidity-controlled, air-conditioned library. Inhale the smell of books. Because they still have real, honest-to-goodness tomes in here. Not just electronic copies. Floor to ceiling, eight levels of knowledge. If I attended this school, I'd set up a cot in the stacks and sleep here. I just want to run around in here all day, collecting big stacks of books to read. I'm amazed at the number of computers. No more card catalogs.

We step inside, but don't see anybody looking for two women. No waves. "Is Quincy still playing piano?" Drew asks me. Quincy took lessons for ten years. She stopped when she was sixteen, but Drew, I realize, doesn't know it.

"No time. Engineering's pretty demanding." A little wellspring of worry bubbles into my stomach, thinking about Quincy. Nope. Can't change it. Not going to think about it.

"It's hard to make a living at music," Drew says, a bit wistfully. "I kind of wish I'd been an engineer, just so I'd have a career."

"No you don't. You hate math. You would have quit the first year." I'm not putting her down—just stating a fact. I'm not a math person, either. My daughter is.

"I wouldn't have." Drew crosses her goose-pimply arms. "I'm good at math. I just don't like doing it."

A young man in the foyer waves. He wears a white T-shirt topped with a blue scarf and black-rimmed glasses. Dark bangs flop onto his goateed face, and his jeans are tighter than Brooke Shields's in that long-ago Calvin Klein ad. He's not much older than my daughter. Wow. I *am* ancient. "Rachel? Drew?"

"Is the name Bond?" Drew raises her brows. "Joseph Bond."

"At least they didn't name me James," Joseph says drily. "Let's find a table." We walk past the circulation desk, and he gestures toward a seat at a long study table where students are lined up with open laptops.

"So how do you know Japanese?" I sit opposite him. "Did you study it in school?"

"I grew up in Japan—my dad worked for Sanyo." Joseph's eyes are blue behind his glasses, the scarf making them stand out even more.

I place the book on the table. "First, I'd like to know who sent it." I point to the return address on the box. There are numbers on the first line: 601-7934. "How do you read the address? Is this a house number?"

"No." Joseph gets out a pad of paper and writes down the translation. "In Japan, they begin with the equivalent of the zip code. The name is on the last line."

The name he writes in his hyper-neat, left-handed print is for a Hatsuko Minamoto in Kyoto. I have no idea who that is. I've heard of Kyoto, at least—it's in central Honshu, southwest of Tokyo. "Hatsuko. Do you know her?" he asks.

"No." I've never heard my mother mention anybody who lived in Japan or anyone in her family. She didn't even really talk about what it was like growing up. I do know that she grew up in the city, and that she's taller than either of her parents, because I'd asked. That pretty much sums it up.

Perhaps this woman knows the secret about my mother that Killian is threatening to reveal. What did my mother do? I wonder. Did she kill someone? Was she a spy? My imagination runs wild, and I inwardly curse my father for deliberately leaving his message so vague. But I wouldn't expect anything less from Killian.

I lace my fingers together and try to let my mind relax. I watch Joseph work, his super long fingers diligently scratching away. Then I sit up straight.

I remember. Yes, there was one time when Killian made some kind of threat to Mom.

I started swim team when I was five, taking lessons at the La Jolla Beach and Tennis Club. Kindergartens were a half day back then, so Mom would pick me up, Drew in tow, and take us over to the club. Often, we'd get a snack afterward. Pretty simple stuff.

On one occasion, another mother invited us to the park afterward to play with her little girls. I remember being giddily excited at having friends. At seeing my mother chatting and laughing with another mother. It got late.

When we arrived home, Killian was already in front of the television, an Old-Fashioned in his hand. The sun was low, sending bright golden light into the room.

My mother set Drew down. "Take your sister to play." I took Drew's hand but lingered on. The scent of chlorine clung to my damp hair. I walked her slowly into the hallway next to the living room, where Drew began rearranging a collection of stone animals on a small table. I could see and hear my parents.

Killian set his glass down. "It's five-thirty."

"Yes," Mom said. "Still light. It's almost summer. Very warm today."

He fingered the rim of the glass. "It's dinnertime."

My mother nodded quickly. She bustled around, picking up the mail he'd left opened and discarded over the coffee table, two used plates. "Yes. What would you like to do?"

"To do?" Killian laughed. "I'd like to eat, that's what I'd like to do. That's why you're here."

"I'm sorry." My mother bowed her head. "I lost the time. We have cold cuts. I can make sandwiches."

"That's not the point." Spittle flung out of his lips. "There's dirty dishes in the sink. Crumbs on the floor. Who wants to come home to that?"

Mom said nothing.

"You're doing too much outside the house," Killian said. He pointed at her. "You can do one activity a week with them. That's it."

My mother stiffened, then turned away. "It's important for the girls to see other children. To play."

He waved his hand. "Drew's a baby. She doesn't care. Rachel sees kids at school and swim. That's plenty."

Mom walked into the hallway.

"You're getting too many big ideas from these other liberated women!"

Killian called to her. "Don't you go thinking you're a feminist. I can send you back where you came from with one phone call."

I remember looking up at my mother, not knowing what that meant. She smiled at me reassuringly, but the plates clinked and trembled.

One phone call? Was his threat idle? What could that possibly mean? I play with the strap to my bag, feeling its scratchiness against my fingers.

All I know is that this is the only memory I have of Mom standing up to my father.

"Did you know that Kyoto used to be called Miyako, and was once the capital of Japan?" Joseph tears off the piece of paper and hands it to me.

I shake myself free of the reverie. "No, I didn't. Thank you." I'll have to ask my mother who Hatsuko is. If she can tell me, which is increasingly unlikely.

Drew reads my mind. "I'll visit Mom today and ask."

I nod at her, take out my notebook. A flicker of doubt about Drew taking that on passes through me. Why do I always feel this doubt wherever Drew's concerned? She's never screwed up my stuff. I am just a control freak. I put my cold hand on top of hers. "Say hi to her, okay?"

She gives me a strange look. *Mom doesn't know us.* "Sure."

"Maybe she'll have a good day."

Drew inhales. "Never has when I've been there."

I put my arm around her shoulder and give her an awkward, stiff half-hug. *Mom loves you,* I want to say, but I don't want to have to overexplain to Joseph.

Joseph takes a pair of white cotton gloves out of his satchel and pulls them on. He opens the cardboard box, gingerly lifts out the book.

"Should we be using those gloves, too?" We've been ruining an antique.

He looks at the spine, at the pages. "I'd say it's no more than sixty years old, honestly. Handwritten. But I wouldn't want to be the one who messes it up." Joseph writes on his legal pad and looks up at us. "This is the story of Tomoe Gozen. *Gozen* means 'lady.' Tomoe's big in Japan." His voice rises. "It's not a letter at all. It's a story."

I look at what he wrote.

Tomoe held the round bronze mirror with steady hands and fought her nervous pulse. A warrior stared back at her, in full battle dress.

"I've never heard of her. Was she a samurai woman?" I whisper. I say her name in my head the same way Joseph did. *TOE-moh-eh go-ZEN.*

Joseph assumes a professorial tone. "The term 'samurai' only applies to men. It means 'male warrior.' The term for women is *onnamusha*, 'female warrior.' You should try not to confuse them."

Great. He's going to be one of *those* guys. Well, at least the translation will be accurate. "I've never heard of . . . *onnamusha*."

"Few have. It's easier for the layperson to say 'samurai woman.'" He glances at me. "Some think this Tomoe was a real person, some don't. Legend says she was the captain of a samurai general named Minamoto no Yoshinaka, also known as Kiso, which basically means 'hillbilly.' He was involved in a big war in the late twelfth century. The Genpei War."

Drew's brow crinkles. She's paying attention now. "Women fought back then? They only just got allowed into combat in this country. I wonder what changed?"

His eyes open wide and the glasses slide down his nose. "Oh, they fought. Empress Jingu of Japan, who ruled from 170 to 260 AD, supposedly led an invasion of Korea while she was almost nine months pregnant. Most fighting women defended their homes against invasion, while the men were off in their battles. If they didn't, they were raped or given away as spoils of war. Women were just property back then."

"Property." That's how Killian treats my mom. How he treated his daughters. Pretty dolls who were supposed to be compliant. Follow his bidding, because he knew best. Was he a samurai in a former life? It wasn't just the samurai who did that. That's how things were.

"Minamoto." Drew clears her throat. "The same name as the lady who sent it to her? So this Hatsuko Minamoto was related to this warrior woman?"

Joseph frowns, but doesn't answer the question directly. "Tomoe was a concubine. Not his wife."

"A concubine?" I purse my lips. "You mean like a prostitute?"

"No. More like a mistress. An official one, not hidden. She had the protection of the family. Like a second wife. Totally the norm in those days." Joseph flashes us a reassuring smile, like we'd be cool with the concept just because it happened in the twelfth century. What would it be like to share Tom with another woman? I shudder. How did this warrior woman feel about it? Did she love the man? She could have just killed the wife. Or were they friends?

I try to write down all the things he's telling me. I'm not used to Japanese names, though, so I'm not sure how to spell any of the words. "Minamoto no—what?"

"Yoshinaka. That would actually be his given name, not his family name. In Japanese, you write your last name first. You'd be Perrotti no Rachel." He takes the pen, writes it down. *Yoshinaka Minamoto.* "When I translate it for you, I'll write it the way you're used to."

"Whichever is easiest."

"I'll make it easier for you, not me." He continues in an intense tone. "Tomoe Gozen was not only said to be an astounding beauty, she was Yoshinaka's most trusted captain. One of the greatest warriors of her time. She was skilled with the *naginata*, the traditional weapon used by women. Basically a curved dagger on a long pole. Warrior monks used it, too." He writes down *naginata*. "But Tomoe was also an expert with the short sword, traditionally a male weapon, and the bow and arrow. Most Westerners haven't heard of Tomoe, but in Japan there are statues and anime and comics and plays and all kinds of art devoted to her."

He turns the page to one of the drawings and rotates the book so I can see. In this one, the warrior woman sits alone amid ruins. Crumbled walls and smoking fires surround her.

"Some people say Tomoe Gozen is only a legend. But I don't think so." Joseph takes out his e-reader and powers it on. "In fact, I have the *Heike Monogatari* right here. That's the history of the Genpei War, with mostly verifiable accounts and events gathered from various people at the time. There's one short passage about Tomoe."

He points. It reads: *General Yoshinaka's wife, Yamabuki, was sick and had to stay home while Yoshinaka went to the capital. His concubine, Tomoe, came with him instead. A woman of great beauty, she was also Yoshinaka's captain—equally skilled in sword as she was in bow and arrow. The best in all Japan, male or female. She single-handedly vanquished hundreds of troops.*

Joseph looks up at his rapt audience. Actually, my sister's looking away, into the depths of the library, at something or someone. I nudge her. "No-body can find a gravestone or any written record of Tomoe except in the *Heike*. Some people think she was an invention to make Yoshinaka look bad. To have a woman doing your dirty work for you—it just wasn't done. It'd be dishonorable for a samurai. But I think she's real." Joseph leans forward. "Why would the writer describe her as beautiful and a great warrior if he wanted to shame Yoshinaka? Why wouldn't she be called ugly and useless? She's described heroically. And all the other people and events in the *Heike* took place. Of course, some of it's exaggerated—one account says she lit-erally tore somebody's head off with her bare hands. But other parts are exaggerated versions of events, too."

A story about a samurai woman. *Onnamusha*, I correct in my head. Mom wants me to read it—obviously it contains something important. "Thanks for agreeing to translate." I slide cash across the table.

"I'll send it along as I finish. That okay?" He's scribbling away furiously. "Let me just do the first chapter for you right now."

We sit where we are, watching. If Mom was coherent, she would be the one telling me this story. But then, if my mother were herself, I never would've found it. Maybe she never meant to tell us. Maybe she only blurted it out because her mind's going.

I turn to my sister. "So you still don't remember Mom talking to you about this book?"

"You were always the one Mom talked to, not me." Drew keeps her gaze on Joseph Bond, who's writing away intently. "I don't really know anything about her."

"You lived with her longer."

"Doesn't mean anything." Drew exhales. "I know facts, Rachel. What year she was born, when she got married. But she never talked to me about how she *felt*. About anything."

I think for a moment. "Didn't she talk about leaving Dad? Ever?"

Drew shakes her head impatiently. "No. Not to me."

"She could have left him," I say. "She would have gotten half. They got married in California." He couldn't have sent her back. You can't just do that to someone who's here legally. Who has American-born children.

"Unless they had a pre-nup. Or unless she didn't really want to leave him. She had it pretty good." Drew sounds matter of fact. "Nice house, all the quilts she could want."

I shake my head. "You think that's what qualifies as pretty good? There's more to life than material crap, Drew."

"I know that, Rachel." Drew crosses her arms. "I didn't say it was to me. To her."

Anyway, Killian was more than just a distracted father, throwing money at his progeny to keep them off his back. He liked to see how far he could push people. What he could get away with.

He used to take me and Drew shopping at the local Fed-Mart sometimes. It's out of business now, but it was like a Target.

First we'd go into the store and get what we needed. Then he'd look around the parking lot for dropped receipts. Scan them for what he wanted. One day, when I was eight and Drew was four, it was a twelve-pack of toilet paper. "Go in and tell them they forgot our toilet paper," he said to me.

I knew what to do. I didn't want to do it. I wanted to hide. I drew my scuffed Mary Jane across the asphalt. "I don't want to today."

He shrugged. "Go ahead, Drew."

"Aye-aye." She saluted him. He saluted her back. Drew, the compliant one, began marching back across the parking lot. A car backing up narrowly missed her. I ran to catch up, snatched up her hand.

In school, we learned telling lies was wrong. Cheaters got punished. When a cashier gave her too much change, my mother would give it back. "Karma will come back to you if you are not honest," Mom would say.

What would karma do to us? I worried. We stood by the manager's desk. Most kids don't know what a manager's desk looks like in the grocery store, that counter in front of the lines where there's a register and a cashbox. Or that the manager always wears a tie. I knew all of this. The store buzzed with register drawers shutting, rattling carts. *Here's your change. Thank you. Come again.*

The manager saw us standing there, came over. "You girls need help?"

I looked at him helplessly, my face red. I wanted to tell him. *Our father's making us do this. It's all a lie.* Before I could take a breath, Drew beamed her dimpled chubby four-year-old smile. "Pardon me. You forgot our toilet paper."

The manager smiled, rumpled her hair. "I'm sorry, young lady. I'll get it right now."

I clutched my sister's hand. She squeezed it comfortingly.

We walked back to the car where Killian waited. I flung the toilet paper at his head, through the open car window. "Here."

"Oh, Rach." Killian sat in front as I helped Drew get buckled. "I'm only trying to make you girls tough. Teach you about life. It's not our fault that some people are so easily fooled. You don't want to be one of them. What do I always say?"

"*Never let anybody pull a fast one,*" Drew chirped. "*We pull it first.*"

We drove away. He never took me shopping again.

Many years later, I told my mother about these trips. She was silent. She simply changed the channel on the television.

SISTERS OF HEART AND SNOW

"Did you know?" I prompted.

Her nose wrinkled. "Oh, Rachel. I knew he did many things, but nothing like this. He has plenty of money." She looked at me, her eyes sad. "I'm sorry, Rachel. I thought he wanted to do something nice, give me a break for once. I was wrong about that, too." Her voice cracked. She shut her lips and swallowed, her hands clenching into fists at her skirt. Of all the things my father had done, this was the one thing that seemed to distress her the most. She spoke again. "You know, he was a little boy during the Depression. Maybe his father made him do it, too."

"Don't you think that was crazy, no matter what had happened to him as a child?" It seemed to me there were plenty of things our parents did that we, as parents, could choose not to do to our own children.

My mother made a swiping motion with her hand. "Your father is not like other people."

We left it at that, never discussing it again.

Joseph puts his pen down, rubs his eyes under his glasses. "Let me go get you those books. You wait here." He gets up and disappears.

I turn to my sister. "Don't you remember what Dad had us do at Fed-Mart?"

Drew stares at me blankly.

"He made us steal groceries," I say. Several people look up, alert to unfolding drama. Rubberneckers. I don't care. "He told us to take the receipts back in and pretend like we hadn't gotten our items."

My sister blinks. Her slender fingers pick at a cuticle on her left thumb. "I vaguely remember doing that. But I thought he really hadn't gotten the stuff." She inhales. "Really? He did that? Why?"

I shrug, relieved that Drew didn't remember, that she hadn't known she was stealing. I'd asked myself why he'd do that many times. "He enjoys getting away with it. Why did Winona Ryder shoplift those clothes she could've bought? Compulsion? Ego?"

117

"I don't know." Drew purses her lips. "I do know that once I went gro-cery shopping with Mom, and her credit card got refused. Dad cut her off at a certain amount. Said she was a spendthrift." She shakes her head. "Can you imagine standing there in designer clothes with a Mercedes in the parking lot and not being able to pay for your cereal?"

My stomach flutters at the thought. "I didn't know that. But he let her do the quilts. She got tons of fabric all the time."

Drew shrugs. "I suppose such a feminine activity didn't bother him. It did kind of keep her happy. Or occupied."

Joseph reappears with several books in hand. *The Tale of Genji*, which Joseph insists is essential for understanding feudal Japan; the *Heike Mono-gatari*, about the civil war; a slim nonfiction book called *Samurai Women*, and a book of poetry by medieval female Japanese poets. "The time during which Tomoe Gozen lived was a very important era in Japan, the beginning of the samurai era. Two clans, the Minamoto and the Taira, fought for the shōgunate. The shōgun essentially made the emperor his puppet and had all the power." His voice rises again in excitement and his eyes practically shoot sparks. I can see why he's devoted his studies to the subject. "The Yoshinaka story is very Shakespearean, full of double crosses and betray-als." He slides the book into a soft cloth bag.

Yamabuki sitting by the fire, mending the coat of her
husband, Yoshinaka, by Utagawa Kuniyoshi
Photograph © MAK. Courtesy MAK–Austrian
Museum of Applied Arts / Contemporary Art

Tomoe put on four layers of clothing, her teeth chattering. The snows had been heavy, starting in early October, and showed no signs of letting up. Tomoe was glad. Heavy snow meant water that would run down to the valleys as it melted, helping the crops and people grow.

She walked to the door, sliding it open to let in what little light lingered in the winter-dark sky. This was her own house, a small one-room bungalow. Nothing fancy, no silk screens or fine furniture, but it was hers, built for her by Yoshinaka. Both of them had hoped, though Tomoe was not his legal wife, that she would be sharing this house with their own child, but no matter how many times they lay together, she continued her monthly blood.

Soon she would be sharing this house with another woman, for whom Tomoe would serve as an attendant.

Yoshinaka had made progress in these few years since Kaneto died, winning over their countryside regions, and was now known as the governor of Shinano, home to about ten thousand. In the cities, Yoshinaka was known as Kiso, a nickname deriding him as a country bumpkin; it was his cousin Yoritomo who was in charge of the Minamoto clan.

At Miyanokoshi, high up in the mountains, tall log walls enclosed a small village of houses. Below the fort stood craggy rocks and a moat. They were secure, but isolated. Tomoe barely remembered what a real city looked like, or even a small town. She wished they could go to war tomorrow, simply so she could get out of this place and the unrelenting boredom of peace.

Snow flurries blew in, coating her face. She closed her eyes against them.

It was quiet today, with everyone busy making preparations for the newest member of the clan, who was due to arrive in the afternoon. Yoshinaka was not a man who liked to sit in silence. He always had friends around him in his house, where they would drink and talk; outside, they played out every military maneuver he could think of in endless succession. But today, he had come here alone.

"We can have a few moments together," he told Tomoe. If he was anxious about the events that were to take place later, he did not say so.

Tomoe had nodded, her tears, always hidden from Yoshinaka, long dried. Today was the day Yamabuki Gozen would arrive. Lady Yamabuki, Yoshinaka's new wife. His official wife, arriving from the city of Miyako.

She wondered what the new woman, arriving from Miyako and accustomed to fine things, would think of it, of this place where there was no powder for one's face, no screens to hide behind, no musical instruments to fill the air with their jangling melodies. This place of mere survival.

Tomoe set her mouth in a grim smile. Perhaps the woman would not last long at all.

Yoshinaka's nostrils flared. "Tomoe. You are making me nervous."

She shut the door. At last, an admission of truth. "You ought to be nervous. We have no idea what this girl looks like."

"Come here." He was behind her now, him coming to her, not the other way around. She did not think she could ever bring herself to come to him again. He looped his arms around her waist and kissed her neck.

Yoshinaka spun her around and kissed her, his warm tongue comforting her cold one. She embraced him, pulled him into her, letting the heat of his body thaw her. If they did this outside, surely steam would rise off their bodies. Snow would melt. They would make a lake.

They moved to her futon, which she had not put away as she usually did. Yoshinaka pulled her with him under the covers, shrugging off their heavy quilted *tanzens* and kimonos, pushing the pile of clothes to one side. Skin to skin. She faced him, side to side, ran her hand over the sinuous landscape of his flesh, the muscularity she knew better than her own.

She wanted to tell him that she was afraid this would be the last time. That he wouldn't love her anymore because he had a novel new wife. Yet it was useless to argue against the fact of Lady Yamabuki.

Besides, Yamabuki was a real noble, a woman from a fine family of Minamoto sympathizers in the capital. Marrying her was a necessary strategic move. Tomoe's analytical brain realized this. It was her silly heart that hurt.

"You will always be first for me," Yoshinaka said. "You must know that."

She said nothing. She would not extract a promise. He would tell her only what she wanted to hear.

Wind shuddered the walls, blowing inside, blasting their faces through the cracks between the timbers. Yoshinaka covered their heads with the blanket.

"If only we could hide in here forever," he said. It was the closest he would get to poetry. Tomoe took small satisfaction in the knowledge that his new wife would never hear a poem of his, either.

She opened her mouth to his, biting ferociously in the way he liked best.

Eight

D rew's phone rings, verboten in the library. Jonah, her ex. Drew holds up a finger to Rachel and steps outside to take it.

"Thank God," Jonah says. His baritone sounds hoarse, as if he's not practicing the good vocal hygiene (no alcohol, only soothing teas, singing from his gut) that Drew tried to drum into him and which he of course ignored. "I went by Dogwarts and it was closed permanently. Your landlord said he hasn't seen you for a while. I thought something bad happened."

"I could've died two years ago, for all you know," Drew points out. She hasn't talked to him but once since they broke up. It's sweet of him to worry. She remembers the way it felt to embrace him, how her head rested so comfortably against his chest, and her throat catches. She's not still in love with him. She can't be. "What do you want?" She sounds harsher than she wants, but it'd be so easy to fall back in with him. If he said right now he wanted her to be the tambourine player again, to scoop up those little crumbs he saw fit to throw her, well, she just might get in her car and drive back up to him.

"We've restructured the band a bit. Drummer's gone." That would be

John, the guy who disliked Drew. "We're thinking of using strings at some of our shows, and I thought of you."

You mean the way I suggested years and years ago? She exhales. Part of her wants to say *Yes, of course.* The other part, deep in her gut, tells her. *This will not end well.*

"It's for Jimmy Kimmel," Jonah adds. Dangling the carrot. "We start rehearsals next week. We might use the strings on tour, too, if it goes well. Drew," his voice drops an octave, "I haven't called because I knew we had to break it off clean. But . . . nothing's the same without you."

"Really? You guys are doing better without me." Drew turns away from the library.

He blows into the phone. "I mean, Drew. You know what I mean. We just wake up and go to the airport and play a show and go to sleep and go to the airport and . . ." he trails off. "I miss you."

Drew feels her bones turning into jelly.

Rachel appears, carrying the books Joseph got her. Drew remembers where she is. With her sister, helping her. Helping her mother. "I've got to take care of some family stuff, Jonah. I'll let you know."

"Okay," Jonah says, sounding surprised. A little hurt. Yes. He expected her to come back, when he wants.

Drew hangs up, her heart beating hard. For a moment she thinks she's done the wrong thing. What if she goes back and everything works out great, and she finally has the career and the life she wants? What if she's meant to be with Jonah? She can't just hang out with Rachel forever. She's got to come up with a plan.

A good plan. A foolproof-no-shit roadmap, telling her how to live the rest of her life.

Her sister holds out her hand. "Everything okay?"

A familiar gesture. Rachel always held Drew's hand when they were little. Up until Drew was twelve, actually—Rachel would grab Drew's hand and steer her through parking lots. *Just in case,* Rachel would say, as if she alone had the power to protect Drew from two tons of solid metal.

Drew takes her sister's hand. It is the same size as her own now.

Rachel drops it. "I've got to carry these," she says, almost apologetically, and hands a few books to Drew. "Help me?"

"Sure." Drew takes the books and follows her sister to the parking lot.

Later in the day, after I take Drew back to my house, where she says she's going to job-hunt online before she picks up Chase, I drive back up to La Jolla to meet my daughter.

I pause outside the bridal boutique, staring at the all-white faceless mannequins in dolloped whipped cream dresses with rib-cage-binding bodices. I'm so out of my element. This is downtown La Jolla, a street of high-end shops and restaurants a couple blocks from the beach—and from my mother's nursing home.

Quincy wants to go on a preliminary dress-scouting mission. When I shopped for my dress, this store wasn't even on my fantasy list. Come to think of it, I had no fantasy list. I'm glad my daughter does. Isn't that what we've been working for, all these years? Anyway, I'm not telling Tom what Quincy's dress cost for at least forty years. Preferably, he won't find out until I'm dead.

Quincy appears now, almost sprinting again. Her face and arms, exposed by her cream-colored tank top, are with dusted with freckles, but her summer tan's gone and she looks chalky. Not her natural skin color, like she's been working too hard. Her sunglasses push back her long, unkempt hair and she's as thin as a fashion model. Normally, my daughter's got a fair amount of muscle packed on from playing volleyball and eating well. I want both her and Drew back at my house, stat, eating. I'll get Tom's mother to help. We'll hold them hostage for a weekend and pack them full of lasagna.

"Hey, Mom." Quincy holds out her arms.

"Hey, Q." I hug her, splay my hands over her ribs on her back. Yep. Skin and bones.

"Stop it. I know what you're doing." Quincy steps back. "I like being this thin. I eat. I'm perfectly healthy. Ryan will love me if I weigh a hundred pounds, or gain two hundred." She shakes her head.

"Sorry. I'm just concerned." I let it go. "Before I had kids, I was too thin. I gained eighty with you and only sixty came back off, which was a good thing." It was true—after my weight went up, post-swimming, I dieted myself back down into skinniness, overdoing it, as I am wont to do. I look sideways at her. "Don't get pregnant for a long time, though."

"Mom. Stop. For real." Quincy laughs me off. "I know. I'm genetically prone to stretch marks and should enjoy my youthful physique while I still can."

"Something like that." We link arms and look in the window. When Quincy was five or so, she poked at my belly. *Why is your belly so squishy? How'd you get all those scars? Were you in a fight?*

I glance at the bridesmaid dresses next to the bridal gowns, the tones of emerald and deep red and brown contrasting sharply with the white. Fall and Christmas colors. "Who are your bridesmaids going to be?" I'm having trouble picturing the wedding party, imagining myself in a mother-of-the-bride dress.

Quincy shrugs. "I don't know."

"Nobody from the volleyball team?" Is she friends with *anyone* besides Ryan these days?

"Didn't I tell you? I quit." Quincy squints at the dresses in the window, a small frown playing across her brow.

"What?" She's been playing volleyball since she was ten. "Did you get hurt?"

"No."

Quincy used to be unstoppable. Nothing held her back. Sort of like Tomoe Gozen, I think, as I look at my daughter. True to herself, doing whatever she wanted, regardless of what anyone else said. What's happened to my daughter? A couple of years ago, Quincy had her wisdom teeth extracted and was supposed to rest for a week. But two days after her procedure, the sound of the blender woke me before dawn. I switched on the light to see Quincy, who'd been in the dark. "What are you doing?" I eyed the eggs, the dirty frying pan, the toast crusts. "But what are you making?"

"Scrambled eggs and toast. Blended." She glopped the thick concoction into a glass. It looked absolutely vomitous.

My stomach turned. "I can make you a fruit smoothie."

"Just leave me alone, Mother. I'm perfectly fine." She tipped the glass to her mouth and drank in loud rebellious gulps, her eyes never leaving mine. I waited for her to gag, to spit the gelatinous goo into the sink, but she kept on drinking until the glass was empty. "I feel a ton better. I'm going for a run."

"The doctor said no exercise for a week."

"That advice is for *normal* people. Not for me." Quincy put the pan in the sink.

Yes, Quincy was tenacious, almost to the point where she didn't care about her personal safety—also like Tomoe. It's funny. I'd always wanted her to be more careful in that way. Balanced. Yet now she's telling me she quit volleyball, and I don't like it.

"I need to focus on my classes." Quincy rolls her eyes. "Mom. Please. It's not like I was going to go professional. Calm down. Anyway, that's probably why I'm thinner. I lost muscle mass."

Well, engineering is one of the most demanding majors. And she's right—she's not going to be in the Olympics. I swallow down my questions. "That makes sense."

Quincy jerks her head toward the shop. "What are we waiting for?"

We step inside. It's like stepping into a wedding cake, and it smells sweet, too, layers of sugar and flowers. Everything is in shades of white—bright whites, warm whites, silvery whites, light cream. There are mirrors everywhere, bouncing the whites back.

I walk around the shop, eyeing the dresses. I will not look at the prices because I am ninety-nine percent sure I will faint. I touch the heavy satin of a Cinderella-type dress, fitted in the bodice, full at the bottom. No idea what sort of dress my daughter wants. A ton of cleavage? Bare shoulders?

Tight skirt or full? Will she go in the modest Princess Kate direction, with long sleeves and lace? Quincy mostly wears jeans and T-shirts. I could barely get her into a dress for prom. "What style do you like?" I ask.

As if on cue, a saleswoman with short red hair appears. "We're having a fabulous sale this week. Ten percent off."

"I brought photos." Quincy fans out some magazine pages that, as far as I can tell, contain a sample of every conceivable type of gown: short, tight, full, trains.

The saleswoman purses her pink-lipsticked mouth. "Let me pull some gowns. I'll show you to a room."

Quincy points to a satiny silver couch where a middle-aged woman sits, dabbing at her eyes with a tissue. "Wait here, Mom."

I sit. Another bride, the one who belongs to the woman next to me, appears in a floofy dress, and the woman claps her hands.

I bought my dress from a wedding-prom discount warehouse, sifting through racks of dresses tried on hundreds of times previously. Tom said he'd ask his parents to buy me a dress, but they were already doing too much. It was ridiculous to spend money on a gown you'd only wear once. We could use that money for tons of other things. I bought an A-line satin dress that skimmed my growing belly, deeply discounted due to the makeup stain by the cleavage. That stain still bothers me whenever I look at our wedding pictures, displayed in our hallway. I don't want that for my daughter.

Tom's proposal was not over-the-top romantic. He actually sort of proposed before we even knew about Quincy. I'm glad he did. Otherwise, I might always wonder if he would have.

He took me to Ocean Beach to go boogie boarding. All day we caught waves until my belly turned lobster-red from my prone position. Waves were high for San Diego, maybe five feet, but I kept up with him, not stopping even when my shoulder told me to.

We sat on a beach towel and drank a couple of Coronas we'd smuggled in Super Big Gulp cups. "I've never had beer through a straw before." I stifled an alarming, nonromantic burp. "Pardon me."

"That was the cutest little burp ever. Like a baby burp." He laughed and put his towel and his arm around me. I put my face in his shoulder. A sense of peace washed over me. With Tom, I never had to pretend I wasn't anxious or afraid. I just was whoever I was. Felt whatever it was I felt.

He squeezed me in close. "You know what?"

I looked at him.

"I want to marry you one day." His face was serious.

I pulled the towel over my head to hide my pleased blush. "Really?" I felt like if he saw me, I'd burst into a million pieces, an iridescent sea-soaked bubble.

"Yes." He took the towel off and raised my head.

I swallowed. *This is too good to be true. Shouldn't it take more tries than this? Is he serious?* My head harped away. "How do you know?"

"I'll tell you." Tom leaned in close, next to my ear, so he wouldn't have to shout over the sounds of the waves and the people around us. "I liked my exes all right. But I was always secretly glad when we were too busy to see each other." He smiled at me and brushed some sand off my face. "I wake up every morning wondering when I'll get to see you."

I took another sip of beer out of the soda container. I pictured us walking down the aisle, college degrees in our back pockets. The sand pushed up against me, hot in the sun. He watched me expectantly. A bit nervous. My heart beat like a marching band drum, shaking me head to toe. I was afraid, but I'd tell him the truth. "I would have walked out of that biology class and gone straight to the county clerk's office if you'd wanted me to," I said softly.

He pushed me down into the sand and kissed me.

One of the first things my sister asked me, after I told her I was engaged, was "How did he propose?" I told her. "Lame," Drew pronounced. "When I get married, I want a big diamond hidden in a glass of champagne during a trip to Tahiti. Or skywriting. If that's not happening, I'm saying no."

"Everything you see on television," I noted drily.

"That's right."

"Well," I said, "would you rather have a 'lame' proposal from a great guy, or a great proposal from a lame guy?"

"I want both," Drew said. Her eyes turned very light brown. "I want everything."

I watch the other bride in the store jump up and down in her dress, seeing, I guess, if her top will stay up. She's got very large breasts, and one slips out, all the way out of her bra. She stops. "Damn. I almost took that one in the chin." Her mother shakes her head. I giggle and clap my hand over my mouth. A thought pops into my head. I should have invited Drew. Then we could laugh at these things together. Couldn't we? Next time, if Quincy doesn't find a dress, we will do it for real. With Drew. If she wants. She'll probably be back in L.A. by then.

A door hinge squeaks from the aisle of fitting rooms. A rustle.

Quincy holds the saleswoman's hand to step atop the carpeted platform by the three-way mirror. "What do you think? Is the skirt too much?"

The dress reflects off Quincy's skin like a pearl, satiny and smooth. Strapless, tight in the bodice but not low cut, curving out over her hips into a full skirt that cascades down to the floor. Quincy fluffs the skirt speculatively. "I could get away with tennis shoes in this. You can't see my feet at all."

How many times did Quincy put on a princess dress and parade around, when she was three? Of course, she got every one of them muddy. "Sneakers would be perfect." I sniffle. What a cliché I am. Mother of the bride crying. But hey—I'm only human.

Quincy finally quits fiddling with the skirt and looks up at me. Her expression is analytical, not joyous. As if she's buying hardware and needs to figure out what size nails to buy. "Nah. Not really me." She pirouettes and heads back to the fitting room. The gown is held together by chip clips in the back. The saleswoman and I watch her.

"It's hard for such a young woman. They look fantastic in everything." The saleswoman purses her lips. "So young."

I just nod. Even the saleswoman thinks she should wait.

"Mom! Can you please help me get this off?" Quincy calls from the fitting room.

"I'll help you. One moment." The saleswoman heads back there. I wonder if she enjoys her job, helping out brides. I glance at the crumpled tissue in my hands and decide I would not last a single day in her position.

Quincy reappears, shoulders down, in a tight mermaid dress. She makes a face and points to her rear. "This is made for someone without hips."

"Your hips are perfect." Again I have my irrational fear. Eating disorder? Body dysmorphia?

"Ah. It's just not me. I'm sorry." Quincy sits on the platform—no easy feat, given the tightness of the dress. "I'm so stressed out, Mom. Too many papers. No time to do anything. My head feels like it's spinning off."

I sit beside her and take her hand. "We've got months. I'm happy to help. Don't rush." I pat her shoulder. "You could even wait years, if you like," I add gently. "Ryan's a great guy. He'll wait."

"I don't know." Quincy is crying now, her eyeliner smearing over her cheekbones. "Ryan's going to hate all of these dresses." She sweeps her arm around the shop.

The saleswoman reappears, a frozen smile pasted on her face. "A groom loves whatever dress his bride picks out, dear." She meets my eyes. I shrug.

"Why do you think he'll hate them?" I ask. Tom wouldn't have cared if I got married in a paper sack.

"Because he thinks all the big wedding stuff is stupid." Quincy sniffles. "Anyway, he can't help me with anything. He's working, and he just told me he might not even be here for Thanksgiving. He's getting deployed in January." She takes a breath. "It's supposed to be for four months, but he says not to be surprised if it's longer."

Quincy introduced us to Ryan at a family barbecue over the summer. A friend of her friend's brother, she'd said, twenty-two years old. Tall, broad-shouldered, with a dazzling smile and close-cut blond hair—it was impossible not to fall for him. He helped clean up without being prompted, got me and Quincy drinks. By the end of the visit, I had a bit of a crush, too.

If only they'd wait just a couple of years. Supportive. That's what I need to be, I remind myself. "You'll get it done. Like every other military wife. It'll be fine."

The saleswoman clears her throat, eyeing the makeup, the white dress. I glare at her and she leaves. I choose my next words carefully, praying my daughter won't get angry. "Does Ryan not want to have a wedding?"

She puts her hand on my arm, cutting me off. "I'm not really upset about Ryan, Mom. I have to talk to you about something else."

Oh no. Here it comes. She's going to tell me she's pregnant, and that's why they're rushing. I take a breath. "Yes."

Quincy wipes her eyes with the back of her hand. "I want to have Grandpa there for my wedding."

Grandpa. It takes me nearly a full minute to realize who Quincy is talking about. Not Tom's father, who passed away years ago. But my father.

"Killian?" I stammer.

Quincy nods. "I was hoping that my wedding would make you guys bury the hatchet."

My body grows cold. How can I call up this man—this stranger—who's blackmailing me? Who wants to stick my ailing mother in a sub-par nursing home? How could I possibly invite him to my only daughter's sacred moment? Just the thought of calling up Killian makes me feel sick to my stomach.

Over the years, I agonized about the kids not knowing my father. Some part of me always hoped for a relationship with him. Something good that might surface in him, burn out bad memories.

Yet I didn't want to subject my children to the grocery store con man, the person who treated my mother so badly, who kicked me out for not being able to solve my own problems at sixteen. At his core, he was unpredictable. Not someone I wanted influencing my kids.

Our children got to know Tom's father, Howard, instead. When Quincy was little, he'd been ill, but after that he spent as much time with the kids as he could until he died. Took them on outings, built birdhouses, cheered at games.

I hadn't realized Quincy felt that way about Killian. Felt anything for him at all.

I stare at my own reflection in the endless mirror at the bridal shop, my reddened eyes and Quincy's teary ones reflected back thousands of times, reflections within reflections, until both of us disappear in the glass. It's not my place to poison her against Killian. "You know your grandfather's trying to get power of attorney for Obāchan," I say with care. "We only talk through our lawyers."

"I know, but . . ." She spreads her hands helplessly. "Don't you think he wants to make up with us now? After all this time? I'm his only grand-daughter, and I'm getting married."

I look at my daughter's open, innocent face, and I don't want to disappoint her. No matter what Killian says or does. Surely Killian has a soft spot, too. He's elderly. Don't we all want to make peace during our last moments? Besides, she's his only granddaughter.

Maybe this wedding will be the bridge.

I let out a long breath, like a balloon expelling air. "Okay."

Quincy smooths her skirt. "Thank you, Mom." She steps down; I hold out a hand, but she walks by it.

"Let me help you unzip." I reach for her, to unclip the contraptions holding the back in place.

"No, thanks. I've got it." She disappears down the hall of fitting rooms, vanishing into the bank of mirrors and half-closed doors.

MIYANOKOSHI FORTRESS
SHINANO PROVINCE
HONSHU, JAPAN
Winter 1174

Yamabuki Gozen arrived as the winter twilight turned a watery blue. Her enclosed litter swayed, barely clearing the sides of the fortress opening, carried by four stoic men moving slowly along the path, their toes scuffing into the snow with each heavy step. Tomoe stood outside, slightly behind Yoshinaka, next to her mother, the chill like knives on her cheeks. Chizuru stood on tiptoe to whisper. "Remember, it's you who has his heart."

Tomoe glanced down at her mother, this woman who had been able to marry her love, Kaneto, a man chosen of her own free will. Tomoe did not recall seeing her father glance toward another woman his entire life. Chizuru couldn't understand what Tomoe was going through, Tomoe thought, and straightened, smoothing out her heavy coat. Yoshinaka's hair, normally wild even when bound back, had been oiled and smoothed. Tomoe wrinkled her nose at its strong floral smell. He shifted from foot to foot. Nervous. She could tell without seeing his expression.

All of Yoshinaka's supporters were here, waiting, dressed in what passed for their best. Mostly threadbare clothes mended and made over for years. All of them wearing layers and layers, their heads tiny above their puffy clothing. They looked so unsophisticated and rough. What would Yamabuki make of them?

Of her?

Yamabuki might want to be rid of Tomoe.

She took a breath so loud and deep it startled Demon, the huge black horse tied to a post on the other side of the courtyard. He neighed anxiously. Tomoe whinnied back to calm him.

After what seemed like forever, the men carrying the litter laid it on the ground. Two of Yoshinaka's retainers opened the door and held out their hands to help Yamabuki step out. Tomoe braced herself for the sight of a plump and powdered white face with shaved eyebrows drawn in close to the shaved hairline. A face used to poetry and music and leisure.

Tomoe could not remember when she had last listened to music. Only when they made one of their infrequent trips into town, stopping at a restaurant, did she catch the refrains of a *koto*, the floor harp, or a voice lifted in song. And there had never been poetry here. Though Kaneto had taught all the children to read, they rarely did so for pleasure. Tomoe didn't see the point of keeping up with such skills. Not when she had so many other occupations with which to concern herself.

One small foot, clad in a cloth *tabi* and a wooden *geta*, appeared first, landing slowly on the snowy ground. Then another. An ice-blue kimono, beautifully woven—Tomoe could see that even from her place in the back—picturing cranes scooping fish out of ocean waves, swished audibly in the still air.

Those tiny feet. How could she stay balanced? Tomoe heard her mother gasp and forced herself to look at Yamabuki's face.

Pale, all right. But not pale from makeup. This woman's skin was pale as that of one who has never seen the sun, nearly translucent with blue undertones. One blue-green vein ran down the center of her forehead. Yamabuki kept her eyes firmly on the ground, her reddened lips pressed closely together. A great length of straight hair swept down her back, shiny as lacquer. She was lovely. Lovely and untouchable as a thin sheet of ice in late spring. When the sun shone on her, this apparition might melt.

The retainers helped her forward to Yoshinaka. True to fashion, the kimono prevented fast movement, so tightly was it bound around her legs. "Yamabuki Gozen," said one of the retainers, his breath visible on the air.

The last bit of light disappeared behind the mountains, the moon straddling its ridge, casting its spectral glow onto Yamabuki. Somehow she seemed more natural in such light. Yoshinaka bowed. "Welcome." Tomoe noticed he was trying to keep his voice low and cultured. It still sounded more like a growl.

But Yamabuki was not afraid. She raised her eyes to his. They glittered like black onyx, the darkest eyes Tomoe had ever seen, yet light too somehow, lit from within.

Tomoe imagined how Yamabuki saw her new spouse, and waited for her to register astonishment or disgust. Yoshinaka had none of the attributes Yamabuki would have prized in Miyako. His face was not round. He was decidedly hairy. "Thank you," Yamabuki said, her tones so high and sweet that Tomoe momentarily forgot this woman was her rival. Her expression was pleasant, as though no terrible thought could ever pass through a mind so pure.

Yoshinaka's great shoulders sagged in that particular way Tomoe recognized. It was the way he looked when he wanted to embrace her. A moment when he let down his guard.

No! Tomoe wanted to shout. She stepped forward.

Yoshinaka straightened. "Please show her to her quarters." Yoshinaka bowed again. "We will see you at dinner."

Was he not going to introduce her? Tomoe stood, rooted to her spot, cheeks hot in embarrassment. The retainer stepped in again, cleared his throat. "This is Tomoe Gozen."

Yamabuki turned her otherworldly gaze to Tomoe. Which world, good or bad, Tomoe couldn't say. "I am pleased to meet you," she said, still keeping that silvery tone. Tomoe should have bowed first, but Yamabuki did.

Tomoe bowed back.

Nine

D rew takes the slow way to see her mother, on a highway border-
ing the ocean. Last night, after they saw Joseph in the morning,
he e-mailed more Tomoe Gozen chapters, and Drew had stayed
up late reading them.

The story swims through her head. A woman who doesn't fit in anywhere. She can relate, though Drew definitely doesn't think of herself as
any kind of warrior. She thinks maybe she's more like Yamabuki, another
out-of-place person, who seems at the moment to be basically useless. At
least Tomoe distinguished herself as a fighter.

Are they related to this Tomoe woman? Is that what Hikari wanted
them to know?

She tries to remember a single time when Hikari mentioned Japan. A
bit of homesickness, a tale about her family. In Drew's family, stories of the
past stayed there. Drew wonders if Rachel thinks about that, too. Rachel
somehow created a whole new family and a whole new way of life.

She finds a parking spot and beeps her car alarm, leaving her giant
sunglasses in the car. Sometimes, if Drew is being very honest with herself, she admits that she can't see the point of these visits. It tears at Drew's
heart to sit there, watching her mother wither away like a time-lapse

movie of a life cycle. As her mother stares at the ocean, unaware of her brain's mutiny.

In the glass-walled lobby, where leather couches face the water, Drew waits to check in behind an older man who leans on a cane. Its top has a silver griffin, the beak peeking out from under a large, spotted hand. Silver threads of hair swirl around a pink-pale skull. He wears a fine pair of slacks, a pressed dress shirt over shoulders that were probably once broad, over a body once tall.

"Let me know how it was," he says to the receptionist in the voice of a much younger man. A familiar voice.

"Thanks for the tickets," the receptionist, a plain woman in her early twenties with light brown hair, says. She smiles up at him as if he's saved her from a house fire. "You don't know how much it means."

Killian.

Drew didn't recognize him. It's the cane—he'd needed one for years. Limping around with bad hips and knees, a legacy of his football days, he'd insist he was perfectly fine. "Only old people need canes," he'd said crossly whenever anyone suggested it. Now Killian turns slowly and maneuvers unseeingly around Drew, as if she's an umbrella stand. In the strong light off the ocean, his skin looks waxy.

Her mouth goes dry. It takes Drew a moment to react. She hasn't seen her father since last Christmas. "Dad." Drew waves. Maybe he's like a dog chasing a rabbit—he can't see things if they're standing still.

He does a comical double take, the motion almost throwing him off-balance. "Drew! Where'd you come from?"

She steps forward and hugs him awkwardly. He thumps her back once, as if he's checking a melon. Whomp. "Were you here to see Mom?" she says, for lack of another thing to say.

"No. I was here painting fences," Killian snorts. "Of course. Why else would I be in an old people's home?" He turns to the receptionist. "Jasmine, have you met my daughter Drew? She's a violinist. Plays in symphonies."

"Viola," Drew says quietly. Killian always gets this wrong. When she was in Out Stealing Horses, he'd tell people she'd founded the band, that she wrote all the songs and sang, too, not that she was the tambourine player. Now he tells people she's in the Los Angeles Philharmonic. Either he can't remember, or he just tells the stories he wishes were true. She thinks it's the latter. Correcting him has done no good.

She wonders what he tells people when they ask about Rachel. She imagines he makes up a story about her joining the merchant marine, or becoming a pirate in the South Seas. Or that Rachel is an ungrateful prodigal daughter who's cut off contact with poor old Killian. Anything's possible.

"I've met your sister." Jasmine shakes Drew's hand. "I see the resemblance."

Drew glances at Killian. He doesn't acknowledge the comment, smiling blankly at Jasmine. "My father got you tickets?" she says in a pleasant voice. "Where are you going?"

Jasmine flushes. "Just a show that came into town. I paid for them. They were sold out."

"Cool," Drew says. Her stomach flops. Was he really trying to be nice, or trying to make allies?

Killian stumps slowly to the leather sofa in the sitting area and lowers himself into it, gripping the arm with one hand, the cane with the other. "So."

He hasn't said it, but Drew knows he expects her to sit, too, without asking what she's doing in San Diego. Drew's stopped expecting her father to think about anyone except himself since childhood. She'd be hard-pressed to name a more self-centered man, even after she lived in L.A. for all these years among musicians and actors. That's saying a lot.

Killian nods at her. "I made a transfer to your bank account. It's time."

"You didn't need to do that." Drew's never had a trust fund, but every year he gives her money for Christmas. And, she's sorry to say, she has asked her father for money in the past when absolutely necessary. Like when she needed first and last month's rent for her studio apartment, a sum she could never quite save up on her own, at least, not unless she had a few years. A ruffling of guilt stirs in her gut. Taking money from your parents makes you beholden. Prevents Drew from being like Rachel, from standing up to her father, lest he take it away again. The worst part is, she desperately needs the money at this moment, and she's already spending it in her head. "Why so early?"

Killian shrugs. "Why not?"

The thought of his money in her account weighs like a lead balloon. How she wishes she didn't need it. Why can't she be the kind of woman who doesn't need anybody, who is a hundred percent independent and able to take care of herself? She feels like a little kid still.

She sits opposite him and concentrates on the brown paisley area rug under their feet. His shoes gleam. "How's Mom?"

"Great. Just fine. She's got no idea who I am." He shakes his head.

They are silent for a bit. Other visitors shuffle through the lobby, families visiting their relatives. Drew wonders if any of them are like her family. She lifts her head. She'll ask him about her mother's life. "Dad, when Mom came over here, how was it for her?"

He settles back into the couch. "Great. Much better than where she came from. She was with me." Killian chortles. "She never had to worry about a roof over her head again."

"I mean . . ." Drew tries to think of how to put this. She never talks to her father like this. It feels as uncomfortable as too-tight jeans. "Was she lonely? Did your family like her? Did you meet her family?"

"Sure. I told everyone I met her while doing business there. Practically true." He smiles at Drew, his blue salesman's eyes sparkling. "She didn't have any family left. But she was fine. Always, until this."

"Do you mean physically fine or mentally fine?" Drew furrows her brow, tries to keep her tone neutral.

He shrugs, then leans forward. "Nobody could do anything about her mental changes anyway. But your mother and I understood each other." Abruptly, he changes the subject. "I want to talk about your sister."

Drew crosses her legs at the ankles, remembering Rachel's story about the grocery store. Her stomach clenches. "What about her?"

"I'm hoping you can make her see reason." Killian strokes the griffin's head of his cane with his thumb. His fingernails are as shiny and lustrous as a waxed floor. He exhales. "If Rachel doesn't relinquish her power of attorney, it's going to be very bad all around. For Rachel, for your mother, even for you."

"So, what do you want to do? Move her into a cheap crappy home? She's used to this one. You can afford it." Drew blinks slowly at him. "Are you bankrupt or something?"

"Of course not." Killian thumps his cane, and his eyes look less twinkly. "Rachel, your mother doesn't know if she's on an expensive beach in La Jolla or sitting in a cargo container on her way to Timbuktu."

"I'm Drew." All these years he hasn't seen Rachel, and he still slips up. A sense of wariness overtakes her. She thinks of Tomoe Gozen. *Ichi-go, ichi-e.* Be ready for anything.

He doesn't acknowledge her correction. "I'm being practical, Drew. Besides, any money we save is money that goes back into your pocket."

Drew's hands are cold, though they shouldn't be. She rubs them together. "What do you mean, it'll be bad all around?"

"Ask yourself this. Is me paying for some cheap nursing home better than paying for no nursing home? Do you want to be cut out of the will, too, Drew?" He squints at her. "Now, I take care of family—but when family stops being family, then I have no responsibility to them."

Drew opens her mouth to respond. What will he do, let her mother be homeless? Is that even possible? *Fuck you and the horse you rode in on,* she wants to say, but of course she doesn't. She just closes her mouth, pressing it into a tight line.

Killian hefts himself to a standing position. Drew doesn't move to help him. He doesn't need any, anyway. "Have a good visit, Drew. I've got to run to an appointment. See you, Miss Jasmine."

"Good to see you, Mr. Snow." Jasmine waves. Killian triggers the automatic doors. "Your father's such a sweetheart."

Drew swallows. For the first time, she fully understands why Rachel doesn't even want to visit Killian. She understands everything. "Sweet as pie."

A *dozen PTA mothers* wait in the middle school auditorium. I recognize all of them, even if I don't know everyone's names. This afternoon is the bake sale planning for the science club, to support the science fair.

One thing I won't miss after my children graduate is the fund-raising. Every day there's a different group selling cookie dough or yogurt or T-shirts. There are dinners in restaurants that give clubs a cut, grocery stores sponsoring teams if you shop there. It's endless, and it never seems to be enough—we still front our kids' costs for entry fees, travel, uniforms, and coach stipends.

I find the table where Susannah, the PTA president, sits beside the little core group: Terra, Laura, and Elizabeth. Some mothers are older than me, some younger, some the same age. Mothers have MBAs, doctorates, associate degrees, and no degrees. Some work, some don't. The thing we have in common is our children. I nod at them and they nod back, lift their hands in greeting.

I don't usually say too much in these meetings. The last time I did was when we were planning the end-of-school-year dance. Hawaiian-themed. Elizabeth wanted to charge an extra dollar for leis. I'd raised my hand. "Don't you think it should be included in the ticket price?" I asked. "It's already ten dollars."

"Well," Elizabeth had huffed, "I guess that's okay. If you want to take money out of our funds so we can't do as much next year."

I'd given up. Too easily. It didn't matter much to me—Chase doesn't like girls or dances yet—but I imagined how Tom and I had felt when

Quincy was little, having to say no to the dance and the extra dollar. Don't they know some people need help, even in a well-off community? Some of the students don't even live around here—they apply to this school because it's better than their neighborhood one.

I'm closest to Laura, who's also our family attorney. Laura's daughter is in eighth grade and has been in classes with Chase since kindergarten. Laura leans over to me. "Prepare for the crazy train," Laura whispers. "It's happening again."

For a moment, I think for sure she's talking about my father. "What's Killian done this time?"

"Oh. Not that crazy. Cupcakes." She laughs.

"We have to get this bake sale figured out." Elizabeth speaks quickly. She's in her late forties, heavyset, her hair cut in the same attractive swingy bob she's probably had her whole life. I have to admit, she's my least favorite person here. In middle school, Quincy was crossing the street in the crosswalk when Elizabeth almost ran into her. "I didn't see her," was all Elizabeth said. Because a kid in a crosswalk before school is a big surprise. "Personally, I think cupcakes are over. Let's do mini pies. And everybody wear pink and black. Black aprons. And we'll need cake stands."

Someone raises her hand. "What about flies? Can't we get a real display case?"

"Good point." Elizabeth puts the tip of her pen to her peach-colored lips and straightens her shoulders in her orange workout top. "We'll see about renting one."

I rest my head on my hands. What they're describing sounds like hours of work. I've been doing bake sales for almost twenty years. At most, we make about two hundred from a bake sale like this.

Now Elizabeth's talking about decorating a plain black canopy with pink stripes. This is what happens when women with MBAs plan a bake sale. The next thing you know, they'll be drawing up a business plan. If they did, though, they'd figure out that it wasn't worth the expense they're proposing.

These kids will get their learners' permits next year. They can make a few cookies, can't they? I swallow. Absurdly, I picture Tomoe Gozen. Would Tomoe go along with the cookie plan, so as not to make waves? Or would she oppose them?

I examine the palms of my hands as I listen, preparing to interrupt. *Go along with it*, my head whispers. My heart rate increases. It's silly, me being afraid to have an opinion. "You know," I say carefully, my voice low, "this sounds like a lot of work."

The women go quiet.

"We're all busy, right?" I nod at each of them, meet each of their eyes. The women shift, listening. "I have an idea. Our kids can work an oven and mix batter. Let's let the kids do their own sale."

I stretch my arms out across the table. "These are middle school kids. They don't care about fancy packages. I know my son doesn't. He just wants to eat a cupcake."

"Mini pies." Elizabeth squints at me. "Not cupcakes." Elizabeth doesn't care about cupcakes or responsibility. She just wants to have something to do. She's kind of like me. Only way worse.

"Their own sale?" Susannah stares at me like I've got a horn growing out of my forehead. "But then it might be . . . crappy."

"And then everybody will blame us," Elizabeth says. "Everybody always blames the mothers."

The others murmur agreement. I forge on. "Because you let them. So what if it fails? They'll learn from what they do." I lean forward. I remember Tomoe Gozen and Yamabuki. The girl who was used to being catered to and cared for. We don't want to make them into Yamabukis. We want Tomoes.

Elizabeth's brow furrows. She's used to being the one who gets her way, even if her way's the wrong way. "The kids make the treats?" Elizabeth repeats. "I want my children studying, not baking cookies."

"If they spent less time on their phones, they'd have plenty of time to bake a few." I smile pleasantly at Elizabeth, but she glares at me. Fine. I stare right back at her. I'm right, and I'm not going to back down today. Let her do her usual arguing—she's a balloon that will run out of air eventually.

Maybe there *is* a samurai in my family tree, in my blood. Maybe that's why Mom left us the book. I mean, this is only a silly bake sale meeting, but darn it if I'm not going to stand firm.

Finally, Elizabeth looks away. I continue. "Don't you agree life skills are important? Listen. They can come over to my house. We'll knock it out in one morning. Boom. You don't even have to worry or do a thing."

"I agree," Laura says. "Make those lazy bums work for a change."

"I don't know." Elizabeth bites her lip. "My Luke throws a fit if he has to set the dining table." She actually seems worried. Like really actually concerned that her tyrant of a son will tell her what to do. Some other mothers murmur their agreement.

I want to shake her, yell, *Grow a backbone.* I blow out a breath. I can't imagine one of my kids disrespecting me if I ask them to help. I'd been asking them to help since they could walk. "All the more reason for him to pitch in with this."

"All right, Rachel." Susannah flips her legal pad closed. "We'll try it your way."

"Good luck with that," Elizabeth says.

I smile at her, suppressing my suddenly overpowering urge to flip her off.

At *home,* I slip off my flats, put them into the shoe cabinet by the door. The same mantel clock we had when we first got married ticks away, and my first thought is to wonder if my sister picked up Chase the way she said she would. Of course she did, I chide myself. Then I wonder if Drew stopped by to see Mom today. Whether Mom recognized her.

I don't remember Drew and my mother getting along well, but I don't remember them getting along poorly, either. When I called Mom, I often asked after Drew, and she'd say she didn't know. That Drew called only on holidays and visited at Christmas. "You could call her," I said, to which my mother said nothing. Perhaps she was from a place that believed kids should call their parents. Perhaps Mom was afraid of rejection.

Now, I drink two glasses of water in the kitchen. This house is just so empty with only me in it. I stop by the guest room, peek inside. Drew's actually made her bed, which she never used to do. But her clothes are still scattered wherever she took them off, exactly as they were when we were growing up. I check the bathroom to make sure she has enough towels and TP, and close the door. I have to admit, having Drew here is different. In a better way than I thought. This morning she made the coffee before I got up and even scrambled some eggs for everyone. Of course, I note drily in my own special ultra-hypercritical manner, the pan's still soaking in the sink.

In my bedroom, three laundry baskets full of clean clothes wait on the bed. I dump it out, intending to fold. Screw it. I push the pile over and lie down.

I stretch out on top of the quilt, stare up at the ceiling fan, see how dusty it is. The red numbers of the clock stare at me accusingly. I feel guilty when I'm not doing what I'm supposed to. Like I'm a downstairs maid in *Downton Abbey* and the head butler's going to yell at me for shirking. I throw a sock on top of the clock. I need a nap.

I look at my phone instead, at the e-mail from Joseph with the samurai book translation. Minamoto is the family name of the samurai in the book.

Minamoto is the name on the package. Was this a descendant of Yoshinaka? Someone who thought Mom could use the inspiration? The bookseller, perhaps?

I look up Hatsuko Minamoto. Nothing. Not even a Facebook profile or an ad for the white pages. Nothing in Japanese, either, but I don't have the ability to type Japanese characters in the search engine. Or understand them, for that matter.

I blow out a breath.

What I should do, to get it over with, is call my father. For Quincy's sake. Try to settle this whole mess once and for all. Maybe he's just waiting for me to make the first move. Maybe we're both too stubborn. Maybe there's a way we can mediate this thing.

I hold my phone in my hand, wavering.

Could Quincy's request have something to do with her wedding? Is she getting married because of our fractured family?

I want her to know that everything her father and I have done for her, we've done so she doesn't have to have the same struggles. And now she's *choosing* to have them, too.

Quincy doesn't remember this at all, but when she was small, Tom and I had gone through a rough time. There was a downturn in his father's business, and his father got sick and Tom had to step in years before he was ready. For years, there was never enough in the bank to quite cover all our bills. Some months we chose between eating and paying the electric bill.

She doesn't remember her father working eighteen-hour days, hammering nails himself, meeting with potential clients. That period when nothing seemed to work.

One night, Tom got home after ten. He had big bags under his eyes, though he was only in his early twenties. It'd been an especially hard day, one of those in which I questioned every life choice I'd ever made.

It'd been a rainy week, and my mood matched. No car, the grocery store too far to walk, I felt like putting Quincy in her stroller and running someplace until I couldn't run anymore. But it was too cold for her to be out in the wet.

Earlier that afternoon, a man from the electric company had knocked on the door and presented me with a pink bill. FINAL NOTICE. He informed me they'd need payment right then, or the electric would be turned off. I wrote him a check, praying there was enough in the account to cover it, knowing we were still three days off from Tom's payday.

I suppose when I married Tom, I thought he'd take care of me forever. I'm not sure why I thought that, exactly, except that of course I was really young. Why I thought I could skip the paying-your-dues time and go directly to the place where my only job would be taking care of my baby. That I'd spend my days driving to playgroups and lessons and preparing gourmet meals and not worrying about anything except my child's development. Instead, we were hard-pressed to afford mac and cheese. We had a house, but we'd been here for three years and it still looked like we'd just moved in. A card table for the dining room, beanbag chairs in the living room.

I should have finished college before I got married. I should have been more careful. I watched my daughter stack blocks over and over, tried to get her to color with the crayons. *This is a crappy life for her.* I walked her to the park every day and schemed with the other mothers about moneymaking opportunities. Having Tupperware parties and whatnot all required start-up capital, and I didn't know of many who wanted to buy anything, much less extra stuff. The pay from any kind of job I could get would be eaten away entirely by childcare expenses.

I lay in the middle of the floor, half-naked dime-store Barbie knockoffs and blocks strewn around me, like a body in a toy crime scene. Three-year-old Quincy slept on the floor next to me. She was in the throes of the Terrible Twos, that period of defiance that pretty much stretched from eighteen months to, oh, seven years. She kept breaking out of her room, refused to be potty-trained, and caused general mayhem. That night, she finally passed out in the living room.

Tom locked the door behind him. "Why isn't she in her bed?"

I shook my head. "I can't go on like this."

"Don't be so dramatic." Tom sat on one of the beanbag chairs that served as a couch, whispering, too. "I'm sorry I'm so late."

My stomach growled and my head throbbed. Either I was going to cry, or I was going to get really angry. I chose anger. "It's all your fault," I said, not bothering to whisper. "That family business is going to kill us. You have to get a regular job."

Tom looked stricken. I didn't care that he'd been up since dawn. That even if he got another job, it'd be entry level and probably pay even less than what he made now. My throat choked tight as I continued. "And did you forget to pay the electric bill?"

"Shit." He shook his head. "I thought we had more time."

"It was three months' overdue! It was humiliating!" I said, too loud. Quincy started in her sleep, her limbs flailing. "The neighbors all saw it. My God, Tom, why would you do that to me?"

"Oh, yeah. I did it on purpose. Against you. Just to spite you." He stood up and stuck his hands into his jeans pockets and stepped on a block. "Ow!" He kicked it, pinging it against the wall. "I'm working my ass off all day and you can't even be bothered to pick up the room. What the fuck do you do all day?"

I glared at him. "What do I do all day?" Both of us, frustrated, exhausted, wanted the release of a fight. "Let me see. I cleaned shit off the bedroom walls, because Quincy is an artist. I read *Chicka Chicka Boom Boom* literally forty-two times. I kept your daughter alive, Tom."

"I'm keeping her alive, too. I'm working." He sat down again. "I don't even tell you half the crap that goes on, Rachel, because I don't want you to worry."

"Do you think your parents would help?" I sniffled.

Tom crossed his arms and all the emotion fled from his face. Stoic. I hated it when he turned into a wall. "No."

"No?" My voice rose. Hysteria. Not a good look. "I know your dad's sick, but they saved while the business was doing well. We can pay it back. We need a little help. We have no food."

Tom turned on the television to the news, and muted it. "I can't. They can't help us, Rachel, and it'll destroy my mother if she knows."

Quincy tapped my leg. "Mommy?" Her little face had marks from the carpet pressed into it, and her rosebud mouth turned down. "Mommy okay?"

"I'm okay." I put my arms around her neck, inhaling the smell of generic baby shampoo.

Tom's shoulders slumped. He got on the floor and crawled over to us. "I'm sorry, Rach."

"Stay 'way!" Quincy said, holding her little hand in Tom's face, her voice loud and distinct. "You are a bad man. Don't make my mommy cry."

I rocked her. "It's okay, Quincy," I said into her ear. "Mommy's fine. Daddy's fine. We just had a tantrum."

But Tom's face collapsed. It was too much for him. Too difficult to keep this family going. He'd put on weight—too much work, not enough sleep, not enough healthy food. My Tom, the happy-go-lucky Tom from biology class, was gone.

He picked up his car keys.

"Tom, wait." My heart pulsed in my throat. "Don't go away mad."

Tom walked out the door.

I closed my eyes into Quincy's hair and said nothing. Not only had I failed myself, I'd made Tom into a failure, too. How much better he'd be without us, I thought. With only himself to worry about. He'd go back to being his old self instead of this defeated golem. Quincy fell asleep in my arms again.

I called Mom, crying. Told her everything. The electric man. How we had nothing to eat now but half a jar of peanut butter and a bag of plain pasta. "Dad was right," I said. "I'll never be anything. It's too hard. I don't know what to do. Maybe I can take Quincy away, go to college, get loans. They have financial aid for single mothers. Scholarships." I was babbling.

Mom hesitated. I heard Killian's show blasting in the background, some announcer shouting scores. "You wait," she whispered.

She showed up not an hour later, her arms full of groceries, a raincoat thrown on over her pajamas. I couldn't believe she'd snuck out away from my father. In the rain and dark.

"I can't do it," I said later, at the kitchen table. I was feeling better, finally, with a belly full of canned chicken noodle soup. "He wanted to take care of us, but we're a burden." I teared up again. "It's too hard."

Mom leaned over and took my face in both her hands. "Rachel."

I looked into her dark eyes. "What?"

She held on to my cheeks. "You're young. Pretty. Maybe you can find a rich man. Like I did. I have a roof and food and clothes. I can buy all the material and thread I want." She releases my face and looks away. "But look. I have to sneak out to see my own daughter and grandbaby." I heard her swallow hard. "I have to be quiet when he's home. Even though he's not."

"Will it get better?" I asked.

"For you, yes." She smiled, her nose widening. I hadn't noticed that before. Like a Buddha. "You must be strong. Stronger than I am."

I didn't ask her what that meant. I buried my face in my arms. Now I wished I'd asked. Maybe she would have told me about Tomoe.

After Mom took off, I found a wad of twenties tucked into my silverware drawer. It got us through.

I went to the grocery store near our apartment the next day and applied for a job. Every night, from ten to three, I stocked the shelves. Mopped the aisles. I went home and slept for three hours until Tom went to work. If I was very lucky, Quincy slept in until seven or eight. Usually she didn't. I did this for a year, until Tom's dad recovered and they were able to get the business back on track.

If Quincy only knew how much harder getting married before they're established would be. Doesn't she know how grateful I feel every time I can fill up my car all the way to "full," without worrying about the card going through? I wanted to spare her that kind of anxiety.

I wish for a crystal ball that could see into her future, all the possibilities of all the different paths.

But maybe it's always hard for everyone, in different ways. I don't know of a couple that's never had problems. I know people married to attorneys who complain about long hours, and I think they should be grateful, because at least they're not working twenty hours a day making minimum wage. But everyone seems to have a unique situation. I only know about my life.

Or, maybe nobody knows how to be happy with what we already have. That's the whole problem. No fortitude.

Tomoe had it harder. Twelfth-century Japan? No modern conveniences? How did she deal with her period, I wonder. And now Yamabuki, who seems far too pale and weak to survive for a day in the world of Yoshinaka and Tomoe. You needed to be tough back then, both in will and in body. All I need is the will.

Hikari sits facing the window, her eyes closed. Should Drew wake her up? That might startle her. Then again, if Hikari wakes up to find some random person in her room, that might scare her, too. Drew never knows quite what to do around her mother these days.

She never did.

It was Drew who told Hikari that Rachel was pregnant. She'd gone into the quilting room. Her mother was bent over the machine. As usual. It seemed to Drew that most every important conversation or fight she'd had with her mother had taken place there. "Do you have any baby quilts?" Drew asked casually.

"Of course I do." Hikari stopped the machine. She looked at Drew, who leaned against the doorframe. Her usual position. At fourteen, Drew was tall and skinny, barely requiring a bra. She kept her hair short. She could pass as a boy and was sometimes mistaken for one. "Why?" Hikari asked, her voice alert. "Do you know someone who's having a baby?"

Drew nodded, playing with the drawstring on her sweats. From the living room, the roar of a football game blasted. Killian. Drew stepped into the room, shut the door.

Hikari grabbed Drew's hand in both of hers. "Tell me." Her mother's hands were icy. Despite all the labor. "I'll help you, Drew."

"Mom." Drew suddenly understood her mother's worry. "It's not me. It's Rachel."

Hikari squeezed Drew's hand once, then released her. "Does she know who the father is?"

This shocked Drew. "Of course she does." But then, her mother hadn't interacted with Rachel in almost two years. She had no idea how Rachel had changed. How hard she worked. Drew wondered what her parents thought her sister did—did they believe her to be a prostitute, entertaining johns in between puffs of marijuana? Didn't they want to know?

Hikari stared at the fabric on her machine. "What will she do?"

"It's her boyfriend, Mom. They're getting married." Drew spoke rapidly. "Don't worry. He's really nice. Boring, but nice."

Hikari smiled sadly at Drew. "Ah, Drew. How can you know what nice is?" She let go of Drew's hand and rubbed her eyes.

Drew swallowed. She felt like she was strangling. Anger flared up, unbidden, at her mother. "You should've just stayed in Japan."

"Yes." Her mother shook her head. "I thought my old life was too hard. Now I'm not so sure."

But then we wouldn't have been born, Drew thinks, and waits for her mother to say she was glad she had her daughters. Hikari pressed the sewing machine pedal, whirring it to life. Drew went back to her room.

At the nursing home, the window's open, the wind blowing cold air straight on Hikari's face, her hair wild. Drew touches her mother's arm. Cold. Maybe Hikari just liked being cold.

Why did Hikari want them to have the story of Tomoe Gozen? It seems to Drew that Hikari's more like Yamabuki. Out of her element, always. Not belonging. Perhaps Hikari thought one of her daughters was like Tomoe, and one like Yamabuki. Which would Drew be?

She feels like Yamabuki, too.

Drew shuts the window. At the sound, Hikari's eyes fly open.

"Hi, Mom." Drew sits down again. Hikari's mouth moves, but she says nothing. She cocks her head to the side. Stares at her. Hard, assessing.

A memory stirs. Senior year of high school Drew was on the Academic Decathlon team. Their mother was pressed into chaperone service to the state competition in Sacramento. While the other chaperone parents quizzed their children and the teammates with practice questions, Hikari sat in the corner of the hotel room, reading. Always quiet. During the tournament, Drew would look up occasionally to catch a glimpse of Hikari in a powder-blue Chanel suit and her hair in a ballerina bun—so striking that everyone asked Drew if that was really her mother—her ankles crossed, a pillar of stoicism in a sea of hyperinvolved parents.

"In 1180–1185, the Genpei War came at the end of what long era in Japanese history that began in 794?" the announcer asked.

Drew was supposed to know this. Her teammates swiveled their heads to look at her. The girl with the Japanese mother sitting only a few feet away. Little did they know that she knew no more about Japan than the average American.

Hikari stared at her hard. Was she saying the answer in her head? Her white throat moved up and down as she swallowed. To Drew, her gaze looked cold. Disappointed.

"Five seconds," the announcer said.

Drew stared back at her mother, trying to read her mind. Abruptly, Hikari got up and left the auditorium.

And then Drew knew what Hikari was thinking. Her mother was ashamed. Of her. The blood drained out of her body. Even if she knew the answer, she could not have reached the buzzer. She watched the blue suit retreat into the darkness, the light of the hallway. The buzzer sounded.

"The Heian Era," the opposing team captain said smugly.

Of course. Drew felt markedly stupid. She hadn't needed her mother to tell her that; she remembered it from her notes. Her teammates patted one another's backs and they filed into the lobby.

She saw her mother waiting for an elevator and ran across, jumped in. One other person was on the elevator, a middle-aged bald man. Drew ignored him. Hikari pressed a number.

Drew inhaled. "You left." She tried to keep the hurt out of her voice. Her mother walking out, Drew realized, felt worse than losing. The elevator walls were a shiny brass, like a mirror. She watched her mother's face in them.

Hikari raised her head. "When I lose, I do not like people to see me. I thought you felt the same." Her mother's eyes were wet. "You had your chance and now it's gone."

Drew was so far from understanding this woman's motivations that she thought Hikari might as well be another person's parent. "Why didn't you ever teach me about Japan?" Drew asked quietly.

Hikari drew an audible breath. She examined her reflection in the elevator, patting a hair that had escaped her tight bun into place. The man with the ear hair shifted his weight from foot to foot.

"Why don't you ever say one word about Japan?" Drew's voice rose. "I don't know where you came from. I don't know your family. It's like you're an alien who got beamed down here. How did you end up in the mail-bride catalog?" The man's eyebrows jumped. He met my mother's gaze in the mirror and she looked away. When the doors opened, he stepped out quickly.

The doors slid closed again before Hikari answered. She turned to Drew. Not angry, not sad. Just the same as always. Closed off. "Drew," she said carefully, enunciating the R too hard as she always did, "living in the past does not benefit anyone. Japan is nothing to me. I'll never go back. You'll never go back. There's nothing there for people like us. There's no point in talking about it."

People like us? "What do you mean?"

The doors slid open. Hikari shook her head and stepped into the hallway. "The only thing I want you to remember, Drew, is that you come from samurai blood. You have that in you. That is all you need to know. No matter what else anybody says." She gestured to her daughter. "This is America. You are what you make of yourself. Come on." Hikari set off down the hallway, walking fast.

Drew looks at Hikari now, in the nursing home room. Her face looks the same as it did then, except for some softening of the jowls, wrinkles between her brows. "You did tell me about us being from samurai," she says excitedly. "Is that why you left the book for us?" She will have to look up the Sato name.

Hikari blinks at her. "I said," she mumbles, "I had the strangest dream."

"Mom?" Drew kneels beside her mother. But Hikari still looks at her blankly. "What's your dream, Hikari?" Drew touches her arm. Her mother's arm is well moisturized, a sign of the good care she receives here.

Hikari looks out the window. "Where is my sister of heart?"

The waves pound the sand. In the hallway outside, a passing wheelchair rattles, a nurse whispers comforting words to someone.

Drew waits for her mother to say more, but Hikari does not.

Sisters of Heart. The book. Or is she talking about the woman who sent her Tomoe's story? "Who's your sister of heart, Mom? Hatsuko Minamoto? Somebody you knew in Japan?"

"Japan?" Her forehead wrinkles.

This isn't doing any good. They have to write to Hatsuko.

Someone knocks on the doorjamb. "Snack time." The nurse has a tray of applesauce and graham crackers. She smiles pleasantly at Drew. "You must be her other daughter. Such pretty girls you have, Hikari."

"Oh my." Hikari claps her hands as though the meal is a grand feast. "For me? All this?"

"Of course." The nurse adjusts the tray table so the food sits over Mom's lap. Mom clumsily grips the spoon, making several attempts at the bowl of applesauce before achieving success.

"Should I help her?" Drew asks.

"Nah. It gives her something to do." The nurse leaves.

"Don't you want some, young lady?" Hikari dips the graham cracker into the applesauce.

Drew takes a bit of graham cracker and does the same. She can't remember the last time she had either a graham cracker or applesauce. Probably back when she was in preschool. She takes a hesitant bite.

Hikari chews and takes another cracker.

They eat in silence for a while.

Drew watches Hikari's placid expression. *Don't you see me?* She wants to ask. She always wanted to ask that. She swallows. Words gather and form at the base of her throat. Things she always wanted to say, but never did. Whether because she was scared of rejection, or because the opportunity never arose. "Mom. I want you to know—I'm sorry we never talked about your life. I wish you would have told me things. I felt so shut out. And you seemed so much closer to Rachel." But perhaps they weren't, Drew realizes now. Rachel doesn't know much more about Hikari than Drew does. Why did she keep herself so walled away from her own daughters?

Was she protecting them from something?

What was it that Killian would tell the judge? Her mother had not gotten so much as a parking ticket, to Drew's knowledge. Drew can't think of anything it could be.

Unless it was something that happened in Japan. Before she came.

She regards her mother. Still, she can't imagine Hikari doing anything. What was she, a gangster? "Mom, if you know what Dad's going to say in court, you have to tell me. Tell me now."

Hikari dips another cracker. "My dear," she says, "you are so very pretty. But you talk too much. You're boring me to death!"

Drew has to laugh. "Sorry." Her face is so hot.

Mom picks up the plate and examines the decoration, a green flowered vine wrapping around the edge. She wipes at it aggressively, and looks up at Drew. "This won't come off. Why did they give me a dirty plate?"

"It's on there permanently." Drew swipes her finger across the vine to demonstrate. "It's a decoration, like wallpaper."

Hikari pushes the tray table away so hard it topples. Drew catches it before it hits the ground. The plate hits the floor, but doesn't break. "It looks like garbage. A plate of garbage!" Her voice rises. "I can't eat garbage."

"Okay." Drew pushes the tray table all the way into the hallway, finds the nurse and gives it to her. By the time she returns, her mother's asleep again.

160

Drew takes her hand. Hikari wasn't a perfect mother. Drew isn't a perfect daughter, or a perfect sister. Or perfect in life.

Drew wishes she could ask her mother many more things. How she felt about Killian, really. What she really wanted for Rachel, for Drew. What kind of motherly advice would she give—she hadn't been one to do that. Perhaps because of Killian. Perhaps because of something else, some constraint Drew has no idea about.

Maybe when Hikari said she hated Drew too that day, what she was really saying was that Drew didn't know her. That Drew didn't understand her any better than Hikari understood Drew.

In her sleep, Hikari squeezes Drew's hand. Maybe this is what Rachel was talking about, about the visits being nice, Drew thinks. Their mother's not here, yet she is here. *She doesn't remember me, yet we're having this moment anyway.* Moments are what matter, now. Not anything that happened before, or anything that might happen in the future.

Drew squeezes her mother's hand back. She listens to the waves breaking onshore, the caws of seagulls and the traffic going by. They sit for a while longer.

Tomoe refused to meet her mother's reproachful glare. She kept her eyes on the sloping riverbank, placing her feet carefully on the slippery new grass. Yamabuki stumbled over the uneven, rain-soaked ground in her *geta* and white *tabi*, carrying a basket of laundry down to the stream.

Yamabuki must learn to be strong, Tomoe thought. *We do her no good by coddling her.*

The girl had been here nearly two months, and this was the first time she had emerged from the house to do anything besides sit on the side-lines, watching. When she volunteered in her spectral voice to help with the day's washing, Tomoe handed her the basket of laundry without a word.

It was spring. The snow had melted. Wasn't spring everyone's favorite time? When the dullness of winter vanished and new energy filled your legs? But Tomoe felt dimmed, rusted as a blade stuck and forgotten in dirt. She scrubbed a kimono on a rock, her hands nearly frozen in the cold water, her legs bent in a squat and her pants hiked up high. In a country fort like theirs, even the wife of Yoshinaka had to do her share of work. This was not Miyako.

"She's used to sitting inside, doing nothing but staring into space as she thinks of poetry," Tomoe muttered to her mother. She couldn't imagine such a life.

"She's barely more than a child." Chizuru wrung out underclothes. They watched Yamabuki pick her way down the bank, waving. Chizuru waved back. "She doesn't know what to do. Think of how she feels."

"Good medicine tastes bitter in the mouth." Tomoe quoted the Japanese proverb. "We must push her into this new life, 'Kāsan. The sooner she gets used to hard work, the sooner she will be happy."

Yamabuki shrieked, took a step, and shrieked again as if the mud was biting her white *tabi* socks. Impractical. "Yamabuki!" she called. "This is not the city. This is the country. We don't wear *tabi* to do chores. You understand?"

Yamabuki bowed her head. "I apologize," she said in her whispery voice. Even the skin on her head was moonlight-white, Tomoe thought. The sun would turn her into ashes.

Yamabuki knelt in the mud beside Chizuru, the folds of her delicate kimono crushing down into the dirt. Tomoe wondered if there was something wrong with her brain.

"Oh, no!" Chizuru said. "Don't kneel. Squat, like us."

Yamabuki tried to imitate them. She managed to sink down only about halfway. "I can't. It hurts."

"Try again," Chizuru urged. "You only need practice."

Yamabuki attempted to squat once more, but couldn't put the heels of her feet down fully to the ground. As Yamabuki's bottom neared the earth, she lost her balance and fell. "Oh!" Yamabuki held up one egg-white hand, covered in mud.

Tomoe supposed Yamabuki had only knelt on the comfortable tatami mats—squatting was customary for those working outside, but was not proper for noble women. Tomoe stood and faced Yamabuki. If the girl was to survive in any capacity, she would need help. "Hold my hands."

The girl did as instructed. Her hands were very small and cold, the skin papery and dry. Tomoe's own hands had long, strong fingers and were warm from her near-constant exercise.

"Now, I will squat, too. You hold on to me." They bent their knees, lowering their bottoms slowly, arms outstretched, until their legs landed in the squat position. Yamabuki's eyebrows went up into surprised curlicues.

Yamabuki squat-walked over to the water, her *geta* squishing in the mud, her white *tabi* splattered brown. Tomoe stifled a giggle. The girl dipped a kimono into the water gingerly, observing how Chizuru was scrubbing before attempting an imitation. "This place is so beautiful, Chizuru-san. I love the mountains."

Tomoe looked about. She had grown up in the north, and after twenty-two years she noticed the landscape only as it practically affected her, assessing the weather to determine if she needed a *tanzen* jacket for the cold or how much water to pack when it was hot.

Yamabuki scrubbed ineffectually at the cloth. Tomoe wrinkled her nose. They would be better off with a toddler's help. She glanced at Chizuru, hoping her mother would correct Yamabuki, but Chizuru said nothing.

Suddenly, the girl stopped scrubbing and spouted a poem:

"Timid, the pines sway in the springtime breeze.
Birds look for their homes.
An iris blooms in the still-hard ground."

The girl blushed, as though embarrassed. Chizuru clapped. "Beautiful! How lucky we are to have such a girl here. Our lives have been too long without poetry."

Tomoe frowned. Chizuru shouldn't encourage such foolishness. The girl needed hard physical labor of the body, not the silly mental convolutions of poetry. "The ground isn't hard. You're in the mud."

Chizuru clucked. "Oh, Tomoe. The poem is about her. She is the timid pine."

"And you are the iris in the frozen ground," Yamabuki said with a shy smile.

"Oh." No one had called Tomoe an iris before. Once, Yoshinaka had told her that her skin was like fresh snow, but he said it in such an impersonal way that she knew he was only describing what he saw. As if he'd said, "The stew is hot."

"Is that what you did in the capital? Sat around and thought of poetry?"

"Sometimes." Yamabuki returned to her ineffectual scrubbing. "It was boring there, honestly. I spent most days alone. When visitors came, my mother made me sit behind a screen. She is very old-fashioned."

Tomoe wondered if Yamabuki had ever come across Wada. He and Yamabuki's father were both courtiers, after all. Wada and his poetry, his round face and earnest air . . . She smiled at the memory. No, she would not ask. Even if Yamabuki were to tell her, Tomoe was not sure she wanted to know. Wada might be engaged to someone else in the capital by now. Besides, Tomoe was glad she'd not chosen court life. She might have turned into Yamabuki herself.

"This must be quite shocking," Chizuru said. "All these people. All these men!"

"Yes, Yoshinaka was quite . . . shocking." Now Yamabuki colored and scrubbed harder, her pale hands flashing in the icy water.

"Don't worry. You'll get used to him. I did." Tomoe giggled, surprising herself with her boldness. It was fun to tease Yamabuki, who bowed her head even lower, her face deepening to crimson.

Chizuru reprimanded Tomoe with a soft slap to her shoulder. "Tomoe Gozen. Ladies don't speak of such things."

"Nor do real ladies wash laundry." Tomoe wrung out the last kimono and stood. "We are far from ladies out here. You'd better help Yamabuki, Mother, or we'll have to rewash everything."

Yamabuki burst into tears, clapping her hands over her face. The pants she'd been scrubbing caught in the stream's current and began to drift away. Tomoe rushed forward and grabbed the material out of the water. "Yamabuki! What has crying ever solved? Your weeping will not finish the laundry."

"Tomoe, hush." Chizuru put her arm around Yamabuki and rocked the frail girl against her side. "She has been torn from her family. I am as close to a mother-in-law as she has. And you are her sister. You have always had your family. You always will."

"My mother sold me to Yoshinaka after my father lost his court job," Yamabuki sobbed through her fingers. "She wanted me to be gone. She hates me. She called me a useless burden."

Shame swept through Tomoe in a hot rush. Going from a life of doing nothing to a life in the north with a huge hairy husband would be wrenching, Tomoe thought. It wasn't as though Yamabuki had chosen Yoshinaka. All things considered, Yoshinaka surely preferred Tomoe's hardiness and practicality to Yamabuki's fragility. And Yoshinaka and Tomoe were close, the product of having known each other their entire lives. Yamabuki must feel like an outsider.

"I wish I could be like you, Tomoe," Yamabuki said, lifting her head. The light bounced off her skin as though it were a precious metal.

"And what am I? Wife to no one. Captain of a farmer army, a soldier in a war that may never come." Tomoe started washing another garment with vigor.

Yamabuki touched Tomoe's arm. "No. Brave and energetic. Good at everything!"

Tomoe thought of how Yoshinaka had not been to see her at night since Yamabuki's arrival. But that was not the girl's fault, she reminded herself. "Not at everything, apparently."

The afternoon sun flickered like candlelight through canopies of tree branches. "You don't know," Yamabuki whispered. "You don't know what you are. How special."

"Yamabuki, you must listen to me." Tomoe peered into Yamabuki's reddened eyes. Why, she was no more than nineteen, Tomoe thought with a pang, yet had no experience in practical matters. Her parents had kept the girl locked away for so long. Tomoe smoothed Yamabuki's cheek gently, as she would an infant's. "We'll go into town today. Buy you some mochi." She lifted the girl's hair. It was as soft as rabbit fur, smooth and glossy. In the sun she saw hints of blue tone under the black. "Maybe a pretty new comb. Would you like that, Yamabuki-chan?"

Yamabuki smiled. "I'd like that very much."

Tomoe handed Yamabuki the pants that had floated away. "But you must finish the wash first."

Ten

D rew waits for Chase to show at the appointed place after school, across the street, under a tree by the yellow fire hydrant. Her sister, as always, was very specific.

She reads the samurai story on her phone. The translator's sent quite a few pages in the past few days. Tomoe—how incredibly resilient she was. If they could bottle that, Drew would definitely drink it. Tomoe had to attend to domestic duties instead of being a kick-ass warrior twenty-four/seven. Even when her love married another, she kept on going. Of course, Tomoe had no other choice. She couldn't pack up and leave when things didn't go her way.

This makes Drew think of her mother. If only her mother had been stronger, surely she could have gotten a good lawyer and divorced Killian. Set herself up well. Taken Drew and Rachel with her. Things would be different.

Chase opens the back door and throws his backpack into the car before getting in. "Can we stop at the library? I need a book."

"Sure. Hello. How are you?"

Chase turns to her, speaking with exaggerated syllables. "Very well, thank you. And you?"

"Great, thank you back." Drew grins at her nephew. "Good manners. I'm impressed."

"As you should be." He bows his head. She drives the short distance to the library and parks. She can't get over how much Chase looks like a man. She doubts he'd be carded at any bar. Dark blond hair covers his upper lip and his shoulders threaten to burst out of his T-shirt. If he was a comic book character, he'd have energy lines zapping out of his restless body.

What a terror he was as a toddler. Drew stopped by Rachel's to say hello to her niece and nephew one Christmas when Chase was two, Quincy eight. Rachel asked Drew to watch him for a moment while she finished something in the kitchen. But Drew had gotten distracted by something— the television, or Quincy showing her a toy—she doesn't recall. Before she knew it, in seconds, it seemed, the boy scaled the seven-foot bookcase in the living room and was tossing down books. "Chase! Get down!" Drew shrieked, and Chase, startled, fell. He needed six stitches on his chin. Her sister had been mad, to say the least. Drew couldn't blame her.

Drew pulls into the parking lot. "What subject is the book for?"

"Uh. Science." Chase leaps out of the car almost before she can get it into park. He slams the door too hard.

She follows him down the flight of steps and inside. The library's one of the smallest Drew has been in, but there's an airy atrium attached and a public meeting room from which soft music floats. Drew peeks in. Toddlers doing yoga with their parents, sort of. Drew smiles at their attempts to do downward facing dog. Most of them fall over.

Middle school kids sprawl out over the tables in the library proper, talking in not-very-library-like voices. It's a sea of overloaded backpacks and instrument cases and unwashed teenage bodies. One kid even lies on the floor, a book in hand. An older patron steps over him, shaking her silver head. "Get up," the older woman says, and the boy ignores her.

Drew can't believe how noisy it is. When she was in school, the librarian would have booted them out for talking above a whisper. "Is it always like this?" Drew asks Chase, horrified.

"Pretty much." Chase shrugs off his backpack at a table. "I've got to find a biography about George Washington." He lumbers off.

"I thought it was science," Drew says, to the air. She makes her way to an empty spot, almost tripping over black musical instrument cases sitting in the aisle. She settles at a round table across from a couple of girls, who ignore her as they text and giggle.

It's October tenth. Drew can't wait any longer to pay rent. She pays it with her phone, using the money Killian gave her. Don't think about it being his money, she commands herself. It would cause more trouble if she didn't take it than it would to take it.

Well, when she gets paid for her viola gig she can stop using it. She's going to have to make a decision soon about the apartment. Give notice or return. She imagines going up back up to L.A., reteaming with Jonah and the band. Would it be different this time?

Would she and Jonah get back together? She allows herself to think about him for a moment. How they cuddled, naked in bed, the exact way his muscles tensed against hers. The sex, Drew remembers, had always been incredible. No matter what angry names had been flung out during their fights.

A boy plops a medium-sized iguana down on the table next to Drew. She glances at it, her brain not processing what it is, looks at her phone, looks back. An iguana? "Hey! Get that thing away from me!" she shrieks, and he laughs. Drew decides maybe she is better off being childless. "What the heck are you doing with an iguana in a library?" Drew says. "They can carry salmonella. Plus, somebody might squish it."

"It's my service animal." The boy has a sly smile. He could be Tom Sawyer with those freckles.

Drew squints at the boy. Honestly, she has to tamp down her impulse to use a bad word. "How the heck is that your service animal?"

"It sticks out its tongue if I'm going to have an anxiety attack." He demonstrates by sticking out his own tongue.

She leans forward. "I don't believe you."

He pets the iguana gingerly. The spines on its ridge look sharp. "What are you going to do about it?"

"Alexander. I must draw the line at iguanas," a deep voice, tinged with a British accent, says from behind her.

"Come on, Mr. Tennant." The boy picks up his iguana. "I swear it's true."

The voice tsks. "Take Iggy home before something bad happens to him. You know better than that."

Alexander picks up Iggy and sticks the unfortunate lizard into his backpack before sauntering off.

"I'm so very sorry." The man moves in front of Drew. She sees khakis, an argyle sweater vest, and a smile hovering above it. He has deep-set dark brown eyes with crinkling lines in the corners and a closely shaved face. A thin, well-shaped nose with thick eyebrows. Strong jaw. He doesn't look like a librarian, Drew thinks. He doesn't even have glasses. But what's a librarian's supposed to look like? She's staring like she needs to memorize his features for a police sketch and forces herself to blink. "Ever since we had this law passed about not being able to ask for pet assistance identification, we've had this kind of thing happening. We don't want to be sued."

Drew swallows and closes her mouth, which she only now realizes is hanging open. "Oh." She clears her throat. He continues to stand there, as if he's waiting for her to say something else, his head cocked to the side. His shock of light brown hair falls into his eyes and he brushes it back impatiently.

She wants to say something flirtatious, but this pops out of her mouth instead. "Whatever happened to being quiet in a library?"

He laughs softly, the sound reminding Drew of a saxophone, and sits in the chair opposite her. He laces his hands together. His knuckles are bigger than his fingers, his hands strong, and he's not wearing a ring. He lowers his voice to a whisper. "I suppose it's my fault."

Drew raises an eyebrow. "Really? I thought the British were very proper."

He leans forward. "In my quest to be American, I may have gone a bit too far. Now it's all gone to the dogs, as it were. You see, these kids had nowhere to go after school to do homework. Their own school library isn't open. I want to keep the library relevant. They asked if they could do study groups. I said of course. But the noise level went up and up and up." He shakes his head. "Now it's irretrievably broken."

Drew glances around at the kids. A few tackle their homework, but they're mostly playing video games. "I guess it's free childcare, basically. Doesn't anybody come in here to study?"

"A few." He holds out his hand. "I'm Alan Tennant. The head librarian."

"Drew Snow." They shake hands. Drew's hands are hardly tiny, given her height, but his still dwarfs hers, envelopes it pleasantly. They shake for a second too long.

It's awfully warm in here. Drew has to restrain herself from flapping her shirt. She looks around for Chase and sees him standing by the encyclopedias, talking to a redheaded girl wearing a basketball jersey that says "Browning High."

"Is that your brother?" Alan inclines his head toward Chase. "Chase, right? He comes in here a fair amount."

"No. My nephew." Drew studies Alan. Surely he can't think she's that young. She figures he's about her age, maybe a bit younger. She glances at the circulation desk and sees a model-pretty librarian with long black hair and teeth that glow white even from this distance, helping out a student. They must hire librarians from the local modeling agency here. She figures he's dating that girl, or somebody else, ring or no. Because nobody this good-looking, with an accent like that, can be single for long. She imagines single mothers bringing their toddlers to storytime, dropping and picking up books while wearing short skirts.

"Ah. Are you a teacher?" He shifts back in his seat and regards her.

"No. Why would you think that?" She cocks her head.

"It's the teachers who want me to do something about it, usually." He ducks his head. "The parents are merely glad that their children have some-place to go."

The noise level crescendos as the toddler class lets out. A middle school boy shouts at another, computer to computer. Drew grits her teeth, mo-mentarily forgetting about Alan. She's neither teacher nor parent, but she can't take it anymore. "Good Lord. You know what?" She has an idea. "I'll bet you I can make this whole library go quiet."

"Yelling won't help." Alan settles back, his keen gaze on her. "Believe me. I've tried it."

"No yelling involved."

He leans forward and his eyes flash wickedly. He lowers his voice so much Drew's sure he's about to proposition her. "I'll bet you—"

Drew holds her breath.

"A cup of coffee." He holds up a hand. "Not that you're obligated to accept."

Drew grins. Why not? Having coffee with an English librarian would be the most interesting thing that's happened to her in, oh, about a year. She holds out her hand and shakes his again. "Deal."

She looks around at all the music cases until she finds the likeliest sus-pect. "A viola?" she asks the girl sitting at the computer. The girl nods, squinting suspiciously at her. "May I please use it?"

The girl shrugs and glances at Alan. "I guess. Don't break it."

"I won't." Drew takes it out. It's a student model, inexpensive, but Drew still handles it carefully. She draws the bow over the strings, tunes it. She's aware of Alan watching her from the table. The library chatters on.

Drew closes her eyes. What to play? A classical song? Her mind goes through what she knows. One of the songs she wrote? They won't recog-nize it. No—they need something they've heard.

A melody settles in her head. "Somebody That I Used to Know," by Gotye.

She plays the first few notes to make sure they're okay. Afraid of being rusty. It's been a long time since she's done a proper performance, like this, in front of live people. No retakes allowed.

Drew climbs up onto the chair. Now the library goes quiet, anticipating something. "Can I get you guys to clap your hands?" She gives them a beat. "Do it all through the song—I don't have a drummer." Only Alan and the other librarian and one mother do it. The students stare, stone-faced.

She smiles at all of them radiantly anyway, feeling a burst of excitement. Her skin tingles. She starts out by plucking the opening notes, as if she's playing the guitar. The kids murmur excitedly as they recognize the song. Quickly she lifts the viola to her shoulder. Her wrist bows with perfect grace and the song bursts out of her viola. She plays with abandon. Acting as if she's onstage before an audience of thousands, instead of in a tiny public library full of rather stinky teens.

She plays as she has forgotten how she could play.

When she lifts the bow off the viola, it is so quiet that she can hear the hum of the fluorescent lights above. She opens her eyes.

The library bursts into applause. "How'd you do that?" "Can you do another?" "Can you play the Big Butts song?"

Smart-aleck. "I actually can, but I'm not going to." She plays the first few bars just to prove it. The kids whoop louder.

Drew takes a little bow. Alan's standing up, sunbursts radiating out from around his eyes. "Well done!" he says.

"Now, kids," she says. "This is a library. That means quiet. If you want to be noisy, go to the park. Nobody will stop you." She points to the kid on the floor. "That means you, too—there's plenty of grass to lie on outside." The boy sits up but doesn't budge. Oh well. Alan will have to handle it.

She looks around for Chase, but he's not in the corner where he was.

Hastily, she returns the viola to the girl, who has been paying the least attention to this performance because she's got her headphones on. Drew walks to the place where he'd been. No Chase. She does a sweep of the room, but he's nowhere.

She goes to the bathrooms and knocks at the men's room. No answer. She peeks in. A single stall—empty.

Shoot.

She exits the library and looks across the parking lot to the wide grassy area between this building and the pool. There, partially obscured by a tree and part of the pool fence, is Chase. With the girl in the high school jersey. Very close together. Drew moves a little closer. Oh shit. They're making out. Not just a little bit, either—Chase's hands move up and down inside the girl's shirt.

Drew bounds across the asphalt like it's a bed of coals. As her feet pound, one thought echoes. *Rachel is going to kill him.*

Or her.

"Hey!" Drew shouts. "Chase!" The girl adjusts her jersey, pulls it down over her belly, and Chase lifts his head sleepily. No time for niceties. "Get over here. Now."

Chase finally looks properly startled. He straightens and lifts his hand in farewell to the girl, who pretty much sprints in the opposite direction. Drew's never yelled at him in her life. She hasn't been around enough to have the privilege. Chase lopes over to her.

When he gets close enough, she leans in. "Just what in hell do you think you're doing?" She's bursting with anger and fear, something she's never felt together. She wants to both shake him and lock him up forever. She motions for him to come to the car.

"I was just talking to my girlfriend."

"Talking. Right. She's your *girlfriend?*" Drew peers after the girl, who's heading away from them, toward the pool, in her high school jersey. "Are you allowed to have a girlfriend? Is she in *high school?*"

Chase blushes. "Yeah. So?"

"What grade?" Drew tries really hard not to shout, but it's not working.

Chase won't meet her eyes. "Junior. We played club water polo over the summer. Look, I have to get my backpack from inside the library."

A junior. Holy smokes. "What is she, sixteen? Seventeen?"

"The second." Chase stuffs his hands in his pockets, heads to the building. "She just turned seventeen."

Seventeen. Lord. This kept getting worse. A girl in high school should have her own peer group dating pool, not scavenge the middle school for a boyfriend. Something's wrong with her. "Does your mother know?" Drew stops so suddenly. "You didn't need a book at all. You were going to meet her." Is that how Alan knows him?

Chase stops moving and sighs, turning to look at her. Christ. He's so tall. "It's not a big deal."

"From where your hands were, I'd say it was." Drew squinches her eyes shut. Should she tell her sister, or keep it quiet? On the one hand, she doesn't want Rachel to strangle her only son. She can just hear Rachel's voice. *You should have been watching him instead of trying to impress the hot librarian. You're unfit for aunt-hood.*

But how could she possibly have predicted this? Maybe she can tamp it down herself. That's all that matters. That he doesn't do it again. "Listen." Drew's face heats. "Do you know about birth control? Two forms at all times. Don't believe the girl if she says she's on the Pill. You need proof." A boy from inside the library emerges and stares. Drew doesn't care. She glares back at the stranger. Maybe he could use a lecture, too. Bring it on.

"Aunt Drew." Chase covers his face with his hands. "Oh. My. God. *Please* stop talking."

She leans into him. "I'm serious, Chase. You're old enough. You could get her pregnant." Scare him straight. That's what she'll do to him. "How would you support a baby?"

"Do you think I'm going to do it with her right in the open?" Chase takes his hands off his face, his face a mottled red. "I'm not some kind of degenerate."

"Okay." She holds up her hands.

"We're in a relationship." He says the word like it means something to him. "She's important to me."

"How? You're fourteen. In *middle school.* I'm pretty sure you're not allowed to date. In fact, I'm a hundred percent sure. Three years is a huge age difference when you're fourteen, Chase. She should know better, even if you don't."

Chase sighs and looks at the sky. "I'm not going to do it with her."

Right. Maybe not at the park, but at someone's empty house? Drew jerks her head toward the building. "Get your backpack."

Chase goes into the library. Drew leans against the car and waits. Chase returns and gets in, slamming the door so hard it hurts Drew's eardrums. She gets in, too.

They're silent for a while. Then Drew says, "You know it can go too far really fast, right?"

Chase closes his eyes. "I will get out of the car if you keep talking." He grips the handle. "I swear to God, I'll roll out onto the street."

Drew clicks the lock. "Stop being so dramatic."

Chase turns his head away. "Are you going to tell Mom?"

"Do you think I shouldn't?" Drew backs out and heads onto the street, bumping the undercarriage on the sidewalk.

Chase shakes his head. "My mother will freak out. She'll lock me in my room until I'm eighteen. Please. You know how uptight she is."

Drew thinks about Rachel and their father and how she got kicked out. "She might be more understanding than you think, Chase." They stop at a light, watching a stream of kids heading to the convenience store pass in front of them. The girls are in middle school and all of them in this group wear tight clothes, low cut, short—the kind of clothes Drew would have worn to a club in her twenties. It makes her feel old and sort of judgmental to think this, but really. She wants to yell at them to have some self-respect. When did this happen? She feels desperately sorry for Rachel and Tom, raising kids now.

"Please." Chase grabs Drew's arm. "I know her better than you do. You haven't been around."

Drew ignores the sting. Maybe he does know her sister better. "I know I can't control you, Chase. But." Drew thinks of the promise she wants to extract. She can't put a chastity belt on him. She can't track down the girl and order her away. "I won't tell Rachel, if you cut it off with this girl. Don't see her anymore. Don't talk to her anymore. Don't text. Agreed?"

He sucks in air, thinking. Drew thinks she even sees relief flicker across his face. Maybe it was too much for him, and he's glad he got caught. He crosses his heart. "Okay, Aunt Drew." The light changes to green.

In the evening, I snuggle up under a blanket on the sectional and pick up *The Tale of Genji*. It's considered the first true novel ever written. A noble-woman, Murasaki Shikibu, wrote it in the eleventh century. It's one of the background books Joseph recommended.

"How is it?" Drew sits and opens up her laptop. "Intriguing?"

"It's kind of dense. She only uses titles instead of names, so it's hard to follow. Plus, everybody tries to talk in verse, which apparently was what people really did try to do." I flip through it. For the first time in my life, I consider just getting the SparkNotes version. Even in high school, even at my laziest lowest point, I'd been too stubborn to stoop to anything like that. This book is very long. "It's about Genji and the Japanese court and all the romances he had. He's a son of the emperor, but he's no longer royal and has to take the name Minamoto."

"Minamoto. Like the clan name in the Tomoe Gozen story." Drew's face lights up. "I remembered today, Rachel, that Mom told me we're descended from samurai." She taps away. "Oh." She purses her lips. "Mom's name was Sato. That's like Smith in Japan. But maybe she was talking about her mother's maiden name."

"I don't know." I tilt my head, curious. "When did Mom tell you that? You never mentioned it."

Drew waves her hand. "She said it during an argument. I forgot—I was more focused on being mad at her." She smiles ruefully. "It was pretty much the most personal thing she ever told me."

"Mom was more about action than words." I lean over to Drew, who's gone from happy to downcast in one sentence. Preoccupied. It's Mom. And probably Drew's lack of a job. I wonder if she needs a loan. "Are you okay?"

She nods.

"If you need to go back to L.A., I totally understand." I smile at her, trying to convey that I really don't mind if she stays longer.

"Well. You know what they say about fish and houseguests." She sinks farther down and clicks on her laptop. "I'm thinking about moving down here."

"Really?" I purse my lips, considering logistics. "What neighborhood? What would you do?"

"I don't know yet." Her tone is terse. "I just thought of it. I mean, there's nothing keeping me in L.A. I can drive up there if I get a music job."

"Okay," I say simply. I don't want to offend her. "You can stay here as long as you like. You're not a houseguest—you're earning your keep. Thanks for getting Chase."

She nods once, focusing on the screen.

I swallow. Sometimes we just seem to be from two different planets, speaking some version of English neither of us quite understands. "Hey." I change the subject. "I stopped by the post office and got airmail stationery. Shall we write to Hatsuko?"

Drew stops typing. "I don't know."

"You don't know? Why? That was really more of a rhetorical."

My sister purses her lips. "I don't know. It's just that when we hear back from her, that will be it. Like really it. This mystery will be solved. Over."

"But we want that. Don't we?" I feel a pang. It's a bit like we're putting end caps on my mother's life, too. I take the airmail paper out of the back of the book, where I've stuck it. "We need to do it. This Hatsuko might know things."

Drew picks up a magazine. "If I write the letter, you can call Killian."

I shake my head. Drew's told me what he said to her in the waiting room. He'd have no problem disposing of us. "I really don't see the point of asking him. He's going to say no."

"But it's his granddaughter. Maybe it'll make him soften. Maybe he's just like that because we never actually invite him anywhere. You edged him out with Mom. It could be a peace gesture." Drew takes the paper, uses the magazine as a flat surface.

Maybe I should phone him, but I don't know if I'd be able to get any words out. I fear it'll turn into an ugly fight. I type up an e-mail quickly, before I think better of it.

DAD,

I KNOW WE'VE HAD OUR DIFFERENCES, BUT I'M ASKING YOU TO PUT THEM ASIDE FOR A MINUTE. OUR DAUGHTER QUINCY [I have to write "daughter Quincy" because I'm not sure he's aware that I have a daughter, much less her name] IS GETTING MARRIED IN MID-MAY. SHE WOULD LIKE FOR YOU TO ATTEND THE WEDDING AND THE FESTIVITIES SURROUNDING.

THANKS,

RACHEL

"How's that?" I show my sister.

She shrugs. "Kind of impersonal, but whatever."

"I don't know him, Drew. I can't be chummy. Are you chummy with him?"

She sighs. She's not. She knows she's not. "Okay. Read mine."

Dear Hatsuko,

We don't know each other, but we might have someone in common. Hikari Sato. She is our mother. Recently, she fell ill, but she gave us the

samurai book you sent. Can you tell us where it came from and how our
mother came to have it?

It would be most appreciated.
Sincerely,
Drew and Rachel Snow

"I'm Perrotti." I hand it back to her.

"That just complicates it." Drew folds it carefully.

"Don't you think you should put in a stamped self-addressed envelope? And have the letter translated into Japanese?"

"First you don't want to do it. Now you're micromanaging." Drew sighs noisily. "Fine. I'll ask Joseph to translate it and I'll include an SASE. It'll cost more. Why'd you bother with the airmail paper?"

I shrug. "I didn't think of the other things."

"But you said them like you had and you were telling me I was wrong."

"Sorry." I hadn't meant to put it like that. Only my sister would scrutinize the meta-meanings of my word choices so intensely. Once she'd asked, after playing a song, how it was. I was busy doing homework and just said, "Okay." She'd pouted and wept for hours.

Drew waves her hand in front of her face. "Never mind. Let me tell you something good." She folds up the letter and speaks brightly. "Did you know that your local library was harboring a very hot single Englishman?"

"Alan?" I think of him. He's always wearing a sweater vest of some kind. I hadn't paid much attention. "He waived a fine for me once. Seems nice."

"Don't you think he's hot?" Drew's disappointed.

I try to remember what his face looked like. "Um. I guess. He wasn't horribly ugly or anything."

"Oh my God, Rachel." Drew throws her hands up. "He's the hottest man in a thirty-mile radius." She puts her hand on my arm. "Single man. I'm not counting Tom or anything."

"Okay, okay." I cross my arms. "What about him?"

"I'm going out with him." Drew draws her shoulders up.

I clear my throat, thinking of how Drew's got to go back to her own home sometime. "Are you sure that's a good idea?"

"It's just for fun."

I kick my feet out in front of me, sending the blanket flying up.

"What?" Drew turns to me. "Say it. I know you're thinking something."

"At a certain age," I begin, trying to choose my words carefully. I want the best for my sister. I don't want her to wander around getting into go-nowhere relationships for her whole life. I trail off. "Don't you think you should concentrate on men with whom you might have a future?"

Drew visibly bristles. If she had hackles, they'd be raised. "You never know. I might move here, like I said."

"True." I watch Chase walk through the family room, a stack of chocolate chip cookies in one hand and what looks like a liter of milk in the other. He's still such a little boy in so many ways. He still plays with his Star Wars action figures sometimes—I can hear him mumbling commands under his breath when I go by his room.

Drew gets up, stomps away. I shouldn't have said anything. Let her make her own mistakes. She returns with a package of cookies. "Want one?"

Chips Ahoy. Crunchy. "Remember when you ate a whole pack of these and threw up?" I ask.

"Totally worth it," Drew says.

"Not really. You did it in my room." I nudge her with my leg. "Every time you were sick, you'd come running to me. Not Mom."

Drew taps my ankle with hers. "I knew you didn't mind."

"Ha."

"Look. Joseph sent us some more of the translation." Drew turns the laptop around to face me.

I sit up and regard my younger sister. She sits facing me, her back against the other corner. Our feet are next to each other's. How long has it been since we've just hung out on the couch together? Years. Decades, already. I lean over and adjust the blanket so it's covering Drew, too. I tuck it under her feet.

"Thanks." She leans back. "Want me to read it to you?"

"Let's see if you're as good at reading aloud as I am." I'd read her the first three books of the Anne of Green Gables series when she was little. I promised her one page for every half hour she left me alone. Once I had to go two hours. By the time I finished the third, she was old enough to read the rest on her own. I did the same for Quincy—without the condition, of course.

"Learned from the best." Drew sinks into the couch.

On a morning early in April, Tomoe and Chizuru hung laundry on the line. Yamabuki had woken up vomiting and was still in bed.

"I hope she isn't sick," Tomoe said. "I will not go near her today."

"Tomoe." Her mother pulled Yamabuki's pants from the clean laundry, her expression excited. "Did Yamabuki have her blood this month?"

Tomoe touched the clothes to see if they were dry yet. "How should I know?"

"You're her lady-in-waiting."

Tomoe made a dismissive noise. "Hardly. She doesn't show me her rags." Though Tomoe cared little about blood, Yamabuki was too embarrassed to let Tomoe help her with such things. Truth be told, Tomoe was glad not to be bothered. Her menses did not appear as regularly as a full moon, like Yamabuki's. Today Tomoe's sides felt as if they had been sliced with a dull sword, and the rags she had pushed into herself to stop the flow needed to be changed three times an hour. On days like this, Chizuru usually let Tomoe rest and made sure she had extra protein to compensate for the blood loss. But Chizuru, as was usual now, thought only of Yamabuki.

"I see nothing. No spots. No rags." Chizuru threw the wet laundry into the basket. Tomoe followed her mother to the house. A suspicion presented itself, a rising jealousy, but she tamped it down.

Chizuru went straight to Yamabuki, who lay on her side, a wooden bucket nearby. "Get on your back," Chizuru commanded. Yamabuki turned, her mouth tight and her face green.

"Leave me alone," she moaned.

Chizuru opened Yamabuki's kimono and felt the girl's flat stomach, pressing her fingertips gently below the navel. Yamabuki stifled a dry heave. "Tomoe, feel," Chizuru said.

Tomoe felt. Her fingers encountered something of medium firmness, the size of a small pear. "What is it?"

"Her womb has enlarged," Chizuru said softly.

Yamabuki wiped at her mouth. "Are you sure that's not my stomach?"

"Pregnant," Chizuru pronounced. She closed the kimono. "I'd say about two months."

Jealousy and joy stormed one another in Tomoe's chest. Why Yamabuki? Tomoe and Yoshinaka had been together countless times. If Tomoe had a baby, though she was a concubine and not the first wife, it, too, would be a legal heir. She longed to see Yoshinaka hold their baby son in his arms. He would love a child from her as much as one from Yamabuki, she was sure of it.

Yamabuki closed her eyes and turned over. Tomoe stood over her, waiting for a response. Her back cramped unpleasantly. "Are you not pleased?"

"Leave me alone," Yamabuki said, her voice high and muffled.

"If I were you, I would be very happy," Tomoe said.

"You are not me," Yamabuki cried. "Yoshinaka is such a demon, I would not be surprised if his spawn clawed its way out of my womb. It is probably spitting fire in there now, causing me these pains."

Tomoe's jealousy evaporated, replaced by shock. It had never occurred to her that Yamabuki didn't enjoy Yoshinaka's attentions the same way Tomoe did. If Yoshinaka heard his wife's words, Tomoe wouldn't be surprised if he did turn into a demon and have the girl killed. Such an insult from a wife to a husband was unthinkable, and invited misfortune.

Chizuru paled, too. "You are asking for bad luck, Yamabuki. If you welcome this pregnancy, perhaps your body won't be sick."

Yamabuki did not answer.

Tomoe took her mother's hand. "Let's go finish the laundry. She will come around."

Yamabuki spent all of that spring and most of the summer carrying the bucket with her wherever she went. Though it didn't seem possible, she became thinner, her ribs sticking out even as her belly grew large. She began refusing to leave the house, saying she was too ill and weak. She no longer played music or helped with the chores. And when Yamabuki recited poetry, she chose the most desolate passages Tomoe could imagine. Her voice no longer sounded like bells, but was breathy and labored.

One night, Yamabuki recited a piece from the ninth-century poet Komachi Ono.

"In this world I am the shadow
Unseen, barely felt
And still at night, as I sleep
I am but
the invisible wind"

Tomoe thought the words beautiful, but the way Yamabuki said them made her soul ache. "What does it mean?"

Yamabuki paused. "It means that self-loathing is terrible, I suppose. If even in your dreams, you hate yourself."

"I don't hate myself," Tomoe said at once. But Yamabuki did, she thought. The idea felt strange. "Neither should you."

Yamabuki bowed her head. "I find it comforting, don't you?"

Tomoe pushed away the sadness and forced a cheerful smile onto her face. She slapped her thigh to jar the air. "You should not examine your life too closely. It makes you unhappy, Yamabuki."

"You, Tomoe, do not understand the point of poetry," Yamabuki replied, and stretched out on her sleeping mat.

Eleven

Y*ou don't know what you are.* Yamabuki's words to Tomoe echo through me.

It's the next morning, and I've just taken Chase to school and come back home to straighten up before Laura gets here for our meeting. Of course, I stopped mid-vacuum to read the Tomoe Gozen book. Laura won't mind a bit of dust.

I finish reading the passage about Tomoe's softening toward Yamabuki. Would it be possible for them to be friends? I can't imagine being generous in a similar situation, but since I don't live during that era, I can't say for sure. It would be more of a benefit if Tomoe and Yamabuki could learn from each other, I think.

My phone's light blinks and I pick it up. An e-mail from my father's attorney.

IN THE FUTURE, PLEASE DIRECT ALL CORRESPONDENCE FOR

KILLIAN SNOW TO ME.

Just like I thought. I'm mad at myself for a second, for even daring to hope. I imagine Quincy's face falling when I tell her, the mask of indifference she'll put on. "It doesn't matter," she'll say. Like Drew and I always did whenever we had to. Damn him for hurting my kid. Damn me for not protecting her.

The box that held *Sisters of Heart* sits on the family room floor next to a basket of clean towels. I realize I never sorted all those childhood mementos Mom stored in the box. I unsnap the lid and begin taking items out. Three small square photos, maybe three-by-three, fall from between the spelling bee certificate and report cards. Old ones I've never seen, the kind printed on heavy cardboard, pre-1970s, certainly.

I sit on the floor to look through them. Mom never showed us old photos. Other households had album after album full of snapshots. My father had a framed photo of his parents on his desk at work, two gimlet-eyed immigrants in flannel coats, dead long before I came along. Their mystery would likely never be solved, and with the way my father's treated me over the years, I never cared to investigate.

But these.

These are Japanese people. My mother's family? A young girl, around age eight. The black-and-white image is stark and printed on heavy board. It has to be Mom. I trace the Cupid's-bow lips, the heart-shaped face, so dark there appears to be no differentiation between the iris and the pupil, so they look solid black. Hikari. I flip it over, scrutinizing the Japanese letters. I think I recognize the symbols from other things Mom had with her name on them. I'll take it to Joseph to be sure.

I study the other two photos. A picture of what must be Mom's Japanese hometown, Mom in a schoolgirl's uniform, standing with a couple who must be her parents. And one more: a portrait of my very young-looking mother, when she was perhaps no more than twenty, holding a baby girl about six months old. Mom's eyes are shining and large. The baby has adorable chubby cheeks and reaches toward the camera.

Who is this baby? A cousin? The child of a friend? Or maybe Mom had brothers and sisters I don't know about. It could be anyone. I put the photos back, but my hands won't release them. I drop them and call Joseph.

. . .

Mid-morning, Laura comes over to discuss my father. I make a fresh pot of coffee, and we settle down in the living room, her briefcase spilling paperwork out across the coffee table. Drew's already left for her coffee date.

Laura claps her hands together. Her fingernails are polished a bright, authoritative red. If I hadn't known her for so long, she'd be intimidating. "I'm filing a response to your father's petition, and I need you to sign the forms." She points with her pen. "I've explained how your mother chose this particular place and how she is entitled to spend '*his*' money, because she's his wife and not his slave." Rolling her eyes, she hands me her pen. "The hearing's set for the Wednesday after Thanksgiving. I'll be out of town for the next couple of weeks, but I'll be back in time for that."

Just three more weeks. I hold the nib above the signature line. My father will tell the judge I tricked my mother into signing over her rights. That I'm using her to get back at him. The judge won't know how Killian treated my mother or me. If you've got food and shelter and clothing, it's very difficult to prove that anything's amiss. "What if the judge agrees with him?"

Laura purses her lips. "I'm not going to lie, Rachel. If the judge agrees with him, Killian can move your mother wherever he pleases. He can also ban you from seeing her."

I put the pen down, add cream to my coffee, and stir it into a cloud. My pulse beats in my ears and my breathing sounds shallow. I take a sip, feeling the hot liquid in my throat.

Laura touches my arm. She has a determined set to her jaw. "Have you found out anything else about this secret your father was talking about?"

"No." The coffee rises back into my throat, burning it. Once again I imagine Mom stuck in the sub-par nursing home, sitting in her own waste, decaying without anyone noticing and me not being able to do a thing about it. "Maybe we should try to compromise," I say desperately. "I don't want to not be able to see her. Isn't there something we can do?"

Laura raises an eyebrow. She's of what she describes as Slavic peasant farmer descent: solid, tall, reliable. I'm reminded for a moment of Tomoe. Like the character in Mom's book, Laura is a fighter. "Rachel, I can ask if he'll talk to you. But my impression is that your father wants what he wants."

"But what if we lose?" My voice is weak. I glance into the backyard, at the leaves floating on top of the pool. If I look directly at Laura, I'm afraid I'll burst into tears.

"We haven't crossed that bridge yet." Laura pokes the pen into my hand.

I think about *Sisters of Heart*. I have to find out why Mom wanted me to have it. Why my name is in it. Talk to her about it, before my father cuts me out of her life. Again.

I sign the papers.

A blue Toyota pulls up outside, parking on the street. I stand up so fast my head spins. Quincy and Ryan. "What's she doing here?" I wonder aloud. I glance at the clock. Ten-thirty. "She has class."

Laura raises her eyebrows as she takes in Ryan walking up the path. "That's the guy she's known for five minutes that she's going to marry?" I nod. "Can't say I blame her."

"Shush." I shove at her playfully. She laughs, zips up her briefcase.

"I'll call you soon. And Rachel—try not to worry." Laura opens the front door.

"Hey." Quincy exchanges pleasantries with Laura and introduces her to Ryan.

"What's up?" She never comes down here midweek. Too much going on.

"I've been cold at night lately. So I thought I'd get that quilt Obāchan made." Quincy smiles at me brightly.

"It's pretty big for your dorm bed." I look at my daughter, her shining hair in the morning light.

"I still want it. Is that a crime?" Quincy threads her hand through Ryan's. He looks terribly tired, his face drawn and thin.

I peer into his face. "You okay, Ryan?"

He nods. "Working a lot."

"You should be sleeping if you have the day off."

"I'm spending the day with Quincy," he says, and Quincy squeezes his hand.

"Don't worry. My classes are under control."

Whatever. She's ditching. I bite my tongue against the lecture about skipping the class we've paid for and just motion to her. "It's in my closet, I think."

We head upstairs into the master bedroom, and I slide open the mirrored door. I know exactly where it is—on the highest shelf. I point. "All the way up there in the space bag, behind the other blankets." Ryan reaches up and moves everything easily. He's helpful to have around, I have to admit. Strong—and tall. He gets down the heavy space bag and hands it to me. I put it on the bed and unzip it. This one is Chase's, blue and white. Quincy's is yellow and blue. "There should be another one up there."

Ryan puts his hand on the shelf and feels around. "I can't find the other one. It must be way in there." He gets the small wooden-backed chair from the corner of the room and steps up; peering into the depths of the closet, he finds another bag, slides it out, and holds it up. "Is this it?"

I take it. It's full of black material. My old wetsuits. I'd forgotten they were up there. I pull at the fabric and wonder if either one will fit anymore. I should get out there into the ocean, use these again. Maybe take Quincy with me. "Nope. See any more bags?"

He shakes his head and takes out a ring box. "This is up in here—is it supposed to be?"

I open the box. I know what's inside. A nugget of gold about the size of a gumball falls into my palm. I turn it over, feel its cold weight in my hand. Sighing, I close my fingers around it and hand it to Quincy. "Gold."

This gold represents my best memory of my father. Why I still hold a bit of hope that one day we can have at least a neutral relationship.

Once a year, during winter break, he'd take us out to the Anza-Borrego desert for a weekend. It was cold in the desert in winter, a fact most people didn't realize, especially at night. But I loved the hotel where we stayed. We stayed in a casita with its own small kidney-shaped pool, heated with solar panels. I stayed in the water nearly all day, emerging only to run into the warm room.

On days Dad didn't play golf, he got me up early for what he called "Desert pirate gold adventures." It was something his father used to do with him, and one of the few times Dad seemed truly enthusiastic and open. "There are still veins of gold out here," he told me, his eyes glinting with something like youth. "Still undiscovered." Mom stayed behind with Drew, who was too young to go out into the desert. It made me feel proud and important.

Usually, I followed Dad to dry riverbeds where he poked around with a pickaxe, whistling happily. Occasionally he came across a small nugget that looked like lead and held it up to the watercolor blue sky. "Wooooo!" He'd crow. I loved it. I loved how engaged he was, how I could pretend I, too, would find a huge vein of gold and make him proud.

Scraps of kindness can keep you hoping that the person will change long after you should've given up. I was like a stray dog whose owner would feed it steak or backhand it according to his mood, following my dad around, always hoping it'd be the steak.

One gray morning when I was eight, Dad drove me out farther, way past any civilization, to where the desert turned back to trees, the pebbles of the unpaved road knocking on the underside of our Mercedes's non-offroad undercarriage. We pulled over amid spiky barrel cacti, fat paddles of prickly pear, and dried-out brown waist-high shrubs. A long-haired white man waited next to an ancient rusted-out military jeep. "What are we doing, Daddy?"

"Looking for our fortune," my father said. He gave the man some cash. I suppose it was the man's land. There was no fence or building anywhere that I could see. Just outcroppings of tan house-sized boulders amid the scrubby landscape and pinkish-brown mountains in the distance. To the right a steep slope led to a gully. Here, near a faintly gurgling stream, an outcropping of bare multitrunked smoke trees grew in gray fingers toward the sky.

The man led us down the slope to the muddy wash. I clung to Dad's hand, my feet slipping in the loose dirt, moving through the clumps of dried-out sage bushes and the sumac with crimson-tinted winter leaves. The creek water moved slowly, so shallow I could see every stone beneath.

"Go ahead, now," the man said. "I'm entitled to half of what you find."

He and my dad started talking about mineral rights, how most people who owned land didn't own the mineral rights as well. That meant if you found gold or oil in your yard, it belonged to the municipality. "It isn't right," Dad said, and the man clucked in agreement. "But this man here's smart," Dad said, turning to me. "He bought all this with the mineral rights attached."

I stared up at the other man, wide-eyed. "Have you found oil here?"

"Not yet." The man chuckled, and lit a stinky cigar. "Haven't looked in every inch of dirt, though."

"When I was a boy, out with my father, I found a big chunk of gold in this very area," Dad told me. Taking my hand, he led me forward. We waded into the stream, the water flowing around our rubber boots, Dad moving his metal detector in slow arcs. "My father took it from me and promised he'd make the house payment. The next thing I knew, he'd drunk and gambled it away."

"Gold makes men do evil things. You can't even trust your own father with it." The old man leaned toward me. Sour breath. "You hear that? If you find gold, hide it from your old man."

I wanted to get away from him. "Can I try?" I asked my father. To my surprise, he handed me the detector. I walked downstream as my father continued talking. The water was silty, the tossed cloudy sand covering smooth round rocks. I peered ahead. The gully where we stood was covered in smooth rocks three times the width of the water. Farther on, the boulders formed walls. It would be difficult to climb out of here. "Is this whole thing a riverbed?" I called back.

The old man nodded. "Yep. We get lots of flash floods."

I glanced up at the sky nervously. "Is that why the rocks are so smooth? From the water?"

"Exactly right." Dad grinned. The wind whipped his gray hair around his head.

I moved the metal detector back and forth across the sand. Nothing. I pursed my lips and kept walking forward, out of the water altogether, toward the big boulders. Overhead, rain clouds thickened, and I thought I heard distant thunder. I ignored it. My metal detector beeped.

"I found something!" I shouted.

The old man limped over and tossed me a spade. "Dig."

I strained to move a large purplish-gray rock partially buried in the hard earth. My father watched, his arms crossed, a faint smile on his face. The same expression he got when his football team was winning on television. Finally I managed to use the shovel as a lever and pry the rock up, pushing it with my foot.

"Nothing there," the old man said.

A scorpion, so pale it was almost translucent, emerged. I screamed and jumped back. The old man stomped it. I looked up at my father, who was staring at the sky. I worried he'd yell at me in the car for giving up. A jittery feeling took hold of my stomach. I held the detector over the spot and again it beeped. The soil was looser with the rock gone. I used the spade to feel around, digging about a foot farther down, until the metal edge of the shovel touched another rock. A small one, less than half the size of a meatball. With my other hand, I snatched it out.

It was a round piece of gold.

"Let me see that." The old man grabbed my wrist with his leathery fingers. "Placer gold. Not bad."

"I found gold!" I shouted up to my father. "Gold!"

"Good job, Rachel!" Dad shouted back.

The old man licked his lips. "Don't forget, I get half."

"It's a small piece, Ralph," Dad said. "I did pay you."

"Half," Ralph said.

I clutched the gold in my hand. How could they break this in half?

"Let me see it," Dad said. I handed it over. He pursed his lips. He looked at me, then took out his wallet and gave Ralph what seemed to my eyes like an enormous stack of bills. "That ought to take care of it."

"I don't know," Ralph said doubtfully. "Gold's worth more these days."

Dad handed him another bill. This one had Benjamin Franklin on it. My heart fluttered.

"Well then." Ralph tipped his hat to us. "If you'll excuse me, I've got to get to the grocer's." With that, Ralph limped back toward his jeep, stomping over the scrub bushes. He revved the engine and took off, sending a cloud of dust up behind him.

Dad ruffled my hair. "Let's get back to work, then. Rachel, you've got a nose for this, just like your old man."

We spent the rest of the morning looking for gold, stopping only after a sudden noon downpour. "We'd better get out," Dad said, loading me into the car. "There might be a flood."

I leaned over the seat as we drove away, the gold in my hand. I felt bad that he had paid Ralph so much money.

"You want this gold, Daddy? You can have it."

"It's yours, Rachel." He grinned at me in the rearview mirror. "I'm not my old man."

Now, sitting together in my old bedroom, I tell Quincy and Ryan the story. Quincy's eyes widen as she passes the gold to Ryan. "I never knew that. You never tell us anything about your family. Especially not about your dad."

This stings. A lot. I cough to hide my distress. "I tell you as much as you need to know. And how much do you tell me about you?" I ask. "You quit volleyball and didn't mention it."

She crosses her arms and looks down. "Enough to keep you off my back, I suppose."

Ryan laughs, handing the gold back to Quincy. "My mother would have a heart attack if she knew about all the crap my brothers and I pulled when we were teenagers. She says she's better off not knowing."

A pang hits my chest. How well do I know my children? How well do they know me? Perhaps Ryan's mother is wise. My children don't need to know the troubling nitty-gritty of my late teen years. It will only disturb them. All they know is that my father was very strict, and didn't like my choices early on. Which is all true.

Do I really need to know every bit of trouble or fun Quincy gets into? I'm her mother, not her confessor. But shouldn't we be getting to know each other as friends now? Isn't this the time? Especially since she's getting married.

Quincy gives me the nugget. "I didn't know your dad took you mining. You should tell us more stuff. I like your stories."

My hands feel cold suddenly, though it's warm.

Maybe that father with the gold is still inside my current-day father, someplace. I look directly at Quincy. "Killian can't make it to the wedding. He'll be traveling."

"Oh." Quincy's gaze centers out the window.

I regard my now adult daughter, feeling like I've been punched in the stomach. My children don't know the whole story. They don't even know that my mother was a mail-order bride. I didn't want to color my kids' perception of Mom. Or me.

I smile at my oldest ruefully. "It doesn't matter. What's done is done."

A silence settles over us, thick as one of my mother's quilts. Ryan sits on the bed motionless, his eyes fluttering closed. Poor guy. A motorcycle roars past on the street below, shaking the single-paned window. After a minute or two, Quincy clears her throat. "We should be going."

I look at her and realize she'll probably never sleep under my roof again by herself. Everything's changed. "If you want to come over this weekend, we could take you guys out to dinner with Aunt Drew."

Quincy hesitates, nudges Ryan.

"I was just resting my eyes." He moves his shoulders noncommittally. "Don't you have a paper due?" he asks, yawning. I hope Quincy drives them home.

"Yeah," Quincy echoes, her voice going strange. "A paper."

"In what subject?" I ask. "Is there something wrong?"

"History. It's just a big project, and I need to get started." She smiles her sweetest at me, showing deep dimples on both sides of her mouth. "I'll see you later, Mom. Come on, Ryan."

"Bye, Mrs. Perrotti." Ryan lifts his hand to me, following Quincy out.

She's never sounded like that about a paper before. Quincy's not a procrastinator—ever since third grade, she's tackled projects as soon as they were assigned. I go to the window and watch them walk down the driveway. An uncomfortable ache settles in my gut, but I can't tell whether it's my too-sensitive Mommy instinct or because I wish she'd stay with me. Probably both.

Ryan feels my eyes on him and turns, waves.

Drew arrives at the coffee shop five minutes early. The place Alan picks isn't corporate-owned. It's called Lestat's (like the vampire, Drew remembers), and it's near Balboa Park, in a neighborhood Drew's not familiar with. When she was growing up, the area was rough and nobody she knew went down here unless they wanted to buy sex toys or illegal drugs, but now it's gentrified and populated with hipsters carting around MacBooks.

She finds it readily enough, though. It's decorated with hanging crystal chandeliers and gold-painted chairs, comfortable couches, fabulous velvet thrones of carved wood. Glass cases of elaborate pastries glisten. Drew's mouth waters. Is it too early for a slice of cheesecake?

She doesn't see Alan yet, so she orders her latte and a slice of cheesecake, and, in case Alan doesn't like cheesecake, a Danish. The debit card goes through without a hitch, causing a pang to appear in Drew's gut. Killian's money is paying for those pastries.

He wants her to talk to Rachel, but Drew won't. First and last and in between, he can't treat their mother like a milking cow past her prime and sent to slaughter. He just can't. It's not fair.

Not that anybody ever thinking something's not fair has changed it.

The door jingles and Alan appears. Right on time. He'd told her the library opened late today, not until noon, so he has this whole morning free. "Drew! Good to see you." He smiles at her and, though he's British—aren't they supposed to be terribly standoffish?—and she only just met him, he gives her a quick hug when she stands. The kind of hug any friend would use. But she also notices how his shoulders feel under his argyle sweater vest. Strong, but not jacked-up.

"Find the place all right?" He sits down across from her. He looks a tiny bit tired around his eyes.

"Definitely. No problem." She smiles, feeling shy, points at the pastries. "I didn't know what you like."

"Oooh. Cheesecake." His cheeks dimple. "I'm sorry I didn't arrive before you. I owe you a coffee."

"You were right on time." Drew sips her latte. The barista has drawn a heart in the foam. Her ears color. It's like they're in a musical. Either of them might burst into song. Like she'd done at the library. Except she didn't bring an instrument, and her singing voice is only adequate.

"My girls were dawdling this morning. Took Audrey fifteen minutes to find one shoe." Alan shakes his head. "She put it in the pantry, of all places. Behind the flour bin."

Drew's heart drops to the floor. "Little girls?"

Alan nods. "Lauren and Audrey. Ages four and three." He digs out his phone and lights up a picture. "Here."

Two little blond girls with cherubic faces beam out. They're eating ice cream cones almost as big as their heads. Drew can't help but smile. "They're adorable."

"Yes." He pockets the phone. "You know, Drew, that viola was amazing. Magical."

Drew takes in another deep breath. So. This coffee is just a coffee. To repay her for the bet. She takes the spoon and swirls the heart away. "Thanks."

"Some of the children have asked if you give lessons." Alan laces his fingers together.

"I've never thought about it." And she hasn't. She's not usually in contact with kids, so it hadn't occurred to her. It might be kind of fun. She wonders how quickly she can find students, if she'll need insurance. She smiles to herself. Rachel would be proud of her for thinking so responsibly.

He lets out a sigh. "Well. I need a coffee. Would you like anything else? Fruit tart? Flask of whiskey?"

Drew shakes her head. "I'm good."

She watches Alan walk up to the register. His corduroy pants make that whisk-whisk noise. Drew's always liked that sound. She had a pair when she was little. And they're hugging him rather well. Is he married? She hates to say it, because Alan seems like a genuinely nice guy and she already enjoys his company, and maybe she's a totally unevolved immature person, but she can't be just friends with him if he's taken. She won't be able to stop thinking about touching his smooth shaved face, what it would be like to put her mouth on his. Asking for trouble. Her phone buzzes with a text.

Jonah.

Haven't heard back from you. Decision?

She puts the phone away. Maybe she ought to go back to L.A. Rachel has things more or less under control. Laura will take care of the legal stuff. Drew shakes her head, remembering what Rachel said. Basically, her sister is letting her stay here to lick her wounds. Because Rachel feels sorry for jobless Drew. She won't abuse her sister's goodwill.

Besides, Rachel could call her anytime and Drew would come right back down. Maybe if she works with Jonah again, she won't have to touch her father's money. She'll give it to Quincy for a wedding present. The thought makes Drew feel better about the situation.

She'll put everything all right.

Alan comes back with a fruit tart anyway, and a cup of steaming coffee. Not tea, Drew notes. "I'll take the leftovers home to my girls. Don't worry." He puts in two Splenda and a ton of cream.

Drew laces her fingers around the cup and decides to be direct. "Do you take care of the girls by yourself?"

Alan takes a sip. He looks down at the fruit tart. He coughs a little, his face screwing up in distress, then has a little coughing fit that he can't stop.

"Are you okay?" Drew asks. Should she pound his back?

Alan gives a final cough, sniffles. "Excuse me. That coffee went down the wrong way." He tries to smile, but his eyes don't. When he speaks, it's soft, almost apologetic. "Sophia, my wife, is no longer with us."

"Oh." Drew sits up ramrod straight and puts her hand on his arm. He nods, no emotion at all on his face, and somehow Drew knows he's used to this question. Used to not reacting. Not crying. "I'm so sorry."

He digs into the cheesecake. "Of course—you'd wonder. With the girls. Silly of me. I always forget to say it." He waves his hand around. "Not that I do this very often. As you can see, I'm a complete imbecile at dating."

Drew allows herself a small smile even as she feels his sorrow for his late wife. So this is a date. But his girls are so awfully young. "When did she . . ." She's reluctant to say it.

"Three years. She passed away when our littlest was born. Childbirth." He takes another bite of cheesecake.

"I'm so sorry," Drew says again. She feels a surge of sympathy. And admiration, for raising two little girls who seem so obviously happy. "Are you here all by yourself? Do you have family?"

"Sophia's parents live here." He sips his coffee. "And I thought it would be important for them to know their mother's family. So we stay here. We've visited my family."

"Do you miss England?" Drew tries to imagine England. She's never been. All she can think of is a photo of a library at Oxford, and the Tower of London.

He takes another bite of cheesecake. "I don't miss the weather, honestly." He closes his eyes. "And I'd certainly miss this cheesecake. Have you tried it? It should be outlawed."

"Well, maybe we should vote Bloomberg mayor and he can outlaw cheesecake here like he did soda in New York." Drew smiles.

"Yes. Only bite-sized pieces should be allowed. Actually, I'll get another piece to take home, otherwise I'll feel too guilty that the girls didn't try it."

"You know, I make a pretty wicked cheesecake. I'll make you one sometime." Drew likes baking. She's better at cakes than she is at regular food.

"Oh. Perhaps I won't bother with this, then." He chews on the cheesecake and smiles, his eyes truly crinkling this time. She can already tell his true smile. Warmth floods through her. She wants him to smile. Drew digs her fork in next to where his just was and lifts it to her mouth.

MIYANOKOSHI FORTRESS
SHINANO PROVINCE
HONSHU, JAPAN
Summer 1177

One day in late July, Tomoe came into the house from cooking breakfast. Yamabuki moaned as the light hit her face. "Close the door!"

Tomoe could not stand another second of this nonsense. She left the door open. The day was fine. It wasn't too humid or too hot. The pregnancy was going well now—the girl was perfectly healthy. She needed fresh air. "Get up, Yamabuki. You missed breakfast." Tomoe refused to bring Yamabuki food—she figured the girl would get hungry enough to rouse herself. But this was the second day she'd stayed in bed. Chizuru had made her drink hot fish broth last night.

"I am too tired." Yamabuki still had her eyes closed.

"If I could have the baby for you," Tomoe said, "I would." She touched Yamabuki's belly, imagining the life was inside Tomoe instead.

A great clattering, shouts, and then the gong sounded. Arrows fell from the sky as abruptly as a sudden downpour. Attack. Tomoe stood up and shut the door quickly. She strapped on her arrows and sword.

"What is it?" Yamabuki pushed herself upright.

Tomoe handed her a dagger. "Stay in here. Bolt the door. Don't come out no matter what."

"And if they come in?" Yamabuki trembled like a tear balanced on the end of a nose.

Tomoe regarded her silently for a moment. "End it with honor. *Jigai.*" *Jigai* referred to the female method of suicide. A woman used the long-bladed *kaiken* to deliver a quick cut to her jugular. *Jigai* was preferable to being raped or hauled off like a bag of rice.

Yamabuki calmed. She nodded.

Tomoe slid the door closed and heard it bolt. The rain of arrows had stopped. Yoshinaka's men were engaged all over the grounds—mostly concentrated at the gate, as they tried to hold off the forces. Taira. These were no better than raiders, Tomoe thought. Kiyomori Taira would love to weaken the Minamoto by doing away with Yoshinaka and his power.

Tomoe ran across the yard, whistling for Cherry Blossom. Almost without stopping, Tomoe grabbed a hank of mane and pulled herself onto the horse.

The enemy had gotten inside somehow. She chased down a samurai on a brown stallion. A beautiful animal. Tomoe wanted to spare it.

The samurai shouted, noticing Tomoe too late. Tomoe brought back her sword and swung it forward, feeling the contact of metal connecting to bone reverberating through her hands.

His head fell cleanly onto the ground, its mouth moving in some silent prayer.

Yoshinaka picked up the head Tomoe had cut off and held it aloft by the black hair. Already the skin was turning an unnatural blue. "The next head I hold will be Kiyomori Taira's!" he shouted, and threw the head into the crowd.

Tomoe's stomach lurched.

"Tomoe?" Her brother trotted up beside her. Kanehira's face was filthy, covered in a mixture of brown and red and black splotches whose origins Tomoe didn't want to know. "Where's Yamabuki? Some enemies may have gotten around us. Didn't you stay to protect her?" He was accusing. And rightly.

"Inside." Tomoe began moving toward the building, her brother following with raspy breath. "Are you hurt?" she said to him.

"Of course not," Kanehira snapped. He took an especially deep breath.

Yamabuki's door was open. Just inside, the girl knelt in the shaft of light, staring out into nothing. She held the bloody dagger, and red covered her front in a thick dark wash.

Tomoe's breathing stopped, her brother thudding into her back. Yamabuki did not move. Tomoe froze in place, watching, waiting for the girl's chest to rise.

Yamabuki was still.

Twelve

fter Alan bids Drew good-bye, she sits there in the coffee shop a while longer. She ought to go to Rachel's and look for a job on the computer. Instead she remembers a local music shop where she used to buy sheet music, and where she'd taken viola many moons ago.

It's in Pacific Beach. Drew doesn't know if it's still there. They sold sheet music and rented instruments and provided lessons in small rooms in a basement. This is also where Quincy and Chase took cello and violin lessons. Drew doesn't know if they still do. She hasn't thought to ask. All she has are broad overviews of the children's lives.

Well, she'll always ask in the future.

The store's not there. A small dive shop is in its place. Drew parks in front of it. Nothing's the same, she thinks. What did she expect? That the world would stop while she lived her life?

Kind of. Because being back here makes her feel like she's a fifteen-year-old girl again, still stuck in a difficult relationship with her mother, standoffish from her father.

She walks in the store anyway.

An assortment of snorkeling masks and signs proclaiming "Scuba Lessons" line the walls. Rachel used to go in the ocean often—her high school swim team sometimes trained out there, meeting in the early hours to swim in a formation.

When Drew was ten and Rachel fourteen, her father took them to Honolulu on a business trip. Their mother came along, though she hated the sun, and spent her time on the beach covered in a gigantic hat and a man's long-sleeved shirt.

Killian took them to Hanauma Bay on Oahu, a protected cove southeast of Honolulu. Once used by ancient Hawaiians for fish farming, it now holds a protected coral reef that serves as a natural barrier, populated with plenty of colorful fish for tourists to admire. They rented snorkel equipment on the beach and headed out.

There were fish everywhere in the knee-deep water, and Rachel and Drew had been content with sticking their faces in and watching the bright pink-and-green parrot fish eat frozen peas out of their hands (which you weren't allowed to do anymore).

Killian kicked water at them. "Come on. We're going out to see the real fish. This area's for babies." He dove in and began swimming, the big black flippers splashing.

The girls didn't protest, but followed mutely. Rachel held on to Drew's hand tight; Drew wasn't as strong a swimmer. They wove through a flock of Japanese tourists in black full-body wetsuits, others with pasty white tourist legs eggbeating underwater.

Killian swam over the coral reef wall that was only inches below the surface. You had to swim against the waves to get over the wide reef, into the open bay. Rachel let go of Drew's hand so they could both hang on to the coral. You weren't supposed to touch it—both to preserve nature and because it was sharp in places. The coral scratched her bare stomach, stinging it, drawing blood. She raised her head out of the water, clearing her snorkel, and saw that her father and Rachel were already on the other side of the coral. Rachel waved.

She also saw the gaps, marked with flags, where you could swim through the coral unobstructed. If only they had thought to look first. A wave hit her in the face, washed over her head. She couldn't get there. Drew's first instinct was to cry. But she couldn't. She gritted her teeth, determined.

Then Rachel was at her side again, grabbing her hand. "Come on. Let's go in," she said, and pulled Drew to shore.

It's funny, Drew thinks. At the time, she felt scared. Panicked. But as she remembers it, the first feeling she recalls is the thrill. Her sister helping her. How she didn't cry, and how brave that made her feel.

She wants to do something that'll make her feel that way again.

She plunks down her credit card and points to a basic mask and snorkel set. "Two of those, please."

Joseph waits for me outside a coffee shop in a strip mall near the bookstore Tom and I frequent. I walk as fast as I can through the parking lot, carrying the plastic box. "Are those the pictures?" He eyes them doubtfully. "We should get you a better box. This kind of plastic isn't good for prints."

"I'll worry about that later." I hand over the photos. "There's Japanese writing on the back. I'm hoping they're names."

"I had a colleague look at the samurai book." Joseph opens the plastic box with a click and peers inside. He looks up at me. "I'm afraid it won't get you onto *Antiques Roadshow*. It's from the early twentieth century, we think. The prints are just reproductions."

I sit down. "I'd never sell the book anyway." Perhaps the woman who sent my mother the book inherited it from her family. Whatever the truth is, I keep expecting Joseph to translate a sentence that reads, "Here is my big secret . . ." But of course there is nothing so obvious. We string together pieces to make a narrative.

I rest my chin on my hand and watch Joseph study the printing. These photos might tell me what I need to know, but they don't look like they're pertinent to what my father said about having something to tell that could harm my mother.

Joseph pushes his glasses back up his nose. From his laptop briefcase, he produces a pen and some address-sized labels in a plastic sleeve marked ARCHIVAL.

I get him a coffee as he begins taking out photos, labeling each one. I notice he's looking at the picture with the baby, turning it over in his hands, and I can barely keep myself from jumping out of line to ask him what he's learned. When I return, I pick up the photo of my mother with the baby, turning it over to read the label. *With Yoshimi.*

"That's it?" I say, turning the photo over again as if I've missed something. I squint at the woman. I've never seen a photo of my mother when she was in her twenties, so maybe she looked different—I'd just assumed it was my mother. "Could it be her sister, and the baby's my mother's niece?" I guess.

Joseph places his cup down carefully, away from the photos. "It only has her name."

Who is Yoshimi? I'll have to take it to my mother. Her lucid moments are increasingly random, but I have to be optimistic. My phone tells me it's already four o'clock. I won't have time today. I gulp my coffee, burning my taste buds. The pain shocks me back to reality. "The others?"

He hands me the photo of the young woman with my mother. "This is her mom, all right. Emiko. And her father, Jun."

"Okay." I'm waiting for more. There seemed to be a lot of writing on the back for just names. But Joseph only shrugs.

"The others don't tell us much, either. *A pretty fall day. Hatsuko and friends.* Things like that." He finishes labeling and puts his pen away. "I'll send you more of the translated story tonight. What do you think so far?"

Mentally, I replay parts of Tomoe Gozen, and how she had to obey Yoshinaka at all costs. "I don't think I could have coped in her place. They treated women like chattel." I trail off, unable to imagine it. "I wish that Tomoe and Yamabuki would leave that place, leave Yoshinaka."

He peers closely at me. "You only exist in the time in which you're born. We can't impose our modern viewpoint to disparage her choices. It's like armchair quarterbacking, nine centuries later."

I sit back, heat on my face. He was right. Do any of us, even today, have unlimited choices? I certainly have the privilege of many options—but I concede that some paths are closed to me, due to my age.

Joseph continues. "Anyway, like I said, even some scholars think Tomoe was a legend. Exaggerated for dramatic effect."

I blow on my coffee. "I think she was real." I want to point to Tomoe and say, "Look at what this woman did—you cannot dismiss her accomplishments." Disappointment wells up in me as I consider the possibility that Tomoe is only a story. As mythical as Athena. I shake it off. "What does it matter if Tomoe is history or fiction, if her story feels true? If it teaches us something we need to know?"

Joseph opens his coffee lid, pours in sugar. "You're getting a lot out of it." He smiles.

I think about the years the story encompasses. Seventeen so far. "They spent a long time doing basically nothing while they geared up for the war."

"But that's life, right? Occasionally, interesting things happen, but mostly it's just day-to-day living." Joseph spreads his hand out to encompass the coffee shop. "Even famous heroes don't spend every day in battle. Look at Odysseus. Ten years getting home, and maybe five big things happened. It's just that people like to skip over the other parts."

I tilt my head. "So, do you have any other books about the culture or Japanese history I can look at?"

He writes a few down for me. "You're getting into this. Catching the history fever."

This is true. I haven't been so enthusiastic about learning anything since I was pregnant with Quincy and read all those terrible pregnancy books that told you every possible thing that could go wrong. Or maybe that one year when I learned how to decorate cakes, made frosting roses and disguised pound cake and ice cream cones as a castle for Chase's tenth birthday. I thought I was just doing this for my mother, but I realize—it's mostly for me. "I guess so," I say.

· · ·

Later that afternoon, Drew crosses the field by the local rec center, heading to the pool to watch Chase's water polo game. This afternoon a group in Renaissance knight costumes, complete with armor and swords, spar next to soccer practices and a dog agility class, as they often do at this community park. Drew wonders how they don't all collide.

She stops for a moment to look at two sparring knights, clanking their broadswords together, unsteady in their armor, holding their shields in their free hands. Rachel, in her research, told her that the samurai sword was lighter and supposedly stronger than these types of swords, that the samurai sword had one edge for cutting and one edge for defending, so they didn't need a shield.

Tomoe Gozen, with her lighter sword and greater skills, could conquer all of them. First she'd shoot them with her arrows, then she'd leap off her horse and fight them, hand-to-hand.

Rachel said that once a year, the Renaissance people hold a festival with welders and sword demonstrations and roasted turkey legs, and everyone speaks in fake English accents. Drew pictures her whole family dressing up like samurai, pulling up in the minivan, and challenging the Renaissance people. Like one of those TV shows, *Who Would Win? Samurai or Knight?*

She enters the pool deck and finds a seat on the metal bleachers in the front row. From here, all the water polo players look the same. Chase's team has dark green swim caps and the other team has blue. The goalies wear red caps. Finally Drew locates Chase and keeps her gaze fixed on him as the game begins.

The players throw the yellow ball around—it's like soccer played in the water, as far as Drew can tell. Chase has the ball when an opposing player jumps on his back, clinging to his neck like a monkey, and Drew stands up, her heart pounding. "Is that allowed?" she asks the mother sitting nearest to her.

The woman shrugs. "It's a rough sport. Kids have to be tough."

Chase throws the ball to another teammate, but still the opponent won't let up. Suddenly Chase sinks underwater. The other boy still has his head up. Drew sees the other boy's shoulder muscles straining. He's holding Chase down.

The parents murmur. *Illegal. Not allowed.* Even the woman next to Drew looks concerned. The ref doesn't seem to notice, not amid all the other activity and churning water.

"Hey!" Drew yells. She starts moving to the pool, ready to jump in.

Chase's face emerges. He takes a gasping breath and shoves the other boy away. "What the fuck?" The ref blows the whistle and points at Chase, says something Drew can't hear.

"Red card for swearing," the woman next to Drew says, shaking her head. "He's out for the game."

Chase swims to a sort of holding pen at the side.

Drew can't stand it. He's getting penalized? She opens the gate to the pool fence and walks in and over to him. His coach squats next to him. Chase has red marks around his throat and angry tears in his eyes. "Are you okay?"

Chase nods, touching near his Adam's apple. "He held me under." His voice sounds hoarse.

Drew looks at the coach, a man in his mid-twenties. "You can't let them get away with it. It's not allowed, is it?"

"Of course it's not allowed," the coach says. He looks grim. "But the ref didn't call it. You better go sit down. He's okay."

"Coach doesn't let *us* play *dirty*," Chase shouts for the other team's benefit.

The ref points at Drew. "Parents. Back in the stands."

Drew feels all the blood rush out of her head, or maybe into it. They can't hurt her nephew and ignore it. For a moment she's about to leave quietly, without a fuss. She thinks of Tomoe Gozen, of the injustice. She's not letting this pass.

Without thinking, she walks in two long strides to the ref, a man dressed all in white. "What the hell?" she asks, her voice low and tight. "That kid held him under by the neck. That's not safe. He could have died. Don't you care?"

The ref won't meet her eyes, just points to the exit. "You're ejected. Get out of here."

"You're not going to do anything?" Drew widens her eyes. True, she's never played a sport, so maybe she doesn't know what things are supposed to be like—but she's pretty sure they're not supposed to be like this.

"I'm going to have your son's team forfeit if you don't get out of here," he replies.

Drew turns and leaves the pool area, her skin tingling. Wow. Does her sister know how dangerous this sport is? "Hey, who are that kid's parents?" she calls into the stands as she goes by. "Come out and talk to me."

Nobody sitting with the other team will look at her.

Drew doesn't think she's ever lost her temper like that. Never gotten booted or shamed like that in public. She felt like she was ready to fight somebody. To defend Chase. She's never had anybody to defend like that before, just herself. She walks by the bleachers, shaking a little bit, a bit ashamed for getting kicked out. *It doesn't matter,* she tells herself. They were wrong. That ref should be ashamed, not Drew.

The woman who'd sat next to Drew grabs her arm as Drew passes, gives Drew the thumbs-up. "I would've done the same thing," she says in a low voice.

Drew looks up at the parents from Chase's side. A few give her nods, their faces set. Drew walks out to her car, her shoulders back.

N o." The syllable rose from Tomoe's throat in a shout. "Yamabuki Gozen!"

The baby, she thought. *Not the baby.*

More than this, she was surprised to find in that moment how much she wanted Yamabuki to live. She had grown fond of the girl from the south. But Yamabuki stared straight ahead, unblinking.

"I'll go get Yoshinaka," Kanehira said, turning and sprinting back toward the street.

Tomoe hardly registered his leaving. She touched the girl's face. Warm. "Yamabuki," she said, and finally Yamabuki's eyes focused and she awakened from her stupor. Tomoe sagged with relief. She looked for a wound in Yamabuki's chest, the telltale torn shirt. Nothing. Tomoe knelt beside her, searching for the source of the blood. Had she lost the baby? Tomoe should have stayed. She could have held off dozens of men by herself.

Then she saw the man behind Yamabuki, his body lying limp in the shadows. The blood ran from his head and into the flooring cracks. Dead. Tomoe put her arm around Yamabuki. "You are as brave as I thought."

Yamabuki shook her head. "I was lucky. Nothing more. I hid and attacked him from behind. He never saw me."

Their fingertips touched briefly. Now Yamabuki was bone-cold. Tomoe grasped Yamabuki's hand and looked into the younger woman's eyes. "Every woman is a tiger when she defends her child," she said softly. "And you are a mother now, so you must be a tiger always." She had to make Yamabuki and Yoshinaka's son healthy. Strong. They could be as strong as Tomoe herself. Strong enough to survive the coming war.

She stood and helped Yamabuki stand, half expecting that she would insist on lying down. To her surprise, Yamabuki stood without wavering. "I'll make tea to calm our nerves," Tomoe said. "Let's go find Chizuru and leave this mess." She offered Yamabuki her arm. The girl took it. Tomoe led her out into the mild afternoon light.

Thirteen

D rew wakes up to the sounds of cake mixers and shrieks from human children. She looks blearily at the clock. It's eight o'clock, two Saturdays before Halloween. Who could be up so early, making so much noise? Chase must have people over.

She yawns and stretches and thinks of Alan with a smile. She's going to see him again tonight for dinner. The girls' grandparents are babysitting. She wonders what she'll wear, thinks the clothes she brought are probably unsuitable. She'll ask Rachel if she can borrow something.

Last weekend, a few days after they met for coffee, they met for a drink. At least, they'd intended to meet for a drink, at a theme restaurant inside a mall. Drew blurted out the name at random—one of those restaurants where everything's fried in butter and the portions are bigger than your head. The place had been ear-splittingly noisy and crowded. Drew looked at Alan and saw a mirrored distaste on his face. Both of them laughed at the other's reaction. *Kindred spirits,* Drew thought. A quote from her favorite childhood book, *Anne of Green Gables. Oh my God, Drew, stop being so cheesy. Put it on a Hallmark card.* Alan watched her patiently. Drew blinked, shook her head. "Want to just walk around?"

He reached for her hand, squeezed it. "Certainly."

They walked to the bookstore first. "What do you like to read?" Alan asked.

Drew froze. Oh no. If she told him the truth, he'd drop her. Should she make something up? They walked past the fiction tables and Alan stopped, looking down at the titles. "I don't read too much," she said in a low, apologetic voice. Her chest felt hot.

He cocked his head, picking up a book with the back of a woman's head on the cover. "Why is that?"

She shrugged. "I honestly don't know. I used to love to read." She had the time. No kids. Rachel read more than she did—Rachel's family room walls were covered in bookcases, so many books she'd made double rows on the shelves. Drew glanced at Alan's face, but he's just reading the back of the cover. "Do you hate me now?"

Alan put the book down with a laugh. "No. I'd hate you if you'd told me proudly that you only read short articles on the Internet. I have a vested interest in making sure people read. I'm a librarian, and I'm working on a novel myself." Now he ducked his head in a shy way.

Drew stood up straight. This was interesting. "What kind of book?"

"Fantasy, actually." He smiled with his mouth closed. "I suppose you don't like fantasy. I tend to read outside of the genre myself, but for some reason I'm writing a book that's got dragons in it."

He had so much going on in his head, Drew thought. She hoped she could keep up. "Dude. Of course I do!" She took his hand. "Show me what you like to read."

They'd spent hours wandering the smallish mall, throwing pennies in a fountain and talking. Alan talked about missing England. How he'd go back if his in-laws weren't here. Drew told him about her mother and her sister and her nephew and niece. She told him about the band.

Alan whipped out his phone. "Wait. I'm purchasing your music right now." He looked up at her, the device dwarfed by his hands. "The original Out Stealing Horses, with Drew on tambourine."

"I wrote some music for that song, 'Irregular Polygon.'" Drew pointed at the screen. The band had already risen to the low hundreds in the Alternative Albums charts since their new album came out. They were doing better without her. She didn't see why Jonah wanted her back. They'd established their sound. They weren't using the song she'd completely written, anyway.

She told Alan about the possibility of rejoining the band. Alan listened thoughtfully. "I think you should do it. If only to show them."

"I don't know."

"Do you want to play with them?" They were in Target now, wandering the aisles. Drew idly picked up a bag of candy corn, chocolate. She'd never had this kind. Candy corn was Drew's favorite Halloween candy. There were two camps of people in this world: those who liked candy corn and those who didn't. One wasn't necessarily better than the other.

She shrugged, playing with the bag. "I sort of feel like I did in high school when somebody told me to join Academic Decathlon so I could put it on my college application. Like, it would be good for me, but I don't particularly want to do it." It was the first time she'd articulated these thoughts, aloud, to someone.

"Well. I guess there are always times when we have to do things we don't want to do because there are bigger things at stake." Alan took the bag of candy corn from her hands. "I would say this is not one of those times."

"It's not?"

"No." He was standing very close to her. "Have you ever heard of the Bus to Abilene?"

Drew looked at him questioningly. "Why would I want to go to Abilene?"

"It's a story. A paradox, actually. There's a group of people sitting around, and they're all bored. Finally somebody says, We should go to Abilene. And so they all get on the bus. They get there and it's not any better. Then somebody says, Whose idea was it? And they all say I thought you wanted to go. Turns out nobody wanted to go—the guy who suggested it only did it because he thought the others might be bored, not because he wanted to, really. All of them only went because somebody suggested it and nobody wanted to be the one to say no." Alan tosses the candy corn into the air. "You should only do this if you truly want to do it. Not because somebody suggested it and it seems like it'd be easy." She could smell his deodorant, a light citrusy scent that, thankfully, didn't make her sneeze. So many men made her sneeze these days. All that body spray.

Drew raised her head and looked at him. His lips curved up, then went back to neutral. "I don't want to join the band again," she admitted. "I don't know what I want to do. But it's not that."

She felt his arms go around her and she closed her eyes.

They kissed.

And then he bought her the candy corn.

Drew puts on a robe and opens the bedroom door warily. Seven or eight middle school kids are in the kitchen. There are multiple stand mixers in shades of bright orange, pink, and red, bowls, and cookie sheets arrayed on the counters, along with cookie ingredients. Chase wears a red-and-white-checked apron with a ruffle around his waist. Cinnamon and butter smells fill the air. It's like Santa's elves have invaded. "What's going on?"

Chase turns from the sink. "Bake sale."

Drew sniffs. Coffee. She stumbles over to the pot. "Does your mom know?"

"Yeah. Of course." Chase shoulders her aside to get out the egg carton. "She said not to bug you."

"What if there's a fire?" a girl with dyed black hair asks.

Drew raises an eyebrow. "Are you planning on starting a fire?"

"No. But accidents happen. That's what my mom says." The girl carefully scrapes off a cup of flour with a butter knife. It's a little under, and she scowls and dumps it out and starts all over.

The kids are of all races. Drew's never identified herself as Asian. She had a few Asian friends growing up, all American-born from families that had already been here for generations. Sometimes people asked her friends where they were from. "La Jolla," they always responded icily (and honestly). Nobody asked Drew where she was from. Her mother didn't speak of it. Claiming her Japanese heritage seemed fraudulent. Drew wonders how these kids identify themselves racially, or if they just categorize into types, like the goths and the jocks and the whatevers.

A sullen-looking boy, his light brown hair hanging over one eye, dumps the flour into the wet all at once. "It works better if you add the dry ingredients a little at a time," Drew says to him. "For next time."

"Whatever." The boy haphazardly attacks it with a wooden mixing spoon. "Whatever. It's all mixed at the end."

Drew takes the spoon out of his hand. "When you add the wet ingredients, the gluten starts developing. Your cookies will be tough. And, by mixing the dry ingredients separately, you make sure the salt and the baking soda are evenly distributed."

The boy looks up at Drew like he's finally noticed that she's a real person. Not invisible. "Oh."

"It's science, really." Rachel appears beside her, already dressed in jeans and a T-shirt with an apron over it all. "Luke got first place in the science fair last year."

"Wow," Drew says, genuinely impressed. Luke blushes a little. "So this is no problem. It's chemistry."

He squints at the mixing bowl. "I'm really more of a physics guy. So, should I dump it out or what?"

Rachel shrugs. "Let's see what happens. We can always make more." She pours herself a cup of coffee.

Chase cracks an egg. "Aunt Drew. Mom. This might go better if you, you know, leave us alone." He stares at Drew pointedly. After she called out the ref, Chase had been embarrassed and asked her to not come to any more games. Though he did admit that she was right. "Nobody's going to get drowned while we're making cookies."

Rachel and Tom were horrified. Rachel threatened to call the water polo organization and report the ref. Chase said he'd quit if she did.

220

"This is true." Drew sits at the counter, sipping her coffee and feeling a bit hurt. She'd only wanted to help Chase. She won't push him now, though.

Rachel sits next to Drew. "That's the boy whose mom said wouldn't help," she whispers, pointing at Luke, who mixes the batter now with greater care.

Drew raises her eyebrows. "You showed her."

Rachel has the grace to not even look smug, the way Drew certainly would have. Drew would have taken a photo of Luke cooperating and posted it to his mother's Facebook page. Rachel takes a sip of coffee. "I heard from Dad."

Drew's pulse flutters in her throat. But Rachel doesn't continue. "Annnnnddd?" It used to be Drew who did that, who made Rachel answer more of the questions she asked. She hopes, illogically, that Rachel will grin and say that Killian said, *Of course, and let's drop this lawsuit and be a real regular family again.*

Rachel just shakes her head, though, signaling she doesn't want to talk about it. Drew glances up at Chase, who is still visibly uncomfortable at the fact that his mother and aunt are hanging around, his back turned to them, every so often stealing a glare backward.

"Oh," Drew says softly. She takes too deep of a sip and coughs. A longing rises in her. When was the last time Drew and Rachel's family was happy? Ever?

She remembers one time, after Rachel won the freestyle event at the state championships when she was fifteen. How Killian took them to celebrate at a fancy steak house in a tower overlooking downtown and the harbor. The fancy tables and the wood paneling and the cigar smoke (back when people still smoked in restaurants). Hikari's beaming face, the small candle on the table making her skin glow softly as the waiter tipped the bottle of champagne into little flutes, the wine bubbling over, Hikari licking it off the sides of the glass like a cat. Her father, already several scotch-and-sodas in, putting his hand on his wife's back. The red setting sun. Rachel looking so proud and flushed, in a white summer dress that exposed her strong shoulders and back and highlighted her tan. Drew felt peaceful. A foreign sensation she only later named. She remembers thinking, *This is what we need to do. We need to win. We need to win all the time. Then our parents will love us and each other. We can be happy.*

But nobody wins all the time.

Look at Tomoe Gozen and Yoshinaka—she could literally be the best fighter in Japan, he the best general—and still they had to exist in the mountains, putting up with all sorts of hardships and setbacks.

Drew's coffee cup is empty. She gets up for a refill and picks up Rachel's. Her sister's is still full. She's just been going through the motions of drinking. Now her sister stares off into space. "Are you okay, Rach?"

Rachel blinks. "Yeah. I'm just a bit tired. I've been waking up a lot during the night."

"Do you want to go see Mom today? Maybe we can take her a few cookies," Drew says. She's visited a few more times, but their mother has been less responsive each visit. Still, it doesn't matter what your mind is like—everybody enjoys a cookie.

"I can't." Rachel smiles blankly at her. "I have to go see Quincy today."

Luke slaps spoonfuls of cookie dough onto a baking sheet. "Okay. My part's done."

"Don't you want to see how they turn out?" Drew asks.

Luke shrugs. "Why? People will buy them and if they don't like them, it'll be too late. Nobody gives refunds at a bake sale." He wipes his hands on a dishtowel and disappears into the living room. They hear the door open and close.

Drew and Rachel look at each other. "Guess that's better than nothing."

Rachel chortles, covering her mouth with her hand. "Ah well." The interruption's stopped whatever funk she was in. "What are your plans for the day? Any new job leads?"

Drew shakes her head. "I'll find something. Don't worry." Maybe she can start giving music lessons out of the house—but no, that won't work for very long. She can call some studios, see if they're hiring teachers. Her brain buzzes.

"I'm not." Rachel traces the edge of her mug with her finger.

Drew thinks Rachel is worried. Drew would be, too, realistically. She takes a long sip of coffee. "Hey. Mind if I raid your closet?" Her pulse rises as she asks. They'd never really gotten to this point, where they were the same size while they lived in the same house. Rachel had left too soon. Drew has no idea how much Rachel values her clothes. Whether she'll freak out if Drew accidentally spills red wine on a shirt. It seems so intimate, suddenly—too intimate.

"Nothing exciting in it, but be my guest." Rachel pours out her coffee, puts her mug in the sink.

My stomach hurts. It's hurt off and on ever since Killian's lawyer e-mailed me, a persistent vague nausea not unlike the feeling I had when I was pregnant, in the early months, when I'd barf if I so much as smelled oatmeal. A lawyer e-mailing me telling me I can't even ask my own father to come to my daughter's wedding—well, that's sure a sign that our relationship is kaput for good, isn't it?

And now, on a Saturday afternoon, I've got this meeting with Quincy's adviser. The professor asked me to come. I don't know why, but I presume that having a meeting on a Saturday when I'm normally not a part of these things can't be good. Tom would have come, but he's finishing up a project that was supposed to be finished last week.

Professor Michelle Murphy's office is in a plain concrete building. I count the doors as I walk down. I'm looking for 214b. Professor Murphy teaches electrical engineering, and Quincy hit it off with her during freshman year.

Quincy is already taking up one of the two guest chairs when I arrive. In the other one, her fiancé Ryan sits. He leans over and cracks a joke that

I can't hear, and Professor Murphy laughs, a booming, hearty sound that echoes down the hallway.

"Knock knock." I lean against the doorframe. Ryan gets up from his chair in front of the desk.

"Mrs. Perrotti. Thank you for coming." The professor stands up and shakes my hand. She's got short dark hair, no makeup, a kind face. She offers to look for another chair, but Ryan demurs, says he'll stand. So he does, sort of lurking behind us like a member of the Secret Service, and I've got the feeling something important is about to happen.

The office is small, all the walls covered in bookshelves which burst forth with books. I sink into the armchair and try to quell this feeling in my stomach, the acid in my throat. Professor Murphy takes off her reading glasses. "Well, Quincy." She looks expectantly at my daughter and I realize—Oh. My kid has called this meeting. Not the professor.

Quincy takes in a giant breath and looks at Ryan. He gives her a small nod. She twists a ring around on her finger, white gold with a tiny diamond glinting in the center. Her engagement ring, bought on credit from the Navy Exchange. "There's no easy way to say this."

Professor Murphy watches my face. She knows what's going on. So does Ryan. Everyone except me. Something about this reminds me of the time Quincy broke a crystal vase when she was about eight years old, playing softball in the house. Tom standing behind her, making her confess. *Mama, I did a bad thing.* "Go ahead," I say gently. I want to add, *You won't get into trouble if you're honest,* like I did then, but I can't.

"I'm going to take a leave of absence." Quincy slouches down and twists her ring faster. Won't meet my eyes. "It's too much with the wedding and I want to move in with Ryan."

I look from Ryan to Quincy and back again, then to Professor Murphy. She nods as if to say she understands. She's got children, too, I remember, about Quincy's age. "You're quitting school?"

Quincy takes Ryan's hand. "No. Not quitting. *Leave of absence.* I'll come back."

I'll come back. I've heard those words before. From my own mouth. I remember telling my history professor I was doing that. He'd been so encouraging—I'd gotten A's in his class. *You have keen insight into relating historical events with current,* he wrote on one paper. I still have it. He'd encouraged me to stay. *It'll be harder later.* I was going to major in history, partly because I loved it (and Killian would have hated it—he'd told me the liberal arts were "useless majors" and I should stick to science or business—but not Drew, with her exceptional talent). Then I told the professor I was pregnant and how it was all too much, too expensive. I'll never forget the look of deep disappointment that flashed across his face, before he controlled it. That made me feel worse than actually quitting school.

Professor Murphy leans over the desk. "I've let Quincy know, and I'll let you know, too, that if she's gone more than just one quarter, she'll have to reapply. If she's gone more than three quarters, she'll have new graduation requirements. That means she'll retake quite a few classes. And with engineering, you know, the curriculum changes quickly."

I think about all the years Quincy studied math. How she worked day and night on the Lego robotics team in high school. Her science project about green energy making it into the state fair. All the clubs she joined and the advanced placement classes she took. I think about the day she got into UCSD, an e-mail showing up in her inbox. How she whispered, "Let's wait for Dad to get home before I open it." *It was all worth it,* I thought then. *All that work paid off.* As if by getting accepted, the hard work had been done, and all she'd have to do was show up at UCSD for four years before she got a lucrative job.

I twist my head around to look directly at Ryan now. I don't care if he is a Navy SEAL capable of breaking my neck with his pinkie. The image of Tomoe pops into my head, unbidden. Tomoe pretending to be someone she's not, to please men. Getting attacked at the wedding, how she had to be ready for anything. If I had a samurai sword in my hands right now, there's no telling what I'd do. "What do you have to say, Ryan? Do you agree?" My voice sounds pretty calm. I'm impressed with myself. I'm practically huffing and puffing, as if I'm back in that useless Lamaze class. "Is this what you want her to do? Quit now? She's almost halfway done."

Ryan shrugs and looks, I have to give him credit, absolutely miserable. He turns Quincy's hand over and kisses it. "You know as well as I do that nobody can tell Quincy what to do. I told her to stay in school."

I blink. Suddenly, it occurs to me that maybe my daughter is the stubborn one. The one insisting they get married now. And Ryan's just going along with it because he wants to make her happy. "How will you pay rent? Ryan doesn't get the housing allowance and all the benefits until you get married."

Quincy shakes her head and looks into a corner of the room. "We—I— I was hoping you'd help us out until we got married."

My heart sinks. As much as I want to help her, I don't think this kind of assistance will benefit anyone. It'll be like she's playing house. Not facing real-life consequences for her choices. "Quincy, your father and I won't pay for you shacking up with Ryan. Especially if you're not even in school."

"Shacking up? He's going to be my husband." Quincy, finding something to be angry about, to take the focus off herself, flares.

Wrong word choice. I hold up my hands and look at Professor Murphy in desperation. She shakes her head slightly as if she, too, has given up. I also notice she didn't answer my question. Which probably means she doesn't have a really great answer. "Well, you'll be a married adult, and therefore we won't help you financially."

"I will get a job. Don't worry about it." Quincy stands up. "I knew you were going to be like this. Why can't you support me?"

"I always support you, Quincy." I remain sitting. Keep my voice calm.

Quincy puts her purse over her shoulder, the Coach bag I got her for Christmas last year. "You know what? I didn't even want to be an engineering major. You made me."

"You chose, Quincy. You're an adult." She's off the rails.

"This is true," Quincy says calmly. "That's why I'm wondering why you need to be here. It's my decision."

Both Ryan and the professor look at me solemnly. I take another breath. "Honey. Look here. Let's talk about this tomorrow. Sleep on it."

"There's nothing to talk about." She turns to Ryan. "Let's go." Quincy offers her hand to Professor Murphy. "Thank you for everything. I appreciate it. Come on, Ryan. Mother, I'll talk to you later." She leaves, Ryan in tow.

I watch her leave. I can't do a thing. "What would you do?"

Professor Murphy smiles sympathetically. "I don't know. I don't know. Just hope for the best, I suppose."

I put my chin on my hand, thinking of Tomoe Gozen. What would she do? She would have done whatever her father told her, that's for sure. I stand up and thank her and I dash into the hallway, hoping to catch Quincy, really talk to her. As if I could get through on my umpteenth try. They're already gone.

T omoe sat in the dirt courtyard of the fortress and waited, shielding her eyes against the warming morning August sun with one
hand. A dozen farmers had appeared so far for their training session. New ragtag soldiers that Kanehira had recruited from the surrounding area.

There were two ways to become a samurai. During times of peace, one
had to be born into a samurai family. At other times, as needed, farmers
could volunteer as soldiers, and a few of the best might become samurai.

Kanehira stood in the center of the courtyard, his sword already
strapped on, his back to her. He didn't want her there. He wanted her to
stay inside with Yamabuki and make him his dinner. But Yoshinaka had
asked Tomoe to help, and so her brother could say nothing.

Yoshinaka at last emerged from Yamabuki's house, his face flushed, his
chest bare. He wore only short underpants. Tomoe swallowed. It was obvious what he'd been doing. Even while the girl was pregnant, Tomoe
thought. He had not been to see Tomoe like that in a month or more. Yo-

shinaka could see whomever he pleased, legal wife or concubine or dance house girl. Yet if Tomoe sought solace with another man, she'd be outcast. The farmers chuckled among themselves, whispered about Yoshinaka's prowess. Tomoe watched for the door to close again, but it did not.

Yoshinaka tossed a sword to Tomoe, spinning it through the air. He intended it to land at her feet, but Tomoe stepped forward, caught it by the handle. The farmers gasped and went quiet.

"Let me be clear," Tomoe said, "that is not the proper way to handle a sword." Why couldn't Yoshinaka be a little more circumspect in how he did things, a little less . . . Yoshinaka-like? She held the sword tightly. Why weren't they going to use the wooden practice swords?

Yoshinaka ignored her gibe. He tilted his head back to the sun. Practically beat on his chest like a monkey. "Ah." He grinned. "Nothing like a good lay to begin the day." He winked at Tomoe. The farmers chuckled again. Tomoe's face heated.

Yoshinaka surveyed the dusty farmers, who gripped their farm tools. "Before you earn your swords," he said, "you must prove yourself. All of you. Come at her at once. With your rakes or whatever you have. Go ahead."

Tomoe glared at Yoshinaka. He was insane. Did he want her to kill all the farmers?

The farmers hesitated for a moment, then one ran up to her with a shout, a shovel swinging toward her. She sidestepped him, tripped him, and kicked the shovel away.

"If you're disarmed, you're out," Yoshinaka shouted, his hands on his knees.

Now the other farmers raced toward her, their sorry implements held aloft. She blocked each one in turn, careful not to stab any of them. They were slow and unsure, either firmly middle-aged or so youthful they still looked like twigs. She broke the wooden handles of their tools, shoved the men away with her foot as though they were overlarge gnats. She felt sorry for them. Surely they'd all perish in the next battle, whether or not they had swords. Yoshinaka would take on anyone.

"Ha!" Yoshinaka clapped his hands. "Now that Tomoe has properly humiliated you, the real training can begin." He snapped his fingers. Kanehira gestured. The men followed him.

"Yoshi," a female voice called. Yamabuki appeared on her porch. She slipped her feet into her sandals and walked, swaying gently, over to Yoshinaka. Her long straight hair smooth as a doll's. She touched Yoshinaka's arm. "Please. Do not have Tomoe fight. She is my attendant now."

Yoshinaka's brows furrowed, torn between wanting to please Yamabuki and not wanting to appear weak.

Tomoe pointed the sword down into the dirt, breathing heavily. Yamabuki intended to own her, body and soul. "I can do both."

Yamabuki narrowed her eyes. She slipped her arm through Yoshinaka's. "Nobody can be the servant of two masters."

"I am the servant of one," Tomoe said. "Yoshinaka."

"Then I want to learn how to fight, too!" A dagger appeared in her hand. "I've already done well once." She approached Tomoe, her belly unwieldy.

Yoshinaka grabbed his wife from behind. "Don't be ridiculous. You're pregnant. Go rest."

"You always tell me to stay inside," Yamabuki shouted. "Both of you." The woman broke into hysterical sobs, wrenching away from Yoshinaka. She sank to her knees, wailing.

Yoshinaka looked at Yamabuki helplessly. He'd never seen a woman carry on so, Tomoe thought. Neither had she. She strode over to Yamabuki and slapped her soundly across the cheek.

Yamabuki stopped wailing. Tomoe glared down at her. A red welt appeared on her pale face. "You ungrateful brat." She'd helped Yamabuki so much. Made sure she got sunshine when she was depressed. Helped her with the most mundane tasks. Apparently all she'd been doing was feeding Yamabuki's ego. "Get up and fight me, then," Tomoe said. Yamabuki wouldn't do it. "You cannot take the pain."

But Yamabuki launched herself up toward Tomoe. She caught Tomoe in the chin; Tomoe bit her tongue, tasting blood. Tears blinded her. The woman windmilled her arms furiously at Tomoe. Tomoe caught one arm in each of her hands and held them still, as though a toddler had attacked.

The two women stared at each other for a moment. Then Yamabuki's face crumpled like a wet origami crane. She went limp. Tomoe released her. The woman's wrists were as red as if rope had been tied around them.

"Leave me alone," Yamabuki whispered. She swallowed. "I thought you were my sister."

Anger flickered up again. "And I thought you were mine."

Yoshinaka put his arm around Yamabuki. "Go back into the house now, Yamabuki."

Yamabuki erupted into tears again, burying her face in Yoshinaka's chest. He stroked her back soothingly. No comfort for Tomoe, she thought with some bitterness. Nothing but crumbs. She turned and walked away.

Fourteen

I t is the Saturday before Halloween, which falls on a Thursday this year. Rachel and Drew drive to the carnival at the park by the pool, Chase in tow. Drew's deliberately dressed casually, in jeans that are form-fitting but not too tight, sneakers, and a purple sweater that looks good against her eyes. Her stomach bubbles nervously. Tonight she's meeting Alan's daughters. Shouldn't she have gone out with him a few more times? What if they hate her? Or what if they love her, and then Drew goes back to L.A.?

To distract herself, Drew turns up the radio. Rachel's playing some music Drew hasn't heard before.

"This is a local band," Rachel says.

"Yeah. My mom's such a hipster. She only likes indie bands nobody else has ever heard of," Chase says, and Drew truly can't tell if he's being sarcastic or kind of proud.

Rachel laughs. "I'm not trying to be. Sometimes Tom and I go to concerts at dives around here. Then we buy the band's music. The concerts are cheap, and we're helping out new talent."

"Really?" Drew figured her sister would just be playing the same CDs she had in high school. But that wouldn't make sense—after all, Drew didn't. Drew had never thought about it. What Rachel likes and doesn't. There's still a lot she doesn't know about Rachel. A lot Rachel doesn't know about her.

Rachel presses the forward button. "Yeah. Like this band, back when they had a really good songwriter." Drew hears tambourine. It's her band. Or rather, the band she was in, she corrects herself.

"He wants me back in, you know," Drew says.

Rachel's eyebrows shoot up. "So he can make you play tambourine for the rest of your natural life?"

"No. For viola."

They park on the street a couple blocks away. Chase gets out. "Meet us back here, ten o'clock, okay?" Rachel directs him.

He salutes her and races off.

Rachel shuts off the car and they sit for a second in the semi-dark, the yellow streetlamps the only light, the moon covered by clouds. Children scream and bass thumps out from the live band. "You believe him?" Rachel asks quietly, and Drew automatically clenches her hands. *You're such a bad judge of character, Drew. Be careful.*

"Yeah." Drew gets out and shuts the door. Rachel follows, beeping the alarm. "They're going to be on *Jimmy Kimmel*. It's real."

"Well, maybe you should do that, then," Rachel says neutrally. She looks at her cell phone, scrolls to a picture of Quincy, puts her finger on it, then shuts it off. "It's what you always wanted, isn't it?"

Drew feels a pull in her gut. Not for herself, for her sister. "Are you okay?" She's been acting distant all week, ever since the morning when the kids made cookies. Drew puts it all together only now—she herself has been mostly thinking about Alan and possible jobs, and thought Rachel was still down about their mother and Killian. They'd gone to visit their mother together, and that was the time Rachel had shown the most animation. "Is everything okay with Quincy?" Drew asks with a spurt of intuition. Rachel hasn't talked about Quincy for days. She usually can't go five minutes without bringing up her daughter.

"Yeah. Everything's fine. Come on." Rachel smiles brightly at her, walking ahead.

It's cooler tonight, for California, but Drew didn't bring a jacket. She never does. The wind stings her skin, and she shivers.

"Are you nervous?" Rachel asks Drew as they walk across the parking lot. He'd said six-thirty, in the food booth area.

"Hell yeah, I'm nervous. I'm meeting his kids. Isn't that a huge event?" She's already seen Alan three times. Warned him she didn't really live in this town. E-mailed back and forth, and talked on the phone more. And so far, only that one kiss that Drew can't get out of her mind. "Aren't you supposed to be engaged or something before you meet someone else's kids?" Alan told her he'd been out with two other women since his wife's passing. Drew asked him why those hadn't worked.

He'd thought about it for a minute. "I saw that these relationships wouldn't go anywhere," he'd answered, "so I didn't feel right about continuing to see them."

"They probably won't start off by calling you Mommy." Rachel links her arm through Drew's. "Don't worry. It's a carnival. It's casual. Not such a big deal in a group, I don't think." She shrugs. "Or maybe he does this all the time, and he's completely screwing up his girls."

"Thanks. Thanks. I needed that." Drew nudges her sister with her shoulder. Yesterday, she stopped by to see Alan at the library, and he'd come out from behind the counter to talk. He wanted to show her some new titles they'd got in, asked for her help in selecting books about music for a display. Afterward, when Alan went into his office, the model-pretty librarian, Brooke, shook her head. "I've never seen him talk that much entire time he's been here," she remarked to Drew.

"You have to think about that. Remember. Children come first." Rachel echoes what Drew said the other day, though Drew doesn't think Rachel realizes it. "You don't want to be the one his girls have to talk about in therapy."

They make their way across the brightly lit concrete path, pausing to watch an artist creating a 3-D chalk picture of a waterfall. It feels like they're standing on the edge of it, looking down into the whitewater. "Wow," Rachel breathes. Drew almost swears that a drop of water hit her. She digs out a dollar and throws it into the artist's donation box. Rachel repeats the gesture.

On the lawn, children race around with dripping caramel apples and ice cream cones. Beyond are a couple of rides, a Ferris wheel and a swing ride. An eighties tribute band thumps out a-ha on a small stage ("Take On Me," Drew remembers). A few portable lights cast everyone in an orange glow.

They walk through the crowd of people watching the band, sitting on blankets or standing or dancing. Drew hears a dissonance in someone's guitar and flinches. Maybe she ought to tell them how to fix it.

"Don't let him crawl on the grass. God. Can't you do anything I ask? Use your head," a woman's voice snaps. Drew looks down and sees a baby in a leopard costume trying to crawl off a plaid blanket. The owner of the voice stands on the other side of the blanket, a woman about Drew's age, wearing a leopard outfit that used less material than the baby's, impatiently sucking on a cigarette. A red-haired teenaged girl in a Robin costume scoops up the baby. Her eyes meet Drew's briefly. It's Chase's girlfriend.

The girl looks away. Drew doubts she recognized her. "Can I have ten dollars, Mom?"

The mother hands her a twenty. "Only if you take your brother with you. Buy him something to eat, too."

Drew wonders what on earth this carnival sells that a baby can eat. The girl nods, walks off, the baby cradled on her hip like an expert. The woman blows smoke, squints at Drew. Her face is hard, all angles, wrinkles on her upper lip from the smoking. Drew wrenches her gaze off the woman.

Rachel tugs on her arm. "The food's this way." They keep walking. Drew says nothing to Rachel. *No wonder the girl's the way she is,* she thinks to herself.

She sees Alan's girls before she sees him, recognizes their white-blond hair and light eyebrows from the pictures. Drew stops, her heels indenting the grass, as if they won't be able to spot her if she stands still.

They could almost be twins, except one's slightly taller than the other. A light illuminates them and their costumes, one in Belle from *Beauty and the Beast* and the older one in a Wonder Woman. They're standing by the cotton candy booth, watching the attendant swirl a poofy cloud of pink onto a paper stick. "Here you go!" Alan hands them the candy. He has no warnings of how they should be neat, or keep it off their faces. Drew smiles. She hates it when parents ruin the simple joy of a treat by warning the kids to be tidy. Once when she and Rachel were little, their parents bought them ice cream cones while on a vacation. Drew's ice cream got all over her face. Chocolate—the messiest kind. Both parents scolded her for so long that Drew had never wanted a cone again.

"Thank you, Daddy," the little girls chorus sweetly, a faint trace of English accent in their tones.

Alan sees Drew, waves at her. Drew lifts her hand but feels a small surge of panic. *Oh my God.* He points at Drew and the two little girls grin and run straight for her, like miniature football players. He follows at a close clip and Drew wonders if she'll possibly be able to keep up with them all. What if they run in different directions? Poor Alan. He looks good tonight, Drew thinks, wearing a soft-looking brown leather jacket, khakis, and a T-shirt. Nothing flashy, nothing hip, but comfortable. A leather-bound book, Drew thinks. The one you want to keep to read again. That's what he reminds her of. He even smells like books. He introduces himself to Rachel, shakes her hand.

"Are you Dad's friend Drew?" Wonder Woman asks her. Already pink candy sticks all over her face in tufts and melted spots.

Drew nods. "I am."

Wonder Woman points at herself. "I'm Audrey. This is Lauren." Named after Audrey Hepburn and Lauren Bacall, Alan has explained to her.

Lauren curtseys in her Belle costume, gold slippers peeking out from under the skirt. Drew's glad to see neither bothered with a wig, their blond hair shining. "Pleased to meet you."

Drew stoops to the girls' height without thinking. She holds out her hand and first Audrey, then Lauren, shakes it. Their hands are tiny and warm. "Pleased to meet you, too. I'm honored to be in the presence of Wonder Woman and Belle."

Lauren tiptoes to Drew. "Know why I picked Belle?" she whispers. Drew shakes her head. "She likes books. So do I."

"I bet your daddy brings you lots of books. What's your favorite?"

"Junie B. Jones."

"Whoa. That's a chapter book." Drew whistles through her teeth, impressed. Quincy had read those in first grade. Drew bought her a set one Christmas.

"I read them myself," Lauren says proudly.

"What a smart girl," Rachel says.

Lauren nods, suddenly shy. She steps back behind Alan's leg. They have Alan's nose in miniature, a slightly upturned version, but both have a heart-shaped face Drew assumes comes from their mother.

Audrey studies Rachel. "That your sister?"

Drew nods. "My *big* sister."

"But you're bigger than she is," Lauren says. "That's not right. She's your little sister. Like mine." She puts Audrey in a headlock, knocking the smaller girl off balance for a moment.

"I'm thinking of enrolling her in judo," Alan says with a laugh, prying Lauren's arm off her sister. "She's a natural."

Audrey grins and holds up the sticky candy. "Want some? We share."

Rachel bends forward, to Drew's surprise. "Yes, please. Thanks. You have such good manners." She takes a small chunk. "I love cotton candy."

Audrey holds the cone out to Drew. Drew pinches off a piece. She hasn't had it since childhood. The sugar crystals crunch, then melt in her mouth. Caramelized sugar. Sort of like the crackle crust on top of a crème brûlée. Her fingers are sticky and she sucks them, which doesn't help much, and wipes her hand off on her jeans. Maybe mothers are just never clean, she thinks. She minds this far less than she would have thought. "Thank you."

"Daddy?" Lauren points to a giant inflatable slide. It's higher than the roof of the rec center. "Will you go on that with us?" She holds Alan's left hand.

"Sure." Alan smiles down at Drew with an expression she can't read. A bit closed off. Guarded. Is it because the girls are here? She wants to kiss him, but of course does not. "You don't have to."

"You're going to have to take off your shoes." Audrey's little hand slips into Drew's. Audrey. Drew's heart skips.

Drew looks at Alan. "Sure, I'll go."

"I'll catch up with you later," Rachel says. "Tom's meeting me by the corndogs."

Drew shoots her a panicked look. That's not a group thing, then. But Rachel makes a shooing gesture. *Go.* Audrey pulls on her, tries to run. "Hurry up, Drew-lady!" she shouts. "We don't want to be late! Pick me up!"

"That would be terrible." Drew picks up the girl. She's heavier than she looks. She runs across the grass to the slide.

"We beat them!" Audrey says triumphantly. She hands Drew a wad of tickets. "Now we go."

They kick off their shoes and climb up the slide steps, which has a rope ladder to help you get up to the top. The girl climbs like a monkey, Drew much more slowly. She looks down and sees Alan and Lauren a few parties below them. Alan is frowning, concentrating on his climbing. She hopes he's not mad that they didn't wait. She was just trying to do what the girl wanted.

"Come on," Audrey yells from the top, and Drew makes it all the way up. A teenager in a red shirt tells Drew to sit down on a felt mat, and Audrey sits in front of her. Drew puts her arm around the girl—she's so small—and peers down. Wow—it's steeper than she thought. Before she can think anything else, they're sliding down, fast, landing against the soft bumpers.

"That was fun!" Audrey stands up and scoots off the end onto the grass. "Let's go again."

"Hold on." Drew waits for Alan and Lauren, who fly down. Neither of them smiles.

Lauren gets off the slide and runs over and punches Audrey in the arm. "Why didn't you wait for us?"

"Ow!" Audrey pulls back. "You're slow."

"Lauren, no hitting," Alan says sternly.

"Sorry," Drew says.

"It's fine," Alan says with a smile, but he's terse.

Drew leans in next to his ear, even as Lauren glares. "Is something wrong?"

Alan shakes his head. "I can't talk about it right now." He looks pointedly at his daughters. He bends and helps Lauren with her shoes. Audrey takes Drew's hand again and she double ties the pink laces of Audrey's glittery sneakers.

"What would you like to do now?" Drew asks brightly, standing. "The jump house?"

"We decide," Lauren says. Her arms are crossed. "Not you."

Drew rocks back on her heels. Oh. Lauren must feel left out. "What would you like to do, Lauren?"

Lauren takes Alan's hand. "She should get her own tickets, Daddy. She's using too many of ours."

Drew blushes so hotly she feels like she's almost knocked off her feet. "Oh. Sure."

"It's not necessary," Alan says, but Drew's already walking to the ticket booth.

"You guys don't need to wait. I'll catch up," she calls over her shoulder.

"Are you sure?" Alan holds a hand of each of his girls, and Drew thinks he looks as relieved as Lauren does.

She waves and walks away.

MIYANOKOSHI FORTRESS / TAKATO TOWN
SHINANO PROVINCE
HONSHU, JAPAN
Spring 1181

W hat's this one?" Tomoe scratched a symbol into the dirt with a stick. The dry, hot wind whipping about nearly wiped out the lesson before it began. Her throat itched in the dust.

When were the rains going to return? A drought had come to Japan. Animals dying because the farmers could not water them. People succumbing not only from lack of food, but from disease as well.

Every morning Tomoe woke and stared at the horizon, looking for rain clouds and seeing nothing but wavering lines of heat. For once she was glad they lived in such an isolated outpost. Illnesses had trouble reaching them here in the mountains. And they were close enough to the scant snow that they still had water.

Shaking away the dark thoughts, Tomoe scratched the symbol again into the dirt. "Come now."

The three-year-old boy squatting next to her did not answer. He dimpled his chubby cheeks into a smile. "I don't remember," he said in childish singsong.

"It's *ki*," Tomoe said, deliberately getting it wrong.

"*Ka*," he corrected.

"I knew you knew it!" Tomoe reached over and tickled him. Yoshitaka, the son of Yoshinaka, doubled over in giggles. He looked exactly like his father had when he was a boy, the eyebrows sticking up at angles toward his temples, the merry twinkle of trouble always in his eyes. Already, his future was secure. Yoshinaka had arranged for his son to be betrothed to his cousin Yoritomo's daughter. Tomoe tickled Yoshitaka some more, kissing his cheeks for good measure.

"Stop! I can't breathe!" he said.

Yamabuki paused at her laundry-hanging, her oversized belly making her off balance. "Tomoe, he's going to pee his pants!"

Tomoe raised her hands. "I've already stopped." Little Yoshitaka picked up a wooden sword lying in the dirt and swung it at Tomoe's legs. She hopped over it effortlessly. The boy was stocky and strong. Already he could climb trees like Tomoe, fire arrows a short distance, and ride Demon as though the horse was a docile pony.

"I chase you down, Kiyomori Taira," the boy said firmly, his hands on his hips. "Yah!"

"See if you can catch me first." Tomoe took off at a run, the boy chasing her and giggling.

For the first time since she could remember, Tomoe hoped that war would never come. And if it came, let it be far from them. Leaning in, she once again tried to get Yoshitaka to focus on the lettering. "Tell me what this is, Yoshi-chan."

He shrugged, concentrating on his fingers. He'd been trying to snap them for weeks and couldn't yet make a sound. "Show me again, Tomoe?"

Tomoe showed him. Yoshitaka screwed up his face. "I cannot!" He stamped his feet. "Ugh. Ugh. Ugh."

"You know what you need?" Tomoe said. "Another hug." He tried to jump away, but she hugged him until he stopped kicking. At the line, Yamabuki smiled ruefully and shook out a laundered kimono.

Yamabuki had long ago given up any pretensions of being a lady. But for her still-weak appearance, she might have been any peasant woman. Her skin had never lost its pallor, almost as though it naturally lacked pigment, like a turnip. Her large belly loomed in profile as Yamabuki leaned over the laundry basket. She was pregnant with her second child. It was easier this time, and Tomoe was glad.

"You should be teaching him with ink, on paper," Yamabuki admonished gently.

"I'll leave that to his tutor. I don't want to waste the materials with my small teachings." Tomoe put her forehead against the boy's and blew air through her lips, buzzing them. He chortled.

This boy would have to be well educated. Someday, little Yoshitaka could inherit much land. Yoshinaka hoped the boy would also inherit from his cousin Yoritomo's leadership position by marrying his daughter. But Yoshinaka's ambitions were endless.

Tomoe was content with all they had now, land or no land. Babies were such a joy. At the sight of Yoshitaka's wrinkled, scarlet, pointy newborn head, covered in sticky afterbirth, she had expected to feel disgust. Instead she found herself eagerly holding her arms out to Yamabuki, who was whiter than ever, the blue-green vein on her forehead throbbing.

When Yamabuki went into labor, all bygones of that day Yamabuki had called Tomoe her servant were forgotten. Perhaps that was the mark of a sister, Tomoe thought. You could be angry, but still be there for one another when needed.

And now that baby was almost four, in the blink of an eye.

Tomoe scratched a symbol in the earth that looked like a kneecap. *"Ko,"* she said.

"Ko," Yoshitaka repeated dutifully.

Kanehira came into the yard. "Uncle!" Yoshitaka called.

"Little man." Kanehira paused to ruffle Yoshitaka's hair. He was the one who rode with Yoshinaka, signing up men, tamping down the Taira. Since Tomoe had been spending so much time with Yamabuki, Kanehira had warmed to her marginally. At least he no longer made jibes at her expense.

But now he barely looked at Tomoe. In one hand, he held a small cylindrical object made of dark brown wood. "What is this?" Tomoe asked, forcing his hand open.

It was a wooden seal, a stamp of bamboo leaves with the kanji symbol for "Kiso" carved into the end. She swallowed hard, her grip tightening until Kanehira's hand turned white and she released him abruptly. "Is this a seal for Yoshinaka?"

Only the royal family and the heads of clans had seals. Yoritomo, the new head of the Minamoto, had one, to imprint official binding documents. Why did Yoshinaka need this? By forging this seal, Yoshinaka had declared himself an equal to Yoritomo. This could only mean trouble within the family. She stared at her brother. Kanehira met her gaze, his eyes cold. His jaw tightened. "Nobody answers to you."

Tomoe's nostrils flared. Kanehira's glance wavered. She kept her voice low. "Tell me, or I promise I'll tell Yoritomo myself."

Kanehira took a breath and glanced toward the horizon. He must have his doubts, too, Tomoe thought, however much he buried them for his foster brother. "Yoshinaka promises the samurai who fight for him land over all of Japan. He writes deeds for these lands, and puts his seal on them. That's how Yoshinaka gets so many to fight."

Her mouth went dry. Yoshinaka could not promise anyone land. He was not the head of the Minamoto. Tomoe might as well be telling people *she* had the right to give away territory. "And Yoritomo gave his consent?" she asked, hoping this was true.

"Of course not," Kanehira snapped. He hid the seal in his fist. "Yoritomo thinks Yoshinaka is overstepping his role. But he is not. The land that Yoshinaka wins rightfully belongs to Yoshinaka—it belonged to his father. If Yoritomo wants it, he can come up here and fight us. He can't win. Not in the mountains, with his soft troops. They'd freeze."

Kanehira sounded like he was trying to convince himself. The problem, Tomoe thought, was that every leader grew a huge ego and needed at least one man to rein him in. But nobody would say no to Yoshinaka—nobody but Tomoe.

This man would be their downfall.

"He is my general," Kanehira said shortly, "and I will follow him to his death, if he asks."

Tomoe looked at Yamabuki, whose face had gone so white it was nearly blue. A pair of wet pants flapped in her loose grip. Little Yoshitaka ran by and snatched the clothing out of his mother's hand, throwing it into the dirt with a laugh.

Fifteen

Alan phones Drew on Monday after the Halloween carnival and asks if she's free for dinner the following night. He surprises her with the Marine Room, an expensive restaurant right on the beach in La Jolla. The last time Drew was here, she was only old enough to order hot chocolate in the bar.

It's dark when they're seated, but the restaurant shines lights onto the breaking waves. The tide's coming in, the water washing right against the thick floor-to-ceiling windows. This is the restaurant's main draw. To be as close as possible to the powerful ocean, yet not leave this air-conditioned comfort. Alan pulls Drew's chair out for her, preempting the waiter. "This is so lovely. Thank you." She sits down as he pushes her chair in, hoping he knows she doesn't expect such extravagance. A picnic on the beach with sandwiches from the local Subway would be fine with Drew, as long as she could be with Alan.

She admires his face as he squints at the menu, that strong jaw, his face shaved very close again. Really, all she wants to do is straddle him and make out. Maybe they should skip the meal and go out to his car.

But no. She's got the sense he wants to talk about something big. Maybe tell her that his daughter freaked out and he doesn't want to push her. After

Drew got her ride tickets, she looked at her phone and found an apologetic text from Alan, saying Lauren wasn't feeling well and they had to go home. Drew gave the twenty tickets to a passing child.

"Lauren feeling better?" Drew asks.

He smiles that quick, slightly sad thing that doesn't hit his eyes again. "She had a bad case of being a brat. I told her if she didn't behave, we'd leave. I had to adhere to my word."

"Of course. Follow-through is important." Drew feels like she's echoing her sister. Follow-through. What does Drew know about it? She mentally shrugs.

They pore over the wine list. Drew doesn't want to admit she doesn't know much about wine. She prefers mixed drinks, dry rather than sweet. "I'm not much of a wine drinker."

"Nor am I." He puts down the list. "Let's do the chef's testing menu. It comes with wine."

"Sounds great." She looks out the window as Alan orders. Almost the same view her mother has in the nursing home, except Hikari's is not as close to the water.

They sit in silence. Drew smiles at Alan. He looks nervous. The waiter brings them an appetizer balanced on a large white ceramic spoon and the first glass of wine. Some kind of shrimp and a white wine. Drew's not listening to the waiter. She's watching her date. Trying to read his mind.

Drew leans over. She's seated next to him, not across, so they can speak quietly. Without anyone hearing. "What's the matter?"

"I have something to tell you." Alan crosses his hands in front of him. "As I mentioned, my contract ends in the spring."

Drew's heart starts pounding. Be calm, she tells herself. Nothing's happened yet.

"It seems . . ." Alan clears his throat. Drew takes a sip of her wine without tasting anything except the astringent sensation of alcohol in the back of her throat. He looks at her with those dreamy eyes. "My life is changing."

He closes his eyes, the lashes thick on his cheeks. Drew waits for him to continue. "My in-laws want to move to North Carolina. They're retired. The cost of living is much better there, they'll run out of money if they stay here." Alan clears his throat. He holds her hand and runs his fingers up the inside of her forearm, making her shiver. "My wife's sister lives out there, and she just had triplets, so they want to see those grandchildren, too."

"And?" Drew waits. She's watching his mouth.

"And I'd love for my family to see more of my children. For my children to know where I grew up. And I have to say—I love it here—but I'm homesick." He stares directly into her eyes. He has such puppy-dog eyes. "I've been offered a job in the Cambridge University library."

"Cambridge . . ." Drew tries to get her muddled brain to think of where that is. Massachusetts?

"England."

Drew's mouth opens and shuts. "When?" She turns her arm over, brings it back to her side. Alan watches it retract.

"January."

January? That's too soon. Drew has trouble taking a breath. Surprised and angry and afraid. "I didn't know you'd applied." Why would she? How many dates have they been on? He owed her no explanation. Her nephew had gotten further with that high school girl than Alan had with her, to Drew's dismay.

"I applied months ago." He swallows. "I only just heard last week."

Drew nods blindly. So that's why he acted so aloof at the carnival. He was getting ready to break it off. Minimize losses, especially for his girls. Who cared if they had a spark—that's all it was, a spark. Not all sparks fan into full-on fires. She takes a drink of ice water.

Take me with you, she thinks, and the thought shocks her. It's unreasonable, and Drew's had enough unreasonable thoughts and actions to last her a whole life. It's time for practicality. For common sense. She forces herself to think rationally. "So . . . what does this mean?"

The waiter shows up and clears their plates, replaces them with the main course. Fish, something something. Both she and Alan stop talking and nod blankly up at the waiter, who seems truly eager to share this with them. She's had only that one sip of the other wine, and a new glass is being poured.

Drew focuses on the crashing waves. England? Part of her wishes that she'd never gone out with him at all. She wishes that she hadn't picked up that viola at the library. She wishes—oh, she wishes she'd done a lot of things differently. What did she think, that Alan would marry her and she'd be a stepmother and they'd live next door to Rachel in San Diego, cozy forever?

She doesn't need anybody to save her. She needs to get her own life. Not co-opt Alan's. Or force him to live out here, without his support system, turning down a job offer that might not come again.

She knows what it means, even as he struggles to answer. She stands up.

He stares at her, stricken. The waves sway in and out from the shore. Suddenly the churning motion of the water makes her feel seasick. Dizzy. Her ears feel like she's up in a plane. She grabs her chair. "Drew." He stands. "Do you need help?"

Drew backs away from the table. Her incautious heart screams at her to stay. *Listen to your mind for once, Drew,* she urges herself. "Alan. I'm sorry. I have to go."

"No, stay. Let's talk about this." He reaches for her.

She holds up a hand, stopping him. "There's nothing more to say. I've enjoyed getting to know you. Maybe more than you'll ever know. You're a very special person." She speaks fast, before her emotions catch up with her too much. The other diners look at them or pretend not to. She inclines her head in a bow. Like Tomoe Gozen. "But I can't do this. Not if I'll have to say good-bye in January. Good-bye, now."

Quickly, she turns and walks upstairs, aware that Alan's trying to follow, but the night's gotten busy and the aisle's crowded with waiters with platters and guests.

She goes straight outside to the valet stand. A cab happens to be there, dropping someone off, and Drew gets in. She doesn't look back at the entrance, both hoping and afraid that Alan will be there, watching her leave.

I sit with my laptop whirring hot on my lap, a lukewarm cup of tea cooling even further in my hands. I've just gotten an e-mail from UCSD, informing me that my daughter's withdrawn from all her classes. I knew this was coming, of course. Quincy's told me they've rented a tiny studio in a bad part of town, and she's promised to have us over after it's fixed up. She's looking for a job. I don't know where.

But seeing the reality of Quincy's withdrawal in black and white almost bowls me over. She really has officially dropped out of college. No refunds, no take-backs. It isn't just a bad dream. I can't stop staring at it like I've just seen Medusa with my bare eyes.

I shut the laptop and set it on the coffee table and take a sip of cold tea. I wish someone was here to distract me. Tom and Chase aren't home, Drew's out having a fancy dinner with Alan, and I don't have anything to do.

I think about Mom and the Tomoe Gozen story again. Did Mom think she was Yamabuki? Is that what she is telling us with this book? Did my father have a lover, like Tomoe? Is that his big secret threat—that he's got another family or three, stashed around the world like Charles Lindbergh had?

Surely the interpretation's not so literal. I just don't know. I open up the manuscript on my computer. It's jumped ahead in time, and now Tomoe's a stand-in mother. I wonder if Yamabuki ever learned how to fight, as she wanted to do when she was pregnant. She should. I'm not sure about

Yoshinaka—he seems to be on the verge of craziness. Who can trust some-one like that?

Besides, with the times the women lived in, they need to know combat skills.

I glance around my safe living room, tucked away in suburban America. Or am I safe? I guess nobody's really safe anywhere. There could be a bur-glar or an earthquake or a plane crash or a terrible drought, like the one that happened in Japan. Who knows what. Well, that doesn't make me feel any better, I think wryly. I look up the drought they're referencing. Yes. The famine of 1181 killed more than twenty thousand people. You can't stop Mother Nature from doing what she wants, even today.

A yellow taxi pulls up in front of my house and Drew emerges, looking wobbly as a sick calf. Without thinking, I run outside. People hardly ever take cabs in San Diego, and especially not cab rides of more than twenty miles. "Are you all right?"

She looks up at me mutely, her eyes red, her carefully applied cat-eye black liner smeared all over her cheeks. "It's Alan, isn't it?" I ask, and my stomach clenches. What had he done to my sister? I'll track him down and smack the life out of him. And here I thought they were so good for each other, that he was so nice, his girls sweet.

Drew nods.

I take care of the cab and go back inside. Drew's already in her bed, the covers pulled up around her, her back to me. I pat her back, thinking of how many times I'd done this with her when she was little and upset or sick. And how many times I've done it with my own kids.

Like I do with my children, I don't press. I wait until she's ready, wedged next to her back, our weight sinking the mattress low, until her silent tears subside and she blows her nose a few times with the tissues I hand her, one after another. Drew had been so happy over the past few weeks. Happier than I'd ever seen her with Jonah. Like Drew was more . . . *Drew*. Drew cubed.

She'd always seemed a little downtrodden when she was with Jonah.

Even if I saw her only briefly on holidays, it was like she was wearing an invisible suit of armor. Back then, it was always: *Jonah says this. Jonah thinks that.* I mean, I know I do that with Tom, but not to that degree. It always seemed like Drew had taken on Jonah's plans, abandoning her own—or that she'd never developed them as she should have.

And frankly, when she first came down after losing her job, it'd seemed like she'd lost all hope in her life, too. She has it back. That's no small thing. If you don't have hopes or dreams, there's no reason to keep living.

She tells me what happened, without looking at me. "So it's over," she finishes. "You were right. I shouldn't have dated him. There's no point in seeing him anymore." Her voice breaks, and I squeeze her arm. "I wish I never went to coffee with him. You were right, Rachel. Go ahead. Tell me your told-you-sos."

I was the one who thought it'd be bad for her to date Alan, if she was living in L.A. But that was before I saw how they were together. I tilt my head, regarding my sister. They make sense. Like my spaghetti and meatballs. If I make my sauce without meatballs, my whole family complains. It's not against the law for me to be wrong, is it? For me, Rachel Perrotti, to (gasp) actually change into a less judgmental, less uptight human being?

Drew turns her head back. "Why are you just staring at me, Rachel? Gosh. Just like you did when we were little."

I grin. "I'm thinking." I shake my sister gently. "Hey, Drew." How could I make her understand all that I'm feeling? I remember when my sister helped me, just by knocking on my door. Brought me back to myself. Maybe I can return the favor in some small way. I think of something. "Do you remember that chalk drawing of the waterfall we saw at the Halloween carnival?"

Drew turns her back to look at me. Her skin's all mottled. "What about it?"

I put my face close in next to hers. Like I'm telling her a secret. "The sprinklers washed most of it away that night. But we still enjoyed it during the time it was there. It's impermanent, but not worthless. Right?"

Drew's mouth pulls downward as she scrapes at the makeup under her eyes with a finger. "I guess not. What's your point?"

"Well." I take a breath, coming up with the right words. I'm not usually this philosophical. At least, not out loud. "No experience lasts forever. None of us knows how much time we have with anyone. It could be years, or it could be days. I think you should see him and enjoy what you have, while you have it."

Drew says nothing for a moment. Then she shrugs. "I understand what you mean, but I know he's going to leave. I know it. And it hurts too much. It'll hurt more if I hang on. I don't want to, Rachel. I just don't." She bites her lip, the way my daughter does when she's sad, and I see in her both my children. A tear comes into my eye, too, and suddenly I feel like I'm talking to both my sister and my daughter at once. I want so much to spare both Drew and Quincy all this pain—I feel like I've experienced it *for* them already. I wish one of them would listen. Let me help.

I'm powerless. I wonder fleetingly what my mother would say to Drew, if she could. Maybe that's a mother's lot in life—to want to shield her kids from the world, and always failing. And to do the same for your younger sister. I bite down my feelings, tangling them in my gut, because I don't want to fight with Drew the way I fought with Quincy. I want to support her, not question. "I understand." I stand. Her eyelids are half closed now. I pull the blanket up over her. "Do you need anything?"

Drew sits up with a sudden burst of energy. "Can you take me snorkeling?" She points to a white plastic bag on the floor. "I bought masks and fins today."

"Snorkeling?" I think of the wetsuits I found. We have fins in the garage someplace. "Where'd that come from? You haven't been since we were in Hawaii, have you?" I remember our father showing us how to spit into the mask, rubbing it clean of fog. Taking off ahead of both of us and me struggling to keep up, struggling to hold on to Drew at the same time. "That time, you almost drowned. You want to do that again? Really?"

"I just want to do something different." Drew fluffs out her hair and flashes me her best, most pitiful pleading look. "Please, Rachel. The water's pretty warm. I can't go alone. Will you go with me?"

I think of Yamabuki teaching Tomoe poetry, Tomoe showing Yamabuki how to defend herself. Their own natural limitations. What Drew and I can learn from each other. This, at least, I can teach Drew.

Besides, snorkeling to get over a break-up sounds a lot healthier than sitting around and eating Ben & Jerry's, though I might prefer the latter these days. And I've got to be there for my sister. I straighten my posture and a genuine smile bursts over me. "Sure. Whatever you want."

We go to La Jolla Cove the next morning. Conditions are clear. I lock the car manually and put the key on a string around my neck. We put on wetsuits in the public bathroom—it's only sixty-seven in the water, a far cry from the seventy-four it was in Hawaii—and go down the steps to the beach. We'll leave our clothes in a shopping bag on the beach—probably nobody will take them, and if they do, it won't be a huge loss. We wore my oldest, most paint-splattered clothes for this trip.

"Oh my God." Drew makes a gagging noise. "It is rank."

"It's the bird and seal poop." I gesture to the hundred vertical feet of large boulderish rocks lining the wall from the sidewalk down, which are white not from the sun but from bird droppings. A fence erected at the top means the birds don't bother flying away when humans are near.

It is stinky, smarting my eyes and mouth. Only a few years ago, when Quincy had her water polo team pictures done here, it wasn't nearly this bad. The whole area has been affected by a nearby beach known as the Children's Pool, a partially man-made cove that has been made into a sea lion preserve, with humans not allowed to disturb them. Often, the water's too polluted for swimming because of the sea lion excrement combined with various other run-off from the land. In fact, there are permanent signs saying things like "Swim at Your Own Risk." Nobody's done much about the pollution, everybody blaming everybody else—sea lion lovers hating the beachgoers, beachgoers hating the environmentalists, on and on, suing the city and each other in a never-ending cycle. I figure we'll be okay once we get out into the open water, and as long as we rinse off afterward. It doesn't stop anybody else.

A single lifeguard sits in the large tower enclosure, wearing a light jacket. Only a few people are in the water, tourists from colder climes, holding their faces up to the sun in hopes of proving with their tans that they vacationed in San Diego. It's high tide, the water licking the sandstone cliffs where the tourists perch, their towels and flip-flops in danger of sweeping out to sea.

Drew freezes. "The water's kind of high."

"You thought of it." I continue down the stairs.

"I think of plenty of bad ideas." Drew follows me slowly. "Doesn't mean I should do them all."

"You'll be fine." I turn and look at her. She's more excited than afraid. "Remember Yamabuki and Tomoe." I think of one more thing she needs to know. "Oh, and we might see some leopard sharks. It's fine. They're completely harmless."

"Okay then." Drew turns and pretends to go back upstairs.

The water's actually warmer than the air, and it seeps into our wetsuits and heats up around our bodies. We quickly put on our fins and masks and snorkels. All I can hear is the sound of our breathing, hard and raspy like twin Darth Vaders, and the pounding of the small waves against my body. Then I get on my belly, Drew following.

The water gets deep rapidly. We can see a few yards around us. Not bad. Sometimes you can't see a hand in front of your face. We swim through a forest of kelp, of small silvery fish, moving farther out beyond the protective cove. A school of orange-red Garibaldi dart past, their fat cheeks puffing.

I float facedown, waves *shoosh*ing me back and forth. The kelp forest ripples in the current, indecipherable forms moving in and out of the twisting fronds. Ahead and below, a five-foot leopard shark glides past, its back marked with distinctive spots. I point to it and throw a thumbs-up to Drew. We follow the shark at a distance as it moves its sinuous body in the water. Suddenly we're in the open ocean. I kick my fins harder. My thigh muscles burn.

I know exactly where we are—above La Jolla Canyon, where the bottom is six hundred feet deep. You really need scuba gear to see it properly. I used to come out here all the time. It's a marine protected area. Once, with my high school swim buddies, I saw a gray whale passing below, its enormous prehistoric form sluicing languidly through the water. More leopard sharks move back and forth underneath.

A wave washes over my snorkel, somehow sending water inside, and I surface to spit. A sea lion rolls in the water, diving into the gully and chasing after a silvery fish. Its whiskered face peers at us adorably, but its adorableness is a ruse. Those things have sharp teeth. The sea lion swims up to the surface for air, dives back down like a rocket, and disappears.

Suddenly, in my peripheral vision, I see a black form on my left. The hairs on the back of my neck rise. It's too large for a leopard shark. Another sea lion? I try to make out its shadow. It's big, maybe twelve feet long, too long for a sea lion, too. A real chill hits me. Black eyes, a mouthful of teeth tasting the water. My heart pounds as I make eye contact with the creature. That is not a leopard shark.

A primeval need to flee makes me shudder. The shark passes so closely I can see the gills moving. Then it loops around and returns, as if it's trying to sense what we are. If it was in a tank and I was standing on the other side it'd be beautiful, with its powerful muscles moving under its sleek skin.

It thinks we're sea lions, I think. I try to remember every Shark Week show I've ever seen. Chase and Tom were always watching that Les Stroud survivor guy. What did he say to do? I turn and grab Drew's wrist, and we start swimming slowly back, but the current's pushing us away from the shore. We have to swim parallel to the beach to get out of this rip current, but I'm not quite able to turn myself, and I'm tired and, yes, panicking. My heart rate goes up and I hear it thudding in my ears and all I can think about is that huge thing somewhere behind us.

The image of Tomoe Gozen enters my mind, as she has so often lately, so real she's become. I see her in a battle. Charging on Cherry Blossom. You must strike first, hard and fast. That's what her father told her. But how? We need to get out of here. The breathing noise in my mask becomes unsteady, panicked, even as I tell myself to be calm.

We're making no progress, the stupid kelp weaving itself around our bodies. A slimy piece wraps around my leg and I kick it free. Where did the shark go? Visibility is terrible now, the waves coming in harder and churning up sand below.

Then I see it, swimming toward us. Its mouth is open. Its eyes, shadow orbs, pupil-less and dark as space. It wants to do another loop around us.

Every nerve I have tells me to get out of there. Or freeze.

I let go of Drew, or she lets go of me. I grab for her and grab nothing. Just water in my hand. I can't see her. Just kelp and clouds. "Drew!" I cry out involuntarily, and this is a mistake, because I choke up on water. I lift my head into the air and cough and see the dorsal fin. I don't see Drew's snorkel anywhere, don't see her fins flapping around. I take a breath and dive.

Drew's by the shark, flailing, her arms a blur. Does it have her? With two big kicks I reach her. I circle my arms around her waist, but she shoves me off.

The shark rolls away, pushing us backward in its powerful wake. Drew surfaces, I follow.

"Rachel! Are you trying to drown me?" She spits and blinks.

"Are you all right?" My eyes sting from the salt. No blood's in the water.

"I punched it." She pushes the mask up onto her forehead, dazed. "I punched it in its eye. It didn't like it."

Relief floods through me, so palpable I sink down into the water, the coolness lapping at my cheekbones. "Drew. You could've gotten killed."

Drew's face contorts. She points at me. "No. *You* could have gotten killed. You're not supposed to fucking swim away from a motherfucking shark." She smacks the water, sending a fan of it at my face. "What's the matter with *you*? I thought you knew what you were doing. Why do I know the right thing to do and you don't?"

I stare at her, speechless. I've never heard Drew sound so angry. I'm angry, too, angry at myself for freezing during a crisis. At her for putting herself at risk. My ears burn so hot the water dribbling out feels warm on my neck. Adrenaline's still shooting through my body, looking for an outlet. I yell. "What's the matter with *me*? Who are you, Evander Holyfield? Punching a shark. That was so, so stupid, Drew Snow. What if it bit your arm off?"

"But it didn't." She blows out her snorkel, pulls her mask down. "We're alive. Come on. Let's get back to shore." She puts her face in and starts swimming fast, diagonally, exactly like she's supposed to.

I watch her for just a second, numb. In the near distance, a plume of blood trails through the water. Sea lion, I think. Fuck. Why aren't we getting out of here? Another dumb move, Rachel.

The sound of a motor approaches and I lift my head above the waves. A lifeguard Sea-Doo. "Hey!" he yells, coming to a stop by Drew, helps her up. She's so far ahead of me. They zoom toward me and I hold out my hand. Thank God. The adrenaline's gone and my body's shaking and useless. They both pull me up, setting me in between them. I put my arms around the lifeguard, his life jacket against my chest.

"Any injuries?" the lifeguard says above the roar of the motor.

"No," I say.

He motors toward shore, where a gaggle of spectators have gathered. I wonder how long they've been out there, watching us, thinking we were about to die. If the lifeguards have been using the loudspeakers, telling us to get out of the water. "We're pretty sure that was a Great White. They've been coming around for the sea lions." He accelerates so I can barely hear him, though he's shouting over his shoulder. "Once in a lifetime," I catch, and then he doesn't try to talk anymore.

Onshore, the lifeguards let us rinse off, then interview us in their wooden tower. Mostly Drew. I sit with a towel wrapped around me, the adrenaline evaporating, leaving my bones rubbery. I need a nap.

They mutter things like *incredible* and *lucky* and look at my sister with the same kind of unbridled admiration she gets when she plays her music. The kind I used to get, a long, long time ago. I swallow. My little sister is the hero. Deservedly so. I should be standing with the lifeguards, cheering for her, too.

"So what did you do?" The lifeguard who picked us up turns to me. He has a mass of red-orange hair, a wild full matching beard, skin reddened from the sun. "Kick it? Or did you punch it, too?"

I am quiet. I failed Drew. I'm the one with experience in the water and yet I'm the one who froze. I shrug. "I froze. I let her save me." A swill of shame rises, hot and miserable as the worst day of summer. Sweat leaks out through my wetsuit. I wait for him to say something, to verify or deny my idiocy.

The lifeguard nods. "Oh." He turns back to Drew, and another life-guard type person shows up and Drew retells the story again, her arms flying, animated.

I rub at my face. I feel nauseated and I just want to go home. I stand and interrupt my sister, who's arrived at the part, again, where she punches the eye. "It felt like punching rubber and goop. I think I actually felt its bare eyeball." She is radiant. Gorgeous. All the lifeguards sort of swoon and look at her like they're about to drop to one knee and propose, en masse.

I tap her shoulder. "Hey. Do you think we could go home? I want to go have a hot shower."

Drew blinks at me. "Can you wait just a second?"

"No. I really can't. I'll be in the car when you're ready." I walk out of the lifeguard shack, clutching the keys, my head down. I tell myself I'm just tired, but the truth is, there's something else secretly bothering me. I wish I didn't feel it. Envy. I'm jealous of my sister because she, what, saved my life? Yes, I admit to myself, barely able to form the syllable, even in my own head. Ugly and true. I walk faster, letting sharp rocks from the asphalt cut into my soles, like a penitent.

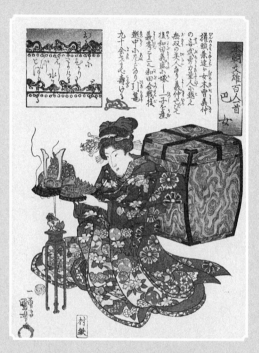

Tomoe, from the series One Hundred Poets from the
Literary Heroes of Our Country *by Utagawa Kuniyoshi*

BATTLE OF KURIKARA
CENTRAL-NORTHERN REGION
HONSHU, JAPAN
Summer 1183

Tomoe checked her appearance in the round bronze mirror and patted her oiled hair. Her armor was in place. She was ready—but inside she quelled a jolt of nerves.

Yamabuki, standing behind her with the comb, smiled at the wavering reflection. "Not even a typhoon will move your hair, Tomoe."

Tomoe frowned. She should stay here and protect the women. But Yoshinaka had ordered her to go. "If anything happens, if we don't return, take the children to Yoritomo's family in the Kantō."

Yamabuki inclined her head. "We will drown ourselves in the river before we let ourselves be captured."

Tomoe kept her gaze from meeting Yamabuki's. Let it not come to that.

She remembered the gift. After setting the mirror down, she went to a corner of the room and retrieved her old *naginata*. "I want you to have this. Remember how to use it."

Yamabuki took the tall weapon in her small hands. She propped it upright and inclined her head toward Tomoe. "It is too fine for me. I am not an *onnamusha*."

"Take it." Tomoe wished Yamabuki would pick up the *naginata* with a yell, swing it around, demonstrate her vigor. Instead, the woman was barely able to hold on to the heavy wooden pole. Surely they would be overtaken if attacked. All the women and children killed. Tomoe squelched the thought.

"*Arigato.*" Yamabuki bowed. She put the sword down and reached into her kimono, pressing something into Tomoe's palm. "I have something for you, too."

An *omamori*. A good-luck amulet. A rectangular envelope made of red cloth, with thin white string knotted at the top of the narrower side. Paper crunched inside. Yamabuki had written a prayer for Tomoe. *To keep you safe from all harm,* it read. Tomoe tucked it inside her kimono, near her heart.

"*Arigato.*" She bowed.

Yamabuki bowed back. "*Do-itashimashte.*" You're welcome. Her voice was as timid as it had been when she was a girl-bride. She reached up and hugged Tomoe fiercely.

Tomoe stepped back and looked into Yamabuki's round, worried eyes. "Don't be afraid. You are a warrior. You are of this family now. You understand?" She sounded fiercer than she meant to, and she feared Yamabuki would start crying, but Yamabuki simply drew herself up and nodded.

"I will remember." Yamabuki clasped Tomoe's hand as Tomoe studied her face. It seemed only yesterday that Yamabuki had arrived, but nine years had passed. Yamabuki had long ago lost her baby fat and delicate air. Her bony hand, in Tomoe's own, was coarsened, the skin rough as pine bark. This was not the life she was born to live. Tomoe felt almost guilty for her own unchanged beauty.

Yamabuki reached up with her free hand and tucked a stray hair behind Tomoe's ear. She began to cry.

"Stop," Tomoe said harshly, afraid she, too, would begin weeping.

Aoi, Yamabuki's two-year-old daughter, tugged at Tomoe's kimono. "Up," she said in her high voice. Tomoe picked up the girl, snuggling her chubby body against her own, taking in the little one's sweet-smelling black hair. Would she see this girl live to womanhood? She felt something break inside her and quickly handed Aoi over to Yamabuki before the toddler could sense her distress.

Tomoe leaned down and pressed her forehead against Yamabuki's. "Take care of my mother and the children." She straightened and took a step away. A retainer sounded a horn. They were leaving. *"Sayonara."* Farewell.

"Dewa mata atode." Yamabuki smiled at her over Aoi's round face.

Dewa mata atode. See you later. What a strange piece of optimism for Yamabuki to show. Tomoe didn't correct her.

Outside, Yoshinaka sat atop a snorting black Demon, in his full battle gear of bearskin shoes and grand iron helmet. Minamoto banners waved in the summer air. Hundreds of soldiers cheered when they saw her. "Tomoe! Tomoe!"

She lifted a hand and their voices rose. Without looking back at her family, Tomoe walked out from the porch and across the courtyard. Cherry Blossom waited, with her scarlet saddle, her silken blankets, her tasseled bridle.

"Let us go!" Yoshinaka shouted. "We will show my cousin who the true leader is!"

Tomoe nodded and swung atop the horse. They began walking out of the fortress, the dust kicking up. Tomoe sat tall. Only once did she turn in her saddle and watch as the figures of the women on the porch grew smaller and smaller, waving at her until they shimmered and faded, like a memory.

Sixteen

They drive to Rachel's house wet, not bothering to peel off their wetsuits. Rachel is quiet, her hands gripping the steering wheel hard, and Drew doesn't talk, either. Both of them are in their own worlds, a mishmash of emotions for Drew.

"You shouldn't have taken such a big risk," Rachel says when they pull into her garage.

"If anyone's going to get killed," Drew says, slamming the door, "it should be me. I don't have any kids. We're alive, aren't we?"

"You know what I think?" Rachel glances at Drew. "You're Tomoe and I'm Yamabuki. I think that's what Mom wants us to know."

Drew shakes her head. That's not right. It can't be. "No, Tomoe's the warrior."

"You're the one who fought. I'm Yamabuki, the one who stays at home. All devastated and messed up." Rachel goes into her house.

Drew follows. Her sister is just upset right now. She'll calm down. If anyone should be riled up, it should be Drew. She's the one who actually felt the slippery gelatinous eye under her nails. Shouldn't her sister be thanking her?

Instead, Rachel stands in the kitchen, dripping sand out of her wetsuit into small drifts on her clean kitchen floor, and ripping open a pile of mail. She tosses one toward Drew.

Addressee Unknown, it's stamped.

The letter to Hatsuko Minamoto.

Drew's hands, holding the letter, sag down to the cold counter. She lets the letter go, palming the granite, holding herself up.

There is no Hatsuko Minamoto. No way to find her. Perhaps she's already gone, dead for who knows how long. Drew thinks of their mother. Even in these past few weeks, she's grown frailer and smaller. She cannot sit in the chair by the window anymore, but spends her days in the bed or being wheeled to the dining room, where she's fed by an aide.

Drew inhales. "I guess that's that." It is as if they've reached another dead end in their small quest to help their mother. Drew wipes her eye. Why is she so emotional? What did she expect would happen—that Hatsuko would write back and spill everything Drew and Rachel never knew about Hikari? Ridiculous.

She tries to sit on the stool, wanting to talk to Rachel more about it. See how she feels.

"Don't sit there—you'll get it all dirty. Go take a shower," Rachel says sharply.

Oh. That's how she feels. Same old prickly Rachel. Rather than argue again, Drew complies. It is not her house, a fact that she feels more keenly every day. Anyway, Rachel's right. She's itchy.

When she comes out, Rachel's already dressed, stuffing a towel into Chase's sports duffel bag. "Can you hand me his phone?" Rachel points to the counter, where's it's charging. She tsks. "He never charges it and leaves it on all the time, then wonders why it dies. I don't know why we bothered getting him a phone at all."

"Guess every kid has one these days, right?" Drew picks it up. Phones hadn't been necessary when they were growing up. If a parent didn't know where they were, well, they just had to keep worrying for a little while. Not have this instant gratification, the tracking apps that use satellites to tell you exactly where your kids are. You'd think people would be more relaxed, but everybody just seems even more wound up than in the past.

Drew unplugs it, turns it over, activates the screen by accident. There's a photo on it and Drew glances at it before she can stop herself.

It is a woman's completely, one hundred percent bare torso, reflected in a bathroom mirror with Wet n Wild nail polishes and Noxzema acne creams scattered over the counter. Just the body. Mostly her breasts, which the women—or girl—pushes together with one arm. The only parts of her head visible are her chin and lips, which are poised in that annoying fake pout like she's wearing waxen ones.

Drew clamps her hand over the phone, as if she's throwing a blanket over the girl. She closes her eyes and feels her face turn bright, hot red. "Ohmygodohmygodohmygod," Drew mutters, and it's really a prayer. A plea for help.

"What is it?" Rachel comes over to her and takes the phone out from under Drew's hand. Her face pales. "Who would send him this? Is this a grown woman?"

Drew gulps and shakes her head. "I'm pretty sure that's his girlfriend."

"Girlfriend? What girlfriend?" Rachel scrolls through the other texts. She blows out a relieved breath. "That was the only one. Unless he deleted them already." Then she looks sharply at her sister. "How do you know this is his girlfriend? Chase doesn't have a girlfriend. He still plays with Legos, for Christ's sake! He's not allowed to have a girlfriend." Rachel's voice rises and bellows through the kitchen. "Fucking hell. What the fuck?"

Drew sits on the stool, feeling like she's about to throw up. She has to tell Rachel. Damn Chase for not keeping his end of the bargain. Damn Drew for not telling Rachel in the first place. Maybe she could have prevented this. Drew closes her eyes to block out Rachel's angry ones. "I saw a girl with Chase. I think it's the same girl."

"What's her name? I'm going to call her parents." Rachel's voice shakes.

Drew's eyes fly open. "No." That girl at the Halloween carnival—a mother like that won't take this well. She swallows. "I don't think her parents are the understanding type. I think they're the type who'd kick her out or beat her."

Rachel shakes her head. She reads aloud as she texts. "*This is Chase's mother. Do not contact him again or I will contact the authorities and your parents.* There." She looks at Drew. "Well? You going to tell me who she is, since you know all about her parents? Why didn't you tell me any of this? What's been going on?" Her voice rises again, frantic.

Drew can't look her sister in the eyes. *Just say it to her.* But Drew finds herself afraid.

Rachel's never tried to get back at Drew when she was angry. Rather, she did something worse. She wouldn't let Drew make amends. When Drew was eight and Rachel twelve, Drew snuck into her sister's room to borrow Rachel's prized Madonna *True Blue* CD, one that Drew was expressly forbidden to touch. But Drew loved the song, "Papa Don't Preach." She made a tape off the CD and returned it.

Later Rachel knocked on her door. "I know you touched my CD. Your greasy little fingerprints are all over it."

Drew had apologized, but that wasn't enough for Rachel. Her sister didn't talk to her for three days. Frozen out. "Good night!" Drew would call out, like she always did, into the wall separating their rooms. Rachel would not answer. The coldness, the withholding, was the worst punishment Rachel could have thought of.

So Drew is mindful when she has to tell her sister bad news, or tell her sister that she made a mistake. They're adults now, Drew tells herself. Rachel's not going to do that. "I caught Chase making out with a high school girl. I assume it's the same one. Like, really making out."

Rachel raises an eyebrow. She leans against the counter. "How old?"

"Seventeen." God. It sounds even worse out loud. That is almost an adult, whereas Chase just started growing whiskers in the past year. "Look. I talked to Chase. He said he would cut it off with her. He *promised*."

Her sister shakes her head. Clearly disgusted with her. *Drew, you're so gullible.* A hormone-addled teenage boy isn't going to give up on a girl so easily. Not a girl who'd send him a photo like that. When Rachel speaks, her voice is low. "You should have fucking told me."

Drew spreads her hands out. "I'm sorry. We thought you'd freak out."

Rachel blinks hard, several times, and familiar dread invades Drew. "No. I only freak out when people lie to me."

"I never lied. I just didn't tell you." It had really seemed like the right thing to do at the time. Why was Drew's judgment always so bad? She feels tears stinging her eyes.

"A lie of omission." Rachel leans forward and glares at her. "Don't you go fucking crying at me. It's not going to work. You really screwed up. How do I know I can trust you with anything?"

Drew wipes furiously at her eyes. "Stop cursing at me."

"I'll fucking curse all the fuck I want! This is my fucking house." Rachel paces around the island.

"Calm down." Drew puts her head on the counter, willing herself to stop crying. *What did crying ever solve?* Tomoe asked Yamabuki. Not a damn thing.

"You know what I'm really sick of?" Rachel says. "Everyone telling me to calm down. Maybe everyone around here needs to get more excited."

"What are you going to do? Kick Chase out of the house?" Drew keeps her head down, the granite against her forehead. "Why is he doing this? Is it just hormones, or is something else going on with him? Too much stress at school? At home?" Or did the opportunity just present itself, and Chase went along with it?

Rachel laughs shortly. "Ha. I don't know. Maybe Chase can save some time and drop out of middle school instead of college, like his sister."

Drew looks at her sister. "Quincy dropped out?"

Rachel nods.

"Why didn't you tell me? When did this happen?" This hurts, too. Rachel withholding.

"Why didn't you tell me about this? Shut up. I don't need to tell you anything." Rachel points at Drew's face. "You are just their aunt. Not their mother. You haven't bothered to get to know them in all these years. It's too fucking late for you to butt in."

Drew grabs Rachel's hand. "I haven't bothered to get to know them? You barely let me see them." Drew recalls all those truncated family visits. The quick birthday calls.

"I let you be around as much as you wanted." Rachel crosses her arms. "It wasn't much." She takes a breath and finishes packing Chase's bag.

"Yeah," Drew says. "But you had to *watch* me the whole time. With your judgy eyes."

"Judgy eyes? What does that even mean?" Rachel sighs and stands up. She brushes off her pants like she's brushing off her tirade. "Drew. Be serious."

"I am." It wasn't the best choice of word but Drew forges on. "When they were babies, you'd tell me I was doing things wrong. That diaper is wrong. And redo it."

"You did it wrong. The diaper would have leaked." She sticks Chase's phone into her purse. There's Rachel again. So reasonable and mature. While Drew's the one who's enraged and shaking now. "You have to do things a certain way."

"You mean your way." Drew crosses her arms to keep herself from jumping up and rushing at her sister, pushing her, the way she did when she was little. "Everything's got to be your way."

Rachel roots around in the papers on the counter, looking for something. "I know I didn't go to college, but I actually know what I'm doing sometimes." She finds a form, puts it in her purse, too.

"College? Why are you bringing that up? Who said anything about college?" Drew watches her sister. She needs to get Rachel's attention. She's always felt that unless she screams or cries, Rachel ignores her. Just like with her parents. Maybe that's what's up with her kids. She grabs her hairbrush out of Rachel's hands. "If it's anybody's fault you didn't finish, it's your own. Nobody made you get pregnant except you."

Rachel pauses, not looking at Drew, and Drew knows the blow landed. She expects a feeling of triumph, but instead she desperately wishes she could pluck those words out of the air and stuff them back down her own throat.

Then Rachel draws out a sigh. "Well, your life hasn't exactly turned out great, Drew. At least I worked hard and fixed mine."

"You think I don't work hard?" Drew glares at Rachel. They always knew where to cut deep, didn't they?

Rachel shakes her head and now looks right into Drew's eyes. She gets close. "We're a soft landing spot for you. You've always had soft landing spots. You're Daddy's little girl."

"I'm not." Drew's nostrils flare.

"You are. Always have been. You know what, Drew? You're thirty-four fucking years old. You've never had a relationship or a job work out." Rachel points at her. "Maybe at some point you should say to yourself, *Hmm, maybe the problem isn't everyone else. Maybe it's ME. Maybe I'm doing something wrong.* But you don't. You always blame everyone but yourself." Rachel's practically spitting in Drew's face. "Take some responsibility for once in your life."

A hot little flame of rage flares up. She wants Rachel away from her. Drew shoves her sister in the upper chest. Not hard. The way she did when she was little. Only they're not little anymore. "Stop it, Rachel."

Rachel glares at her and picks up the duffel bag. "I need to go pick up my son now." She walks toward the door, then pauses and addresses Drew again. "I don't need a stranger telling me I'm a crappy mother."

Drew turns her head away. Rachel knows which words will hurt the most. And so does Drew. The words hang in front of her. She chooses to say them even as her heart screams at her to stop. "You know what, Rachel? It's so ironic. You hate our father, but you've turned out exactly like him. Mean. Controlling."

Drew watches her sister's face crumple at the sting. Maybe they're both like him. They tried not to be him. They have become him anyway. Nasty and bitter. A lump fills Drew's throat. Drew holds up a hand. "I'm sorry, Rachel."

Rachel's mouth clamps shut. Her whole body seems to drop thirty degrees in temperature. "Okay, then." Rachel looks down for a second, then speaks calmly. "Go back to your own home, Drew. I don't really need any more of your help. Such as it is." She opens the door, her form silhouetted by the sun, before she shuts it.

KURIKARA PASS

CENTRAL-NORTHERN REGION

HONSHU, JAPAN

Summer 1183

As they approached the Kurikara Pass, Tomoe could hear the voices of the Taira bouncing off the rocky walls. She swallowed. Yoshinaka had perhaps eight hundred soldiers, while the Taira still had several thousand. They were hopelessly outnumbered.

Her fingers grazed the good-luck amulet near her heart.

They began ascending the pass, toward the waiting Taira. Demon snorted and stomped, ready as his master for a fight. "Whatever happens," Yoshinaka swung about in his saddle, "be prepared for battle when I give the signal. Understood?"

Tomoe did not answer. Around her, the men shouted *"Hai!"* in one fierce voice.

"Do you know what's going on?" Tomoe whispered to Kanehira.

"Yes, but you don't need to," Kanehira answered. "You're just a figure-head." With those words, he spurred his horse ahead of the rest, declaring, "Taira warriors! I am Kanehira Imai, son of Kaneto Nakahara, foster brother to Lord Yoshinaka Minamoto! Behold the best archer in all of

Japan!" He bowed. "Who will challenge me? Who can bear the shame of losing to a Minamoto?"

An archery battle? Of course. This would take hours. The samurai were foolishly proud men; they loved to see whose forces could boast the best swordsman, the best archer.

The Taira broke into an excited murmur, rearranging their troops to either side. This contest was but a distraction, she thought, to keep the Taira from noticing Yoshinaka's pitiful numbers.

A Taira mounted on a black mare ran forward. "I regret to inform you of your misinformation!" he shouted. "I am Takamune Kazurahara, son of Shinnō, and it is I who is the best archer in all of Japan!" His horse pranced and snorted, kicking up a cloud of gray dust. The Taira cheered lustily.

At its widest, the pass was only as big as a dozen horses end to end. Near the beginning, the pass had no walls of mountain, but narrowed into a natural bridge over a steep, tall ravine. One misstep would send a rider to his death. But Tomoe supposed it was no more painful than dying in a battle.

The matches wore on into the afternoon. No one fell into the canyon. Tomoe sat down on the embankment and ate her ration of rice cake as Cherry Blossom chewed the grass into stumps all around her. Below, the men felt no such boredom. They cheered enthusiastically at each new match and even broke out the sake.

So this was war. Tomoe dozed. *I get more rest here than at home*, she thought.

The line of soldiers volunteering for the arrow battle grew shorter as the day progressed. She gave up listening for Yoshinaka's battle charge. Obviously it would happen later. Perhaps tomorrow. Tomoe dabbed at her perspiring forehead and considered mounting Cherry Blossom and riding into the distance, never to be seen again. She'd fly back home, retrieve little Yoshitaka, Aoi, Yamabuki, and Chizuru, and take them to the Kantō. Yoshinaka wouldn't notice for weeks.

But then Tomoe thought of the farmers who had joined their army, of her father—his dream of helping the Minamoto overthrow the Taira rule. Of the Taira putting the child puppet-emperor into place. Of the indifferent government that heavily taxed its people and let them die of starvation and disease. Of the Search and Destroy troops who killed innocents like Kaneto.

Kaneto's voice came back to her on the wind, whispering in her ear. *You must watch over Yoshinaka,* he had said. She was her foster brother's keeper, then as now.

She watched Yoshinaka, his broad back as he sat on Demon, gesturing to her brother. Whenever she looked at him, a flutter of anticipation went through her, as though she were still a girl mooning over her first crush.

She knew she would stay even if Kaneto had released her. She would stay if Yoshinaka told her to go home.

The Minamoto *horagai* sounded, the conch trumpet. A roar rose from the other side of the mountain. Yoshinaka had sent soldiers up around the other side, to surprise the Taira from behind, Tomoe realized. The duel had been a ruse, an all-day distraction.

Now the Minamoto cut down the unsuspecting soldiers as if they were stalks of grass. The Taira soldiers pulled out their swords and tried to shoot arrows, but, caught by surprise, they tumbled about like a spilled bag of Go pieces. Tomoe mounted Cherry Blossom and urged her forward to help.

A Taira warrior galloped at Tomoe, his sword whipping viciously through the air. Tomoe had just enough time to unsheathe her sword and block him; the clang of their blades nearly knocked her off Cherry Blossom. She swung, aiming for the vulnerable part of her attacker's armor, where the helmet connected to the neck, and drove her blade up and under. She made contact and he fell from his horse. His head, freed of its body, thumped against her thigh; a long hot trail of blood soaked through her pants. Tomoe gritted her teeth, breathing through her nose. The air smelled of sour sake and blood, of fear.

She concentrated on navigating Cherry Blossom past the ravine. A man came at her and she shoved him with her foot, sending him screaming over the edge onto the sharp rocks far below.

Still, she feared there were too many Taira to defeat.

But now something else was happening below. The ground shook. In-human shrieking reverberated up from the front, down the pass, and Tomoe thought of legendary trolls who ate passersby. What was happening? The entire battle paused.

A herd of oxen charged in, up from the valley, flaming torches tied to their horns, their massive bodies hurtling up the mountain pass like boulders flung from a catapult.

Hundreds of Taira, surprised on the bottom of the pass, leapt out of the way, falling headlong to their deaths with high-pitched screams. Others were trampled. A few men tried stabbing at the oxen, but the oxen were maddened from the torches on their heads and stampeded blindly, snorting and bleating in terror as they charged through the pass.

Tomoe fought her way back down into the valley. Only a hundred or so Taira were still standing, the Minamoto putting them down in final skirmishes. Suddenly Tomoe was alone among the Taira dead and wounded, the battlefield soiling the peaceful valley like black mold on rice. The sun hung heavy and red, searing its last rays through the clouds.

Tomoe began walking among the wounded, searching for those she could help. She bandaged wounds and set broken bones as the injured rasped out their new, undying support for the Minamoto clan.

An old man lay on his back, his feet and arms splayed limply, like a crushed doll's. He caught Tomoe's attention because, although his face was deeply creased and liver-spotted, his hair was a curious jet-black. An inky black substance ran over his cheeks and forehead.

"Yoshinaka!" Tomoe gestured at Yoshinaka. "Come and see this one."

Yoshinaka squatted down next to her, squinting. "An old man? What is he doing in battle?"

The old man had dyed his hair to look younger, she realized, so that the enemy would treat him as an equal. To do otherwise would lead to dishonor. "Who are you?" Tomoe shook him gently. "Tell me. Let me help."

"A woman on the battlefield? It must be Tomoe Gozen." The old man opened his eyes. They were so opaque with cataracts that Tomoe wondered how he could see at all. He smiled toothlessly. "I am Sanemori Saito. I have something to tell you."

Sanemori Saito. Though she had not heard the name for many years, she recognized it instantly. This was the samurai who had rescued Yoshinaka as an infant, bringing him to live with Tomoe's family. She did not remember that day, of course; she was too young. But Kaneto had talked of him often.

Sanemori closed his eyes. "Your cousin Yoritomo will betray you just as his father betrayed your father."

"What?" Yoshinaka leaned closer.

"It was your uncle who killed your father, Yoshinaka. Not the Taira. Your own family stole your father's title and land. You must not trust him. You must be the new leader of the Minamoto." The man coughed, struggling to speak through his agony. Tomoe gently wiped at his face. "Or they will kill you for certain."

Sanemori went still. Yoshinaka lowered the man's body to the earth. Still, he said nothing. Yoshinaka rose and walked off, disappearing among the dead.

Seventeen

I manage to hold myself together, acting normal and calm when I pick up Chase and a couple of his teammates, and drive them out to East County for a tournament. Sit there clapping and chatting with the other mothers and fathers though I just want to ask them all, *Has this happened to you? What should I do?*

When Tom finally gets home in the late evening, he finds me in our bathroom, sitting on the toilet lid and staring blankly at the wall. I'm blowing my nose with a wad of toilet paper. It's where every mom goes to weep privately, without interruption.

"What happened?" Tom asks. "Can you move, please? I have to . . ." He gestures to the toilet and I stand up.

"The world fell apart while you were at work." I splash cold water on my face.

"Uh-oh." Tom flushes the toilet and washes his hands.

I look at his face in the mirror, touch his five-o'clock stubble. Drew was gone when I got home, just like I asked. Everything gone.

I made a mistake with Drew. Drove her away just because I needed to be right. I don't know what's happened with Chase and Quincy—do I act the same with them, without realizing it? I need to stop needing to be right. It's a disease, this thing. My sister was right. I am as controlling as Killian, in my own special way.

I tell Tom about Chase.

His jaw tightens. "I'll talk to him."

"Talk? That's it?"

"What else can we do? Beat him?" Tom shakes his head. "I'll take his phone and his computer away."

We're silent for a moment. Then I speak. "All know is, if Quincy had been dating a high school junior when she was in eighth grade, you would have broken out the shotgun and gone over to that boy's house."

He nods. "But she didn't. And maybe I'm more reasonable now."

"No. She's just getting married at age twenty. We are doing a spectacular job." I turn on the cold water, splash it on my face again. "How did this all get so fucked up?"

Tom spins me around and takes me in his arms. "Rachel. It's not all as bad as you think."

"That's because you're a pathological optimist." I push my forehead into his shoulder, like my kids would do when they were little and tired. How I want to be a kid again. To be loved and carried around. But I'm not. I have the kids now. Sometimes I feel like I'm pretending to be a grown-up. "I think I should talk to him." I lift my head. "Is it different for boys? I mean, people always think it's okay for boys to do that, but not girls."

Tom puts his cheek on my head. "Yeah. You get called a stud for sleeping with girls, and a girl gets called a slut." He sighs. "I remember the pressure to do it, like I should sleep with the first girl who'd let me, but after—feeling like it wasn't all that great."

I nod. Tom and I don't really talk about our past lovers. They are, after all, in the past. "I know what it's like to fool around before you're ready."

Tom tightens his hold. "Maybe you should share that with him."

I swallow. I'm his mother. He's supposed to hold me in high esteem. Compare all other women against me. If he knows I slept around so much, will Chase become disillusioned? "You want me to tell him about——me? I don't want him to think I'm a slut, too."

Tom said, "But I don't think poorly about you, Rachel. I didn't care about your past. Why should you teach your son to judge people by what personal mistakes they made decades ago? Is that what you do?"

I think about the chastity-only movement. The ones that visit schools sometimes. That say you're used, a piece of trash, a worthless piece of chewed-up gum, if you've ever been with someone other than your husband. That's how I felt, actually, coming out of the other end of it. I felt like there was no forgiveness, no grace. No penitence strong enough.

I don't want Chase to have these devaluing thoughts. I have to offer myself up.

I have to come down off my pedestal.

I knock softly on Chase's door. On the outside are signs he's been posting since age ten. A sign about the Zombie Apocalypse. A crayon sign saying "Stay Out, This Means You Quincy."

There's no sound inside; he's probably listening to music on his headphones. Finally I hear him galumph across the hardwood (the boy would make a terrible cat burglar) and he opens up the door.

"Hey." I look right at him, seeing him as I haven't seen him for a long time. He's taller than I remembered. With my mother and his sister and everything else, how much have I seen my son this year? Not much. I've watched him play sports and driven him to school, but how well have I really gotten to know him lately?

Soon, too soon, he'll be gone, off to college, hopefully. "You've been growing up behind my back."

He goes to his desk, sits. "Quincy always said she was sneaking caffeine into my food, so I wouldn't get taller than her."

"It didn't work." I lean against the doorframe, dig my fingernails into my arms. Having a sex talk with my daughter felt awkward, but this is in a whole new stratosphere. I don't know how I got so straitlaced. It seems like I spent so many years corralling Wild Rachel that I've become Prude Rachel. "Chase, you got a text today. A photo, from a girl."

The blood drains out of his face. "Why are you looking at my phone? It's private."

"It's technically my phone, Chase. That was part of the deal." The deal we made when he got his own phone: his father and I could look at it whenever we liked. Electronics are a privilege, not a right. All that good stuff. He's been signing Good Electronics Moral code since he was in third grade. "She was naked."

He goes very still. Then he brushes his hair back, puts on a Padres cap backward. "I didn't tell her to."

"No." I take a breath, close my eyes.

"You deleted it, right?" He's talking fast, nervous.

I open my eyes. "Of course." I swallow. "Has she done it before?"

He nods, not looking at me.

"You didn't . . . share them, did you?"

"Of course not. I deleted them." He stands up again. "I told her to leave me alone, just like Aunt Drew said. But she wouldn't. She kept calling and e-mailing and sending those . . . pictures." His voice quivers, full of tears. "She wouldn't stop."

"Well. She'll stop now." Oh my God. She's been harassing him. "I wish you would have told us. Let us help."

"It would make it worse." He sits on his bed, wipes at his eyes, embarrassed. "What's my punishment?"

I clear my throat. I don't want to punish him. I want him to understand. "I want to tell you something about me. I mean, that's not the punishment." I allow myself a small grin, which he returns. "It's related but not related."

He angles his head to the side. Listening. No headphones, no phone, no car. Just me and my son.

I tell him. Everything. About me and my father. About the drinking, drugs, boys. How I got kicked out.

Chase tilts his head back and squints at me. "That was a long time ago."

"I know."

"I mean, a really, really long time ago. A whole generation ago."

I spurt out a laugh. "Yeah. Prehistoric."

He shakes his head. "Did you think I'd, like, shun you or something?"

I shrug. "I don't know what I thought. I was ashamed. I didn't want you to know."

"Mom, the only time I'm ever ashamed of you is when you dance. Seriously." He lies back on his bed, putting his hands behind his head, grinning.

I sit on the bed next to him. "I just don't want you to get hurt. In body, mind, or spirit. I want you to be safe. Never be afraid of us. Okay? I promise. We will always be there for you."

He wrinkles his brow at me. "Okay, Mom. I get it."

Does he? It's hard to tell. Nobody can really tell anything about anyone—all you can do is hope and trust.

Chase pats my arm. "Don't worry. I'm not hiding any other deep, dark secrets." He sighs. "Well, Mom. I'm glad we could have this talk. I feel very much wiser now."

"I think it's just 'feel wiser.'" I pat his arm back.

"Way to ruin my moment, Mom." He smiles a half smile, one corner crooking up. "Now can I finish my homework?"

I take his phone with me and look at it to see if the girl responded. She has not.

The last text is from Drew. My breath catches. I open the thread.

Chase: You left without saying good-bye.

Drew: I know. I'm really sorry. I had stuff I had to take care of up here.

Chase: We had fun. When are you coming back?

Drew: I'm not sure. But we'll keep in touch. I
promise.

He hasn't answered.

I slump against the wall. *We had fun. When are you coming back?* is Chase-speak for *I'm glad I got to know you. I love you.*

But it's too late to do anything about Drew right now. I turn off the phone and head for bed.

Drew stands in the middle of her studio apartment, wondering where on earth her basket of clean clothes can be. She knows it's in here somewhere. She shifts a throw blanket, finds it under there.

For the first hour and a half of her drive home, Drew stewed about Rachel. Of course Drew had a part in the fight, but Rachel was the one who told her she wasn't part of her family. Fine. Let her live her life with her kids. Apart from her. Drew had no family anymore. She thought, for a moment, of Alan. Alan didn't count.

But by the time she passed the false snowy fiberglass peak of the Disneyland Matterhorn in Anaheim, halfway up to L.A., she was feeling regretful. She should have told Rachel about Chase. Drew would have wanted to know, if she had a son. Drew had messed up. But she only wanted to keep the bond she and Chase had developed, and prevent a Rachel meltdown. Rachel spent so much time trying to be the perfect mother and wife that her children were afraid to mess up. They wouldn't come to Rachel with problems while the problems were still little. They were secretive, even if they didn't intend to be—as secretive as Rachel was about keeping her past hidden. And look—she'd had a meltdown anyway.

All their family kept parts of themselves hidden. Afraid of rejection and pissing off the others. "Tomoe Gozen wouldn't do that," Drew says aloud to her empty dwelling. Tomoe not caring whether her brother hated her. Whether Yamabuki was displeased. She was simply Tomoe, unapologetic.

A fine layer of dust covers all the belongings in her small studio, the bed, the couch, and the kitchen all in one space. Drew puts her hands on her hips and takes a mental assessment of her belongings. Most of her furniture is from the thrift store, painted white so everything matches. The couch is ancient, obtained for free from a curb and slipcovered to hide its crumbling interior. The television's prone to conking out. The appliances aren't hers. Drew's afraid to look in the fridge. She probably doesn't have much in there. She doesn't even own a plant.

She could walk away from these four hundred square feet and not think twice. If she had anywhere else to go.

A message from Alan appears on her phone. *Drew, I want to see you again. Please. I need to talk to you.*

She texted him back. *Bad idea. Sorry.* This, at least, she could do right. Stick to her guns.

Her gaze falls on her viola case. Sitting right where she left it, next to her bed.

This is her most precious possession. It has a spruce top, and cost thousands of dollars. Why didn't she take it with her?

Drew doesn't have an answer. She snaps open the latches. The warm wood shines up at her and she puts her fingertips on it. This instrument has seen her through since she was sixteen. It was her birthday present. Drew remembers opening the red package in front of her mother.

"Do you like it?" At the time, Drew thought her mother's tone was neutral. Now, as she thinks back, she remembers the emotion hobbling her mother's eyes. The hope and the fear.

"I do." Drew hugged the viola to her. "I love it."

"You better like it," Killian said. "It cost more than a year of college."

Drew puts her hand on the strings and plucks one, thinking of the *koto* that Yamabuki played, how she still found some beauty in her difficult new life. This is what Yamabuki taught Tomoe. Together, they formed the warrior-poet. Tomoe found satisfaction from being a domestic nurturer as well as venturing out into the world. There was no reason she and Rachel couldn't do both, too.

A text comes in. Chase. Oh no. She hadn't said good-bye. But really, she *had* to leave right then, not wait until he got home. And she thought he wouldn't care. That he'd be angry with her for getting him in trouble, and besides, there was that whole water polo thing. Wasn't he glad to have her out, not interfering with his business?

When are you coming back?

Drew shuts her eyes, pinches the bridge of her nose. A lump in her throat.

She loves this boy.

She loved him before, of course. In a more abstract way. But now . . . Everything's different. It is like how Tomoe loves little Yoshitaka, Drew thinks. Loves him even though he's not hers biologically. Loves him like he's a piece of her beating heart, existing outside of her body. Vulnerable and scary as that is.

And now Drew wouldn't want it to go back to how it was before. She can have a good relationship with Chase and Quincy even if their mother doesn't like her. She sets her teeth. She will. She texts him back.

Drew gets her purse, takes out the little black notebook and gets her favorite pen, a gel roller with a medium point. She thinks of Rachel. Of Alan. Of Tomoe and Yamabuki. Their mother. Of finding and losing people.

Without thinking further, she begins to write. Sometimes she stops and picks up the viola, plays a string of notes. The music will come later. Her lyrics come first.

T omoe watched cousin Yoritomo's soldiers march into the fortress. Four carried a litter with a cabin on top, big enough to hold two or three people. These men were accompanied by a dozen more soldiers on horseback.

They had been home for only two weeks. Yoshinaka won all his battles with sheer guile, against huge numbers. The victories made his cousin nervous. Word got to him that Yoshinaka wanted to oust him as the head of the Minamoto clan.

Yoritomo had decided not to do away with Yoshinaka—his skills as a general were too badly needed. No, there was only one other way to control him.

Yoritomo was taking little Yoshitaka as collateral.

If Yoshinaka was to try to take over, little Yoshitaka would be killed. If Yoshinaka behaved, then Yoshitaka might have a chance.

The men set the litter into the courtyard. A cloud of dust rose. Tomoe felt as though ice had replaced her blood. She put her hand on her sword without realizing it.

Chizuru grabbed Tomoe's wrist. "You must be strong."

"Of course." Tomoe folded her hands in front of her and quelled her stomach.

Chizuru glanced at the sky. "At least the weather is kind for the journey. It is before the frosts. That we can be thankful for."

Tomoe regarded it, too. She hoped the wind wouldn't blow between the litter's bamboo planks, that they had some kind of insulation. It was October, and the temperature had begun its inexorable drop. Wind-scudded feathery clouds drifted past the fortress and ruffled Tomoe's clothes. She knew her mother had packed several thick woolen blankets and Yoshitaka's heavier kimonos and jackets for the boy, but still she did not feel reassured.

Little Yoshitaka was playing in the yard, chasing the curly-tailed orange-and-white Akita dogs and barking like them, his straight black hair flying out behind him. His feet were bare and dirty, kicking up reddish dust, his pants covered in mud; bean sauce stained his mouth. Just like his father. Tomoe watched him with a mix of love and dread. He was six years old, still young enough to be sweet and give plenty of hugs, but all boy. Her eyes filled and she bit down sharply on her tongue. Behind, his little sister, Aoi, chased her brother the best she could on her chubby short legs. Sometimes Yoshitaka allowed her to catch him, making her scream with delight.

Who would be her playmate now? The new baby coming, Tomoe supposed. But nobody could replace their firstborn son.

Behind her, the door of the house slid open and she sensed Yoshinaka's presence. Another set of footsteps—Kanehira.

"I hope you look at your son and see that trying to defeat Yoritomo is not worthwhile," Tomoe said. If Yoshinaka had not tried the stunt with promising land, this wouldn't be happening. Her voice was cold. "You may be an excellent general, but you're a horrible politician."

Yoshinaka did not answer. He pushed past her and went into the courtyard, her brother following. Tomoe felt light-headed, sick with helpless anger. They waited.

At last the retainer Yoritomo had sent struggled out of the litter, shaking his skinny legs as though they were numb. He was better dressed than the others and wore a short black cap set upon his head. "Lord Kiso?" he called. Kiso, hillbilly of the north.

Yoshinaka grunted, but kept his expression neutral. *"Hai."*

"Are they here?" Yamabuki came outdoors, shielding her eyes against the sun.

"Yes." Tomoe held out her hand to help Yamabuki down from the porch, but Yamabuki waved her away. Instead, Tomoe put her arm around Yamabuki's thin shoulders. "Are you well, Yamabuki-chan?"

"Of course not." Her voice was all blades. "Why would I be?"

Tomoe watched Yoshitaka throw a stick for his dogs. If Yamabuki fell apart, he would mirror her terror. "Have courage."

"Do not tell me to have courage, Tomoe." Her voice rose, mocking Tomoe. *"Be brave, Yamabuki. Be like the great warrior Tomoe Gozen."* Tears spilled onto Yamabuki's cheeks. "I never ask the gods for wealth or power or to have my beauty back. All I want is to raise my children. Is this so grand? So unattainable?"

"Yamabuki." Tomoe clutched Yamabuki's shoulder, trying to think of what to say. There were no words.

The dogs stopped their game and barked at the strangers. Yoshinaka clapped his hands twice, and the dogs fell silent. Tomoe wished she could bark, too, could have that outlet, running and screaming until her voice and body gave out.

Yamabuki stood up straight and approached the retainer. "I am Yama-buki. Know that you will answer to me if any harm comes to him."

The retainer's mouth twitched in amusement. Yamabuki's hair was wild, her kimono askew. No doubt they considered Yamabuki to be the female Kiso, a good wife for the crazy Yoshinaka. The retainer humored her with a slight inclination of his head. "I will treat him as my own son during the journey."

"Some sons are not treated so well," Yamabuki said darkly.

Kanehira helped the soldiers load the boy's trunk. No man spoke. How could they be like tree trunks, all solid and unfeeling? Next to Tomoe, Yamabuki trembled. *Do something,* Tomoe felt Yamabuki plead. Or perhaps it was her own voice in her head.

Tomoe stepped forward, her fingers closing around the hilt of her sword. The soldiers looked at her cautiously. Tomoe would hold on to Yo-shitaka with her life. She would fight the men with her teeth. Until they kicked her into ashes. "Wait," Tomoe said.

But she could not do anything. Yoritomo had thousands of men. They could not fight his army. And if they resisted now, all of their heads would be cut off. Even Yoshitaka's.

Yamabuki held her arms out to Yoshitaka, burying her face in the boy's shoulder. "Will you do nothing, then?" she whispered shakily to Tomoe. "The brave *onnamusha?*"

Tomoe swallowed, anguish fighting its way up her throat. If they fought now, a bad outcome was certain. If they waited, at least they had hope. "This is his only chance to grow into a man. Let him go and he may come back to us, or we to him."

"What's happening?" the little boy asked. He glanced from face to face, all of them stern and sad. "I must go alone?"

"Cousin Yoritomo is your new *otōsan,*" Yoshinaka answered in his stern-est voice. "You must do as he and your new mother say."

"They are exceedingly kind to their children," the retainer piped in.

Yoshitaka's eyes grew as big as the moon. "No Okāsan?"

Tomoe met his eyes and remembered him as a tiny baby, his head still pointed from birthing. "Yoshitaka-chan," she said, "it is all right if you are afraid. We are all afraid."

He screwed up his face in that way he had when he was trying not to cry and nodded mutely. Tomoe knelt. "Remember, this feeling will not last forever. But our love will." She had to make him understand. Give him something to concentrate on. She saw a stray black thread on his dark kimono, near his chest, and touched it with her fingertips. "See this thread, near your heart?"

He nodded.

She plucked it out. "There is a thread like this that no man can see. It goes from your heart to your mother's, and to mine. If you are afraid, pull on it." She gave a tug in the air on her imaginary thread. "And we will be there, in your mind. Just like that." She snapped her fingers.

"Like this?" he snapped his fingers. "I did it!"

"You did it." She put her arms around his sturdy body and held him. "Now you tug the thread," she said. He tugged the air. Tomoe clutched her heart. "I felt it!"

Yoshitaka grinned. "Me too! Did you, Okāsan?"

"I did." Yamabuki smiled. Kanehira helped her stand.

"Yoshitaka!" Yoshinaka called. The boy leapt over to his father, his small feet scuffing the dirt into clouds. To Tomoe's surprise, Yoshinaka bent and kissed his son's forehead tenderly. "You will grow up to be a brave and strong man. We will meet again."

Yamabuki turned her face into Kanehira's shoulder and collapsed; her brother-in-law had to hold her up. Tomoe went in her stead, embracing the boy. She felt his heart skittering like a jackrabbit's. "Good-bye, little son of my heart," she whispered.

The retainer took Yoshitaka's hand, led him into the litter. The last thing Tomoe saw was his smooth blue-black hair disappearing, like a dark stone falling into a well. The men picked up the poles. Tomoe did not want to watch. Yet she must. Yoshitaka's small hand stuck out, the fingers grasping air.

"Okāsan!" he screamed. *"Okāsan! Obasan!"* Mother, auntie! He broke into wordless wails, like a small animal who knew it was going to be slaughtered, shrill and loud.

Yoshinaka's stern face softened. "Wait!" He called a dog to him, the orange and cream one called Nariko. "Let him take his dog." Yoshinaka bowed deeply to the man inside the litter. He handed in a bag of coins. The retainer opened the door and Yoshinaka hoisted the dog inside.

Yoshinaka caught up his son's hand through the opening, walking beside the litter as the men carried it away, holding Yoshitaka's tiny palm in his big, rough, hairy one. He held his son's hand through the gate and beyond, not letting go until they reached the trees.

Eighteen

E arly the following afternoon, I sit in my kitchen drinking a cup of coffee that I've rewarmed. It's slightly disgusting, but I'm too lazy to make a fresh pot. I dip a shortbread cookie one of the kids had baked and rejected for being a little too well done. The bake sale, held last week, was a success, netting almost three hundred dollars. I did not dance around and yell *In your face!* at Elizabeth, though I sort of wanted to.

This morning I visited my mother again, hoping, as I always do, for another moment of sentience. "Drew's gone home, Mom," I'd said to her softly, but my mother continued to sleep, never opening her eyes once, her breakfast untouched on the tray table.

Now I'm trying to keep my mind off my sister. It's impossible—I've just stripped the sheets off the guest room bed, and the smell of the fruity apple shampoo she uses still clings to them. She left a hairbrush here, too, the bristles embedded with her hair.

I put my head on the cold granite, staring at my mug. "#1 Mom," it says, emblazoned with tiny handprints from both of my children. Made for Mother's Day when they were little. I turn the mug so I can't see the words.

My phone rings, vibrates so hard it almost falls off the counter. Quincy. I grab for it, sloshing coffee. "Q!"

"Hi, Mom." There's a lot of static, as if she's very far away. "How are you?"

I adjust the phone, trying to hear her better. "Good, honey." Please tell me you're going to get back in school, I think at her. "How are you doing?"

She sucks in a breath. "Mom. I wanted to say that I'm really sorry about how I acted."

"Oh, honey. It's all right. We needed time to cool off." I smile into the phone. My reflection moves in the stainless-steel refrigerator. I fix my hair needlessly. "Are you ready to talk? Did you move out of the dorm? Where are you living?"

"Well. That's the thing." On her end, a car honks and music plays faintly. "I'm calling to tell you that you were right about the whole wedding. I really do plan to go back to school. I just don't care about it right now."

"Okay." She's working up to something.

"So. I'm making it really simple. Like so simple you don't have to worry about anything. And we'll get benefits right away."

"Quincy, just tell her." A male voice. Ryan.

Quincy clears her throat, coughs, clears it again. "Mom, I wanted to let you know. Ryan and I are on our way to Vegas."

I blink and my brain can't catch up to what she's saying. So I say something dumb. "You're not twenty-one until next year. What are you going to do there?"

She makes a funny noise in her throat—to me it sounds like holding back tears. "We're getting married tomorrow, Mother. I thought it would make everything easier on everyone. To have it settled."

I can't speak. Vegas marriage? Quincy? Thoughts of Tom walking her down the aisle in a white dress, in front of her family and friends, poofs away. "I don't understand."

"You know Vegas, right? You can get married there really fast." She gets sarcastic when she's nervous.

"Q, wait." I stand up and pace. Think. I have to think of a plan. Quincy can't elope. She just can't. "You caught me off guard is all." I put my hand on my hot forehead. "Wow. This is big news." What should I do? What will stop her? "I'm sorry. I wasn't expecting it." I switch my phone to my other ear, my sweat clouding its surface. "I guess that will cut down on wedding costs by a long shot."

She laughs. "Right."

She tells me they're going to the Little White Chapel, off the strip by Circus Circus. That they're only by Barstow. "Love you, too. Man, she took that better than I thought," I hear Quincy say as she hangs up.

I press End and put the phone down. What should I do? Automatically I think of calling my husband.

Conventional wisdom would be for me to do nothing. Let Quincy make her own mistakes. I'm sure that's what Tom will say. That hasn't worked. It's simply not in Quincy's best interests.

I think of Tomoe Gozen. Of her going into battle. All or nothing. Committed.

I finish the cookie and go upstairs.

Drew writes all day. Sometimes she plays a few bars on her viola, too, as the melody takes shape in her head. This is a new way for her to work, she thinks. The rest of the band was always telling her what to do. It was a group effort.

Finally, she has to stop, because her fingers ache. She stretches them and gets a drink of water. Her foot is numb, too.

She yawns and looks at her lyrics. As always, she can't tell if they're good or not. Not yet. They have to sit for a while. But the important thing is, this heaviness on her is starting to let up a little bit. Cobwebs clearing. Her brain's waking up.

Outside the studio, traffic blares by. A motorcycle revs and stops. The ceiling shakes as the people upstairs walk around.

A knock on the door. Maybe a neighbor telling her to take care of the mail because her box is full—Drew forgot to have it held or forwarded. She opens the door.

Jonah stands outside. Drew takes a step back, shocked. He looks good—better than she remembered. Tall and rangy, his dark curly hair in need of a trim. Drew used to remind him to do that. He must be in between girlfriends. He's wearing mirrored aviator sunglasses. "Hey," she says, feigning casualness. She leans against the doorframe. "I haven't seen you in a while."

"Hey." He shifts from foot to foot. Jonah isn't used to doing the asking. The pursuing. Even at smaller venues, dive bars and county fairs, there were girls lining up to see him after the show. He holds up a sheaf of mail. "You didn't collect this."

Drew narrows her eyes in mock distress. "Surely you've got better things to do than stalk me and collect my mail." She takes the mail. Mostly junk.

He laughs, glances down, back up at her. "Maybe I don't."

She gestures. "Come on in."

He comes inside and takes off his sunglasses, his so-blue eyes lined with black lashes making her stomach flutter. Just a little. A tiny bit. His eyes are puffy, which means he drank too much the night before. Everything shows on your face in your mid-thirties. He shrugs off his leather jacket. His arms are covered in tattoos. She knows all of them but one. A tiny viola on the inside of his right wrist, just the outline. She catches his arm. "New tattoo?"

He flexes and unflexes his hand. "Yes."

Is it for me, Drew almost asks. Then decides she doesn't need to. Who else would it be for? Unless he started dating another string player.

He sits on her couch, on top of the blankets and laundry. "You haven't been home. Are you moving?"

Drew clears off a spot on the couch and sits. His body indents the couch in a way both familiar and strange. She can feel his warmth, warming her. She swallows. "I don't know."

"Oh." He leans away, to better see her. "You look wonderful."

Drew has to laugh. She's wearing tattered workout clothes, no makeup, and her hair's in a ponytail. "That's some sweet sarcasm."

"No. Really." He smiles at her. Sincere and regretful. He catches her hand and kisses it. "I missed you."

She's not going to get sucked back into this. Into him. She looks around at her disordered apartment. She's got so much to do. "What is it that you wanted to tell me, Jonah?"

He takes out a piece of paper from his pocket. Tri-folded. "You know that song you wrote? 'Out of Bounds'?"

Drew lifts one corner of her mouth. "The one that you guys said wasn't your sound? Yeah."

Jonah has the good grace to blush. "We want to play it. Everybody loves it. I'd wanted you to play your own part in it." He unfolds the paper and hands it to her.

Drew studies it. It's a contract. She would get the standard rate, a percentage of what the publisher makes. Only about eight cents per sale. She wouldn't really make much unless the track sold a few million copies. It's standard, actually. Drew folds it, hands it back. "Do you have copies?" She'll do it. After all, she'd rather it be played than not. Eight cents per sale is better than zero. It's a start for her.

He nods, but doesn't get any more papers out. "Have you been playing a lot?"

"Here and there." She leans back and looks at his arms. The way they connect to his shoulders.

"Have you thought about rejoining the band?" He puts his face very close to hers. His breath is minty, as if he chewed gum on the way over.

Her eye travels to the viola case sitting by her bed. It was dreary to travel from town to town, never getting enough sleep. The only familiar people were her bandmates, and not all of them liked her. They bickered over everything—where to eat dinner, what towns were worthwhile, the set list. Endless little arguments that whittled chips out of Drew.

Everyone kept telling her what an honor and a privilege she had, getting to be in a band that got any gigs at all—yet Drew remembers only how empty she felt. Always bending to the band's wishes. Never able to quite be herself.

Her ambition was supposed to keep growing, wasn't it? That's what Drew was taught. Be bigger, stronger, faster. Once one goal was accomplished, another goal would move into view. Unending. Drew was tired of it.

Like Tomoe with little Yoshitaka, Drew longed to have a more domestic life. And if she was totally in love with music, well, she would have taken her viola with her to San Diego. Music is *a* love, but not a hundred percent of her. Once, when Drew performed well in a college biology class, she briefly considered changing to pre-med. "Go volunteer at a hospital," her professor told her. "A lot of people can't stand to be in hospitals. If you don't like the environment, you can't do the job. That environment will be your life."

Maybe, by choosing a smaller goal, Drew's life will actually get bigger.

"I don't want to have that life anymore," Drew says aloud. She looks Jonah in the eyes. "I wasn't happy. Never happy." She swallows, trying to find the right words. "It was never my dream. I felt useless." Perhaps uselessness is the worst feeling of all—to understand that everything would continue on perfectly, maybe even better, if you were never there.

"Okay." Jonah folds his hands. "You're not useless, though. You know that? Everything's changed. The dynamics are better."

She nods, mute.

He talks quickly, the words spilling out. "I want you back, Drew. You, whether or not you're in the band. I miss you. Nothing feels right. Nothing's felt right."

Drew goes very still. Jonah's so close now she can feel the texture of his afternoon stubble on her lips, his exhaled breath on the sensitive skin around her mouth. She thinks of Alan for a moment, but only how he's moving to another continent. How they're not a couple.

She raises her chin and kisses Jonah, hard, her tongue finding its way into his mouth.

He kisses her back, putting her flat on the couch, his hands all over her body. It's been at least half a year since Drew was with anybody. And that was just someone she'd met in a bar, something, if she had to do over again, she would not. The weight of Jonah's body on hers is a bit different from what she remembers, the way he kisses her slightly different. Not as hard and probing. She used to complain about that and wonders if he'd changed his method, for her, or if it was just a matter of maturity.

He undoes her bra with one hand and Drew throws it to the floor. He stands up and undoes his belt, the metal jingling, unzips his jeans, looking at her. "I've missed you," he repeats, and he falls to his knees and kisses her. She sits up, putting her arms around him.

Jonah stands and she takes him in her hands, sitting in front of him. His taste, metallic and salty, seems unfamiliar. She pauses, her hands clasped around him. She has a surreal feeling of being outside of herself, like she's looking down on Dream-Drew, doing this. She puts a hand on his belly as if to make sure he's really still there. His abdomen is as taut as ever.

"What is it?" Jonah asks.

She hears her own breathing, his ragged breathing.

She looks down at him again and he feels strange and too different, all at once. She can't help wondering where he's been. Who he's been with. Why he waited so long, if he really loved her so much.

Without wanting to, she thinks about Alan, and it is this vision that takes her breath away more completely than Jonah in the flesh.

She lets go and wipes her mouth and creaks back on the couch. A spring sticks into her bare back. "I can't," she says softly, and Jonah sits beside her.

"Are you okay? I couldn't hear you." He strokes her hair and she lets him for a moment, just for the comfort.

"I can't do this." Drew finds her shirt, puts it on. She shakes her head. "I'm sorry."

"It's too fast." Jonah pulls on his jeans. Drew's grateful, at least, that he's not pointing out that Drew's the one who kissed him. Who initiated. "We need to get to know each other again."

"No." Her hands tremble. "I need something different, Jonah."

"What do you want me to do? Quit music?" He takes her hand, kisses it. "I'll do that for you."

"No!" She takes her hand away. "It's part of who you are. You can't change yourself like that. It'll kill you inside."

He swallows, the Adam's apple moving up and down. She touches his jaw briefly. He nods and looks down at his hands. The callused fingers. "I'm too late."

It's not a question, so Drew doesn't answer. They don't speak for a few moments until he says, "What will you do?"

"I don't know." This is what's hardest to admit. That she's turning down a solid offer of paying work.

"Well." He draws in a breath. "I had to try. One more time." He kisses her forehead, softly, and he gets up.

"Leave the contracts," Drew says. "I'll sign after I look them over."

He nods once, places an envelope on her table, leaves.

Drew sits motionless for a minute. Waiting for her morass of self-doubt and second guessing to kick in.

Nothing. She feels peaceful. A bit sad. She blows her nose, then gets an empty box out of the closet and begins cleaning up the mess.

I *throw a change of clothes* and my toothbrush into a small bag. I use my iPad to find a flight. Bam. Purchased, just like that. My anxiety's gone. Excited, that's what I am.

"We're home!" Tom yells from downstairs. I take my bag and go to see him. He won't stop me now that I've bought a ticket.

Chase and Tom stare up at me and my travel bag. "Hey." I look down at my hands, expecting them to shake, but they're as steady as a surgeon's. "I have something to tell you."

. . .

The cab takes me into the depths of the Strip. Past the small-scale Eiffel Tower. The faux verdigris Statue of Liberty. The huge water fountains spurting up twenty stories in front of the Bellagio in a multicolored light show. Christmas decorations on acid. The pulsing lights make my eyes ache. The sidewalks are jammed with tourists walking around in everything from shiny cocktail minidresses to Hawaiian shirts, teetering on platform spikes or trudging in Birkenstocks. It's been years since Tom and I came here, and Vegas has exploded like a giant boozy piñata. The driver stop-and-goes through the slow red lights all the way along the Strip, turning at last down a side street.

The flight to Vegas took only an hour; driving conservatively, it takes five. More if there's snow in the Grapevine, the long mountain pass on the I-5. It's ten o'clock. Quincy should have only just arrived.

Circus Circus, with its white plaster clown statues and giant archway of throbbing red and yellow lights, shimmers into view. The Little White Chapel, which looks like a sweet steepled white clapboard country church set down improbably in Vegas, is across the street. I pay the cabbie and head into the lobby, with its polished cream and black floors. I fully expect Quincy will not be pleased to see me.

The front desk clerk rings their room. "No answer," he says.

"Thank you," I say, my phone already to my ear, calling Quincy's cell. She doesn't pick up. "What room is that?"

"I'm sorry, I can't tell you." He smiles apologetically, answers another line.

Well, I suppose I don't want any hotel telling a stranger what room I'm in. I sit in the lounge so I can see the front door, the bank of elevators, and the entry into the casino. I either have to find her in person or hope she answers her phone. My plan B is nonexistent. I rub the chair's arms with my fingers. From the adjacent casino floor, the smell of cigarette smoke and alcohol drifts in, along with the clang of slot machines and tipsy, overly loud conversations. If I leave my position, I may miss them. I wipe my brow. I'm getting more and more nervous. Maybe this is a stupid plan. For a second I wish Tom had stopped me, but he didn't say a word.

"At least you'll get to go to Vegas, even if you can't stop her," he said on the way to the airport. He was trying to not be worried. He reached over and patted my thigh. "Play some blackjack."

"I'm not good at blackjack," I reminded him.

"You can still have fun," Tom said.

An hour passes. I reread Tomoe on my phone. *Ichi-go, ichi-e.* I never thought I'd welcome those words, not after my father said them. I look up at the clerk. He's bent over the desk, writing something. He's a bit older than me. Balding, reading glasses. Maybe I can talk him into it.

I go up to him again. "Hi there. I'm sorry, but I wonder if I could ask you again for Quincy Perrotti's room number. You see, I'm her mother. She's here to get married."

"I'm sorry, ma'am. I really can't do that." He looks at me over his glasses. One hand, no doubt probably getting ready to push some hidden red button.

He has a wedding band on. I lean over. "Do you have any children?"

He nods. "Two. Boy and girl. Nineteen and sixteen."

I nod slowly back at him. "I understand your policy, and I think it's a good one. But understand this—my daughter is twenty. She's here getting married. She just called me and told me over the phone. What would you do, as a father? Would you sit there and wait, or try to find her?" I let this sink in as he considers. I think about bribing him, but figure there are too many security cameras and it might get him into trouble. "Please. Help me out. As a parent. I can show you my ID. We have the same last name." I look at him pleadingly.

He nods once, his glasses sliding down his nose, and writes a number on a Post-it. He sticks it on the desk in front of me.

P erhaps this will be a new beginning," Yamabuki said from her bed-roll. She and Aoi were supposed to be napping. Yamabuki's third pregnancy had taken its toll. She was nearly eight months along, and Tomoe thought—as always—that she needed to eat more. Yamabuki's face was thin and tired. She wore an old kimono of Yoshinaka's, baggy and stained. There was little resemblance to the girl she had been when she arrived.

They had moved out of Miyanokoshi to Shinowara Town last month, in late November. There were no memories of Yoshitaka here. Shinowara was closer to the western shores, not up in the mountains, not far from the ocean. They could get fresh fish. Life felt more possible, Tomoe thought.

"We will finish off the Taira, and everything will go back to normal," Yamabuki said. "Cousin Yoritomo will make Yoshinaka a lord, and we will get little Yoshitaka back."

Yamabuki moved her legs restlessly. "I want to get up. There are chores to do."

"No. You rest." Tomoe examined the woman's appearance with concern. Yamabuki grimaced as she turned over. "Remember when you couldn't even wash a kimono?" Tomoe said abruptly, hoping to distract Yamabuki from her pains.

Yamabuki nodded. "How far I've come."

"And you have been blessed with children," Chizuru said, entering the house with a jug of water in her liver-spotted hand. "You have enough children for both you and Tomoe."

Tomoe frowned. Her mother should not speak like that. But Yamabuki laughed. "If only Tomoe could carry this child for me. I'm sure she wouldn't have to stop riding horseback or fighting. I'm afraid I'm not made for these burdens." She lifted a leg. "Look at my ankles."

Tomoe and Chizuru gasped. Yamabuki's ankles were swollen to twice their size, laced with bulging blue veins. Even her toes were swollen, like the daikon roots. She couldn't bend them. Clucking, Chizuru rolled up a blanket and tucked it under Yamabuki's feet. "No more chores for you until after the baby," she said sternly. "Keep your feet elevated."

Yamabuki struggled to sit up. "I will not allow these ailments to trouble me."

Despite her outwardly weak nature, Yamabuki could be very stubborn. But she needed bed rest. All of them had seen pregnancies where swollen ankles led to swollen limbs, sweating, a high pulse, and a terrible headache. The woman and baby both died.

"There are times when being strong means you must accept your weakness." Tomoe put her hand on Yamabuki's forehead. She had a fever. Tomoe and her mother exchanged a concerned look.

This life was too difficult for poor Yamabuki.

Yamabuki's face softened. "I hope one day I can watch over you as you have me."

From outside, loud men's laughter rang out. Yamabuki sighed. "I wish they would be quiet. All they do now is drink."

Tomoe's stomach knotted. "I'll speak to them."

She left the house. A campfire crackled in a stone circle in the clearing. Yoshinaka, Kanehira, and about twenty other men sat around the flames, drinking.

Yoshinaka looked a wreck. He wore pants and a kimono jacket in material too light for the cold weather, the ends of the pants caked in mud. His hair was filthy and matted, and Tomoe could smell him from yards away. He raised his sake cup in salute.

"Tomoe! About time. Guess what? Yukiie lost Muroyama." His tone was gleeful. He stood and waved his clay sake cup. "I am the best general the Minamoto have! A toast. To me. The only one who can win."

"*Kanpai!*" the soldiers shouted.

Yoshinaka took another swig of sake. "I will show him what poor old cousin Kiso can do."

"To Yoshinaka, our new shōgun!" Kanehira cried.

Yoshinaka turned with a smile. "That is right, Kanehira. The Taira have abandoned Miyako and taken the child emperor with them. This means the retired emperor is the acting emperor again. If we go to Miyako before cousin Yoritomo and receive the emperor's blessing, I will become shōgun!"

"You cannot hold off the entire Minamoto army and the Taira. You'll lose." Tomoe planted her feet. Somebody had to tell Yoshinaka the truth, and it seemed it would be her.

Yoshinaka scowled. His hand tightened visibly around his sake cup. "When I'm shōgun, my cousin Yoritomo will do as I say."

"No. He'll kill you and take over. And he'll kill your son." She tasted copper in her mouth, rising from her throat. If this threat did not reach Yoshinaka, nothing would.

The men went still. They looked from Tomoe to Yoshinaka. Yoshinaka appeared to be holding his breath, his face turning a peculiar combination of red and blue. "I will have the support of the emperor," Yoshinaka said in his deepest voice. "If Yoritomo kills Yoshitaka, I as shōgun will have the authority to execute him."

Tomoe stepped closer to Yoshinaka. "You bluster and bluster, but you will not take good advice when it is shoved in your face! I say we stay here, show cousin Yoritomo that you are trustworthy." She looked around at the gathering, at the houses beyond. "Join forces with him and conquer the Taira for good."

Yoshinaka put his face next to Tomoe's, his hot and sour breath on her. She stared directly into his swollen eyes, eyes that had once been more familiar than her own. But not today. Today they were strange. Cold. She tilted her head up. "Be reasonable," she whispered, so close that her lips brushed the coarse hair of his beard.

Yoshinaka didn't blink. "I want revenge."

Tomoe heard her heartbeat pound in her ears. Ever since Kurikara and the taking of Yoshitaka, Yoshinaka had become more and more unstable. Perhaps this had all pushed him into some wild territory from which he, the real Yoshinaka, was unrecoverable. There was only the beast Yoshinaka in his place, like some shape-shifting *obake* monster out of Japanese legend.

"Revenge will not solve your problems," Tomoe said, her voice loud.

Yoshinaka walked away. She thought he was going to the house, but instead he turned suddenly and pitched his sake cup at her. Tomoe held up her hands, deflecting the blow with her forearms. The cup bounced with a sound like sword hitting bone, and it stung as badly as the stick Yoshinaka had hit her with when they were small.

"Your father should have told me!" he shouted. "He should have told me the truth about my cousins, instead of letting me think the Taira were the real enemy! Yoritomo will kill me now or kill me a year from now. It makes no difference. He will never trust me. With good reason! I will kill him!"

Tomoe rubbed her forearm. Heat exploded over her, inside her. "My father wanted to protect you from exactly this type of madness."

Striding forward, Yoshinaka grabbed her by the hair and yanked her head back. Her neck made a snapping noise and she let out a cry. So let him hurt her, if it came to that. If he could. Tomoe hit the wrist of the hand holding her hair, forcing him to release it, ducking under his arm. Then she shoved at his chest with her foot. Yoshinaka staggered backward and nearly fell into the fire, landing in a heap of ash piled next to the stone ring.

Yoshinaka lifted his broken face to Tomoe. "You are nothing but a woman," he said, his eyes watering. "I only keep you because your cunt has not been stretched by children."

Tomoe's face burned. "My father," she said, "would be ashamed of you. The only reason I stay is that he told me to watch over you. Let me have Yamabuki. I will take her and my mother and Aoi and leave."

"You want Yamabuki?" Yoshinaka spat at the ground. "Have her." He threw down his sword and walked off toward the center of town. Kanehira cast his sister a desperate glance, and then followed his foster brother into the maze of streets.

Nineteen

D rew wakes with a start. She was having a dream about Rachel. Rachel standing next to her, wearing a white kimono with white irises on it. Drew in the same. Holding hands, they walk through a city street, a place filled with garbage and flies. Somehow the stench doesn't bother Drew.

It's three o'clock in the morning.

A strain of music floats in Drew's ears. Something from the dream. She turns on her light, grabs her pen and notebook, writes.

When she's done, she reads it over.

You were always in the lead
Follow follow follow me
I was glad to be your shadow
Always flying like Peter Pan
You never let go of my hand
Together, forever, the way it should be
Until one day
When you left
Left me all alone

Maybe I left you, too
Good things, they never stay
But now I've found you again
I want you back in my life
I want you to let me in
Forget all the anger and strife.
Time is always wasted
Dwelling on our sins
But all we have is now
Never what might have been.
Please—let me in.
Let me in.
Let me in.
I'm your shadow.
You're my shadow.
Always in my heart.

She rubs her eyes and looks at her phone. Five o'clock. At last her fatigue hits her—she hasn't stopped to make coffee or anything. She's gotten out her musical notation paper and jotted down the beginnings of the melody, before she forgets, the notes coming to her like Morse code.

She turns off the light and lies in the dark, but sleep doesn't return. Just that melody still.

The afternoon she played in the library comes to mind. Alan. How he makes her feel somehow more Drew-like. His acceptance of Drew for who she is, not how he thinks she ought to be. And she for him. How time passes like it's nothing when they're together.

Her heart sounds loud in her ears, as it often does when there's no other sound. But she remembers something else, from Tomoe Gozen.

"Do you love him?" she asks aloud, into the darkness of her apartment, and waits for her inner heart to answer.

Yes.

She's in love with Alan.

She takes in a deep, surprised breath.

Dammit.

She's in love with him.

It's crazy and maybe it makes no sense, but it's real and true and Drew knows it. Just like she knew turning down Jonah was the right choice. She wants so much to be strong. To be like Tomoe and do the right thing, like when Tomoe let little Yoshitaka go.

But if she does that, she'll regret it for as long as she lives.

She gets dressed. If she leaves soon, she'll miss most of the morning traffic. This time, she packs her viola.

The corridors of the hotel are empty and quiet. Everyone's out or sleeping the daylight away, waiting for night. I find Quincy and Ryan's room and knock. Our special family code: TAP (pause) TAP (pause) TAP-TAP-TAP. It's from the Crest commercial in the eighties, where the little plaque monsters sang, "We make holes in teeth. We make holes in teeth." The commercial's been off the air for decades, but that's how Tom and his brothers knock on doors, and therefore how we do it. Nobody answers. I give it a minute, knock again, normally this time. Nothing.

I sit down in the hallway. I could go down and try my luck with the slots, or attempt to play blackjack—but I'm so terrible at cards that the rest of the table invariably rises against me, like I'm Alice in Wonderland playing against the Queen of Hearts. I settle against the wall, consider calling my sister. But what can she do?

I think about Chase and try to work up a little self-righteous anger. *She should have told me.* I remember the days when I'd get angry at Drew and shut her out. Hear her pitiful voice at my bedroom door. *Please let me in, Rachel,* she'd plead, sobbing. I'd put on my headphones. It didn't matter what the transgression was. If she did something I didn't like, that's what I would do.

Then she'd write a note and slide it under my door. *Sry I Am a bad Sistr,* read one in her childish, misspelled crayon. God. Why was I so mean? Quincy had never acted like that with Chase—both kids relented and made up quickly.

"You're not a bad sister," I whisper.

She probably doesn't want to hear from me at all.

I open up the Tomoe Gozen story to the chapter about little Yoshitaka and reread it.

Little Yoshitaka was going to be used as insurance for Yoshinaka to not throw a coup. I swallow. I'd learned from some of the history books that this was commonplace. In fact, Yoritomo, the leader, and his brothers had something similar happen to them when they were young. Their father was killed by Kiyomori Taira, and he'd planned to kill Yoritomo and his siblings. But Taira's wife had pleaded with him to spare them. So instead, Taira sent them to live in exile, where they grew up plotting revenge and a new takeover.

I keep reading. A sentence sticks out.

Let him go and he may come back to us.

A couple walks by, smoking, laughing. My eyes water and I cough. They don't even glance at me. Apparently women sitting in hallways by hotel room doors is not an uncommon occurrence. Probably they wouldn't bat an eye if I was sprawled in the middle—they'd just step over me. I stretch my sore back, read the sentence again.

Let him go.

My legs feel numb. I stand up, shake them out.

If they fought now, a bad outcome was certain. If they waited, at least they had hope.

I imagine the scene: Tomoe and Yamabuki watching the little boy being carted away. Tomoe could have perhaps defeated the group of soldiers who came to pick up the boy, but doing so would destroy their future. The battle would be won, the war lost.

I imagine myself confronting Quincy again. Her shutting the door on me, literally and figuratively. Never speaking to me again because I tried to control her. I'm the intruder here.

Becoming like my father to her.

Flushing red, I slump against the wall, staring at the beige wallpaper on the opposite wall.

I thought I knew better than Tomoe, in my modern age, with my ability to travel and my Western-style hubris. I thought that if Tomoe had a choice, she would have done what I'm doing.

But it's Tomoe who has all the wisdom. Even now.

"Mom?" Quincy stands in front of me in the same sweats she wore to Thanksgiving, holding a large brown mailing envelope stamped with CLARK COUNTY MARRIAGE LICENSE BUREAU in red. Ryan stands behind her, his forehead wrinkled, his hands at her waist. "What are you doing here?"

My throat closes. I look down for a long moment at my feet in their black sneakers, considering my next words. Trying to sweep away the debris of what I want versus what my daughter wants. What *am* I doing here?

At last, I figure it out. The core of why I wanted to come. What matters the most. I stand up.

I take Quincy's free hand and look into her hazel eyes. When I speak, my voice is steady. "I want to be there when you get married. I want to be a witness."

The words seem to have physical form. They're a rope, a lifeline between me and my daughter.

My daughter stares at me in shock. For a brief second I think she'll turn me away.

Then she bursts into tears and hugs me tight.

The next morning, I walk down to Quincy's room. I stayed down the hall from them. Today, all we have to do is walk across the street to the chapel, pay the fee, and order the service. It will be done. I wonder if Quincy needs help with her makeup or hair. What will she wear? For all I know, she's getting married in her sweatsuit. She said she didn't need help. For the ceremony itself, I've promised to call Tom on speakerphone. I'll also get the chapel to record it on a DVD, so we can share it with everyone. A plan. Plans are good, I reassure myself. Even if you have to change them later.

I do the family knock. There's no answer. I knock again. Muffled footsteps. The chains rattle. At last Quincy pulls the door open. She wears a white robe and her hair is unbrushed, her makeup not done. Her face is drawn. "Hi, Mom." She does a shuffling turn away.

"Where's Ryan?" I step inside, onto the red carpet that looks the same as the one in my room. Only one light is on, and the curtains are drawn. A single king-sized bed sits in the middle, the red cover pulled up. Her duffel bag sits on the dresser, next to the dark television set. Ryan's bag is nowhere.

Something's wrong.

The bed creaks under Quincy's weight. She stares at her bare, ringless fingers. "He's not here."

I put my purse down. "He left you?"

Quincy's jaw flexes. "Yeah. He went home." Quincy's eyes have purple bags under them, and she won't meet my gaze.

I sit down, sinking deeper into the bed than I want, and put my arm around her. "Q, what happened? Did you have a fight?"

She flinches away. "I don't want to talk about it right now." Quincy goes into the bathroom and shuts the door firmly.

I should be relieved. Thanking my lucky stars. Instead, a deep chasm opens in my chest. I remember how in love I was with Tom. The excited flutter I felt on our wedding day. *I love making him laugh. I love how he makes me laugh.* We looked into each other's eyes as the clerk read the marriage text, and again, as I had when I first held my newborn sister, I felt that inexplicable sense of connection. As if we could touch each other with only a glance. That was the yardstick by which I measured every loving feeling I'd had since. How devastating it would have been if he'd left like that, right before we got married.

I put my head on my hands. I'm suddenly paralyzed by the possibility that I've had it all wrong, that my presence here has ended the relationship. Tom's mother hadn't interfered with us—perhaps she'd wanted to—what would have happened if she had?

I get up and knock on the door. "Quincy?" I call. "Are you all right?"

The water runs. "Go away."

I rattle the doorknob. What is she doing in there? I'm afraid, momentarily, that she's hurting herself. She wouldn't, I think—but then, I don't know my children as well as I thought, either. "Q, I need to make sure you're okay."

The bathroom door opens. Quincy's dressed in jeans and a UCSD sweatshirt. Her hair is brushed and bound back. She's dabbed concealer under her eyes, put on some lip gloss. "I haven't eaten since yesterday afternoon. Can we get some food?"

I smile at her. That sweet, brave baby girl who was always so quick to shake off a softball hit to the head is still there. "Of course."

We leave the casino and head to a diner down the street. In the sunshine, the lights of the strip try to compete with the sun and fail. Everything looks more like a fading carnival than a multibillion-dollar tourist attraction, the plaster statues chipped, the sidewalks gray and littered with flyers for strip clubs.

Quincy says nothing. Our feet move in unison, right-left, right-left.

We sit in a booth, slightly sticky with pancake syrup, and I wave down a busboy. Quincy slides in next to me, instead of opposite. We sip our coffee, watching people wander by the window, elderly tourists, parents with young children, homeless people with their carts. I'm waiting for her to talk. Or not talk.

The waitress puts down our pancakes in front of us, three each, with a great glob of butter on top, plus scrambled eggs and bacon. Quincy smears her butter into the pancakes and pours out what looks like two cups of syrup, making a lake on her plate.

When her pancakes are gone, Quincy blows out a breath so powerful it moves the empty creamer tubs, spilling their last white drops onto the tabletop. "So. This is what happened."

I put my fork down on the side of my plate.

"Last night, after you said you wanted to see me get married," Quincy crumples her straw wrapper, "Ryan realized he wanted his parents to see it, too. He said we should put it off. Like, until after I graduate. He said we should 'rethink things.'"

"Then I said he should have thought about that before we drove out here. Before I got out of school and gave up my dorm room. I didn't want to wait. Then he said . . ." Quincy's lower lip trembles. She begins sobbing, real big nonverbal sobs, the kind I haven't heard her emit since she was two and couldn't form words to express what she wanted to say.

I put my arm around her. "It's okay, Quincy."

"Are people looking?" She blows her nose with her napkin.

I glance around. Nobody has blinked an eye. "It's Vegas."

"Then . . . he . . . said . . . he . . . loves . . . me." She begins hiccuping. I pat her back until she can talk again. Her breath is hot. "And then he called it off." She takes my napkin and dabs at her nose again. "He said we're not ready to get married. *He's* not ready. He said he has a lot of training to do, so it'd be best to wait. And I said it was all or nothing—we already got our license—and he chose nothing."

"Oh, honey." Seeing your kids in pain is the worst. Even necessary pain. I put my hand over hers. If I could, I would absorb every bit of her angst so she wouldn't have to experience it. This is that invisible thread Tomoe spoke of, the one tethering us to our children forever.

Quincy wipes at her swollen eyes. "Well. I'm waiting."

I dig out the tissues I keep in my purse. "For what?"

"The *I told you so.*" She blows her nose. "You were right and I was wrong. Yay, Mom."

"Quincy." I lean in close to her. "All I want is for you to be happy. The only reason I objected—well, the biggest reason—is because it seemed like you were losing yourself in him."

Quincy's face goes splotchy. Her eyes flash. "You think I'm so perfect and sweet. Well, it was my idea to get married. *Mine.* Not his." She shakes her head. "He's in the military. You don't understand. When he's gone, he's *gone.* No phone a lot of times. No e-mail. No texts. Sometimes for a couple of days, sometimes for weeks. We don't always know beforehand when he'll go."

I nod.

She spreads out her hands. "So while he's gone, I get busy doing my own stuff, seeing my friends again." Quincy takes a sip of water. "But when he gets back, I want to see *him.* I drop everything. I blow off my friends. Of course, my friends got tired of it. I blow off my classes. I can't just ignore Ryan, not when he might leave again at any time. Possibly to *die.* You know?" She rubs her eyes. "He wasn't controlling me, Mom. It was me. I felt so guilty if I had to do anything else while he was home. I thought if we were married, then I'd feel more secure. We could be together more."

She inhales. I wipe her cheeks with a fresh tissue, touched that she can open up so much to me. "I understand."

Quincy puts her hand over her face. Her left ring finger bears no trace of the engagement band, no tan line or mark. "Will they let me back into school?"

"Yes. Do you want to go back to school is the question?" I kind of hold my breath for this.

Quincy thinks about this for a minute. She shrugs.

I put my hand on her arm. Tomoe's words come back to me and I say them aloud: *"It is all right if you are afraid. We are all afraid."*

"What's that supposed to mean?" Quincy asks grumpily. Grumpy means she's almost back to normal.

"It means you'll get through it, Q. We all will." I hug her from the side. "I love you and always will, no matter what."

"What if I'm a secret serial killer?" Quincy takes her bacon between her fingers. "Will you still love me then?"

"I refuse that hypothetical." I finish my coffee. "You are not a serial killer, nor will you ever be."

"Moooommm. You're no fun." Quincy rolls her eyes.

My phone rings and I lift it to my face.

SHINOWARA TOWN
CENTRAL-NORTHERN REGION
HONSHU, JAPAN
Early Winter 1183

During the night, Yamabuki went into labor. Tomoe awoke to soft sobs coming from Yamabuki's mat. She crawled over to Yamabuki's sleeping roll and touched her leg. "It's time!" Tomoe called to awaken her mother.

In the dim light from the fire, Yamabuki looked greenish red. She lay on her back, her legs apart, already pushing. Tomoe touched where the baby's head should be and felt a cold foot sticking out. She withdrew her hand. The birth water smelled foul. Infection and breech. They needed to get this baby out.

Yamabuki gripped Tomoe's forearm. "I cannot. It hurts too much."

Chizuru ran over with rags and began manipulating Yamabuki's stomach, trying to coax the baby to turn. Tomoe spoke to Yamabuki. "No. It's not in your nature to give up. Your body remembers what to do. Remember the iris blooming in the frozen ground?" She stroked Yamabuki's forehead. "You told me that, remember?"

"True." Yamabuki shifted and shot Tomoe a bittersweet smile. "Long ago. When I was young." She shouted as the baby's foot poked farther out, then retracted. Panting, she gripped Tomoe's arm. "Don't leave me."

"Never." Tomoe knelt beside Yamabuki's head, pulling it into her lap.

Chizuru's gaze met Tomoe's. Her mother shook her head. Yamabuki screamed as though someone was stabbing her in the throat.

"You must fight," Tomoe said sharply. "Push him out!" Yamabuki screamed again, but this time it was more of a loud moaning shudder. The baby slid out into Chizuru's waiting hands, the umbilical cord gleaming like an oyster shell in the light.

Chizuru's face fell as she held the bloody infant close to her breast. "A boy," she said sadly.

She handed him to Tomoe. He weighed no more than a handful of green beans, his limbs scrawny. She swept his finger through his mouth, sucked the liquid out of his nose with her own mouth, spat. He did not take a breath. Tomoe slapped him on the back. Nothing. She put her lips to the boy's and blew, feeling his chest move up and down. Again and again. Her fingertip on the boy's chest waited to feel a pulse. Stillness.

The baby's head was round and perfect, but too big for his tiny body. His nose was squashed and slick, the eyes white and unseeing. Tomoe had thought his skin red, but no, that was the reflection of the fire. His skin was the perfectly pearly blue of an early winter sky. She pushed more air into the tiny lungs.

"What is it?" Yamabuki said. "What has happened? Let me see. Let me see!" Unexpectedly, the woman sat up and clawed at the baby, wresting him from Tomoe's arms. The umbilical cord was still attached to the placenta, which glided out of Yamabuki's body, her uterus convulsing, then fell onto the bedclothes. Chizuru quietly cut the cord away from the baby.

Yamabuki rocked the limp boy. Her mouth moved to make words. She shook her head and sobbed without sound.

"He will be all right." Yamabuki rocked the baby harder. "Wake up, little one." She rubbed his chest furiously. The baby lay, wilted, in her arms.

"Yamabuki-chan." Tomoe knelt. She tried to come up with words. But there was nothing to say. She put her arm around her friend. "I am so sorry."

Yamabuki stopped moving and held her baby silently, staring at the small face. Her shoulders shook. It looked like a dozen men had died in here, blood running off the bedroll and onto the tatami, leaking through the woven straw. "It is my fault," Yamabuki said hollowly. "I should have taken better care of myself."

"Yamabuki-chan. You don't mean that." Tomoe embraced her hard, stopping her shaking. "It is not for us to say."

"I did this." Yamabuki's mouth twisted. "I did it." She hit her own face with a closed fist, smacking it over and over. Tomoe gasped and tried to catch her arm, but the woman had surprising strength. Yamabuki felt feverish, five times as warm as the night air. "I am bad luck."

From behind, Tomoe looped her arms under Yamabuki's armpits and grasped her hands together behind Yamabuki's neck. "You did nothing. Stop!" The woman thrashed, but could not move. Chizuru took the baby. Yamabuki collapsed, falling into unconsciousness or sleep; Tomoe could not tell. Still she breathed.

"Let him spend this one night with his mother," Tomoe said. Chizuru wrapped the baby in a silken blanket and placed him under Yamabuki's arm. Cries rose up in Tomoe's throat, but like Yamabuki, she had no tears. She took the baby from Chizuru and placed him on the mat next to Yamabuki. In the dim light, both were the same color.

Twenty

D rew doesn't show up on Alan's street until she's sure he's taken the girls to school. It's one of the days when the library opens late, and she takes a chance that he'll return home after drop-off.

He does, but not in the way she expects. He pulls up behind her car and stops and walks around to the window before she realizes what's happening, so focused is she on what's ahead of her instead of what's around her. "Drew?"

She jumps.

He pulls open her door and she unbuckles her seat belt and stands up. He puts his arms around her and squeezes her tight, and it's like she's finally home after a ten-mile trek in a blizzard. Well. Maybe that's too dramatic. She can smell his green citrusy deodorant, his natural scent underneath. She inhales automatically, as she would if she smelled coffee. My God. Never in her life has she wanted to smell a man's natural smell. She is attracted and bound to him on a chemical level. Any small bits of anxiety over what she's going to do dissipate.

"I thought I'd never see you again," he says into her ear. His breath is warm, nuzzling.

She shakes her head, unable to speak now.

He pulls back and looks at her. "I can turn down that job."

"No." She puts her head on his chest again. Listens to his heart, which is beating fast. "You have to do what's best for you and the kids."

"Maybe you're what's best." He lifts her chin and kisses her.

Drew trembles. Then she lets go of everything else and kisses him back.

He takes her hand and they go inside his house.

Only later, when they lie in his queen-sized bed, does she notice what kind of house it is. It's a small Craftsman bungalow, with built-in bookshelves and lots of natural woodwork. Light comes into the bedroom through an eyelet lace curtain that flutters. "I like this house," she says appreciatively. He puts his arms around her from behind. The fine hairs on his chest and belly tickle her back and she nestles into him.

"My in-laws own it. We live here very cheap. But they're going to sell it when they leave."

Drew turns. Those lashes. "Then you can't possibly stay. You'll be homeless."

"Things will work out." Alan kisses her mouth gently.

Drew leans back and looks at him. Memorizing his face. *Just say it.* She's afraid. She thinks of Tomoe, being so brave when Yoshitaka was taken. This is nothing. She won't turn into a pile of ash if he doesn't respond.

She runs her fingers over his unruly eyebrows, puts her hand on his newly shaved, smooth jaw and takes a deep breath. "I love you."

He closes his eyes, just for a moment. When he opens them, the deep brown seems lit from within, the sunlight reflecting into them. Maybe— relief? "I love you, too."

It hadn't scared him away.

It kind of scares her. But here, she feels brave. And there's no going back now.

He leans his forehead over so it's touching hers. "Do you know when I knew?"

Drew holds her breath.

"When you walked into the library, I knew. And when we talked, I knew. And when you played the viola, I knew." He talks rapidly. "And when you were so sweet with the girls, I knew. I've only felt like that once before in my whole life." He smiles. "I know you must think I'm hopeless and crazy, talking like this, but some things you *feel* first, with your heart. Your brain follows later."

She draws her head back and regards him. "Well," she says at last, "you've already seen me at my worst. Jobless and totally adrift. If that can't chase you off, I guess nothing will."

He faces relaxes. "Drew. This is hardly the worst." He speaks with the perspective of someone who's lost his dearest thing. She holds on to his face with both hands and kisses him all over it. His face wet with her tears.

The phone call drew us home early. A stroke, her doctor said. Vitals strong. No organ damage. Stable. I feel like I'm watching this scene happen through glass. A dream. The peculiar antiseptic soap and baby powder scent of the hospital choking me.

Chase and Quincy are in the ICU waiting room and Tom's out in the hallway talking to the doctor, with the understanding that he'll be able to recall more than I can at this moment.

My mother lies covered in wires and tubes like some kind of supercomputer robot, tethered to various boxes that blink and blip. But these boxes help keep her alive, not the other way around.

Her breathing sounds soft and even, the heart rate an even mountain range. The faded blue cotton curtains are drawn around her in an ellipse, forming a small room between two other patients. I can see feet on both sides, hear other machines and coughs.

All I know is that I'm holding my mother's hand and I'm memorizing how her fingers look. The slender knuckles—her wedding ring was always slipping off. I used to play with it, beg her to remove it so I could examine the diamond. A small diamond, she said. A bigger one would get in the way.

I forgot about that.

I have a memory, then, of Mom stitching together clothes for my Ken doll when I was maybe four. That darn Ken—he never had good clothes. I cried when I tried to put Ken's polyester pants over his sticky vinyl legs.

My mother never played with me when I was little. She attended to her own chores and expected me to entertain myself or knock on a neighbor's door. I'm pretty sure that's half the reason she had another baby, to give me a playmate. Anyway, just one generation ago, nobody's parents played with them. Kids were meant to entertain themselves.

That day when I cried, I was sitting on the floor of the living room, my doll clothes spread out over the coffee table. I expected no help, but to my surprise, Mom appeared from the kitchen, drying her hands on a flour sack dishtowel. "Are you hurt?"

I shook my head. I had knotted my hair into pigtails, which pulled at my scalp. My mother looked at me as though surprised, as if somebody had deposited me in the living room that morning. Even then, we had green flowered couches and the dark wood furniture Dad preferred. Everything dark—the wood paneling on the walls, the blue carpet, the cabinets. I suppose it was his cave.

Mom threw the towel over her shoulder and walked over, knelt beside me. She took Ken in her graceful hands and turned him over, trying to pull the pants up his sticky legs. "Such poor quality," she said. "I'll make you some."

"You can make doll clothes?" I said in wonder. I had no idea where doll clothes came from, but my own mother making them seemed magical.

"Of course." Mom smiled at me, unfastening my pigtails and smoothing the hair with her fingers. I relaxed as my scalp unpinched. Later, we went to the fabric store and bought a doll clothing pattern. I got to choose the material, and Mom made Ken a pair of pinstriped pastel slacks and a ridiculous flowered shirt in pea green and orange. Now that I think about it, it must have taken her hours to sew. All those little stitches, turning minute sleeves and legs inside out. I tried to make Barbie clothes for my daughter once and gave up, my stitches falling out hopelessly. "The Barbies are nudists," I told Quincy. "They live in the tropics."

Something hard lodges in my throat and makes it hard to speak. I lean over Mom. She's a pale shade of gray, her sunspots standing out against her skin. The hollows under her cheekbones are deeper than the last time I saw her.

This morning, the nursing home reported, Mom began acting strangely, repeating words, staring into space. The right side of her face went limp and stiff—she couldn't blink that eye. The nursing home called an ambulance.

Tom pushes aside the curtain and puts his warm hand on my shoulder. I put my hand on top of it. "How's she doing?"

"All right, I guess. What did the doctor say?"

"We should go home," Tom says. He scratches his face, the five-o'clock shadow standing out in salt-and-pepper tones. "There's nothing else we can do. They'll call us when she wakes up."

"I want to be here." I glance up at him. "What if she wakes up and needs help and they're busy?"

His face is concerned, his brows drawn together. "Rachel, they're taking good care of her."

"I'm fine." I want to be stubborn. With a pang, I think of the photographs, the mysterious people smiling out at me. Stupidly, I had still hoped Mom would have a coherent day and tell me about them. I may never know who the people in those pictures were. If that baby is a niece or a friend or a little sister. I could have relatives I don't know. I want to cry, but nothing comes out. I'm angry, too, because my mother never told me about these people. Why didn't she share her life with us?

Right now, my worries over my children fade. They're good kids. I raised them as best as I could. Still raising them the best I can. But I'll never have total control over them. I never did, even when they were babies and I all wanted them to do was sleep and poop regularly. I used to focus on their achievements. Quincy headed toward being an engineer, Chase getting good grades and college-bound, too. Now all I want them to do is be good people. The kind of people who help, who have open hearts. The rest doesn't matter.

Tom puts his arm around me. "I called Drew, but she didn't answer. I didn't want to leave a message for this. I'll try again later."

"Thanks." I lean into him. Of course Tom understands deeply how I feel because his father was sick and died, too, but only Drew understands all of this. She is the only person on this planet who shares the little microcosmic culture of the Snow Household—the half-Asian dysfunctional samurai gold-digging tribe. Though her memories of our family may be different from mine in some ways. And I'm sure my mother's and father's accounts would be different from mine. Like we're all writing our own fiction, in the history of our lives.

I press my hands against my face. I want Drew. I need her like she's needed me—to comfort me, to hug me, to tell me everything will be okay.

I wish I hadn't been so mean to her. I wish I hadn't been so scared and petty.

My breathing's ragged, and I force it to be even. I think of Tomoe riding into battle with hundreds of men, to fight an army outnumbering her. I lift my head.

I've let fear control me for far too long.

Mom looks so weak lying there on the bed. Those pictures—who are the people in them? Hatsuko Minamoto was a dead end—maybe we'll never know. "Tell me your story," I whisper. "I'm listening now. I promise."

The machines shudder and blip. For one awful brief moment, I wish Mom would have passed away with her stroke, just to end the suffering. Selfish of me to want to keep her here, just so I can have an ending.

Some stories don't end so neatly.

But what I can do is this. I call my sister.

She answers on the first ring. "Rachel?"

.   .   .

I'm still at the hospital, in the common waiting room, when Drew arrives with Alan. She's carrying her viola case. Quincy took Chase home. No use in everyone being here.

I stand up and hold out my arms. Drew puts her case down and we hug. Hard.

"I'm sorry," I whisper.

"Me too." Drew's voice sounds husky. Her face is shiny and flushed. I bet she didn't even bother to eat.

I hold her by the shoulders and look into my sister's eyes, the way I did when she was a newborn. And then I think, even if Drew hadn't been born my sister, even if I'd met her as an adult, I'd still want to be her friend. That's something worth keeping safe. "Thank you."

Drew pushes the strands of hair that have fallen out of my ponytail back behind my ears. "Everything's going to be okay, Rachel. You'll see." She smiles at me and I am reassured, as if Drew is God and can promise that. I sit down as she goes in to see our mother.

I sip my watery coffee. All this time, I'd pushed away help. But accepting help didn't make me weaker—it made me stronger. Just like Yamabuki letting Tomoe help her made her stronger. And Tomoe opening herself up to Yamabuki made her stronger. How easily they could have been rivals. Instead, they became like sisters.

I throw the remnants of my coffee into the trash and go in to be with Drew and my mother.

Kiso Yoshinaka and Tomoe Gozen, by Utagawa Yoshikazu

Photograph © 2015 Museum of Fine Arts, Boston

MIYAKO, THE CAPITAL
CENTRAL REGION
HONSHU, JAPAN
Winter 1184

They left for the capital at daybreak, on a day when the wind blew bitter snow into their faces. Tomoe forced her mother to stay inside, to not see them off. She kissed Chizuru, Aoi, and then knelt next to Yamabuki and picked up her hand. Stiff and cold. All the words that needed saying had been said long ago. There would be no changing anything in the hard days to come.

Without Yamabuki, Tomoe thought, she would have turned out like Yoshinaka and her brother. Bitter, inflexible, battle-hungry, unable to take pleasure in anything but a fight. It was because of Yamabuki that Tomoe had learned to enjoy the daily humdrum routine of life. To find the poetry hidden in laundry day. To learn how to become a mother. To love somebody better than you loved yourself.

Tomoe stroked the long fountain of hair under Yamabuki's head, so white now it might be snow-pale by the new year. Her skin hung like empty kimonos on a clothesline. Tomoe put her ear gently against the woman's face. She still breathed. "Yamabuki!" she said. "Wake up. Please."

I cannot go on without you. My sister of heart.

Yoshinaka and her brother Kanehira went to the palace on their own. Tomoe wandered the streets with Cherry Blossom. She had dreamed about Miyako as a girl. The capital city seemed so glamorous. Sophisticated. This was where the court was, the hub of life. Never had she imagined she'd be riding in as an invader, against her own clan.

She came across a stall selling a beautiful orange silk material with bright red flowers and fans woven in. Tomoe touched the luxurious folds. How Yamabuki would adore this. She imagined Yamabuki healthy again, wearing a kimono made of the beautiful silks. Perhaps it would help her get better. She gave the vendor, an older woman with blackened teeth, a few Chinese coins for it.

Tomoe had started back to the palace again when she smelled smoke. Not smoke from vendors cooking food or lighting fires to keep warm, but the hot odor of many flames. She looked up, and felt her body stiffen in horror.

The palace was on fire, its slanted roof blazing. Men ran about, carrying goods in their hands as Yoshinaka's men pillaged the city.

"This cannot be. This cannot be." Tomoe mounted Cherry Blossom and headed inside the palace grounds.

Yoshinaka stood in the courtyard with her brother and a half-dozen other men. They faced away from her, firing blazing arrows almost lazily into the palace walls, watching as each melted through the shoji screens, through the beautiful wooden scrollwork.

Beside Yoshinaka, a shrunken and stooped old man stood, bald and thin, his back marred by a hump. He was covered in soot and blood and dirt; at first, Tomoe thought he was a beggar. "Tomoe Gozen. Help me," the small figure pleaded. She looked down at him. It was the retired emperor, Go-Shirakawa.

"Yoshinaka! You've gone mad," Tomoe cried. She was so out of breath, so in shock, that she couldn't hear her own voice. She yanked on Yoshinaka's arm. "Stop this." He was focused on the fire, eyes bright. He sniffled and ran his hand along his nose. Tomoe thought of Kaneto, of how disappointed he'd be with all of them. "No!" she shouted, her voice loud now, ringing through the courtyard, battering against the burning building. She had been saying words like this to Yoshinaka since he was a toddler. Tomoe had no more words for him, and no more strength. She wanted to weep, and she wanted to be done.

"I am destroying the city," Yoshinaka said calmly, shrugging off her hands. He spoke as if he had told her he was fishing or going for a walk. He took a swig from a bottle one of the men offered. His dark eyes reflected the flames. Go-Shirakawa is my prisoner until he makes me shōgun."

Tomoe took a step back. His face was like the face of one of these stone dragons decorating the garden. Unrecognizable. For the first time in her life, she truly feared Yoshinaka.

But she stepped in front of him anyway. Her lungs ached from the fire. "How can you rule a lost city? What good does it do us to destroy everything? This palace has stood for hundreds of years! Look what you have done to it, to Japan! You might be shōgun, but you're not the emperor."

He looked down at her, finally seeming to recognize her. His gaze softened. "Tomoe Gozen," he said in a low voice. "You must understand. Yoritomo will kill me either way. No matter if I stayed out of Miyako or took it over or found the child emperor Antoku or killed off Munemori Taira. This way"—he stepped toward her—"this way, I had a chance."

Yoshinaka clasped her arms with his dirty hands and forced Tomoe to meet his eyes. The palace flames danced in his irises. She remembered when she'd conquered him as a child, put her foot on his chest. His eyes full of pleading then. His eyes simply resigned now, blank, reminding her of her father's, after he'd fallen.

She turned her head away. She hadn't wanted to admit it, but he was correct. Yoshinaka was necessary only for victory, not for the ruling of a country. Yoritomo would kill Yoshinaka, just as his father had killed Yoshinaka's.

Tomoe rested her head, just for a moment, on Yoshinaka's shoulder, trying to breathe in his familiar smell once more. But the smoke was too strong. There was none of him left. *Oh, Yoshi*, she thought. *Where did you go?*

"You must leave, Tomoe," Yoshinaka said. "Take Cherry Blossom and go; return to our family and protect Yamabuki." He embraced her roughly. Tomoe's eyes watered, flushing soot away, streaking the front of his dirty armor.

She nodded numbly. "Yes. I will go back to Yamabuki and await you there." Tomoe's mouth had a bitter taste. She swallowed and stepped away. Go-Shirakawa, held upright by two soldiers, swayed in their arms.

Twenty-one

A few days later, their mother is stable, moved into a semi-private room, next to a window overlooking the Life Flight helicopter landing pad, a big red cross painted on top of an adjoining building. It's Tuesday at ten and already one chopper's come in. The other bed's taken up by someone who sleeps silently, no visitors yet.

Rachel dozes in the uncomfortable wood-and-vinyl chair next to the bed, her head resting on the bed next to Hikari. Hikari sleeps upright, one hand loosely wound in her daughter's hair.

Hikari's woken up and looked around and eaten. She's spoken two words, "It's fine." She acknowledges their presence in the same way she acknowledges her nurse: she knows they are here, but not who they are.

"Knock knock?" a male voice says behind the curtain. Drew draws it open. A doctor appears next to her, bearing an iPad. He's blond and young, way younger than Drew is. Dr. Hakiyama. A person of Japanese descent with blond hair. Maybe this is what Chase will look like, Drew thinks.

Rachel lifts her head sleepily at the sound and Hikari opens her eyes. Drew introduces them.

"It's fine," their mother says softly. She clears her throat, repeats. "It's fine." She looks listlessly out the window.

A furrow appears in the doctor's brow. It makes him look older and somehow more competent. He should have frown lines stitched into his forehead. "The stroke affected the language portion of her brain." He looks down at his iPad again, though Drew thinks he already knows what he needs to say. "That phrase seems to be all she can say."

"It's fine." Mom struggles to sit up. She gestures at the water pitcher and Rachel pours her a cup, helps her with the straw. "It's fine." She doesn't appear distressed at having the ability to say only two words. Maybe she doesn't realize she's only saying "It's fine."

Rachel puts the cup down. "Can she do speech therapy?"

He hesitates. "We can try. But it probably won't make a difference, honestly. Her heart's very weak."

Rachel's phone buzzes. "It's Laura," she says, and she steps into the hallway. That's right. The hearing for custodianship is next week.

Dr. Hakiyama touches Drew on her arm. "We'll make her as comfortable as possible."

She knows immediately what he means. What he's not saying. He doesn't have to. Her mother's bones seem smaller than Drew could have imagined, lying there with the skin on them. The room feels like it's caving in on her. Drew closes her eyes for a second. A scene from the samurai book springs into her head: Yamabuki lying on her bedroll, covered in blood.

This life was too difficult for poor Yamabuki.

Or for Hikari.

Drew and her mother will never have the kind of warm relationship Drew longed for, but Drew has this. This time she spent with her sister. How Drew feels about her mother now. No resentment. No remorse. Just the understanding that Hikari had done the best that she could, with what she had. They were limited, both of them, and that's all there was to it.

She puts her hand on her mother's cool arm, covers it with a blanket. "Thanks, Dr. Hakiyama."

He gives her a small smile and pats her shoulder.

. . .

Later in the day, Drew meets Alan and the girls at the park. Audrey hugs Drew's knees, but Lauren, once again, glares from a distance away.

"No training wheels?" Drew asks when she sees the little pink bikes in the back of the car.

"I think they're crutches. If you know you're always safe, there's no incentive to learn how to stay upright." Alan lifts the bikes out of the back of the minivan. He pats the car. "The cars aren't so big in England. I'll miss this, surely."

Drew feels a pang, but she lets it pass without comment. She helps Audrey buckle her helmet. Lauren does it on her own.

"Come on!" Audrey shouts, wheeling her bike to the path. To Drew's surprise, it's not the older girl who gets on and starts riding. It's the younger, pedaling madly down the path.

Lauren pushes her bike by hand, her face furrowed. "Ready to try again, Lauren?" Alan asks brightly.

"No," she says. "I don't want to."

"She fell off once and skinned up her knee," Alan whispers. "I can't get her to try again."

"So she's going to walk the bike forever?"

Alan shrugs. "When she's ready, she'll ask for help."

Drew watches Audrey zip around the path, Lauren trudging behind. Suddenly Audrey, swerving to avoid a dog walker—her control isn't so great yet—zooms off the path into the grass and tumbles down. Alan and Drew freeze, and a second later, she lets forth a mighty wail. Alan runs across the grass to her.

Lauren is beside her. "Is she okay?"

Alan picks up Audrey, flashes them a thumbs-up, carries her to the bathroom. "Yes."

"Okay." Lauren starts pushing again.

"Hey." Drew bends down to the girl's eye level. "Do you want me to show you how to ride? I know a trick."

Lauren cocks her head. "A trick?"

Drew nods. "My sister taught it to me. She taught me how to ride a bike. Of course, I was a lot older. It's good that you're learning now." She'd been eight, Rachel twelve. Rachel pushed her across a field like this one, until Drew learned to balance. "Come on." Drew wheels the bike to the center of the field so it's facing downhill.

Drew has the girl balance on the bike without moving. "Hold your legs out," she instructs. "If you need to, just put your feet on the ground to slow down." She pushes the bike forward and it starts rolling downhill.

Lauren shrieks and puts her toes down, but doesn't fall. She lifts her legs up again and keeps going.

"I did it!" she shouts when she rolls to a stop. "Can I do it again?"

"Sure." Drew starts her off three more times, and on the third time, Lauren puts her feet up on the pedals. Drew crosses her arms and feels a surge of pride for the girl so strong it brings tears to her eyes. She smiles. At eight, Drew was still scared of the bike. *I'm going to fall, Rachel!* Rachel yelling back, *So what?* And then Drew fell and the wind got knocked out of her, but she wasn't hurt because of the grass. She got right back on.

Lauren starts teetering. "Push backwards to brake!" Drew yells, but Lauren puts her feet down. Oh well. That part will come later.

Alan watches her from a picnic table, Audrey on his lap. He's smiling so big that Drew can see his teeth from all the way across the field.

Drew runs over to Lauren. "Great job, sweetie!" She puts her hands on the bike. "Want to go again?"

Lauren, however, is not smiling. Again. She looks up at Drew with those serious eyes, the same color as her father's. "I remember my mother. You're not her."

Drew kneels on the ground, hitting the grass with her palms, as if she's been shoved over from behind. Of course that can't be true—Lauren was only one—but the girl's remembering the photos. Alan's done such a good job of telling the girls stories about their mother that she is real. Bless him.

"No, I'm not your mother." She stops, not sure what else to say. Drew looks carefully at Lauren, this tiny articulate girl. Her fists are clenched and her brows knit. Maybe she does hate Drew. Or maybe she's just afraid. Drew speaks what's in her heart. "But I'll take care of you and your sister like I am."

Lauren tilts her head.

Drew opens up her arms, ready for rejection.

To her surprise, Lauren walks into them and hugs her tight. It's brief and she turns and runs away. Drew smiles. It's a start.

They stay for a while longer, Lauren venturing out onto the concrete path while Drew and Alan walk behind. Drew watches the girls with a mix of wonder and sadness. "Are you sure we should be doing this? I mean, me? I don't want them to get too attached." She swallows. Already she feels the hole where they will be, when they leave. Ghosts to her.

Alan takes her hand. "Drew, I want you to come to England."

She stops moving so suddenly another walker has to jump aside to avoid hitting her. "What do you mean? Move there or visit?"

"Move." Alan puts his hands on her shoulders, all seriousness. "I want you with us. I won't lose you."

Drew's mind races, thinking of her current lack of job and money. "But . . . I need to figure out stuff. Get a job. Be a strong independent woman. Like my mother wanted me to be." She must have, Drew thinks, to give them the Tomoe Gozen story.

"You are a strong independent woman. Look at what you've already done, Drew. Your music is wonderful. You've overcome a decidedly fucked-up childhood more gracefully than most." He smiles at her. "Besides, you'll have to be strong and independent. I'm not rich enough to fully support you. I am just a humble librarian."

Drew laughs.

"So." He leans down to her. "Are you planning to drastically change your personality?"

Drew shakes her head. No. That, she realizes, has already happened. It happened when she came down here to help Rachel. Somehow, this period of lost-ness has resulted in finding Drew.

"Then why on earth can't you figure yourself out with me?" he asks.

Drew considers this. She can continue songwriting wherever she is in the world. Maybe she'll sell some, maybe not. There is a pretty big music industry in England, too—surely Drew can get some gigs over there. Maybe she can teach music. There are just as many possibilities there as there are here for Drew. A little wellspring of hope bubbles up.

Alan puts his arm around her shoulder and they resume walking. A soccer ball rolls across the path and Alan kicks it back without pause. "I know you need to think about it. When my wife and I were thinking about having a baby, we talked ourselves out of it for a good five years. Too soon, we thought. Plans too up in the air, we thought. We want to travel the world first, we thought." He draws her into his side. "You're never ready. The timing is never exactly perfect. But life is too short."

Drew looks at the girls across the field. Lauren braving a quick lift of her hand. Drew waves back.

She thinks about Tomoe choosing not to go to the capital with Wada. How, to the outsider, this might have seemed like a bad decision, but was right for Tomoe. She thinks about her mother, and Quincy, and Rachel. No choice has a certain outcome. You have to do what feels right and true. Actually, Drew made up her mind a while ago, she realizes. "No," she says.

Alan stops. "No?" His voice goes sad and he takes her face in his hands.

"No. I don't need to think about it." She grabs his wrists. "I'll do it. Yes."

A man jogging by lets out a whoop. "She said yes!" he shouts, pumping one sweaty arm in the air. "Whoo-hoo!"

"That's step two," Alan whispers into her ear. She kisses him.

omoe awoke to a dull rumbling in the morning light. She stirred in her heavy wrappings, disoriented. Cherry Blossom stamped and neighed. Tomoe put her ear to the frigid ground, now covered in a shallow layer of white snow. Horses were coming.

She jumped atop Cherry Blossom, not bothering to gather up her pack or meager belongings. Should she flee? Stay? She had to know. She had to see. They trotted to the road facing the city.

In the peachy morning light, gray leftover smoke inked over the sky above Miyako. A cloud of dust moved toward them. Soldiers. White banners. Tattered.

Her soldiers, and not many of them. Perhaps fifty at most.

Her heart quickening, Tomoe waited for them to reach her. Yoshinaka must have changed his mind. He was going to go out and fight the Taira as Go-Shirakawa and cousin Yoritomo wanted.

She saw Kanehira first, in the lead. He made no attempt to slow. As he came closer, she made Cherry Blossom run and brought her to a gallop beside him, catching up. He didn't seem surprised to see her. His face was drawn, white, too frightened and cold to perspire. She knew the news was not good.

Her brother confirmed this. "Yoritomo's sent an army into Miyako. There are too many. We are fleeing."

His words, so simple, sent her stomach heaving. She swallowed. Yoritomo would not be satisfied this time with a son, or a promise. He would kill all of them.

They galloped on in silence, the landscape passing in a blur. She looked behind and saw Demon, the largest horse there, with Yoshinaka atop. He did not glance in her direction.

She concentrated on riding. If they could get over the Awazu River, they might have a chance. Across the bridge. They could burn the bridge after they crossed.

Tomoe looked over her shoulder. She saw Minamoto banners, not tattered but fresh and clean, rising high. Their horses galloping toward them, faster than Yoshinaka's. Yoshitsune and Noriyori, two of Yoritomo's brothers, were coming. Yoshitsune was the lead general, a master tactician. And ruthless. She pressed forward against Cherry Blossom's heaving flanks.

The river was coming up, wide and frozen near the shore, its bridge still intact. But the bridge was too narrow for them to all pass quickly. She slowed and let the other soldiers with horses go ahead. *"Hayakata!"* she shouted. Go faster.

They clattered onto the bridge, the faces of the men grim, their eyes unseeing. Here the other army was below them, coming up fast. Tomoe knew that Yoshinaka's small band could not make it across the bridge in time. She counted Yoritomo's soldiers, then counted again, but there were too many. Tomoe gave up. Her side was outnumbered at least ten to one, she realized.

Yoshinaka and Kanehira did not try to cross the bridge. All they could do now was buy time to let their troops get over to the far side of the Awazu. She saw her breath rising in a hot cloud before her face, heard Cherry Blossom's excited snorts and the thunderous noise of the approaching animals.

Kanehira stood next to her, Yoshinaka on his other side. They did not have to look at each other or exchange words. They were united again, fighting with a single mind, as they had in childhood training.

But then Yoshinaka paused. He locked eyes with Tomoe, and he smiled, just as he had that day he brought her the mochi. A hopeful smile, tinged with tenderness. She returned it. Gone was the man from last night. The slightly mad one. Here again was the man she knew. The one she loved. No matter what happened, she would stay by him.

As one, they drew their swords, and with a shout, ran straight at the approaching rival Minamoto.

Tomoe deflected an attack to her left, then ran her blade through the man's heart. He sank with a sigh. This she repeated, again and again, like a terrible machine, without thought or language.

The Minamoto troops surged among Tomoe, Yoshinaka, and Kanehira. She looked about for Yoshinaka, afraid he'd already been felled. She did not see anyone familiar. Some of the opposition troops went over the bridge. Perhaps Yoshinaka had crossed, and they were pursuing him.

Then, without warning, a gnarled splintery tree branch swung at her face. She reached her left hand up to stop it, thinking she was running into a tree that had come out of nowhere. No, someone tried to hit her. The splinters cut into her hands as they wrapped around the thick wood.

Tomoe gripped the branch and ripped it from the hands of the other samurai. She swung the branch and smacked the man in the chest. He fell from his horse with a loud shout, rolling down the muddy bank, all the way to the water.

She jumped off Cherry Blossom and slid after him, her sandals catching in the muck. The man scrambled, trying to get away, but the mud had pinned down his armor and he flailed like a beetle stuck on its back.

Tomoe reached the samurai, her sword pointed down, ready to finish him. The man held up his hands. "Tomoe!" he yelled.

The voice sounded familiar. She kicked off the metal helmet that partially obscured his face. The surprised countenance of Yoshimori Wada stared up.

Shock coursed through Tomoe. She loosened her grip on the sword. It had been years since she'd last seen him, but she would know him anywhere. The softness had left his face, and he was all angles and bones now, his neck strong and wrapped with muscle. He looked up at her, his face a mixture of fear and warmth. "I've said," he said, his fingers scrabbling through the thin ice of the river as he tried and failed to stand, "that if I had to die at the hands of a Minamoto, I would much rather it be Tomoe Gozen than either of her brothers."

Tomoe sheathed her sword. "It takes more than a stick to defeat me, Wada-chan," she said heavily. "You should know that."

His mouth twitched. Wada nodded.

She left him in the muck, walking back up the bank to Cherry Blossom and the rest of the fray. The soldiers fought on the bridge, on the far side, on the near. Tomoe turned once and looked back at Wada, but he was on all fours, still trying to stand up. The only way she would behead Wada, Tomoe told herself, was if he was about to kill Yoshinaka or Kanehira. She simply could not otherwise.

Yoshinaka fought near the bridge opening. Despite their inferior numbers, his troops were a hardy bunch and acquitting themselves well. Yoshinaka was engaged with no fewer than nine men, who all seemed to attack at once. More enemy seemed to spring up as Yoshinaka cut one down.

But a samurai on horseback approached from Yoshinaka's rear, intent on stabbing him in the back. "Yoshinaka! Watch out!" Tomoe yelled, but her voice was lost in the din.

She dug into Cherry Blossom's ribs. *"Aiiii!"* They leaped forward toward Yoshinaka.

The samurai turned to face her instead. Hachiro Onda, the samurai who had taken little Yoshitaka. He was dressed head to toe in armor, only one small part of the side of his neck exposed.

Tomoe's blood seemed to go as cold as the ground. Hachiro growled and swung his sword at her. She saw the flash of the blade as it passed by her face. Yoshinaka shouted something. Time seemed to stop, and then Tomoe was swinging her sword and falling from her horse. For a moment, she thought she'd been beheaded, her head tumbling toward the ground, but then she saw Onda's head rolling away toward the river.

Kanehira was beside her on his horse. "Well done! That was Hachiro Onda!" Her brother was splattered in blood and guts. Tomoe wondered fleetingly if they would ever have the chance to talk of this later, at a campfire. She wouldn't even begrudge anyone getting drunk. Tomoe wished she and her brother could have been closer, but both of them wanted Yoshinaka's friendship and attention. Both of them wanted to be the captain. Only one could have him. She was the one who had Yoshinaka, body and mind. Perhaps her mother was right, she had been put into the wrong body, and so had he.

Yoshinaka dismounted Demon and strode over to her. He took her by the arm and helped her up. "Get out of here, Tomoe!" His face was pained and drawn. Blood came from his shoulder, soaking his bamboo armor.

"I won't leave you." They were backed up against the supports of the bridge. She shot an arrow into an approaching soldier.

"I cannot die with a woman at my side. It would dishonor me." Yoshinaka's lips curled into a snarl that dissolved into sadness. "Go."

It wasn't dishonor Yoshinaka was worried about, not after all he had done, making Tomoe a captain and taking over Miyako.

Yoshinaka did not want her to see him killed.

She shot another soldier with an arrow. Her fingers were numb and flecked with blood. It had grown even colder. The river was turning into frost before their eyes. A glance around the battlefield told her what she knew inside. The situation was hopeless. The men were decimated. Even the ones who had tried to cross the bridge had been overtaken and slain.

No, Tomoe would not leave Yoshinaka, she decided. She looked at her brother. Kanehira drew himself up and spoke with conviction. "Go, Tomoe. I'll stay with him. Go."

Why shouldn't she die next to him? Without him, she was nothing. She had nothing. She thought of Yamabuki and her mother and her resolve returned. She had to see if they were all right and save them.

She moved toward Yoshinaka. One more embrace, she thought. One more.

Yoshinaka mounted Demon. "Leave now! While there's a break." He leaned down and his strong hand squeezed her shoulder for the last time, the imprint of his fingers remaining there forever.

"I do not want to leave you," she said again. Tomoe remembered when they first professed their feelings for each other, that afternoon by the riverbank. A lifetime spent together.

Yoshinaka blinked rapidly. "I command you to!" He spurred Demon head-on into the next wave of soldiers, leading them away from the bridge. Kanehira followed on his heels without a glance toward his sister.

"*Sayonara,* Yoshi-chan," Tomoe said. She mounted Cherry Blossom.

She turned and trotted away, over the bridge.

Tomoe would not look back.

Twenty-two

The following morning, I park in front of my father's house, wishing that I had a Cherry Blossom to ride into this battle. I ring the doorbell.

Yesterday, Laura called me while I was at the hospital to tell me that my father was ready to talk. Tell us what this big bombshell was. To show his hand. He'd asked for a conference call, actually. Laura thinks Killian's attorney finally convinced him, at this late hour, not to spring it on us at the hearing—judges don't like unfairness.

"No call," I said, not thinking about it. Just saying it, right from my gut. "Tell him I'll see him in person."

And so I'm standing here. Alone. Drew offered to come, but somehow I know I need to do this on my own. Finish it. In my purse, I have the address of the Japanese woman, and the photos. I want some other answers, too.

A woman no more than five feet tall and perhaps twenty-five years old answers the door. She reminds me of a sparrow, with her small, sculpted nose, the way she holds her head to the side. Even her bones are tiny, down to her petite fingers—she must shop in the girl's section. She looks young and mature at the same time in navy blue slacks, a red-and-white-polka-dotted blouse unbuttoned to the top of her red bra, and navy blue socks.

Who is she? I stare at her, my mouth open. An aide? A cook? No. I shut my mouth, a violent flush creeping up my chest to my face. Killian already ordered my mother's replacement. I grip my handbag so hard the surface crackles.

"The daughter?" she says in heavily accented English. She extends her hand toward the living room. Her nails are painted a deep red, cut short and rounded. "I'm Lucy."

I begin to take off my pumps, but she waves. "No need. Not unless it is for comfort." She regards me with her deep-set almond eyes, her irises so dark they are nearly black. I cannot tell what she's thinking, if she feels welcoming or is being polite. Nor do I particularly care. Nodding, I follow her in, wondering what it's like for her to live here with my elderly father. What she left behind, where she's from. If she has a personality, it's as hidden as my mother's was.

The curtains are drawn, letting sunshine into the cavelike room. The television blares a *Matlock* rerun, Andy Griffith's kindly gap-toothed grin spreading across the giant screen.

That's when I spot him, sitting on the far end of the long brown couch opposite the window, his head turned toward the television. He wears reading glasses far down on his nose and a sudoku book is folded open in his lap. His hair is mostly gone. What remains is silvery, his scalp covered in liver spots and scabs. Still, I recognize his posture immediately. The curl of his upper lip as he works out the sudoku with little effort.

"Killian?" Lucy walks over and puts a hand on his shoulder. I remain standing, alone, at the far end, awkwardly poised by the door. "Your daughter is here."

I stand with my hands by my sides. I'm not going to hug him. I study him up and down, taking in the shrunken limbs, the blue veins under his skin, going over the plan in my head. "Hello, Killian."

My father puts the sudoku aside. I notice a walker parked near him, the tennis balls on the ends still a bright brand-new green. He peers at me with his watery, red-rimmed eyes. Still sharp at age eighty-nine. A clearer, lighter version of the blue he used to have. "You've gotten old."

There was a time when that would have hurt, but it strikes me as funny today. Kind of sad, that he thinks this way. I laugh. "Not as old as you."

A reluctant smile plays at his lips even as he makes a harrumphing sound. "Well? You going to come all the way in or what?" His voice is the same, more gravelly, still strong.

I sit opposite him on the other brown couch. "It's good to see you, too."

Lucy pats at his shoulder as if she's pulling back on a rearing horse. "Tea?" she asks. "English or herbal?"

"Herbal, please," I say. Lucy nods, leaves the room.

I lace my hands together, my fingernails digging into my knuckles, fighting the urge to get up and leave forever. I think of my children and my mother. I have to do this for them, not me. "I know you don't believe me, but Mom chose that home and she chose me to have power of attorney. I want her to stay there, and I'll keep filing appeals for as long as she's alive. I can make things difficult for you, too, you know."

He rolls his eyes, slapping his newspaper hard on the couch. "Oh, boy. Here it comes. The great reckoning with your old man. What do you need? Money? Do you want me to put you in my will? Or do you want to blame me for all your problems?"

I shift, getting that familiar nausea, like when I was little and had to deal with my father's unreasonableness, his demands. "That's not why I'm here. I'm here because you asked me to be here." I get the feeling he's provoking me, trying to make me react. He can't. "I can see how keeping Mom alive would be inconvenient." I jerk my head toward the kitchen. My voice rings off the hard surfaces in the room. "I wonder what the judge would think of you already shacking up with a new woman?"

"It's not like your mother's going to get better." He enters another number in his sudoku, jabbing at the paper now.

His bluntness is jarring. My insides feel like they're spilling out.

He's right. I knew it in my head, of course. Drew told me what Dr. Hakiyama said. We discussed hospice options just last night. But right now is the first time I've really felt it in my bones. Admitted it fully to myself. *My mother is never going to get better.*

I take a breath, put my hand on my purse, on the address and the photos.

My heart pounds. I bring out the photos, fanning the black-and-white images out on the coffee table. Killian leans over and picks them up. The one of the parents and the little girl in Japan is on top.

"Your mother and her parents." He smiles briefly, nods. "She was a cute kid." Killian raises an eyebrow as he looks at the photo of Mom with the little girl. "But I thought you knew about this. Didn't your mother tell you?"

I don't answer. My body goes still, hoping he'll keep talking. This is it.

He flutters the picture in his liver-spotted hand. "This is the baby your mother had back in Japan. The one that died."

He says it so casually I almost don't comprehend the meaning of his words. A baby who died. As it sinks in, the truth of what he's saying, my head snaps back on my neck. "What?" I clutch the seat cushion to steady myself.

"She never told you?" Killian hands the photo back. "It's why she was damaged goods, more or less."

The baby gazes at my mother adoringly. She looks so tender. Of course. I squeeze my eyes shut. "She never told me."

"Baby got a fever when she was about a year old." He shifts. "I gather your mother's boss knocked her up. He was married. Gave her some money to keep her quiet."

This was my half sister. My mouth is dry. "Poor Mom."

"It worked out okay for her in the end, though. She got to live here. We had a part-time maid so your mother didn't have to ruin her manicure. She quilted the hell out of everything. What a life she had." He chuckles, shakes his head. "She had no good way of supporting herself there—you have to understand."

"She wouldn't give the baby up for adoption?" What had my mother's options been? I would have given up Quincy in that situation, I think. If Tom had turned out to be an ass and left me without any means of supporting myself, I would have made sure my daughter had a better life. As much as it would have hurt.

He frowns. "We never talked about that, but no. In Japan there's a stigma against adoption, too, unless the baby's in your family. The Japanese think that if you adopt, you don't know what you're getting. There might be bad blood in there someplace. They put kids in institutions instead."

"I didn't know." My stomach clenches. He's delivering this information as casually as he might deliver a weather observation. My mother—the mother of his only children—is dying, and he does not seem to be affected at all. Yet it's typical of him. Maybe he's closed himself off so completely from real emotion, he can't feel it anymore.

"Hell, I wouldn't have married her if she'd had a kid with her. You never know how someone else's kid will turn out." He looks out the window, his expression impassive. "She would have been banned from the catalog if anybody knew."

"You never know how your own kids will turn out, either," I say softly, but Killian doesn't hear or chooses not to. I take out the address. "Hatsuko Minamoto." As if the name meant a real live person to me.

He nods once. "You know."

"Tell me."

He squints at me, seeming to consider whether he really wants to tell me. At last he relents. "This is what I was going to talk about at the hearing. How she got here."

"What do you mean? She was a mail-order bride." I look down at the address.

Killian makes a so-so gesture in the air. "Eh. Sort of. What happened is she changed her name. She wanted to cut off all her bad associations, otherwise the catalog wouldn't have accepted her. It was a high-class catalog." He lifts the piece of paper with the address on it. "This is her real name. Hatsuko Minamoto."

"Minamoto is her name?" Minamoto, like the Minamoto in the story? My fingers tingle. I reach for the paper as though it's a talisman. Killian releases it.

"Yup. She's here illegally, through and through. She lied her way to the catalog and lied her way to me to get here." He shakes his head.

This is why Mom never talked about her past. It was too painful. Too shameful. She didn't want to admit to an affair or her name change any more than I want to tell my children I got kicked out for fooling around.

But if Mom had only told me . . . I don't think anything less of her, now that I know.

I know this now. We all need someone with whom we can be our most core selves. Unhidden and honest. When you hide parts of yourself from other people, they can't fully know and love you, nor you them. You construct a false version of yourself. Then your true self remains unknown. Isolated.

You become a stranger, like my mother was to me and Drew.

Killian coughs before he speaks again. "You know, the Snows are too strong for that Alzheimer's crap." He rubs the sofa arm with his fingertips. "Nope, you won't get it from my side of the family."

I gape at him. I shut my mouth.

Killian shakes his head. "I know you think I'm a monster. But think about it. I did you a favor when I kicked you out."

I am still silent, waiting for him to spew out his whole tangled thought.

He pushes himself upright. "If I hadn't kicked you out, you wouldn't be who you are. You wouldn't have your husband or your kids."

I sit up straight, too, heat flashing through my belly. Would I want Quincy to, say, get hit by a car just so she can appreciate life better? I shudder. "Who would wish a hardship on their children?"

He looks at me like he genuinely can't comprehend the question.

Lucy returns with the tea on a small wooden tray. "I put a little honey in yours, Rachel."

"Thank you." I smile at her.

"Hand me mine," Killian says. She gives him the mug. He sniffs it with a dour face. "You know, I gave Lucy her name. She had some awful-sounding Thai name. Those languages, they sound like grunting. Can't make head or tails of it." He slurps.

I look up at Lucy, who wears a familiar expressionless poker face, like my mother's. A well of sympathy rises up in me. "What's your real name?"

"I like 'Lucy' better." She turns and leaves the room.

"'Pakpao' was her name," Killian supplies. "Sounds like gunshots."

"Killian." I turn back to him. "Don't treat her like that. She's not chattel." My voice cuts through the air.

"Huh?" He sips some tea. "Ah, she's fine. She's happy. She's a lot better off here than in Thailand—her parents run a stir-fry stand or something. She sent them enough money for them to buy a house. She shops online all day. When I die, she'll be set for life."

I take a sip of tea. Despite the honey, it tastes bitter. My father shakes his head. "You know, we were a happy little family until you messed it up, Rachel."

"Me?" He's trying to make me feel guilty. I lean forward. "You live in a fantasy world if you think *that* was a happy family."

He squints at me. "When I kicked you out, I forbade your mother speaking with you. Told her if she did, she'd be out on her ass, too. But when you were pregnant with what's-her-name . . ."

"Quincy," I supply again.

"Quincy. I knew it was some boy's name. Quincy. Then your mother rebelled. Started talking back." He makes a smacking noise with his tongue. "You think I didn't know she was seeing you? Do I look like an idiot?"

My throat closes against the acid rising in my stomach. I want to leap up, grab his sudoku, hit him across the head with it. How Mom must have suffered, staying with him. For the first time, I know the real cost of Mom's defying my father and coming to see me. She risked being kicked out of this country, sent away from me and her grandkids forever, shipped back to a place where she'd have no family and no means of support.

I wish she would have left. I would have fought for her. She could have lived with me. My voice comes out, loud and strong. "Yes, you kind of do look like an idiot, if you want to know the God's-honest truth. You're just saying that to save face."

"But your mother never told you what you needed to know, did she?" Killian takes another sip of tea. I look at him, feel the sourness seeping from him like juice from a lemon. It'd be easier to have an emotionally open conversation with my car. I am not going to fight him or defend any-body or do anything except what I came here to do. I need to get this set-tled and then I need to leave.

I put down my still-full teacup with a shaking hand. "Here's the deal. I highly doubt that anybody is going to deport an elderly woman with dementia."

Killian snorts. "Really? We deport kids' parents all the time."

I lift my hand in a stop signal. Put on my best, calmest poker face. Tomoe, you're up. "Okay. Like you said—Mom probably isn't going to live for much longer. This is what we do. Put her in hospice care. Her doctor thinks that's the best bet. Call off this hearing. It's pointless and it's already costing you too much." I hold my breath.

Killian's mouth thins into a hard line as he considers this, probably going over his checking accounts in his head, the probable short life of my mother versus the costs. "Fine. You learned one thing from me." He sighs and glances at the clock on his cable box, as if he's bored with this whole interview.

It's over. I breathe in and out slowly through my nose, folding my hands carefully in my lap. I've gotten what I wanted. More than I wanted. "Thank you," I say, with genuine gratitude in my voice. "Thank you for telling me about Mom."

He nods. "She wasn't the saint you thought she was, huh? Guess I'm not so bad." His tone is a bit gleeful, and I realize he told me all that only because he thought it would make me hate my mother.

I don't respond to that. Won't engage that kind of emotion. "Do you ever feel regret?" I ask him. "For how you treated us?"

"Regret is a useless emotion, Rachel." Killian shakes his head and puts his hand back into his lap. "I told you what I expected and what the consequences were if you made the wrong decision. And both you and your mother did."

"Ichi-go, ichi-e." I thought I'd feel sad or bitter, but all my emotions collapse. This person sitting before me is who my father is. However he came to be this way. Even in his old age, he has no grace. I watch him with a kind of pity. Resignation. What a waste.

I remember one more thing from the Tomoe story. The latest installment, in which Yoshinaka loses his mind and tries to take over Kyoto, defying his clan. Nothing Tomoe can do will stop him. Nothing she can say will change him. She can only back off and watch the palace burn.

He'll never change. It's useless to hope otherwise.

Tomoe learned from Yamabuki that she didn't have to be all warrior. She learned how to nurture. To find joy in her daily life. And Yamabuki learned to be brave. To defend herself with tooth and claw, if need be. Like these women, I am a combination of both. A fighter and a mother. Imperfect. But loving. With a family I love, who love me, too.

My father has nothing compared with what I have.

Killian picks up his mug and drains it. "So, Rachel, do you ever go looking for gold anymore?" He smiles, the flash of that once kind father flitting across his face. The afternoon sun has begun to slant in the windows behind us.

I shake my head, my muscles weak. I suppose I should feel victorious, but all I want is to go home and cry into Tom's neck. Is this how Tomoe felt after a battle? Empty and worn out? "Never."

"There's still some out there. If you know where to look." He sets his empty mug down. "Lucy! Come shut these curtains! I can't see the television." Abruptly Killian extends his hand again and I take it. It will be the last time, I already know.

He grips hard, a firm businesslike handshake. "Thanks for coming by, Rachel. Lucy will see you out. I'm glad we could settle this favorably, without any hard feelings."

And with that, I'm dismissed. "Good-bye," I say, and he releases my hand. Entering the room, Lucy pulls the drapery strings, blacking out the world beyond. She walks me to the door, her sock feet soundless on the dark hardwood.

"Thank you for coming." Lucy opens the door.

I step onto the porch. "You know, Lucy—if you ever need help . . ."

She draws herself up straight, meeting my eyes. "I know how you see me, but it's what I want."

I take a step away. Shouldn't she want more than for her material needs to be met? But it's not my business. Not at all. "Take some of that clothing money and get a good immigration attorney."

"It was nice to meet you." She bows her head and begins closing the door. I glance back toward my father, but he faces the window, and I can see only his back, his spine poking through his shirt. With the blinds shut, I cannot see what he is staring at, except the darkness.

I walk to my car, away from where my father lives. That is it. That will most likely be the last time I see Killian.

I start the car. I think about what Lucy said at the end, about her needs being met, and I think of all the types of relationships I've seen lately. Chase and that girl, coercion. Quincy and Ryan, where she almost lost herself. Drew and Alan, where she's sort of found herself. Mine and Tom's, which strives to be balanced. My mother's and Killian's. Tomoe, Yamabuki, and Yoshinaka's.

Rachel, Drew, Mom wrote in the book. The book's title, *Sisters of Heart.*

Mom must have read the story, too, just as I did. Maybe she identified with Yamabuki—that careful, domestic creature. But then she realized that even Yamabuki had to fight sometimes.

I can see it in my imagination as clearly as if it is happening in front of me. Mom reading the book, thinking about what she could and could not tell. Yet wanting her daughters to know anyway. *Please understand me,* I hear Mom say in my mind. A phrase Tomoe said, as Miyako burned and Yoshinaka went mad, comes to my mind. *I don't care what happens to me, as long as my family survives.*

Mom, I think, gave me that power of attorney so I'd finally have to stand up to Killian. She wanted me to be brave and finally put all the years, all the pain, to rest, so I could move on.

I put my purse with the photos in it on the front seat beside me. *I will not forget you, little sister.* Tomorrow I'll go see Mom and tell her I know everything. Maybe she'll hear me from wherever my real mother exists.

With that, I drive away.

Without battles to fight or men to wait for, Tomoe made the long journey back to Shinowara alone, moving as though in a dream. Sun and darkness passed without her notice. One morning, faithful Cherry Blossom reached her limit and began to stagger, knees buckling. Had they slept even once?

Tomoe vaguely remembered her eyes closing, Cherry Blossom stopping to graze at whatever paltry winter grass she could find. Poor Cherry Blossom. The mare was better off alone. Tomoe dismounted and walked. "Go on," she told the horse, hoping Cherry Blossom would abandon her, but she merely followed at her own slow pace. They must have made a sight, the two of them like half-dead ghouls trudging the empty roads.

At last, the houses of Shinowara came into view against the dim January sky, a tiny cluster nestled at the bottom of a hill among the still-bare trees and evergreens. Or what remained of Shinowara. It had been burned almost to the ground. A dozen structures still stood, their roofs blackened. Tomoe paused, listening for any sound of life. Nothing.

She walked slowly into the town.

Not even a dog remained, only a few chickens that continued to peck for bugs and plants as though their world had not ended. Tomoe knotted her hair back, the silt and grease coating her fingertips. Perhaps this moment was the dream, she thought, and she would soon awaken and find Yamabuki and Chizuru chatting as they prepared breakfast, Aoi and Yoshitaka chasing the dogs across the packed dirt of the compound. Where had they all gone?

"Yamabuki?" she called, her voice rising with the winter wind, using the last of her strength to scream. "Yamabuki! Chizuru! Aoi!"

Her voice echoed and reverberated back to her. She staggered on, following the paths to their house. It was still standing, part of the roof caved in, the doors broken off and lying askew.

She went inside. A pot of rice stew sat on the table, along with their chopsticks and bowls. One rice bowl was broken into quarters, dropped on the floor, bits of rice still clinging to it.

Tomoe picked up Aoi's miniature pair of chopsticks. Yoshinaka had bought these for her. They were black lacquer, inlaid with tiny enameled cherry blossoms on the handles. She closed her hand around them. The women had left suddenly. She searched the chest for kimonos. Only a few spring robes remained. All of Aoi's things were missing. Tomoe shut the heavy wooden trunk lid and sat down on it with a sigh of relief. At least Chizuru had managed to grab most of her clothing. That meant they had had some time. That meant that the Taira had not taken them or the women had not all killed themselves to avoid capture.

That meant Yamabuki and her mother and surely Aoi were alive.

Everyone she knew was gone. Her brother and Yoshinaka. Her father. Now her mother and the closest thing she had to a sister and daughter, Yamabuki and Aoi. She hoped they could bring each other comfort. That they were safe.

"Yamabuki," she said aloud, as though calling the woman to her. Louder still. "Yamabuki."

If she were a ghost, surely she would appear to show Tomoe she was at peace. But no apparition made itself known. Tomoe rubbed her bleary eyes with dirty hands. She needed a fire. But she was too tired, and she lay down on the porch where she was, and slept, Cherry Blossom standing close beside her.

When she heard a horse clomping into the fort, she was not alarmed. Enemy or friend, she had no idea. She considered drawing her sword, but her hands were stiff, and she no longer cared what happened to her. Let it be up to the fates. She thought of how Yamabuki would have laughed to hear Tomoe talk of fate. Tomoe, who had never believed in destiny. Who thought it could be changed. She smiled despite herself.

The horse halted in front of her, its chestnut skin glistening. Cherry Blossom was calm, a good sign. The rider spoke in a baritone. "Tomoe Gozen. We meet again." The sun shone behind him, obscuring the man in a searing halo of light.

"Who are you?" She did not lift her head.

"Don't tell me you've forgotten me so soon. I'd never forget you." The voice was warm, with a hint of laughter in it. Tomoe did not think she would ever laugh again, and she resented this voice's good humor.

She stood slowly. The courtyard spun around her, the walls bowing out in her vision. She blinked. "No games. Tell me your name, or I shall have your head." She put her hand on her sword. It might as well have been covered in grease, for all the purchase she had.

The man swung a leg off his horse. "I have been writing poetry to you all these years. Of course, nobody's seen it but me. It's terrible."

Tomoe tried to stand, and stumbled. The man caught her in his arms. A flash of white teeth. Yoshimori Wada. The boy from her childhood. Wada-chan.

"Wada-chan," she said, with a glimmer of her old humor, and he laughed.

"You're weak." He stated the obvious. He dragged her back inside. With one hand holding her up, he got out a blanket and placed it on the floor, then placed Tomoe on top of it. She went as limp as a wilted flower. He lay next to her, his body heat warming her, and put another blanket over both of them. "I thought I would find you here. They told me you hadn't died alongside Yoshinaka and Kanehira."

"Yoshinaka didn't want me to stay," she said. "Neither did I."

"You are a liar," Wada said. "You would have stayed and probably fought off the rest of the battalion alone."

"Untrue," she murmured, slipping into unconsciousness. When she awoke some time later, her head rested on something soft and steady. Startled, she realized it was Wada's lap.

"Tomoe." Her name settled toward her lips like a snowflake. He was rubbing her hand between his, and had built up the fire. A pile of wood stood ready nearby.

Clearheaded, Tomoe struggled to sit up. "Tell me what happened to Yoshinaka and my brother."

He hesitated.

"Don't leave anything out," Tomoe said. Her lips were chapped and bleeding. She tore away the dead skin. Nothing hurt anymore. "I have imagined it all."

Wada inhaled. Softly, he began his story.

After she left, Yoshinaka fled, Kanehira with him, intending to outrun the army with their strong horses. They escaped by running into a forest, where they thought they were safe. But before long, Yoshinaka realized they were in an unfamiliar area. Demon's hoof sank through a layer of ice with a crack, and the horse fell with a terrified whinny.

"A bog!" he shouted. "We are in a bog." He flailed, trying to get Demon to free himself, but the horse only sank deeper, all of his hooves stuck. The mud sucked the horse down like quicksand.

Kanehira stopped his horse from following. "Abandon Demon and I'll pull you out!"

Yoshinaka tried to dismount, but now his own feet at the sides of the horse were stuck, too, the pressure of the mud pushing in on him. "Get away!" Yoshinaka shouted to Kanehira.

Kanehira urged his own horse into the mud and tried to dig at Yoshinaka's legs. Now Kanehira's horse cried out and sank, too.

Yoshinaka cast one last desperate look at Kanehira. Kanehira dismounted and crossed to Yoshinaka's side, the bog sucking him in waist-deep, knowing what was about to happen. He nodded.

Yoshinaka tore off his armor and threw it into the mud. Without hesitating, he plunged his sword into his abdomen, pulling the blade toward the earth.

Kanehira's sword swung at his milk brother's neck. "I follow you into death as I followed you in life, Yoshinaka!" he shouted, and cut his own abdomen, Yoshinaka's blood still hot on the steel. No one was there to help Kanehira end his pain swiftly, his life flowing out of him before the somber eyes of his enemies. At last the legendary general picked his way over to Kanehira, as he gasped desperately for air, and took pity on Tomoe's brother. Loyal to the last to Yoshinaka.

Exactly as he had promised.

Wada stopped talking. He held Tomoe's hand somberly. "I am sorry it had to be this way, Tomoe."

It was as she had imagined. At least her brother had been with Yoshinaka in his last moments. Tomoe covered her face with her hands. "Have you heard about the others? Little Yoshitaka?" It hurt to say the name.

Yoshimori held water up to her mouth. "Who?"

"The son of Yoshinaka. Yoritomo took him." She rolled her head, avoiding his touch.

Wada frowned and looked at the fire. He drew his hand over his eyes. "Do you remember how we spoke about the Taira leader who spared the lives of the boys, only to have them grow up to challenge him?"

Tomoe nodded. Her heart jumped into her throat and temples. "We thought he was foolish," she said, very faintly.

Wada pursed his lips, his eyes distant. "I'm afraid Yoritomo is not so foolish."

The boy, too. Yoshitaka, lost. Tomoe's eyes hurt. She put her fingertips on her temples and pressed in, her breathing fast and shallow, until she regained control. She swallowed hard. "And what of Yamabuki and my mother and the little girl?"

"There were a few who arrived at the Kantō from this village. I heard of an older woman with a girl child. They are staying with Yoritomo's in-laws. I don't know their names, but I think it must be them."

Tomoe closed her eyes and breathed. Aoi and her mother were alive. Not Yamabuki. She felt a flash of relief. Yamabuki was no longer in pain. "I must get Aoi," she whispered. Retrieve the girl and raise her. Tomoe wasn't sure how. Her head swam with sorrow. What could she do, here alone? Her choices were to become a beggar prostitute, or join a convent. Neither would let her raise Aoi.

She closed her eyes. Her mouth tasted metallic, like blood. "And why are you here?"

He leaned toward her and took her face in his hands gently. "I wanted to find you."

Tomoe laughed in spite of herself, but when she opened her eyes she saw his face was earnest. "Are you insane? I am an old warrior woman, no longer a great beauty."

He blushed, as he had when he was a boy. "Tomoe. I, too, am older and wiser."

"Wada-chan, don't be silly." She sat upright. He tried to help her, but she pushed him away.

"It is Lord Wada now. Will you come with me?" He looked at her pleadingly, then bowed his head. "I will not keep you from your sword or hide you away."

"I never want to see a sword again." Her vehemence surprised her. "But do you not have a wife? Am I to be your concubine?"

He inclined his head in affirmation. "But other women are pale imitations of you, Tomoe."

She closed her eyes again. "You would let me get my mother and Aoi? That's three more mouths to feed, Wada. Be practical."

"You know poets are never practical." Wada bent his head toward her, his breath warm on her ear. "Tomoe. Come with me. We will make our world new again."

She thought of Yoshinaka. The homeless orphan. How he had hit her with that stick, knocking into motion the beginning of her warrior journey. Like a tremendous landslide begun by moving the smallest rock. His last act was a generous one, saving her.

A convent would provide a peaceful life. She would not have to fight or think or be concerned about anyone or anything except prayer. Shut away from the world. Wouldn't it be nice? Perhaps. But it was wrong for her.

Tomoe opened her eyes. She picked up a piece of the broken rice bowl. All of them had used it, she remembered. It was greenish-brown earthenware, made by a ceramist in the capital, brought here by Yamabuki.

Wada took it from her hands and put the pieces back together. Only one small chip of a hole was missing. "I know of a man who can repair this with gold. It will be more beautiful and stronger than it was before."

Tomoe bent her head. "Can he repair me as well?"

"Only you can do that," Wada said.

Sister of heart, a familiar voice said in her head. *Live.*

"Yamabuki," Tomoe whispered for the final time, her voice so faint only her mind heard it.

Wada sat still, his head bent over hers, his eyes shut.

She reached for him.

Twenty-three

SAN DIEGO

Present Day

D rew awakens early on Christmas morning, the way she did when
she and Rachel were very small. When she still believed in
Santa. Her stomach thrums in excitement. It's barely dawn.
They went to midnight mass last night, yet Drew feels alert, like she's had
a full eight hours of sleep instead of four. After breakfast, she's going over
to Alan's house, where she'll meet his in-laws for the first time. See the
girls have Christmas for the first time. Begin her part in making the girls'
childhoods better. Never worse. She can't wait. She wonders if people have
children, in part, to have a sort of do-over of their childhoods. Later on,
she and Rachel and everyone will go over to the hospice home where their
mother is. Bring her some Christmas spirit.

Drew opens the door. The Christmas tree in the family room glows
softly, strung with a thousand white lights that took forever to put up. Especially the exacting way Rachel wanted it done. Drew smiles wryly.

She sees the back of Rachel's head as she sits on the couch. A log's burning in the fireplace. *Just like a Christmas card,* Drew thinks. Like no Christmas she's ever had before. "Hey." Drew shuffles over. "You're up early."

Rachel pulls the blanket back and lets Drew inside. It is warm, almost
hot. "I always get up early on Christmas. Even though my kids sleep in now.

I just like being the first one up. Besides, I have a present for you." She pulls out the Japanese samurai book, and a leather-bound notebook beside it. "Completely transcribed into English."

"Oooh." Drew rubs her cold hands together and opens the notebook. It has parchment paper pages with deckled edges, and feels good on Drew's fingers. Joseph wrote the story out in careful handwriting, the kind of neat script you don't often see anymore. "Thank you. I haven't been this excited about a present since Spanish Barbie."

Rachel cocks her head to one side. "You remember that?"

Drew nods, her eyes skimming the pages.

"Mom and I got that for you, you know. I told her to get it after Dad said you were bad." Rachel's arm lies warm against Drew's.

"You did?"

Rachel nods.

Drew looks down at the samurai book. Her eyes blur. All this time, even when she didn't know it, her sister had been looking out for her. She puts her arms around Rachel. "Thank you."

Rachel hugs her back. "Stop it. You'll make me cry."

"Let me get mine for you." Drew goes into her room and returns with her iPod and a gift box. She hands Rachel the gift box and plugs her iPod into the stereo on the bookcase.

Rachel tears open the paper and takes out a small earthenware bowl in shades of brown, green, and blue. A crack of gold runs around the outside in a jagged pattern. Rachel looks up at Drew with shining eyes. "Is this—?"

"Kintsukuroi pottery." Drew touches it with her forefinger. "Like what Wada was having repaired for Tomoe in the book. The breaks aren't hidden. They're beautiful. Part of its history." She chokes up a bit now and has to look at the ceramic instead of her sister. "I want us to be like this."

"Drew—Thank you." Rachel reaches for her, but Drew's stood up and gone to the bookcase. She presses play.

Drew's song. She made her own recording—amateur for now—with Drew playing all the parts and then mixing them together. Guitar, piano, viola. Drew singing—passable, Drew thinks, not professional, if she's honest. Drew looks at the fire, feeling shy.

The song ends.

Rachel says nothing. The fire crackles, sending a spark to the hearth. Drew's mouth is dry. Finally she can't stand it and looks at her sister. "Well? Did you like it or not?"

Rachel's face is wet, her nose swollen. She mops at her face with a handful of tissues. "Holy shit, Drew. What do you think?"

Drew runs over and puts her arms around Rachel. They hug each other. She thinks of what her sister will look like when she's very old, when Drew is also very old, their skin loose and wrinkled. On another Christmas morning, in the past, they ran to the tree, Rachel faster. *I'll be as big as you someday,* Drew said. *No—you'll always be my little sister,* Rachel shouted.

Will they ever sit here again, early on a Christmas morning? Everything's changing. Like always. She's going to enjoy every minute of what they have. She hugs Rachel harder.

A week after Christmas, Tom and I sit alone in the living room. We're wearing formal clothes for a Saturday, Tom in a loosened tie and dress shirt, his black suit jacket off, and me in a dark blue dress with long sleeves. He has his arm around me and I'm staring at the large photo of my mother resting on the sideboard, propped up against the wall. I took the photo one Christmas about a decade ago, forcing her to stand in front of the Christmas tree with the kids, my children looking everywhere but at the camera—they're blurred. Next to it, I've framed the photos of Mom with her long-gone baby, and with her parents.

Sympathy cards stand around the photos of my mother. Macaroni and cheese, enchiladas, cookies, and salads cover the kitchen counter. Most of these are not even from people who knew my mom, but people who know me. Who want to comfort my family. I'm touched—even Elizabeth and her son Luke came by with a tray of cookies. "I made these," Luke whispered at me. "Mixed the ingredients separately."

I put my arm around Tom's midsection and exhale, feeling his breath move my hair. Everyone's gone home. Drew and Alan took the girls out to the zoo—some fresh air, something to do.

Two days after Christmas, Mom had a massive stroke in the middle of the night, passing away peacefully in her sleep. For this I'm glad—glad that it wasn't drawn out.

"I'm going to get a soda. Do you need anything?" Tom squeezes my shoulder. I shake my head. We disentangle and he gets up, goes into the kitchen.

I look around for something to do. It feels better to be occupied. There's a stack of unsorted mail on the table by the front door. I go through it, flipping ads and coupons directly into recycling.

There's a community college catalog stuck in among all the grocery store circulars, addressed to my daughter. She's still not sure if she'll go back to school, so she's staying here for now. She got a job working at the local Nordstrom for the Christmas season, paying us a bit of rent.

I sit on the couch and open it. If I were to go back to college, what would my major be? I pick up a pen from the coffee table. It's four-thirty and almost dark, cloud cover making the light thin and watery. Wind blows at the trees, bending them back slightly. Two neighbor kids, a boy and a girl, shriek past on the sidewalk, their Big Wheels rumbling over the concrete, their red curls flying. They are like skipping shadows on film, a glimpse of my once small children. I smile as they pass.

I circle the classes I'm interested in. *Survey of Asian History. Japanese Language. Asian Art.* I'll have to reread the Tomoe Gozen story when I'm through with these courses. Maybe eventually I'll be able to read those first-person tomes Joseph was talking about.

Thudding sounds on the stairs as Chase and Quincy clomp down. "Hey, Mom. What's that?" Chase comes over and throws himself onto the couch next to me.

"I'm thinking about taking a class or two." I hold up the catalog.

"You can sign up online these days." Quincy perches next to me, puts her arm around my shoulders.

Chase points to the photo of Mom and her baby. "Is that you, Mom?" It's the first time he asked about it.

I expect to feel the familiar flutter of nervousness I always did whenever I spoke of Mom, but I only feel a surge of gladness. "No. Her name was Yoshimi." I pause to collect myself. Quincy hands me a tissue. "Before 'Bāchan met my father, she had a little girl who died."

"Oh." His mouth turns down. "That's too bad."

My daughter tightens her comforting grip. "How come you never told us?"

"I didn't know until I talked to my father," I answer. They know all about him now. Everything's out in the open.

"Well," Quincy says with a sigh, "like Grandma Perrotti says, a leopard can't change his spots. His loss."

Chase squints at the photo. "The baby sort of looks like you."

I peer at the photo, trying to see the resemblance between me and the fully Japanese girl, the same way I tried to see the resemblance between Mom and me or Drew and me. "How?"

"In the chin," Chase says. He sticks his out. "I have it, too. So does Quincy."

I hadn't seen it before. We all have a slightly heart-shaped face: Mom, me, Drew, my children.

"It is by far the superior chin," Chase says. "I'm glad we didn't get Dad's."

"Hey," Tom comes back, "what's wrong with my chin?" He squeezes in next to Quincy and hands me the papers. "Mine is perfectly functional."

Chase grins. "No offense, Dad, but you have that little dimple in the middle, and you always have whiskers in it."

Tom feels the offending spot with his index finger. "True."

The kids and Tom talk about nothing, about time-traveling phone booths, sports, what they should watch next on TV. A comforting hive buzz. They decide to watch television and all of them decamp into the family room. "Coming?" Tom says.

"In a minute." I smile. I pick up the original Tomoe book from where it sits on the coffee table. Good-bye, Tomoe. It's time for you to go into the special archival box and be stored away. I can take you out whenever I need to.

My house makes that creaking noise it sometimes does, its old framing with its new plumbing settling down for the night. The sun's almost gone. Outside, all the trees are bare, a few just beginning to bud. A gust of wind stirs up grass and leaf clippings on the lawn, swirling it all up into a cone, about the size of a person. It hovers for a moment, a spectre made of dust, and then collapses, once again, into the earth.

EPILOGUE

T omoe wiggled the fishing line in the clear blue water of the bay. "You must not give up," she said to the young boy sitting beside her in the light brown sand. Beyond, the imposing mass of Mount Fuji rose out of the waters, always snowcapped even when it was so warm they wore little more than their cotton *yukata*.

The boy scowled, drawing his grubby knees up to his face, picking at a scab until Tomoe caught his hand. "It's no use," he said. "We've been at this all day." He picked up a rock and skipped it across the water.

"That will scare the fish." Tomoe knew there was only one remedy for her son's grouchiness.

Yoshihide had been born two years after Wada found Tomoe at Shinowara. The boy was the miracle she and Yoshinaka could never achieve. Sometimes, Chizuru said, such things occurred. Just because they were rare did not mean they never happened.

Now Tomoe lived here with her family, in this small fishing village near the bay. Their house was off the beach. Wada had offered to keep her in a finer home in the capital, apart from his wife, but Tomoe refused. She was happier here, far from the crowds and Yoritomo, who was now shōgun. Far from the memories.

The beach house had turned into Wada's vacation home, with Wada visiting when he could. His trips had become more frequent of late, with Wada coming often to see Yoshihide, his only child, and staying longer and longer.

Tomoe reached over and tickled Yoshihide. He tried to resist, holding his body stiff, but before long his mouth wiggled and he began to giggle helplessly. "I'll teach you to scare the fish," Tomoe said. He laughed and tried to scramble away, clawing at the sand and throwing it about dramatically, but she held on to his ankles. "You will not escape me!" Yoshihide broke away. At eight, he was almost stronger than she. "Come back!" Tomoe leaped on him again, her belly landing across his legs in the sand. She growled like a monster. Yoshihide laughed so hard he stopped making noise, which amused Tomoe all the more. She went for his belly, his most ticklish spot.

"*Ai*, Tomoe, stop. You'll make him wet himself," Aoi called from where she hung up the laundry. Tomoe paused, her skin prickling. Once Tomoe had tickled another little boy, just a bit younger than this one was now. Tomoe felt her eyes well with unexpected tears, even as a laugh escaped her belly at her son's joyous expression.

Tomoe looked at the girl with the black hair blowing in the breeze. Aoi pulled a strand away from her smiling mouth. Her black eyebrows curved up, nearly as thick as her father's had been. At thirteen, Aoi resembled her mother, with the same pale complexion and lustrous black hair. But Tomoe was determined to help Aoi weather life well. Already Aoi was used to hard work, was smart and practical. She could fish, cook, and fight as well as anyone.

Next to Aoi, Chizuru, a stooped and white-haired old woman, sniffed the wind. "I smell rain coming, Tomoe. Perhaps we should stop this work."

Tomoe smiled fondly at her mother. "All I smell is fish."

Yoshihide pitched another rock into the water. She leaned back into the warm sand as though it were a hammock and closed her eyes, remembering sitting near another fisherman, another time.

Fat drops of water hit her forehead. Tomoe's eyes flew open and she sat up. The children shrieked in delight. "A big rain!" Yoshihide shouted, dancing around his mother. "Come on!" Thunder shook the sand, and a flash of lightning arced across the bay. Her mother had known, of course. Chizuru was already at the house, shaking her head at their stubbornness. Aoi pulled down the laundry as quickly as she could, flinging the clothes into a large reed basket.

"Tomoe!" Wada-chan stood at the door, beckoning her. Even from this distance, Tomoe felt the warmth of his smile. "Hurry, before the lightning gets here."

Wada's hair was more gray than black now, and his face leaner, but Tomoe saw the young man who had so carefully courted her. Aside from her mother, he had known her longer than any other person alive.

"Race?" Yoshihide asked hopefully. His adult front teeth were just beginning to come in, pearly-white and slightly serrated.

"You can't catch me!" Aoi slipped past them, the heavy laundry basket of wet clothes tilting precariously on her head. Yoshihide took off after her.

The humid, warm wind blew hard across the bay, sending up plumes of mist, bringing the storm closer to shore. Tomoe heard Kaneto's voice in her head. *Your will to live is too great . . .*

She tilted her head and peered at the roiling gray clouds above her. She thought of running inside to Wada-chan's waiting embrace. How they would gather around the table to have the smoked eel Tomoe had caught and prepared. How Chizuru and Aoi would sing as they washed the dishes. How Yoshihide still didn't mind, even at his age, getting on his mother's lap during a thunderstorm. How he still allowed her to kiss him on his downy cheek when she put him in his bed at night, the snug weight of his arms around her neck. She swallowed away a lump. "You were right, Otōchan," Tomoe whispered.

"Hurry, hurry!" Yoshihide shouted. "You're dawdling, Okāchan!" He began running in slow motion. "I will let you catch up."

Tomoe turned her back on the dark clouds and the water, and broke into a run for home.

ACKNOWLEDGMENTS

Novel writing, while a solitary practice, requires a veritable behind-the-scenes legion, providing logistical and moral support. Thank you to my supportive editor, Christine Pepe, and to Ivan Held for believing in me—and huge thanks to everyone at Putnam: Meaghan Wagner, Ashley Hewlett, Kate Stark, Lydia Hirt, Mary Stone, Anna Romig, Christopher Nelson, Amanda Dewey, and the rest of the team.

Many thanks go to my agent, Dan Lazar, and to Victoria Doherty-Monroe, Genevieve Gagne-Hawes, and the rest of the Writers House crew. To Julie Kibler, thank you for the moral and reading support beyond the call of duty. Appreciation goes out to the rest of our Oregon Women's Writing Retreat, where I wrote some of the first draft and whose members provide ongoing support: Marilyn Brant, Sarah Callender, Sarah McCoy, Jael McHenry, Kristina McMorris, Erika Robuck, and Therese Walsh. To my writer friends Jean Kwok, Susan Meissner, Patricia Wood, Jamie Ford, Ben Brooks, Kristan Hoffman, thanks for your sympathetic ears and advice. Thanks to my assistant, Frankie Masi, for freeing me to write. Tracie Masi, Brenda Radder, Jennifer Kurpiewski, Carly Garrett—you all helped in ways you probably don't even know about. Thanks to The Naked and

Famous, The Airborne Toxic Event, and Tokyo Police Club for providing my writing sound track.

Randy Schadel, scholar at the Samurai Archives website, and his wife, Dr. Ayame Chiba, read an early draft of the historical portion and offered suggestions and corrections for many things great and small, like the fact that green tea was had only by nobles and monks during Tomoe's time. Any errors in this book are mine.

Finally, I want to thank my husband, Keith, who reread each scene twenty times without complaining once and bought me all the chocolate I wanted; and our children, who tolerated countless microwaved dinners with cheerful understanding. You mean everything.

AUTHOR'S NOTE

People often ask me which parts of my books are "true" and which are "made up." My answer to this question is this quotation from Maya Angelou: "Facts can obscure the truth, what it really felt like." I'm more concerned about the emotional truth that my characters experience.

That said, I've tried to keep the historical details as accurate as possible, except where keeping historical data intact would disturb the story—that "truth" I tried to pursue. So some facts have been purposely fudged. For example, Yoshinaka had another concubine, named Aoi, whom I left out purposely (though I gave her a nod by naming another character after her). Other historical members of the Minamoto clan have been omitted for the sake of simplicity.

I anticipate some readers will discover historical inaccuracies that they may be tempted to write to me about. However, please remember this is a work of fiction, not a history book. If you find my liberties disturbing, I invite you to write your own book.

If you're interested in reading more about the samurai era, check out the e-book companion piece, *Tale of the Warrior Geisha*, the full book-within-a-book, which expands on Tomoe and Yamabuki's stories.

To read more about samurai, Japan, and the mail-order-bride industry, look into some of these sources:

Chun, Christine. S. Y. "The Mail-Order Bride Industry: The Perpetuation of Transnational Economic Inequalities and Stereotypes." *University of Pennsylvania Journal of International Law* 17, no. 4 (1996), pp. 1155–1208.

Englander, Itta C. "The Search for June Cleaver: International Marriage Brokerages and Mail-Order Brides." 2008. Available at: http://works .bepress.com/itta_englander/1.

Farris, William Wayne. *Japan's Medieval Population: Famine, Fertility, and Warfare in a Transformative Age.* Honolulu: University of Hawai'i Press, 2006.

Joly, Henri L. *Legend in Japanese Art: A Description of Historical Episodes, Legendary Characters, Folk-lore, Myths, Religious Symbolism, Illustrated in the Arts of Old Japan.* London: John Lane, 1908. See especially p. 374.

Ruch, Barbara. "Unheeded Voices, Winked-at Lives: Shamans." In Kozo Yamamura and John Whitney Hall, eds., *The Cambridge History of Japan*, vol. 3, *Medieval Japan*, pp. 521–540. Cambridge, England: Cambridge University Press, 1990.

The Samurai Archives. "Minamoto Clan." http://wiki.samurai-archives .com/index.php?title=Minamoto_clan. Consulted October 2013.

Shikibu, Murasaki. *The Tale of Genji* (1021). Translated by Royall Tyler. New York: Viking, 2001.

The Tale of the Heike. Translated by Royall Tyler. New York: Viking, 2012.

The Tales of the Heike. Translated by Burton Watson. Edited by Haruo Shirane. New York: Columbia University Press, 2006.

Turnbull, Stephen. *The Book of the Samurai, the Warrior Class of Japan.* New York: Arco, 1982.

_____. *The Samurai Sourcebook.* London: Arms and Armour Press, 1998.

_____. *The Samurai Swordsman: Master of War.* North Clarendon, VT: Charles E. Tuttle, 2008.

_____. *Samurai Women, 1184–1877.* Oxford and Long Island City: Osprey, 2010.

Villalpando, Venny. "The Business of Selling Mail-Order Brides." In Michelle Plott and Laurie Umansky, eds., *Making Sense of Women's Lives: An Introduction to Women's Studies,* pp. 178–184. Lanham, MD: Rowman & Littlefield, 2000.